Birdhouse
Jesus

ISBN # 978-1-940189-32-1

This is a work of fiction. Names, characters, businesses, places, events, locales, and incidents are either the products of the author's imagination or used in a fictitious manner.

Cover design by Babski Creative Studios

Cover image courtesy of iStock photos

Printed in United States

Twisted Road Publications

CONTENTS

Part I

Aunt Jean's Jesus
Six Years Old—1967

One

Outside my bedroom window, Mr. Hickory has a special spot just for me. He crosses his branches the way we girls in Mrs. Mayer's first-grade class grab each other's upper arms to weave a basket seat for one of us to sit on. Mr. Hickory is even better because his seat curves where three branches meet. Sitting with my back against his trunk, I'm perched so high cars pulling into the parking lot at Shorty's Store look like toys.

From this spot, the field next to my house is a lost world divided in two by a poisonous creek filled with deadly salamanders. One touch and their slick, electric blue tails could turn me into white dandelion fluff, ready for any-old-body to blow me into yonder, where no one could ever put me back together again. The wind would lift the pieces of me on her back and carry me all over the world. I'd have to live wherever I landed: with the lions in Africa, the kangaroos in Australia, and even tigers in India. It would be confusing to be in one hundred places at once and never know which one was the real Mary Alice. Every day, I'd have to ask each of my selves, "Are you the real one?"

Being one girl is so much better than being split into a hundred, or even into two.

Curled up in Mr. Hickory's lap, my spyglass fist sees over the treetops, all the way up the Cedartown Highway, over the whole town of Rome, Georgia, all the miles away to my Aunt Jean's house at 714 North Broad Street. She's leaning over the gas stove to pull out a tray of sugar cookies. While I'm stuck here at home, a batch of sweetness waits for me to sprinkle it with red sugar dots. I just know it!

At least I have my friends with me. I reach into my shorts' pocket and take out my Snap card game. Each card has an animal, and my favorite, Buzzy Squirrel, grins up at me. I always keep him on top. He's my best friend.

The cards are all bent and faded from me playing pretend with them. Today, we're going to play school. I pull six cards from the pack, lay them out on my lap, and re-pocket the rest of the deck.

"Hurry up, class. Everyone to your desks." I clap my hands. My students stampede. Tim Elephant stomps down on Joe Giraffe's toe. "Slow down. Find your seat. No pushing. Act like good little children. Not animals."

Teaching is hard work, but I smile at all of them. "There. Class, today we're going to practice our alphabet. I know you remember. Let's all sing it together."

Buzzy is the smartest. He knows every letter. "Very good, Buzzy. You get a star." He sticks it on his shiny, blue coat. Freddy Fox's cheeks turn red, so I keep an eye on him. "Freddy, you need to study your letters. I'll help you. Then you'll earn a star, too." But he's talking to Tommy Tiger and not listening to me. "Freddy, be quiet. You're bothering the other children." Freddy reaches out and pinches Buzzy, and with me watching! "Freddy, you come to the front of the class this instant." He stares right at me, like he's daring me. "Disgusting brat!" I throw a hickory nut at him. It hits him smack in the middle of his forehead. He yaps out a loud cry.

I clap my hands over my mouth and squeeze my eyes shut. That wasn't what Mrs. Mayer would do. Biting down hard on my thumb, I mutter, "I'm a bad, bad teacher."

When I open my eyes, Freddy's looking at me like he hates my guts. "I'm sorry, Freddy. Really, I am. I'll help you with your letters." He turns his back to me.

Class is over. I shove the cards back into their box. All of them, except Buzzy, who sits in my lap.

We look out over the field. The air turns a shade darker. The crickets crank one twist higher on the dial. How did night come so quickly? A drizzle of rain taps the leaves above our heads and a splash hits my arm. Now they'll call me inside for sure. My stomach hurts. Buzzy looks scared.

The wind picks up. If I were a hundred dandelion puffs, the wind would blow all of me into outer space.

Mama's voice rides out over the gust. "Mary Alice, time to come in." The leaves mumble and reach for each other. They don't want bedtime to come either. More raindrops find their way to me.

"Buzzy, we have to go in." He won't meet my eyes. The sky is the color of Miller Mountain Road that runs by my house. I imagine Coca-Cola trucks driving upside down across the line of clouds and dropping bottle bombs on top of us.

Down by the house, jasmine flowers are opening up. They love the night and leak out happy smells. Mama hollers again. "Mary Alice!" Her voice is a sharp tack. "Get in here!"

If Mama calls again, I'll get a whipping. I slip Buzzy into the pack. "You'll be safe in here."

I climb down three branches, grab a rope hanging on the lowest branch, and ready myself to swing over and walk my feet down Mr. Hickory's trunk. Mid-swing, the bottom drops out of the rain cloud, and Mama's voice jabs at me. "Mary Alice Lydell!"

Wrapping my hands and legs around the rope, I slide down it like a fireman's pole. My palms burn. The ground comes at me fast. I land on my feet. Fall to my knees.

No time to waste. Jump up. Run at a gallop. Hands and knees stinging. The downpour is soaking my hair, face, and shirt. "Coming, Mama!"

Mama's standing at the carport door, waiting. I'm a drenched pooch. She always looks like somebody from the Sears wish book. Today, navy blue slacks show her bare ankles, flat loafers, and a baby blue, long-tail, long-sleeve button-up blouse. Most moms have bangs to their eyebrows and brush the top of their hair straight back. My mama grew her bangs out and has her hair parted on the side, with a wide band of hair tucked behind one ear and a pointy curl flipping towards each cheek. She says bangs are out of fashion. With hands on her hips, she taps her right foot. Her metal shoe buckle flashes.

I try to scoot inside, past her. "Oh, no you don't." She grabs me by my shirt. I plant my feet so her grip doesn't jerk me backwards. It's not that she wants to hurt me. She wants to get my attention. "I know you have sense enough to come in out of the rain." She doesn't say it like a question, but I know it is one.

"Sorry, Mama." I duck my head and scuff the toe of my dirty Keds against the top brick carport step. A stream of rainwater trickles from my forehead to my shoes.

"I was up my tree when it started." I wipe my face and raise my head. Her brown eyes are not blinking. "It takes a while to get down from there."

"You're to come when I call you." She steps back and looks at my skinned knees. The rain pouring down the carport gutter sounds like a train coming to a fast stop.

"Just look at you. All banged up and bruised." As she talks and shakes her head, I move my hands behind my back to hide the rope burns.

"Let me see your hands." Mama doesn't miss anything.

I hold my fists out, knuckle side up. She doesn't say a word, just raises her eyes from my fingers to my face. I turn my palms up.

"Good God!" Mama takes my hands and cradles them in hers, careful not to touch the raw, red welts running across my palms. "Look what you did to yourself. What am I going to do with you?" The tightness around her eyes softens.

"I didn't mean to. It was a shortcut, down the rope." She cups my elbow and guides me to the kitchen sink. I scope out our kitchen and den to see where Daddy is. He's laid back in his old brown recliner. His snores rumble through the house.

"If you'd come the first time I called you, you wouldn't have to hurry, now, would you?" Mama twists the cold-water faucet, then puts her hands around my waist and boosts me up. I reach for the bar of soap. "Good Lord, you're growing like a bad weed. I won't be able to lift you much longer."

The suds set my hands on fire. I suck my teeth, so I don't cry out as I rinse my hands.

She sets me down and hands me a dry dish towel. My hands are smarting blue blazes. I pat instead of rubbing. Squinting at my knees and palms, she says, "That needs doctoring. Come on. Quiet now.

Don't wake your daddy." I follow Mama through the den on tiptoes, dodging Daddy's chair and not making a sound.

In the bathroom, I dry my hair with a towel. Mama wets a washcloth, hands it to me, and points to my knees. I dab. They're sore, but not like my hands. Mama squirts Bactine on all my cuts and scrapes. I love the way it mists out onto my skin. It's a hundred times better than the orange stuff Aunt Jean uses. Her stuff stings worse than alcohol. Mama hoists me up onto the bathroom counter and puts Band-Aids on my knees. Aunt Jean says bandages keep a wound from getting air and healing, but I don't tell Mama. She doesn't like it much when I tell her what Aunt Jean would have done.

"Nothing I can do about your hands." She shakes her head. "If you do battle with that tree, it's gonna win every time. You have to be more careful, or I'll have to keep your feet on the ground."

My breath freezes. "I will be, Mama. I promise. Cross my heart and hope to die." I make an x-mark over my heart and hold my pointer and middle finger up to show my pledge.

Mama lifts me down and pops her hand across my bottom, but not to hurt me, like Daddy. "Come on. Let's change your wet shirt, then you can set the table while I finish supper."

The second we get back into the den, Daddy's open eyes stare at us. I slide over to Mama's far side, away from him, as we walk by.

He grabs her hand and says, "Come give me sugar."

Mama leans down, pecks him on the lips, and pulls away.

"Mmmmm." Daddy circles her arm with his big hand. "That all I get?"

Mama yanks away. "I have supper to get on the table."

I hurry into the kitchen, with Mama following behind. Daddy's still trying. "Come on, Marva, dinner can wait."

Pulling an apron over her head, she mutters under her breath, "Ain't enough I'm slaving over this stove," hands me three plates, and turns back to the range. I set the plates on the table and lay out three napkins folded into triangles.

When I turn around, Daddy motions for me to come over to him. He pushes up the sleeve of his stained work shirt, balls up his fist, pumps up the top of his arm into a camel's hump, and says, "Mary Alice, come feel your daddy's muscle."

My daddy thinks he's a strong man, but he ain't nothing but a show-off. Wants Mama to think he's working hard at the Pepsi Cola plant when everybody knows nobody drinks nothing but Coca-Cola 'round here. Even if they drink RC or Double Cola, they never drink Pepsi. But he thinks he's special, bringing home cases of the stuff and hefting them up over his head. Any time Mama pours me a glass, I carry it outside and spit it into weeds. That should kill them.

Daddy watches his muscle. "Look at that. Get over here and feel this whopper." I don't move. He jerks his head up. "I said, get over here!"

I turn to Mama. She's looking at the ceiling and shaking her head. The snap of Daddy's footrest coming down makes us both jump. I spin my head back and forth between the two of them. She pipes up real quick, in her cheerful voice, "Hold on, Carl. We're coming."

Daddy's half out of his chair. When he hears Mama, he shoots me a shadow look and plops back down. Her hands are in a bowl of flour and chicken livers. Tossing the bowl into the refrigerator, she rears back and slams the door. The box of Trix cereal on top of the fridge shakes and tips over. A rainbow of colors pours onto the floor. Mama doesn't even seem to notice.

She turns the heat off under her sizzling iron skillet, leaving white fingerprint smears on the stove knob. He raises his footrest back up and grumbles, "You'd think I was asking Christ to come back from the dead, the attention I get around here."

She slaps her hands against her apron. Flour shimmers around her fingers.

He raps his knuckles on the wooden arm of his chair. "Any day now, Marva."

"I'm coming!" She snatches her apron off, rinses her hands under the tap, and wipes them on a dish towel she throws onto the counter so hard that it slides off onto the floor, next to the Trix.

As she passes by me, she crooks her finger for me to follow. She breathes in, twists her face into a smile, and walks over to Daddy, swishing her backside. "Let me see this muscle."

He pumps it back up. Mama squeezes, then runs her hand up and down his hairy old arm. "Mary Alice, come feel. Like Superman. Like the Man of Steel's."

Daddy puckers up his lips for Mama to give him sugar. I bet they hear the icky smack all the way next door.

I sit at the kitchen table and spin the top I found in a Cracker Jack box. Mama pulls away, but Daddy grabs her with his gorilla arms and drags her on top of him. At first, I think Daddy's hurting her, but she's still smiling. She always lets him do whatever he wants. How can she like him touching her?

I wish she'd come back and finish cooking, instead of them doing the gushy stuff. But she never looks this happy. I spin my top and hope it never falls down.

They wrestle around and smack some more. Mama's giggles tinkle toward me. "Come here, baby." She's lying sideways over his lap with her legs hung over the side of his recliner, holding her arms out to me.

Half the time, there's no telling what Daddy's gonna do when it comes to me. I take a close look at him. He lifts the back of Mama's hair and kisses her neck. This don't look like the time to be bothering him.

Mama's smile gets smaller, and she waves at me. "Come on. Join the fun."

Daddy pulls her tighter. When he talks to Mama, he's staring at me with his green eyes. "Leave her be. We got our own fun going on here." He turns his head away as if I was an old dog he'd told to stay and lays his cheek down on her shoulder, the same as a little baby.

But Mama insists. "Don't be silly, Carl. Mary Alice doesn't have to sit all by herself. Besides, I want to spend time with her before she goes to Jean's tomorrow." Her smile is gone, and she jerks her hand in a "get over here now" move.

I scoot my chair back. The pots of potatoes and turnip greens boil away on the stove. How long before we eat now?

I grab Mama's outstretched hands and scramble up her legs onto her lap. Daddy doesn't help me up, doesn't look at me. But he does open his arms from around Mama until I get settled, then wraps them back around both of us. We all lie back like turtles stacked up on a creek log: me on top, Daddy on bottom, and Mama between us.

I lay my head back against her chest, close my eyes so I don't see all the black hairs on Daddy's arms, and breathe in Mama's White Shoulders. Every day, when she gets home from work, off goes her girdle and on comes her powder. Mama says she can smell Firestone tires for hours after she leaves work. The powder's sweetness clears out her nose.

Aunt Jean wears White Shoulders, too. Mama buys it for her every Christmas. It smells better than anything, even better than summer nights when the whole neighborhood's outside grilling up hamburgers and hot dogs, and all us kids get to run around catching lightning bugs and playing Ain't No Boogers Out Tonight.

Mama rubs her hand down my arm over and over as she talks soft and low into my ear. "What'd you do at school today?"

"Made Easter baskets for sick kids in the hospital."

She crosses both arms around me in a hug. "What a nice thing to do. How'd you make the baskets?"

"Oh, it was fun." I'd like to see her face when I tell her about the project, but I don't want to see Daddy. I talk straight ahead. "We cut a plastic milk jug in half. The bottom part was the basket, and we cut around the top half to make the handle. Mrs. Mayer stapled the handles on, so we didn't stick ourselves." I wanted to staple it myself, and my right foot starts bouncing back and forth as I talk. "Then we put in green grass, not real grass, but plastic, and the Easter eggs we made yesterday from long strips of paper wrapped around and around. Mrs. Mayer called it 'paper-that-played.'"

Mama laughs and says, "That's papier mâché, you silly girl."

"Pa-per muh shay." I nod. "Then I painted my eggs blue and green, not yucky pink." I don't tell her I tied yellow yarn around the handle and wouldn't let go when Mrs. Mayer came to take it. I wanted it for myself.

Daddy's loud voice comes from behind my head. "Stop your infernal wiggling or you're getting down. And quit yakking. Can't hear myself think with all your damn babbling."

I press my foot against an invisible brake. "Yes, sir." Daddy doesn't say much, but when he does, he means for me to listen.

Mama presses her lips against my ear. It tickles, but I don't move an inch. "Your Easter basket sounds real pretty." She gives me a squeeze and settles herself against Daddy.

Lying with my back against her, every breath she takes moves both of us up and down. The three of us lie there for a while. I begin to breathe in time to Mama's chest rising and falling, until the oven timer goes off.

"Shoot, the cornbread." Mama pushes Daddy's arms away and moves her hips for me to get down.

"Shit." Daddy wraps his arms back around us. "Who cares?"

"You'll feel different with burned bread on your plate." Mama pulls Daddy's hands loose, hugs me around the middle, and rocks one, two, three times to stand us both up. She motions for me to hop back onto Daddy's lap. "No reason for all of us to tend to supper."

"I'll help you cook." I say it fast.

She barely looks back over her shoulder at me. "I've got it. You spend time with your daddy."

With a slap of his hand on his thigh, he shows me I'm to climb back up. I grit my teeth and look at the floor.

"Well, come on then, if you have to." I don't move. "What's the matter with you?" he says louder. "Get up here." I look up and shake my head. He brings his face right in front of mine so close his cigarette stink makes me gag. "Think you're too good for your own daddy?"

"No, sir." There's a grass stain in the shape of a lion's head on the toe of my left tennis shoe. It's ready to pounce on Daddy and eat him up.

"Well, you sure as hell ain't." He grabs my wrists and yanks me toward him. I stumble and fall into his lap.

"Watch it!" Daddy stands up and I fall to the floor. I don't drop far, just enough for my bottom to bang on the wood floor. As he steps around me, he tugs hard on my ponytail and hisses low, "Disgusting brat." Low, Mama doesn't hear.

When his hand comes away, his watch catches in my hair. He jerks the metal band loose, taking a plug of my hair with it. "Youch!" I rub the side of my head. "That hurt." Tears sting my eyes.

He turns away and goes off down the hall.

The bathroom door slams shut as Mama scurries in and leans over me. "For goodness' sake, you know he didn't mean to hurt you."

I glare at her. "He did, too."

"No. He didn't. He was trying to play with you. Why do you have to treat him that way?" She puts her hands on her hips and frowns down at me. "Get up from there and help me get dinner on the table."

I stare at the floor, push myself up with raw palms, and rock onto my sore knees. He never lets her see him being mean to me. So, she's always on his side. No fair. Nobody ever takes up for me. No matter what he does, I'm the one who gets in trouble.

—

After a quiet supper, the scrapes of our forks were the loudest sounds, Mama's cleaning the kitchen and Daddy's back in his chair. I wipe down the table, then slip through the den to take my bath.

When I'm clean and in pajamas, I creep to the den door. "Mama, I'm ready for bed." She's sitting on the couch with the ironing board down low, pressing our clothes. Daddy's staring at The Gomer Pyle Show and sipping a beer. He doesn't move.

Mama's shoulders go up and down. She sets the iron with its bird beak nose pointed up and wipes a loose strand of hair out of her eyes. "Go kiss your daddy good night."

I slide over to him and don't look at the TV. That Gomer Pyle kind of looks like my daddy. Daddy moves his cheek toward me, without taking his eyes off the TV show. I touch my lips on it as quick as a blink.

Mama takes my hand and leads me down the hall, into my bedroom. "Can I have a book?" I crawl into bed. She sits on the side, pulls my chenille daisy bedspread over me, and kisses my forehead.

"Honey, Mama's done in tonight. How about two next time?" Seeing her sleepy eyes, I nod. "Good girl."

"Can you lie down with me?" I grab her hand and pull it towards my heart. "Just for a little while?"

"No, baby," she says with a yawn.

"But I could scratch your back for you. It'd feel really good." Sitting up and reaching around her, I rub my fingernails across her shoulders.

"You're a sweet girl, but it's time you get some shut-eye." She stands up. "Now you sleep tight. And don't let the bedbugs bite." She cuts the light off. I'm in the dark.

I lie in my twin bed, holding myself perfectly still. Night noises flow around me. Mama comes out of the bathroom and slaps down the hall in her house shoes. Daddy's TV hums. Mama's voice rises above it, "No. I'm exhausted. Maybe I'd have more 'sugar time' if you helped out around this house."

He growls something, and she's louder than before. "Let me remind you. My alarm goes off at five-thirty. I have to work tomorrow while you're off fishing."

I shut my eyes and listen. If they start screaming, I'll get in my closet. But Daddy doesn't say anything. Mama's heels pound down the hall, and their bedroom door bangs shut.

Bit by bit, the house quietens, except for Daddy's TV. I tune my ears in. Witch fingernails scratch across my bedroom windows. I tug my bedspread up and hold it hard. My knuckles drill into my chin. My eyes work overtime. I count my windows and doors over and over—one, two, three, four, one, two, three, four.

At first, I count slow and stare with wide open eyes to see if anything's coming in the front window. But then I might miss something at the side window or the bedroom door or the closet door. I use supersonic speed, until everything's one big blur. It makes me dizzy headed, and I have to slow down again.

Why am I such a chicken? I'm six years old. A big girl now. Not scared of climbing the tallest tree. Not scared of the boys at Pepperell

Elementary. I can outrun most all of them anyway. But bedtime makes my heart beat out of my chest and my skin itch all over.

My pillow's name is Mr. Sand. I hold him against me and pull the covers up until they cover my nose, with my eyes still searching the room. I whisper into the sheets, "Now I lay me down to sleep." But that's as far as I can get.

It's hard to breathe under here. I must have been lying awake for days. Out in the hall the sounds come: squeak, bump, pop. A monster coming after me. I yank the covers all the way over my head.

But it's not really a monster who shows up. Just my Daddy. What have I done wrong now?

He flips the covers back and squeezes in next to me, wearing nothing but his t-shirt and underwear. "Daddy?" He grabs hold of me. So tight it hurts. Slaps his hand across my mouth.

"Shut it," he hisses into my ear. If only Mama was awake.

I lay as still as a statue. The nasty, black hairs on his hand itch and scratch my nose. He lies on top of me and starts shaking and having a fit, the way a girl at my school does. I breathe in and don't breathe out again until spots fly in front of me.

He mashes against me and jerks up and down, squashing me flat as a flitter. The whole bed moves. Whatever he's doing, I want him to stop. But I know better than to make a peep.

Instead, I go away in my head and think about Aunt Jean's Jesus. Aunt Jean says He's our Savior. I wish He'd come save me right now. He'd sweep me out of bed with one hand and hold me safe up against Him. We'd fly down Cedartown Highway to Aunt Jean's house. When we got there, she'd have breakfast cooked, and we'd have French toast with butter and maple syrup, just the way I like, all golden brown. Then Aunt Jean's Jesus would fade back into His picture on her wall, like a genie's smoke sucked back into its bottle.

Daddy rolls me, facing away from him, with his head above mine. His fingernails cut into my hip bones like he's using my bottom as a washcloth to scrub his stomach. He's bumping against my sore bottom, from where he dropped me. He pants the way the old hound at Shorty's store does. He smells sour as a dirty dishrag.

I feel horrible bad the way I do when I've done something wrong and Mama says, "Now aren't you ashamed of yourself?"

There's a big lump in my throat when I try to swallow. Squeezing my eyes shut, I try not to cry.

I poke one finger out to trace and count the puffy daisy petals on my bedspread … one, two, three, four, five, one, two, three ….

"Carl?" Mama's voice sounds from their bedroom across the hall.

Daddy drops on top of me as heavy as a horse, knocking me from my side onto my stomach, my arm caught up underneath me. His hand slaps across my mouth again.

"Carl?" Mama's feet hit the floor.

He springs up. Pushes me away. Hard enough I have to grab onto the edge of the bed to keep him from shoving me off.

He pulls up my covers just as Mama opens their door.

She crosses the hall into my room. "What are you doing?" Mama rubs sleep from her eyes.

"Just tucking her in."

I open my eyes and look at Mama but she's looking at Daddy.

"Well, that's nice, but don't wake her." Mama turns and goes into the bathroom.

When the bathroom door shuts, he grabs me again and brings his face close to mine. He pulls his fist back. I squeeze my eyes shut, waiting for him to hit me. Instead, he whispers near my ear, "I was sleepwalking. Don't you tell." He squeezes me tighter and pinches my arm. "Not anyone. Never. You hear me?" I try to nod my head, but I'm shaking all over. My teeth chatter the way they do when it snows. "Say it. Say 'Yes sir, Daddy.'"

I manage to croak out "Yes sir." When I open my eyes, he's gone.

For a minute, I remember Daddy coming in my bedroom and doing something like this before. But, like a bad dream, the thought fades away.

I need to go tee-tee. My legs won't move.

If I can count all ten of my fingers, then maybe I'll be able to get out of bed. One. I touch my thumb. I can't feel it. I pinch until it hurts. Two. I press down hard on my pointer … until I count all the way to ten. Taking a deep breath, I try to swing my feet out of bed, but I'm frozen solid. I can't budge.

I force myself to stretch out my fingers to grab Mr. Sand and hug him up tight against me. We stare out into the dark room. It's like my eyes are glued wide open and my nose won't work right. It sniffs in but doesn't sniff out. It finally sniffs out, but won't sniff in.

The witch's fingers scratch at my windows again. I don't care. If only she'd cast a spell and turn me into a squirrel. Then I could live in my tree, alone with Mr. Hickory and Buzzy.

I try to figure out what just happened. Did Daddy come in here? But he never tucks me in. Then I remember. He was sleepwalking. I wonder why he doesn't want anyone to know.

Car lights shine in my window, moving along the ceiling from left to right. I pretend they're falling stars and make a wish Daddy would go away forever.

Two

The next morning, I spring out of bed extra early to go see Aunt Jean. But then I remember something. Something bad. Something about Daddy. But I can't tell anyone, not even Mama, not even Aunt Jean.

Mama's bedroom door opens. She comes into my room and puts her finger to her lips, "Shhhh. Your daddy's sleeping. Get dressed. Hurry up."

Mama drives me to Aunt Jean's to spend the night and go to church with her on Sunday. Mama says Aunt Jean's a "holiness person." Aunt Jean says I'm her little angel.

It's still mostly dark when our baby blue Malibu crunches up Aunt Jean's gravel drive. But she's sitting outside on her glider in the brightness of her porch light, waiting for us. As I fling open the car door, she stands up straight as can be. My Aunt Jean's tall. She has on a thick black sweater. Her brown dress comes down almost to her ankles and buttons up to her neck. Her long, black and gray hair is piled up so high it about touches the ceiling. All the women at the Church of God wear it that way. I know from watching it takes practically a whole box of bobby pins and hairpins and a can of hair spray to hold her beehive in place.

"Aunt Jean!" The dirt and leaves fly underneath my sneakers. When I leap onto the porch and into her, she falls backwards a little and makes an "umph" sound. I squeeze my arms around her waist and press my face onto her flat stomach. My hands sting from sliding down the rope yesterday, but I don't care.

I step back from her and spread my arms out as far as I can. "I love you this much!"

She throws her arms out as wide as the porch. "But I love you this much."

I rise up on my tiptoes and try to stretch my fingertips even farther. "But I love you as wide as the whole wide world."

She leans down, gathers me to her, and whispers in my ear, "But I love you forever and ever, and a day." It's what we say every time I come to visit, and it always makes my heart the happiest.

After giving me a bear hug, she pulls me away and puts her hands on my shoulders. "You're a sight for sore eyes. Just let me look at you. Grown a foot since I saw you two weeks ago. Looking more like your Mama every day."

"Really?" My mama's pretty. I want to look just like her.

Mama walks up holding my Sunday dress on a hanger and the baby blue pillowcase I packed the rest of my things in. Aunt Jean looks back and forth between the two of us. "Same pretty brown hair and eyes, high cheekbones, and sweet smile. But when are you two gonna get some meat on your bones? You could do with beef roast and potatoes to fatten you up."

"That's the pot calling the kettle black." Mama crosses to the glider and sits down.

Aunt Jean ignores her and plants a dry kiss on my cheek. I breathe in White Shoulders … and Listerine. "You're as sweet as sugar candy. Yes, you are." Then she turns to Mama. "And here's my other sugar girl."

I still can't believe they're sisters. Aunt Jean has gray grandma hair. One time I asked Mama about it. She said Aunt Jean was a teenager when she was born. That's why Aunt Jean seems much older. I wish I had a big sister like Aunt Jean.

Mama hands me the dress and my pillowcase tote bag. "Go put your things up and find yourself something to do. Give Jean and me a chance to talk for a spell. Then she's all yours."

I hold the sunshine yellow dress up high, so it doesn't drag on the floor, tuck the pillowcase under my other arm, and pull open the screen door. Aunt Jean's house is split down the middle by a long hall. On the left side is her bedroom and kitchen. On the right side is her bathroom and a living room she never uses. I skip into her bedroom and drop my tote onto the floor by the bed.

Her house is chock-full of Jesus pictures. I go over to the one with the sheep. He looks like a person I could talk to. I'd pet all those wooly lambs, and they'd curl up in my lap, tuck their little hooved feet under so they wouldn't hurt me, while Aunt Jean's Jesus sat beside me and stroked my hair. He'd undo the elastic on my ponytail and comb His fingers through. But it would never pull, never tug, never hurt. We'd sit there in silence—not a word needed. And when the sheep scampered off, the two of us would walk down to the pond and skip stones. He'd show me how to hold the pebble between my thumb and pointer finger—how to snap my wrist so the stone did the walking-across-the-water thing.

And that's the first words we'd say. As my stone skipped, we'd count each hop aloud, "One, two, three." He'd be real proud of me. Then He'd point towards the pond with His eyes. I'd be looking at the water when His magic trick appeared. We'd count, "... four, five, six, seven, eight ..." all the way until we couldn't count anymore, because the stone was clear out of sight, the pond spread out into eternity before our eyes.

Then, Jesus could come home and take my Daddy's place. He'd sleep in the bed with Mama and go off to work at the Coca Cola plant, not Pepsi, every day in His red truck. I bet His truck would glow sunshine gold when He drove up every night. He'd blow the horn, and Mama and me would hop in and go for a ride. Mama would be happy and lay her head on His shoulder. But she'd pull me close to her, too, and Jesus wouldn't mind at all. He'd drive all the way to the West Rome Krystal, and we'd be laughing, and singing Be My Little Baby. Jesus would let me place the order through the drive-in's little speaker. And when the waitress brought out our food, she'd have to wear sunglasses, because our truck would be shining firetruck bright.

Mama and Aunt Jean's voices drift in through the screen door. I leave Jesus and sneak down the hall. They can't see me listening.

Aunt Jean's talking. "Take some time off. You look close to the dropping point."

"Can't do it. Never know how long Carl will stay on a job. Mine keeps us going." A moth flutters outside the door, batting itself against the yellow porch light bulb.

"Then let Mary Alice stay here every weekend. Give you the Lord's Day to rest. You know how much I love having her."

"Sunday is really the only time I get to see her." A milk truck rumbles by. The metal glider clangs. "My heavens! A quarter 'til seven and I'm opening. Gotta run!"

I bolt out onto the porch and grab Mama around the waist. "Bye, Mama. Love you."

She kisses my cheek and hugs me. "See you tomorrow. Behave for Aunt Jean." Then she's gone.

Aunt Jean and I stand on the porch waving bye as Mama backs out of the driveway. The split second her taillights disappear, I pull Aunt Jean by the hand. "Come play!"

Into the kitchen we go. I take my Snap cards out of my pocket. Buzzy's on top of the deck, as always. He's happy to be at Aunt Jean's house.

"Settle your little self down. We aren't playing until I've fed our growling stomachs." She pulls out her black iron skillet and sets out a bowl, a carton of eggs, milk, sugar, cinnamon, and a loaf of bread on the kitchen table. Then, she starts breaking eggs. She can do it with only one hand.

"Are you fixing French toast?" I cross my fingers.

"What do you think?" Her hand pauses in mid-air with a half-cracked egg jiggling in its shell.

"I think you are, hope you are, and am absolutely for-positive you are!" I'm bouncing on my toes, then stop. "Aren't you?"

She lifts her head and grins. "I absolutely, for-positive am." Her big hair looks like a turban, from a movie I once saw. She'd just need to paint it white. "Here," she hands me a fork, "you beat the eggs while I get the bread ready. Careful now. Don't let them spill."

After breakfast, we play ten Snap games in a row. She says cards are the work of the Devil, but since no money's changing hands, it can't hurt. We head outside to visit on the glider and sing all our favorite songs with hand motions: *This Little Light of Mine*; *Climb, Climb Up Sunshine Mountain*; and *Say, Say Oh Playmate*. We're sliding down the rain barrel when the phone rings. It's a sister from the church. She'll be gabbing for a while.

At lunch time, we eat egg salad sandwiches made with green olives, just the way I like them. For dessert, fruit cocktail, the kind with red cherries. After that, we lie down to take a nap, because Aunt Jean needs her rest. I'm six now. Not a baby anymore and too old for naps. But I don't tell her. And anyway, when I'm at Aunt Jean's, it's like there's a switch on the pillow. It closes my eyes and puts me to sleep every time I lay my head down.

I wake when I hear the bedsprings squeaking from Aunt Jean getting up. We like to have quiet time after napping. It's back to her kitchen table to work on a jigsaw puzzle, read, and play tic-tac-toe.

As we play, I tell Aunt Jean, "Mrs. Mayer's the best teacher ever."

"Now, why is that?" Aunt Jean scratches out another O on the back of the fruit cocktail label she tore from the can.

Searching the nine-square, I mark an X so hard my pencil tip breaks. "Tic tac toe, I win!" I pat her hand. "Play again? You might win this time."

"All right. But just one more. I must call Sister Gladys and Sister Thelma." She hands me her little plastic pencil sharpener, and I twist my broken tip while she draws another board. "Why is Mrs. Mayer the best teacher?"

A curl of wood rolls off the tiny, silver blade, and I smile a secret smile. Aunt Jean always listens to me and remembers what I say. "Because she reads us books and nods her head when we get it right but doesn't yell if we get it wrong, not even when Sammy misses every one. She just has the rest of us color, while she leans over Sammy's shoulder and talks to him in a quiet, inside-voice."

Aunt Jean pushes the label between the two of us. "She surely does sound like a good teacher."

I nod and, before she can say anything, I mark an O in the middle square. "There. You get to go first, and I made your first mark for you, in the middle." I wink at her, but both eyes come down at the same time. "A sure-fire way to win."

When she circles in her last O, I jump up and hug her neck. "You did it!"

She pulls me onto her lap. "I think I had help."

"Oh, no, you won, fair and square." My stomach growls, and we laugh.

"How can you be hungry?" She sets me down and picks at a loose thread at the hem of my skirt.

"Just a little bit."

She hands me an apple and sends me outside to play by myself, so she can make her phone calls.

I race marbles down the drainpipe in the backyard, then push acorns into a little hole in one of the birdhouses her neighbor, Mr. Bledsoe, nailed together. He has them all over the place, up on his porches, on tall poles in the yard, and even on the clothesline post. I stand on tiptoe and fill every hole I can reach with acorns. Maybe the robins will find them, and sing thank you songs.

Buzzy and I crawl under Aunt Jean's weeping willow, where no one can see us. We pretend we're Indians living behind a waterfall.

When I hear Aunt Jean calling me for dinner time, I stay hidden. She opens the back door and yells, "Mary Alice!"

"Boo!" I jump out from under the branches.

Surprised, she holds up her hands. Then she laughs. "Boo yourself. It's time to come in."

I'll be glad when I can tell time. Then all these times won't sneak up on me.

———

After dinner, we wash and dry the dishes. I'm wiping the last plate when she says it's time for my bath.

"Oh, no. Not yet." I spin around to face her. "Let's finish our puzzle first. Please."

She looks at the half-finished puzzle spread out on the end of her table and laughs. "We'll probably have to finish next time you visit. It's 250 pieces. But we can read after bath time. Remember, we're visiting the Lord's house tomorrow. Cleanliness is next to godliness." She takes the plate out of my hand and sets it in the dish rack. "Scoot,

scoot. Off to the tub for you." She holds my hand and walks me back to the bathroom.

Grunting and twisting, I tug at my shirt. "Don't want no rotten bath," I mumble under my breath.

"Be still and stop your complaining." I hold my arms straight up while she pulls the shirt over my head and sneaks a tickle under my arm. I laugh and grab myself around the middle.

After dropping my panties, I scramble over the side of her clawfoot tub. Stretching my legs out, I tilt my head back, ears under the water. My periscope rises above the waves. A sea monster! Man the torpedoes! All hands on deck!

Aunt Jean fishes my arm out and pulls my head from under the water. "You're flooding the floor! Stop splashing." She soaps up a washcloth and hands it to me. "Hurry up now. Don't make your old Aunt Jean stand here for long." As I'm bathing my arms, she stops me and takes both of my hands in hers. "What in the world happened here?"

The rope burns in my palms look even worse than they did yesterday. "My horse tried to get away."

"What horse?" She leans back on her heels.

"Trigger." Aunt Jean doesn't let me climb trees. She says it isn't lady-like.

She motions for me to stand up. I can do the bottom half. Pointing toward my bruises and skinned knees, she says, "You are a walking wreck." I look down and see the bruises on both of my hip bones. "You better stop your rough playing, or your cowgirl days will be over."

I almost remember where those marks came from, so I sit down fast and water splashes in Aunt Jean's face. "Mary Alice! Settle your horses. Right now!"

I squeeze my eyes shut and smell shampoo as she lathers up my hair. A few streams of soapy water trickle down my face. "Arghhh! My eyes!"

"Stop squirming!" She fills a plastic cup with warm water. "Here's a clean washcloth to put over your face. Tilt your head back." Cup after cup rinses the suds from my hair. "Okay. Out you go."

"Do I have to? I didn't even get to play!"

"You beat the band. Don't want to get in, then I can't get you out. Come on now. I'm tired and still need my bath." When I crawl out, she wraps a towel around me. My baby doll pajamas are warm from her space heater. She sits on the toilet seat. I stand facing her, cringing each time she pulls the comb through my long, tangled hair.

"Ouch!"

"Be still! Where do you get these rats' nests?" She combs and combs, more knots than smooth spots. "Okay, I'm finished." I bolt from the room.

When she comes back in the bedroom, her wet hair really is wrapped turban-style, and she's changed into her night clothes. I'm in the middle of the bed, ready with a stack of books. Her shoulders hitch up with each wheeze of breath. Mama says a long time ago, Aunt Jean had TB. TB is something that makes them cut out part of your lungs. Now, she can't breathe so good. She stumbles to the armchair by her bed, leans back, and closes her eyes.

When the rise and fall of her chest slows, she opens her eyes. "What are you up to? Scheming your bedtime story already, I see." Between her words she makes a sound like Lawrence Welk's accordion.

After un-wrapping the towel and brushing through her hair, it falls to her hips. I get down and sit near her feet. "Get up off my nasty floor. Here." She pats the ottoman in front of her chair.

With me facing her, she bends from the waist, and brushes forward until her face is hidden behind a sheet of hair. Then she leans over and covers me with it. I squeal, and she shakes her hair all over my head and shoulders.

After jerking my head out, I edge forward, grab the wavy strands in the middle with both hands, and pull her hair apart, like the Desoto Theater's red velvet curtains. "Peek-a-boo!" It's our old game from when I was a baby, but I don't care. It's still fun.

Giggling, I hop up and run away. Her hair curtain swings closed. I ease towards her and pull it open again. "Peek-a-boo! I see you!"

I make to run, but not really going anywhere. She grabs me with one arm and pulls me into her lap, wet hair and all. I pat her smiling face and lay my cheek against hers. "I love you the mostest."

"Oh, no, you do not. I love you the mostest, forever and ever, and a day." She gives me a gigantic squeeze. "Do you know what?"

"What?"

"I'll tell you what. God sent you to me when I needed you most." Her dark eyes shine behind her thick, black-framed glasses.

I yawn. "What'd you need me for?"

"To have somebody to love."

Three

The next morning, after Sunday service, Aunt Jean and I change out of our church clothes. She starts frying up pork chops for lunch. I wander around. While she's busy cooking, it's my chance to go into the closed-up living room she almost never uses.

I rub my arms. This room is always cold. Her old green vinyl couch sits next to her fancy antique covered up with a light blue sheet. Underneath the sheet is a red velvet chair, with a tiny seat, skinny wooden legs and a curved top outlined with fat screws. I'm not supposed to sit on it but I like how it feels.

The bookcase in here has knickknacks I can play with if I'm careful. The little black and white china dog with the broken foot fits in my open hand. I rub his head and speak his language, "Woof." He woofs back. I sit him down and pick up the little wooden crate that came all the way from South Georgia. Holding it up to my eye, the real peanut in there shows through the slats. I sing to it, "Found a peanut, found a peanut …."

That's when I see the crucifix above the bookcase. I'd forgotten about this one—the sad, scary Jesus up on a wooden cross, nailed up there. This Jesus reminds me of the birdhouses her neighbor, Mr. Bledsoe, builds. But it's a bird house gone wrong. It has a little plastic doll hammered onto a wooden cross.

I feel sorry for Him and reach out my hand for Him to come skip stones with me at the pond. But He just stares at me with a lonesome look and all bleeding. No Bactine. No Band-Aids.

And then it comes to me. This Birdhouse Jesus needs me near as much as I need Him. If He came to my house, then I could help make Him better and He could help make my daddy not be mean to me. I could ask Aunt Jean, but she might say no.

I pull over a wooden stool Mr. Bledsoe made. Stepping up on it, I reach tall on my tippy-toes and grab Jesus with both hands, the way

Aunt Jean taught me to carry my dinner plate from the table to the sink. He wobbles when I step down, and I think for a minute I'm gonna drop Him. That scares me bad. My spit dries up quick as a peanut butter sandwich. Aunt Jean says He is the light of the world, so I know if He got broke it'd be dark all night and all day long. We wouldn't have recess outside anymore, and there'd be no sunflowers, and the lightning bugs would have to work twice as hard all the time, or nobody'd be able to see a thing.

I squeeze Him tight and walk all careful-like, listening to Aunt Jean singing *Nearer My God to Thee* while she makes lunch, until I get to the pillowcase with my dirty panties and pink polka dot PJs inside. I wrap Him up with my baby doll top, same as a mummy, give Him a little hug, and whisper, "Me and You will take care of each other, and everything's gonna be different." It wasn't really stealing Him. I would just borrow Him. Then I slide Him in with my things and sit the pillowcase by the front door. "You wait here, and when Mama comes for me, I'll take you home."

"Mary Alice, come eat!"

I hop into the kitchen on one foot.

"Well, aren't you chipper?" Aunt Jean smiles and motions with her metal spatula towards the sink. "Wash your hands and come eat while it's hot."

After washing up at the sink and saying the blessing, I dig in. I squirt ketchup on my plate to dip the pork chop patty in and push the crowder peas back, so they don't touch it.

"Did you have fun at Sunday School?" Aunt Jean spoons chow-chow onto her plate and cuts my pork chop into eight pieces.

"Uh huh. Can I use a toothpick?"

"Go ahead, but you're getting too old. You need to start using a fork." She squeezes a wedge of lemon into her sweet iced tea. "What was today's lesson?"

"Oh! It was a good one." I sit the toothpick box down. "There was this giant named Goliath. A little boy named David told the king he'd kill that old giant. He sure was brave, and he did it! Using a rock and his sling." Holding my right arm straight up, I circle a pretend sling around and around fast over my head, then let go. Wham! I imagine a rock flying into Aunt Jean's cabinet and breaking her dishes.

Aunt Jean holds her palms out, facing me, like she's protecting herself, but she's grinning. "You store your weapon away before you put my eye out and tell me what you learned from the story."

Learned from it? I bite on my bottom lip and think. "Good guys win if they're brave?"

"Why do you think David was brave?" Aunt Jean raises her eyebrows.

"Because he wasn't scared." Using the toothpick, I jab a piece of pork chop, dip it in ketchup, and pop it into my mouth.

"Why wasn't he scared?" She sits back and waits for my answer.

I look up at the ceiling. Why wasn't he scared? Oh, yeah! "I bet it was because God was on his side."

Smiling big, she nods her head yes. "That's right. He knew God would keep him safe. But don't say that— 'I bet.' Remember, betting is a sin."

"Okay. I won't say it." My toothpick is Goliath's sword. I spear a pea. "And Jesus, He'll keep you safe, too. Right?"

"Yes, ma'am. Jesus is God's son." Aunt Jean takes a bite and dabs her lips using a faded white cloth napkin covered with yellow daffodils.

"And God's a good daddy?" I hold my breath, waiting for her answer.

"Well, of course, He is, you Silly Willy." She puckers her lips and shakes her head. "You can ask the strangest questions. I wish I was a marble rolling around in your noggin."

A tap comes at the front door. "Yoo hoo!"

Mama! Though I get up and run to let her in, she's already in the house and turning the corner into the kitchen. I throw my arms around her waist. She gives me a quick hug, pats my back, and moves my hands away. "Ready to go? We gotta get a run on." I grab her right hand with both of mine and hold on to her, my left cheek pressed up against the soft skin of her arm. She smells good. Like tires.

Aunt Jean stands and pulls Mama into a big hug, causing me to drag along like the little red caboose. "I fried up a few extra big chops for you. I'll get you a plate while you pour yourself a glass of tea."

But Mama shakes her head. "Sorry. We can't stay. Carl's in the car waiting on us. Wants to run by a friend's house and borrow some tools while we're in your neck of the woods."

"Well, then have him come in and grab a bite first. No need for him to sit out there in the hot car." Aunt Jean doesn't look mad, but she doesn't look happy, either.

"That's good of you, Jean, but we ate a sandwich before we left." Mama yanks away from my grip and points at me. "Sit down and eat. No lollygagging. Your daddy wants to get on the road, and you know how he gets."

Aunt Jean sighs. "Let's plan a nice long visit next time. I don't see near enough of either one of you."

Mama rubs Aunt Jean's shoulders with both hands and lays her cheek against Aunt Jean's. "I know. We'll do better. But it can't be helped this time."

I have to get my pillowcase before Mama does. I poke two pieces of pork chop at a time and shove them into my mouth. "I'm done."

They both look down at me and say at the same time, "Eat your peas."

The mound of peas on my plate must be a mile high. I don't want them. They taste like dirt. "But I ate all my meat."

A horn sounds from the driveway. "See. We gotta go." I gulp my glass of milk, start to wipe my mouth with my hand, and think to use my napkin instead. "May I be excused?" Aunt Jean loves it when I say that before leaving the table.

"Oh, all right. But don't think you'll get by without eating your peas next time." Mama gives Aunt Jean one last hug. I shoot out of my chair, around her, and into the hall.

Aunt Jean's calling for me as she makes her way from the kitchen to the front porch. "Who shot you out of a cannon? Get back here. I want a proper goodbye, you rascal."

I grab my pillowcase in one hand and my David and Goliath coloring page in the other. Have to get Birdhouse Jesus in the car before Mama feels an extra-heavy somebody in there. I tear off to the car and sit Him in the back seat.

Daddy scowls at me. "What's taking so long?"

I stay out of his arm's reach. "We're coming, Daddy. Just one more minute." I back out of the car before he can tell me to sit down.

Aunt Jean is waiting for me on the porch with both hands on her hips. I dash back and hug her waist, peck her cheek, and give her an extra squeeze to hold my place until I get to see her again.

Mama hustles me into the car. I roll down my window. "Bye! I love you!"

As Daddy backs fast out of the driveway and into the street, Aunt Jean throws kisses from the porch. I throw them back. She acts like she catches them, patting them onto her cheek, all the while waving her other hand over her head. Daddy screeches off. When I get up on my knees to look out the back windshield, Aunt Jean is still waving, still throwing kisses, until she gets so small I can't see her anymore.

Four

When we finally get home from Daddy's friend's house, it's dark, and Mama shoos me into the house. "I want you in and out of the tub lickety-split. It's already past your bedtime and a school night."

I clutch my pillowcase to my chest and skip straight to my room and close the door. But not all the way, just almost, so Mama won't come around saying, "Now what trouble are you making in there with the door shut?"

While she's running my bath water, I take Birdhouse Jesus out of the pillowcase and hold Him tight, while I spin in a circle, looking around the room for a place He might like to live. Have to think quick. I can't lay Him on my pillow, can't prop Him up on the dresser or slide Him behind my striped yellow curtains. Somebody'd find Him. And I can't let it happen.

What about my closet? I open the door and see it, the perfect spot. Kicking my school shoes out of the way, I drop to my knees and sweep aside my stack of games: Cootie, Uncle Wiggily, and Candyland. I lean Jesus against the back wall and crawl in there with Him. "This'll be a good place for you. I come in here sometimes when it gets loud. Won't nobody hurt you in here."

Maybe He won't be afraid of the dark. Just in case, I pull my Snap cards out of my pocket and slide Buzzy off the top of the deck. "Now, the two of you can keep each other company." I prop Buzzy up next to Jesus. That should make both of them happy.

Mama shouts from the bathroom, "Mary Alice, where are you? Get in the tub this instant."

I throw kisses to Jesus and Buzzy and dash out of the room for my bath.

———

On school days, I wear a house key on a beaded chain around my neck. After riding the bus home, I change into my play clothes and walk through the woods behind my house to my babysitter, Mrs. Middleton's. That way, I don't have to walk on the narrow country roads. Mrs. Middleton is an old lady who lives on Booger Hollow Road, catty-corner from my house, but far enough I can't see her house from my backyard.

The rule is I change clothes and go straight to the sitter's, unless Daddy's home. If he's there, I have to stay at my house. Once, when Daddy was home and asleep in his chair, I acted like I didn't know it and went to Mrs. Middleton's anyway. Daddy got real mad when he had to pay her. Mama isn't ever home early, no matter how many times I hunt on my hands and knees until I find a four-leaf clover to wish on.

I don't much like staying at Mrs. Middleton's either, because she uses mounds of moth balls that make my eyes and nose burn. Plus, there's not another girl there my age, just a few babies and some older boys who won't let me play ball with them. I wish my mama was like my friend Carolyn's mother and stayed home all the time. I could come home, and Mama'd be waiting for me. Then, Mama and me would make construction paper decorations to match the holidays. Orange, red, and yellow leaves. Pumpkins. Strings of popcorn and pipe cleaner ornaments. Hearts. And on Mother's Day, we'd make the biggest bunches of tissue paper flowers you ever saw, one for Mama, and one for Aunt Jean.

Monday is art day. I get home from school and dash to my room to show Jesus the picture I drew at school. "See. It's me and You and Buzzy. We're riding the Ferris wheel at the county fair." I hold the drawing out towards him. "It was funny. Mrs. Mayer thought You were my mama, because of Your long hair and robes. I didn't tell her no different. Here, you can keep it." I tuck my drawing behind Him. "I have to go to the babysitter's, but I'll be back later."

Daddy picks me up at five o'clock and drives me home. Mama won't get off until seven, or later. The minute he gets in the door, he goes to the laundry room, then comes out screaming and grabbing at me.

"Towels don't fold themselves! You must be the laziest ass little bitch on Earth. No better than a damn nigger!" His hands on my shoulders bear down hard and spit splatters onto my face.

I gulp. "But Daddy, I was at the sitter's. Mama just washed them this morning."

He pulls his eyebrows down low. "You arguing with me?" He takes two steps towards me. "Think you're gonna sass me. Well, I'll show you who's boss."

Before I can say anything, he unbuckles his belt, whips it off in one fell swoop, and pushes me onto the couch. "Get your pants down."

A flurry starts in my head. Not that. "No, Daddy …."

"Think you're gonna tell me no." He grabs me by the arm and twists. I flip face down. "Pants off! So help me God, if you sass back at me one more time, you will regret it the rest of your short life."

I tremble. Can't feel my hands. Fumble with my zipper. Look back at him over my shoulder.

His face turns bright red. "Now!"

Yanking the zipper, I rush to tug down my pants and panties. I can't breathe as I wait for the sound of the belt whizzing through the air. It comes down hard. I gasp and bite my tongue. He hits me again, and again. My ears buzz. My nose runs.

He tosses the belt to the floor. "Now. Get out of my sight."

I jerk my pants up and run to my room.

Opening my closet door, I sit down with Buzzy and Jesus and wipe the tears and snot from my face. "Jesus." I pick up the crucifix and look Him in the eye. "You have to help me. If you can't make Daddy love me, can you at least make him not hate me?"

I kiss Jesus' face and place Him back next to Buzzy. Maybe that will work.

I have to get away from Daddy. "Buzzy, you can't come with me today. Jesus is a secret. He can't come and He needs company." Looking around the closet for something for them to play with, my black patent Sunday shoes shine in the darkness. "Here, you two can ride bumper cars." I sit Jesus in one shoe, Buzzy in the other, and point the shoes at each other. "I'm sorry. Daddy leaves me alone when I'm outside."

Grabbing my bag of marbles, I take off my shoes and slide down the hall in my sock feet. I peep into the den and see Daddy already asleep in his chair, three beer cans already empty on his end table. His feet propped up on the recliner footrest have socks with a hole. One of his big toes sticks out. Inching around him, I hold the marbles tight against my stomach. They don't clink. I make my way out and sit on the carport steps to put my shoes back on.

In the backyard, I grab a stick, draw a circle in a bare spot of dirt, and dump my marbles onto the ground. Where's my shooter? I pluck my giant cat's eye from the rest, roll it between my thumb and pointer finger, and drop down low on the grass to aim.

It's not as much fun playing by myself, but living in the country, I'm used to it. Once, I asked Daddy if my friend Carolyn could come over, but he said, "It's enough trouble for me to watch you, much less have to babysit a house full of snot-nosed brats."

My friend, Imaginary Carolyn, is winning when Mama calls me in to supper. When did she get home?

Today, I don't scoot behind the cedar bushes to hide. I run right in and wash my hands, fronts and backs, and scrub my face, without nobody telling me. Holding my head like there was a book on top of my noggin, I walk to the table the way Mama said little ladies should. I sit down, spread my napkin on my lap, and look to see if Mama's watching, but she's scraping the crisped-up bits and pieces out of the frying pan onto a plate of chicken. I cross my hands in my lap with all the fingers lying on top of each other, as patient as chalk at the blackboard.

Daddy comes to the table dressed in his grease-stained work shirt and rubbing the back of his neck. He sits down and wipes at a cut on his left thumb. I don't think he washed his hands.

Taking in a breath, I hold it until I think I'll smother half to death and the kitchen gets all wavy. I think, okay, Jesus, now's the time for You to change Daddy.

Mama brings over the plate of fried chicken and sets it next to mashed potatoes and gravy, English peas, and biscuits. All my favorites.

My mouth curls up. "Oh, boy, Mama. Thanks."

Jesus is already working. I bet Daddy's going to act like my friend Carolyn's daddy now. He'll smile at me and say, "How was school today for my best girl? Tell Daddy all about it."

Then he'll nod his head and look right at me the whole time I talk about the birds we cut out of red construction paper and hung from the ceiling with yarn and how I drew little lines of feathers on mine. I'll say, "Mine was the daddy bird." That will make my daddy so happy he'll tell Mama and me funny riddles, and we'll all laugh and have the best supper ever. Then, he'll act the way real daddies act every day from now on.

Daddy takes a big swig of sweet tea and wipes his mouth with the back of his hand. "Mary Alice, get me some lemon since your mama makes a point of 'forgetting' it every damn time." Mama glares at him.

"Yes, sir." I hop up. I need to hurry before Mama and him start going at each other. Grabbing the bowl Mama keeps in the fridge, I take him the lemons as fast as I can.

He takes two pieces. His fingernails have dirt under them. "That's a good girl."

My daddy said I was a good girl. I smile at him, but he's squeezing lemon into his glass. My feet feel light and happy as I set the lemons on the table, in case he wants more. I take my seat.

And then, because Jesus is here, and He's already making things better, I get brave like David facing Goliath.

"It all looks real good, don't it, Daddy?" I turn my eyes right toward him, right where I can see him, and he can see me. His eyes edge over me the same as when my teacher's not gonna call on me, never mind my raised hand waving in the air and the answer on the tip of my tongue.

He spears the biggest chicken breast and flops it onto his plate, spoons up taters and peas, crumbles two biscuits and pours gravy over them, and begins to eat. He looks straight ahead the whole time, like

Walter Cronkite's sitting across from him dishing out the evening news.

Mama finishes cutting up a cantaloupe and brings it over to the table. Another of my favorites! She takes off her red apron with the white rickrack outlining its kangaroo pocket and sits down between Daddy and me. She asks Daddy a question with a chirp in her voice, "How was your day?"

He grunts.

She doesn't give up. "Anything new happen?"

Daddy sets his fork down and turns his head slow towards her. "What would happen that don't happen every damn day at that shit hole?"

Mama's cheeks frost up all pink, the same as when she brushes makeup on. "Carl, there's no reason for you to be such a grouch. I just wanted to talk."

He turns back to his plate. "What's to talk about?"

I sit there wishing she'd talk to me. Except she doesn't. Instead, she says, "Well. Let's all eat before it gets cold." And she has on a smile that doesn't match her eyes. Her face ends up looking crooked.

The whole time, I've been sitting with my hands in my lap waiting for it to happen. But I've never been half as slow as Daddy says. I catch on real quick nothing's changed and likely never will.

As I stare at my plate, I wish it would start shining like the moon, and a robot would shoot up out of the light and take me away to another planet, where I could learn robot-talk and float across the ground without my feet touching.

Mama pokes me. "What are you doing, staring off into space? I fixed this dinner special for your first night back home from visiting Jean. Now eat up."

I spoon potatoes and peas onto my plate and pick the littlest chicken leg. When I take a bite of potatoes with my heavy fork, my throat becomes a closed trapdoor, and I can't swallow. Holding the bite in my cheek, I stare at my plate and imagine the peas forming a line like marching ants over the table, down to the floor, outside, away from here. I stare at the peas and count them by two's: two, four, six, eight, two, four, six, eight.

Mama's taking fast bites. Her fork clicks on her teeth. She shakes her head and turns to Daddy. "I will never understand how you can run hot and cold the way you do. You know, you're not the only one who had a hard day."

She taps my plate with her fork, and I jump. "Stop playing with your food and eat."

Daddy chews his food. Mama folds and refolds her napkin. The kitchen sink's leaky faucet drips. She sips her tea. He takes his cigarettes out of his front pocket, lights one, throws the match onto his dirty plate, scrapes his chair back without saying nothing, and goes into the den to watch TV.

Mama looks at the refrigerator and tells it, "A mighty fine dinner, if I do say so myself." After that, she gets up, squirts dish detergent into the sink, and clears the table of Daddy's and her dishes.

While her back's turned, I spit a mouthful of food into my napkin. Then I take a real bite and eat enough Mama will let me get by. I want to go hug her waist, but I know it'd be like hugging one of the pine trees in the backyard. Instead, I drink half of my milk.

"Can I be excused?"

She doesn't answer me.

Taking my plate to the garbage can, I scrape the rest of my food in, along with my napkin full of potatoes and peas. She stands there, rubbing the same plate over and over in circles and looking out the kitchen window.

When I check to see where Daddy is, he's lying on the couch with his eyes closed. The TV's blaring. I make myself small and quietly leave the kitchen, pausing before I walk by him.

The hardest part is always when he's behind me, and the first steps are the worst, because the back of my head waits for a slap. Three deep breaths, and I put one foot in front of the other. I make it without him moving ... all thirty-three steps from the kitchen, across the den, down the hallway, and through my bedroom door. I'm home free. Olly, olly, oxen free.

Birdhouse Jesus is still in the same place in the closet. But He's like one of the lightning bugs I find on the bottom of my jar in the morning, after they'd gleamed so bright the night before. Look what I've done.

I lift Him so I can look in His eyes. He's still bleeding, and nothing's changed with Daddy. Even Jesus can't shine here. Mama would say it's time to fess up. I tell Him the truth. "You can't stay here. No way I can take care of You near as good as Aunt Jean. I'm real sorry."

I set Him down long enough to rub my fists at the corners of my eyes. I don't want Him to think I'm a baby or nothing. Then I scoot down on my stomach and prop myself up on my elbows close to Him. "Don't You go worrying over me. It's not Your fault nothing's different. I've heard my mama say it time and again, 'Just can't be helped.' Ain't nothing nobody can do." I nod at Him. I'm doing the right thing. I have to get Him back to Aunt Jean's as quick as I can.

I take Him into the kitchen, stepping fast past Daddy, who's lying turned on his side, with his back to me. "Mama." I have to say it twice before she turns around. "Mama." I hold Him out to her.

When she sees Him, her forehead scrunches up, and she puts her soapy hands on her hips. "Did you ask Aunt Jean if you could have that?" When I don't answer right away, she closes her eyes and rolls her head from side to side. "For Christ's sake, could anyone ever cut me a break?" Seconds tick by.

The carport door is only a few steps away from me. I make myself curl my toes up or I'll run.

She opens her eyes and glares at me. "Did you take it without asking?"

"But, Mama, I didn't steal it."

"What do you want to call it then?" She shakes her finger at me and soap suds land on my nose.

I talk fast. "Mama, it wasn't for me. It's not my fault. I was trying …."

Her eyes snap open wide. "No. Nothing's ever your fault, is it?" She grabs Him out of my hands before I can warn Him. "I guess this appeared in your room like a ghost. Is that it?" She shakes Him in my direction.

I have to duck to the floor, so He doesn't knock me in the head.

"You get up from there right now. Don't you dare act like I tried to hit you, or I'll get out my belt." Her face is splotchy red. "I can't believe you'd steal this after all Jean does for you. Well, young lady, you're the one's gonna call her and tell her what you did."

My stomach drops into Little River Canyon in one second flat. Tell Aunt Jean! What will she do?

Mama lays Birdhouse Jesus on the kitchen counter, and with her mad and all, I can't tell her she shouldn't lay Him near the stove that way. He should be propped up next to the African violets on the windowsill. At least He'd be watching over me when I talk to Aunt Jean.

My feet won't move. Mama takes my arm and pulls me to the phone. While she dials, I wipe my nose on my sleeve and screw my head around trying to see Him, but He's face down.

"Jean. I got Mary Alice here with something to tell you." She holds the phone out. It's like a snake she's trying to hand me. I grip my hands behind my back.

"For heaven's sake." She yanks my right hand from behind me, wraps it around the phone, and moves the receiver to my ear. The long turquoise cord drums against my legs.

"Aunt Jean." I can't help it. My eyes fill up. There's nothing I can do. I start boo-hooing.

Aunt Jean's voice sounds the same as when she's tucking me in at night. "Now, you know you can tell me anything. Gather yourself up and say your piece."

"Aunt Jean. I took your Birdhouse Jesus from the living room. I'm sorry. I didn't mean to." Then I wail like a big baby.

She waits until I quieten down. "What in the world did you call my Jesus? That's our Lord and Savior you're blaspheming. None of your childishness when dealing with the Lord. You hear me?"

I nod my head yes.

"I'm waiting on an answer."

"Yes, ma'am."

"What come over you? You know not to take something without asking, now, don't you?" She sounds like she did the time she caught me pulling strips of paint off the back of her house.

"Yes, ma'am." Mama's staring a hole through me. I turn my back to her and pull the phone in closer to my ear.

"You've been taught better." Then her voice comes over the line seeming less hickory-switch-like. "You could've asked me if you wanted to borrow the crucifix. You know that. Don't you?"

"Yes, ma'am." Mama's foot taps behind me, and she makes a humpf sound.

"Well, now. That's all we're gonna say about this. It's water under the bridge. But I expect you won't be doing nothing like this again, right?" The disappointment in her voice almost turns me into an earthworm.

"No, ma'am."

"Good. I'll talk to you later. I love you."

I snuffle real loud. "I love you, too." She hangs up without asking to talk to Mama or nothing.

Mama jerks the phone out of my hand. "She's always too soft on you." She slams down the receiver. "But you're not getting away that easy. You go to your room and stay there the rest of the night and think about what you done to the person loves you better'n most."

"But can't we take Jesus back now?"

"You think I'm going to work twelve hours, cook your dinner, clean this kitchen, and then take the drive over to Jean's and back, just so you can take back something you stole?" She rolls her eyes. "You. Go." She points. "Now."

I want to ask if I can keep Jesus in my room until He goes back to Aunt Jean's, but I see from her pressed lips I've pushed things as far as they'll go. He's on His own. There's nothing I can do but trudge back to my room. I hear Daddy snoring on the couch and pass by on racecar feet. The growling sound coming from his throat can't nip me.

Five

Tuesday is music day. I get off the school bus singing *Get Along Home Cindy Cindy* all the way up the driveway. I wonder if Jesus misses Aunt Jean. She's a mighty fine person to have around, always talking and humming. Mama says the smell of Aunt Jean's pound cake is Heaven on Earth. That must keep Jesus from being homesick at her house.

It must have rained earlier. There are puddles trickling down our driveway. When I lean down close to them, they look like jungle rivers. I keep my hands away, in case one poke of my finger wipes out a herd of tiny elephants.

Using my key strung on a silver-beaded necklace, I let myself in the carport door. Daddy's sitting at the kitchen table, and I stumble backwards when I see him. He should be at work.

"Hey, Sport." Daddy isn't wearing his greasy work clothes or his old white T-shirt. Instead, he has on a clean, red shirt with a collar, and he must have just washed his hair because it's shining blue-black. He tilts a Pabst to his lips.

The muscles between my eyes relax. When he talks to me and calls me Sport, it's usually okay. "Hey." Why's he home? I lower my head and take a step away from him but keep my head aimed where I can see him from the corner of my left eye.

"Where do you think you're going?"

I stop. "Nowhere." My knees start to shake.

"Kicked off work early to run a little errand." He swipes at the foam on his top lip with the back of his hand. "I'm taking you with me. What do you think of that?"

"You are?" He didn't ask me if I wanted to go. If I say I'd rather go to the sitter's, he'll be mad.

"Come on, we gotta get going." Daddy's keys jingle in his hand. I toss my book satchel up onto the counter.

"Yay!" I pretend to be excited he's taking me, and he actually grins. Maybe he has changed.

He turns up the beer can. "Run and get in the truck."

"Where is it?" It wasn't on the carport. That's why I didn't know he was home.

"Across the street at Wally's. Think the transmission's going. Having problems with reverse, so I parked there. Taking the wreck to my buddies to get fixed before your Mama finds out and has those jackasses she works with at Firestone mess it up." He reaches on top of the refrigerator. When he brings his hand down, he's holding Birdhouse Jesus. "And take this with you. We're dropping it off at Jean's."

I breathe in and don't breathe out.

"Go ahead. Take the thing. It's just another damn crucifix." He shoves Him at me.

I take Him with two hands. Aunt Jean better not hear Daddy talking that way.

"See. Won't bite ya." His hand snakes out real quick and pinches at my waist, causing a shudder to go clear through me.

"Don't break it or your mother'll have a conniption fit. I ain't listening to her bitch another two hours tonight." He rolls his eyes. "We're getting this thing done now." A sharp point of his finger says he wants me out the door.

We head over to Wally's. His house is across the street and two doors down. The upstairs has one window on top. It looks one-eyed, like Popeye. At the truck, Daddy opens his door and motions for me to climb in.

I have a special, quick way to get up into Daddy's truck by grabbing the door handle to help heft me up, at the same time I push off from the running board. Then I scoot, scoot, scoot across the seat as close to the other door as I can. If I'm not fast enough, he takes both hands around my butt and lifts me up and over with a push that sends me headfirst. I don't like him behind me where I can't see him. Don't like him lifting me up. Don't like feeling like I'm going to crash through the car window.

This time, I make it before he can take hold of me, because I hand him Jesus while I get in.

Once Jesus is back in my lap and we're on the road, Daddy starts whistling. I look at him from the corner of my eye to see if it's true. He looks funny, like his cheeks are held up by clothespins.

"Yes sir! I'm glad to be rid of those jackasses. Won't miss them ordering me around." He glances at me and nods his head once.

I don't know who he's talking about. Daddy calls anybody and everybody a jackass, especially the guys he works with. But he's sure happy about something.

"Daddy."

His eyes are on the rear-view mirror. "Uh huh."

"Thanks for taking Jesus back to Aunt Jean's."

He hits the brakes at the top of the hill for a stop sign. "Well, it's not a federal case like your mother always wants to make out of everything. It's a dime a dozen Christ on a stick. Lighten up, Sport." And he reaches under the seat and pulls out another can of beer. "This here beer's our little secret. No need for your mama or Aunt Jean to know nothing about a man wetting his whistle. Now, is there?"

I giggle. So that's where the whistle comes from. "Okay, Daddy."

A Coca Cola truck rumbles by, and he looks at me. "Now there's a company for a real man. No more Pepsi shit." He hands me the beer. "Pop it open for me. Careful. Don't get cut." Then, with a smile, "Unless you want to take the steering wheel?"

"I'm not old enough to drive!"

"You sure?" He takes both hands off the wheel for a minute and motions for me to take the wheel.

But that's scary. I shake my head really fast and pull the tab all the way back. The beer makes a bottle rocket sound and little drops spew onto Jesus. I wiggle the curved part of the tab. It breaks free, and I hand the can to Daddy, drop the tab into the ashtray, and wipe the beer off of Jesus with my shirt sleeve. Aunt Jean would have a fit if she saw.

Daddy motions with the beer towards the hill in front of us. "Want a ride on Thrill Hill?"

I shrug my shoulders. "What's that?"

"What's Thrill Hill?" He revs the truck engine, then guns it, racing down from the top of the hill we were sitting on and back up the next hill. "Whoo hoooo!" He's laughing like crazy, and the whole thing takes my stomach for a flip, but the same way a ride at the fair does. I start laughing, too.

While Daddy's not in a bad mood, I take a good look at him. Jesus must have done it after all. Daddy doesn't seem so scary today.

I like his tan. Mama says she sunburns just thinking about a swimsuit, but the more Daddy's outside, the darker he gets. Once Mama said he must be half-colored, and he got so mad he pulled his fist back. "Shut your mouth before I shut it up for you."

But he's not mad today. He's got on a pair of dark sunglasses, his neat-o tomato red shirt, the tan slacks Mama keeps ironed in case they need to go someplace special, and his shiny loafers. He could be a Hollywood movie star.

I can't believe he's taking up for me and having fun. It feels like having Lassie come home, and double good cause I get to see Aunt Jean, even if I have to face up to her in person about taking her Jesus.

Daddy slips the beer can between his legs and drives with one hand. He turns, sees me looking at him, and winks. "Daddy's got a new start."

He wants me to say something. "That's good, Daddy. You look all shined up today."

"Not bad, if I do say so myself." He brings the tips of his right-hand fingers to his lips and blows on them. We both laugh. He takes a drink and tucks the beer can back in its spot.

We pass by the road that goes to the lock and dam. "Lookee there, Sport." He points with his head. "I've got me some good fishing days in my future." With one hand on the wheel, he acts out he's reeling in a big one and jerks on his make-believe line until he lands it right in my lap. "Don't let it get away!"

I wrap my arms around his catch and play like it's flopping me around with it.

"That's it. Hold on." The can flashes to his lips and back down again. "Wear the sucker down." Turning the can up, he finishes it off, leans forward, and pokes it under the seat.

Bending all the way over, I trap his fish between my chest and Jesus in my lap. "I got him."

"That a girl. We'll have us some good eating now." Laughing, he reaches towards me. I shy away. "Come on over here and sit by me." He pats the seat next to him. "If that monster tries to give you any more trouble, he'll have to answer to me."

Looking at his hairy hand and smiling face, I edge myself over. My heart's thumping so fast at the base of my throat, I can't count the beats. When he squeezes the back of my neck, I stiffen up, but it doesn't hurt. He leaves his hand lying easy on my shoulder, the way I've seen him do with Mama. I know it should feel good. I want it to feel good.

I stare at him. He's whistling again. His cheeks puff in and out. I don't know why I feel like I'm going to cry. I bow my head. Jesus is looking up at me.

Daddy takes his arm away to get another beer from underneath the seat. I'm so glad he moved it. But then, I wish he'd put it back.

When I raise my head, we're passing the Church of God and getting closer to Aunt Jean's house. My stomach feels fizzy thinking about Aunt Jean and Jesus. I know she said it was water under the bridge, but it's different now I'm here to give Him back.

At her little faded-white house, Daddy doesn't pull in the drive, but goes right past, then swings around in a u-turn. Aunt Jean is in the shade of her big old oak, sweeping her front walk. She stands up long and tall, like a pine needle. She always says, "I'm all bones."

And she mostly is. Bones covered with a blue and green plaid dress that buttons up the front to her neck and comes down past her knees halfway to her ankles and with her hair piled up like a whole stack of bird's nests. She has on her house slippers, as usual. Doesn't like shoes, says they hurt her feet, and she only wears them to church or town or to catch the city bus for a visit with a brother or sister from her Sunday School class. Her house shoes have ragged circles cut out of the terrycloth sides for her corns. I can't figure those corns out because the warts do not look like corn. Not one bit.

Daddy pulls up in front of Aunt Jean's house and parks on the curb. She turns her black-framed glasses towards us, props her broom against the porch, and hurries to the truck. I'd usually throw open the door and leap down, but what with Jesus in my hands, I stay put. Daddy slides his beer down next to his door.

Aunt Jean comes right up to the rolled-down window, sticks her head in, hair first, and kisses me on the cheek. "Now, look here who's come to see me. What a nice surprise. A grand surprise!" She smiles wide, and shows her crooked teeth, the side ones overlapping the front ones, the bottom ones crowding around each other, and the one empty spot at the top right where she says Dr. Webster got slap-happy with his pliers.

"Carl, come on in and have a glass of tea." She waves her hand towards the house.

"Can't stay, Jean. Come to drop off a certain package I think you're missing." Daddy doesn't much care for Aunt Jean.

I heard him talking to Mama one time. "She's a Bible-thumping old maid bound and determined to save my soul, and the only kind of saving I need is to have a seat waiting for me down at Smitty's."

"You have something for me?" Aunt Jean points her long nose at me.

I hold Jesus out to her. "I'm sorry. I didn't mean no harm." My voice comes out low and sputtering.

Her eyes always look two sizes bigger with her glasses on, and she only takes them off to go to bed, so giant blue eyes turn on my daddy. "Where you off to in such a hurry there's no time for me to visit with my heart's love?"

"Errands to run."

"Here in town?"

"Yep." The side of Daddy's jaw is tight now. He looks straight ahead. That happy look went away fast. He doesn't like people asking him questions. If it was Mama, I bet he'd have told her wasn't none of her business what he was doing or where he was going.

"Well, you don't want Mary Alice tagging along under your heels, slowing you down, do you?" Aunt Jean takes Jesus from me. "What say you just leave her with me, and you go on off and take all the time you need to run them errands of yours, while the two of us have a little talk?"

"Suits me."

I can't believe it. Daddy will stay gone for hours and it'll just be the two of us. Before he can change his mind, I jump out of the cab and wave bye to him. "See you later." I push the door shut with both hands, but it doesn't close all the way.

Daddy stretches across, slams the door, and pokes his finger at me. "When I get back here, you be ready to go when I hit the horn. You're to get your fanny out here and into the truck pronto. I got better things to do than wait in the road for you. You hear?"

"I will, Daddy. I promise."

He drives off without telling either one of us goodbye. I skip along beside Aunt Jean.

"Now. You're gonna help me put Jesus back where He belongs, and then we're warming up some supper. You hungry?" She motions for me to hold the screen door for her.

"Uh huh." We step inside.

"Yes, ma'am?" She turns to me, waiting.

"Yes, ma'am."

"Good. I have vegetable soup Sister Young made fresh from her garden I can take out of the freezer. How's that sound, with half a peanut butter and jelly sandwich?" She opens the living room door. It's all shadows in there except for daylight coming in the side window.

"Uh huh." I catch myself. "Yes, ma'am. Sounds really good." My eyes start getting used to the dim room.

An un-faded patch on the living room wall that's the same size and shape of the Jesus on the cross waits for Him to come fill it up, like my fairytale sticker book, with the blank shapes on the page outlined in dots for gluing on the pieces. A rusty nail sticks out at the top and Aunt Jean angles Jesus so she can hang Him back on.

"I'd be hurt if I thought I couldn't trust you. You know that?" She squats close to me, making a little grunting noise, and balances herself with one bony hand against the floor.

I drop my head. Dust specks dance in a sunbeam.

"You raise your head and look at me." Using her pointer finger, she lifts my chin.

When I look up, Aunt Jean and Jesus are watching me. Aunt Jean's chest moves up and down with each wheezing breath as I answer her. "I won't do it again."

"Exodus 20:15, 'Thou shalt not steal'." She stands and takes my face in her hands. "Do you understand?"

"Yes, ma'am." I smell White Shoulders powder on her arms, and lean closer to sniff more of it. It makes me sneeze.

"God bless you." She doesn't let my face go, but it doesn't hurt. "Tell me what you understand."

"No taking things without asking. I promise."

She holds my face tighter, and it hurts a little. "Don't promise unless you mean it. Never break a promise."

With my pointer finger I make a cross over my heart. "I swear."

"No." Her hands move to my shoulders and press down hard. "Don't you ever let me hear you swearing."

A bead of sweat drops from her chin onto my hand, and I want to wipe it off. "But I wasn't swearing. I didn't say a bad word."

Her hands loosen and she straightens up so tall I think the top of her hair will touch the ceiling. "Swearing is bad words. And swearing is making an oath to anybody or anything except the Lord. You can make promises, long as you keep them. But you only swear to God." She takes my hand and leads me into her bedroom.

"I've been holding back on giving you this until you could read better, but I figure the time's come." She crosses over to the chifforobe, opens the skinny, mirrored door, pulls out a little white box with a clear plastic top, and hands it to me.

Inside is a tiny Bible with gold letters on the front. "For me?" I hold the box in my hands, like holding a baby bird.

"That's the New Testament for you to study on and take good care of." She takes a baby blue handkerchief from the top shelf of the chifforobe, before closing the door with a soft push sets the whole thing shaking. "Let me get the soup on. Then we can sit down and have a talk about this Bible."

As we walk into the kitchen, she wipes the sweat from her face and tucks the handkerchief into her dress, next to her heart. Sometimes grownups are disgusting.

While she starts cooking, I climb onto a chair at her old scratched-up table. I set down the Bible and run my fingers over the deep cuts in the table's wood, pressing my fingernails down into the grooves. I like to imagine shrinking small enough to explore those dried riverbed cracks. Then, if Aunt Jean spilled her water, I'd be washed away.

Mama doesn't like Aunt Jean's table. She told Aunt Jean it was pitiful.

But I love that old table, the feel of the rough wood. Different from our shiny Formica table made to look like wood. Our table is pitiful.

I could sit running my fingers over this table, counting the cracks, for half an hour.

I stick my whole fingertip inside the extra-wide crack where Mama says the table is going to split wide apart one day, leaving Aunt Jean's breakfast dishes on the floor.

"Stop fiddling with my old broke-down table and pay attention." Aunt Jean washes her hands, sits down, takes my new Bible out of the box and lays her hand gently on it.

I make my hands be still but keep one fingertip dipped into the giant crack so I can wiggle it there.

"This is your first Bible. Soon, you'll be able to read it by yourself. Then you'll have Jesus with you all the time. You read His words—all the red ones—and He'll be with you. You understand?"

I move to pick it up.

"No, ma'am. You wash your hands every time before you touch God's word." She pulls the Bible back to her, rises, and sets a chair next to her kitchen sink for me to get up on, so I can reach the sliver of Ivory soap in the chipped saucer by the faucet. I scrub my hands pink.

Back at my seat, I take the Bible and flip through it. This isn't Jesus. Nothing like Him. All big words I can't read yet. No pictures. No shine at all. I bend down like I'm studying hard on it. "It's real nice. Thank you." I don't want to hurt her feelings.

"It is not nice. It's the word of God. Your salvation." She lifts her glasses and rubs between her eyes.

"Yes, ma'am." There's a fly buzzing over her head, and she keeps shooing it away, while I puzzle on that Bible.

"You read from this every day."

"Yes, ma'am." Does she understand I'm only learning how to read Dick and Jane? There's a thin blue ribbon sticking out of the bottom of the book, the same kind of bookmark in Aunt Jean's grown-up Bible. I pinch it between two fingers and tug.

"Mornings are best. You begin the day with the Lord. And then again, before you go to bed, so you're protected through the night."

Protection? That must be why she gave it to me! I can bring it to bed with me. I open it again to figure out how it will protect me.

"Now, let's the two of us talk about what's troubling you so much you're feeling such a strong need for Jesus."

I jerk in my chair. "What?"

She bends close to me. "You can tell your Aunt Jean. What's wrong?"

"Nothing." My heart runs crazy like Mrs. Middleton's bird dog. I can't tell her about Daddy. Then she'd know what a bad girl I am.

"If it was nothing, you wouldn't have wanted Jesus." She pats my hand. "You can tell me. Something at school?"

"Nope." Her eyebrows lift up. "No, ma'am."

She leans back, stretches her legs out, and doesn't say anything. Just looks right at me like she sees me, really sees me. Not like Daddy, who hardly ever sees the color of my eyes. Not like Mama, who looks for a second and then goes off to do the dishes or the ironing. Aunt Jean looks at me like she has all the time in the world to hear what I'm going to say.

"Well?" She keeps quiet, not smiling, not frowning.

"I thought Jesus could help with Daddy." I look right at her. There, it's out.

"You're worried about your daddy?" Behind me, her refrigerator's humming loud and sounds as if it will come off the wall at me.

I shake my head. "No."

"Then why'd you want Jesus to help him?" Why did I want Jesus to help my Daddy? I remember him mashing up against me in my bed and push that thought away.

My Aunt Jean loves me. I know that. And she doesn't seem to like my daddy so much. She doesn't say it, but when she talks to him, I see it in the way she pulls her shoulders back, the same way she does when she talks about sinners. So, I tell her.

"Did you know Daddy sleepwalks?"

She scratches her ear. "No, and that's nothing to bother your silly head over. But if you want Jesus to help him, just add it to your bedtime prayers."

She doesn't understand. I don't know what to say. If I told her I really want Jesus to help me, she'll think I'm selfish. Mama's always telling me, "You are the most selfish girl I ever saw. Never think about anybody but yourself." But I want somebody to do something so bad. It must be Aunt Jean just doesn't know how rotten my daddy is to me. If she did, she'd make it right. I know she would.

Something's bad wrong with my daddy. Thinking about it makes me want to crawl under Aunt Jean's house so nobody can see me. I blurt it out. "Daddy's mean. He's downright horrible to me. You just don't know...." But she cuts me off.

"I know your daddy can be ornery. But you know the Ten Commandments. Exodus 20:12, 'Honor thy father and thy mother.'" She sits up straight in her chair. Not leaning towards me at all. She draws back her stretched-out legs and puts her feet flat on the floor. She pulls away from me. "He's your daddy. I know he don't rightly know how to handle children. But he didn't have a good family like you do. Wasn't treated right as a boy. His mother died when he was just eleven. Then he was kicked from pillar to post. It means he needs my love and your love and God's love even more."

"Yes, ma'am." I try to make my stomach small, so it won't shake. Try to hold my eyes still, so they don't blink. I count the stitches on my new Bible cover and tug on its blue ribbon. But I want her to listen to me. I try one more time. "But, Aunt Jean, Daddy doesn't like me. He comes in my bedroom. He …."

She's shaking her head and she interrupts me again. "Mary Alice! Your daddy does too love you. You pray for your daddy! Pray he comes to Christ and the Lord shows him The Way."

If I talk anymore to Aunt Jean about Daddy, she'll just think I'm breaking one of the Ten Commandments so I tell her, "I will. I'll pray for Daddy. And I'll read my Bible every day." But I have my fingers crossed behind my back. It's not really a lie. No way am I going to pray for my daddy.

"That's my girl." She opens her arms for me, and I rise up and into her hug. As I bury my face into her shoulder, I have to gulp hard to keep from crying.

I know then, there isn't anyone who will listen to me when it comes to Daddy. Not Mama. Not Jesus. Not even Aunt Jean.

Six

After dinner, we play two games of Old Maid, and I win both of them. "Let's play one more. Maybe you'll win this time."

"You're the boss." Aunt Jean shuffles the cards and deals them out. Then I hear a horn outside. One short beep and two long ones. It's Daddy. The cards in my hand become blurry. Mama's always telling me not to cross my eyes like that or they'll stick in place. But I like the blur. I like not seeing everything clear. It makes things look better, especially when it comes to Daddy.

Aunt Jean sits her cards down. "You run on out there before he busts a blood vessel." She stands and opens her arms wide. I run into them and press my cheek into her stomach. "Can I take my Old Maid cards home?"

"No, then you won't have any here, and I know how much you love to play with them." She draws me close for her extra squeeze, then stoops a little and looks into my eyes. "Study hard and you'll be able to read your Bible every day. Even if you don't know the words, hold it in your hands, and the Lord's love will come pouring out."

I nod yes and bury my face in her neck. If Birdhouse Jesus couldn't help, there's no way that book's going to work. When I pull away, my ponytail holder catches in her hairnet. "Ouch."

"Stand still." I drop my head, so she can work it loose.

She hands me the Bible and her phone rings. "Now who could that be? You run on out, and I'll get the phone." The kisses she usually throws to me from the front porch, she blows on her way to get the call.

I skip out of the house. The second I hit the sidewalk; Daddy lays down on the horn. My ears fill up with uh ohs.

It's almost dark, but I can still see. He doesn't have the door on my side open wide as usual. I duck my forehead and run.

The truck windows are down, and as I get closer, he's a growling shadow in the truck. "Come over here and get in. We ain't got all night." He swings open the door on his side, and I run behind the truck.

A second horn blasts from a car coming down the road. I stop so fast I fall forward onto my knees. Fire flashes in the dark behind my eyes, as car lights blaze by. I keep hold of my new Bible and scramble up, look both ways, and limp to the door, with my knees bleeding. He's looking down at me with his lion face.

"Can't you watch what you're doing? Last thing I need's you splattered all over the road. Your mama'd never let me hear the end of it." His hand waves me in without him getting out. He's gonna make me crawl over him.

"What you waiting for?" He sees the Bible clutched in my hand. "Oh, good God. More of her infernal Bible thumping." Snatching it from me, he tosses it into the floorboard and holds out his hand for me to grab.

I take it. I take his hand, and before I can pull myself up, he yanks me by the arm and across his lap. My panties go wet with tee tee.

With me flat across his lap and my feet sticking out the door, he puts his mouth close to my ear. "I'm gonna tear you up when we get home. Then next time I tell you to be waiting on me, you'll be ready. Hear me?" He pinches my butt, and I twitch.

"Yes, sir." I scoot as fast as I can across the seat, close to the door.

"No, you don't. You, get over here where I can keep an eye on you before you make any more trouble. Instead of over there next to the door making out like you're scared of me."

I wish he would act like he did today after school, but he doesn't have the same face on, and the space between us already looks too small. It would be a good time for it to part like the Red Sea.

"I said get over here. You deaf and dumb?" He grabs me by my other arm and pulls me to his side. Now both arms burn ten times worse than when I hang too long from the bar on the school gym set.

As I curl my head like a roly poly bug, I hear the truck gears grind. Daddy doesn't smell like beer. He smells the same as the bottles at his

Uncle Bobby's house. His whistle went away, and his hair's sticking out all over his head. There's a tear in the sleeve of his good shirt. All the happy shiny from this afternoon is gone.

"None of this is for your Mama to know. Not the truck or the job or the beer. I find out you told, and you'll regret it the rest of your life. I shouldn't have told you. I'll get this damn truck fixed tomorrow. She won't never need to know."

The job? The truck? I don't know what he's saying. In the dashboard light, I fix my eyes on my scraped knees and watch the little blood bubbles pop up and trickle down my shins. Since the day's turned to night, it's cooled off, and he has the heat on full blast.

When we get out on the highway, he reaches one arm around me and holds me right up against his side. "Aw, come here. I know you won't tell. Let Daddy give his girl a hug."

I don't want his hug. It was all right this afternoon, but his mean hands are back. I turn my head and look out my window at the cow pastures passing by. The sky is purple with no stars shining.

As soon as he gets me as tight as can be, he moves his hand down to my lap. His skin feels hot under my skirt on my leg. "Don't move."

What's he doing? Is he gonna spank me right here, driving down the road?

But he doesn't swat my legs. His fingers are an inch worm going up my leg, and I start to shake. "Hold still." He sounds like he means it. I keep my head down low and don't move and don't look at him. But I can't quit shaking and he doesn't say anything else. The heater keeps blowing hot air right in my face. I try not to choke.

He rubs his fingers against my panties, where I go to the bathroom. My head is a balloon blowing up bigger every second until I think it will bust. The heater blows and blows in my face. Hot air pushes each breath back down my throat. I can't breathe. I'm smothering.

I don't know what I've done wrong. This is a hundred times, a million times worse than when he spanks my bare bottom with the belt or squashes me in my bed.

As we pass under streetlights, I stare at the blood trickling from my knees. One, two, three dried bloody lines running down from my left knee. One, two lines on the right. One, two, three, four, five, one, two, three, four, five … the blood becomes a blur, and I keep counting. I keep counting until everything becomes a blur and I'm safe in a white world, far away from here.

Seven

The next day, when the school bus pulls up in front of my house, Daddy's truck must be fixed, because it's parked nose front on the carport.

Daddy's in there. Mama's at work. My stomach hurts. My breathing stops like Aunt Jean's when she's having a spell. Last night… I remember Daddy's hands on the drive home. I scratch my arm hard. It makes a long, red mark. A shooting pain fills my head. I blur my eyes and count to eight over and over until last night is invisible in my head.

Slowly, my eyes tune back in, and I see the truck's tailgate spelling out DODGE. Why can't I stay at school? Or Aunt Jean's? I kick a stone across the road with the toe of my Mary Janes. I wish I could run down to the creek, take my shoes and socks off, tie up the corner of my skirt, and wade. Wish I could kick, kick, kick the water and watch it spray out in front of me. Wish I could pick up one pebble after another and throw each one as hard as I can.

Or I could run away. Would serve them all right. But then Mama and Aunt Jean might miss me.

Taking my time up the hill, I watch the cloud shapes. A mountain. The Cheshire Cat. A coiled-up snake. I don't like snakes. Even the sky is scary now. And that's been one of my best games.

Ahead of me, the front door is getting closer no matter how slow I walk. I stop, drop my satchel, untie my shoe, and re-tie it. But it won't do for Daddy to catch me lollygagging around. I swing my satchel over my shoulder and head for the house.

As I open the door, I don't yell out, "I'm home." Instead, I ease the door shut. Maybe he'll be asleep.

I tiptoe in, peeking around every corner before going into each room. It's like he's playing hide and seek. But Daddy's never played hide and seek with me, not never. If he's here, I can't find him.

I don't know what to do. Go to Mrs. Middleton's? Stay here and wait for Daddy? No. I do know what to do. I run out the door and into the woods to the sitter's.

After we do homework, play dominoes, and watch the Bob Brandy Show, the phone rings. I keep my eyes on the TV. Mrs. Middleton calls out, "Mary Alice, your daddy's home. Get your things. He said just to walk home. See you tomorrow." Just like normal.

I come in through the back door. He's watching TV but motions me in. "Go turn that TV down." I twist the knob and turn to face him. His leg is jerking up and down, the same as Aunt Jean's sewing machine bobbin. "You listen up good. My truck was not here when you got home."

I stare at him with my mouth open.

He glares at the ceiling and does this thing where he chews, but isn't chewing on anything, and shakes his head. "You're 'bout as dense as a board, ain't you? Totally worthless."

Then he looks at me straight on, and one eye is higher than the other. "Your Mama's not to know nothing about my truck being here when you got home. That's for me to tell her." He jabs his chest with his fist, then punches it out at me. "Not a word out of you, or I'll take my belt to you so hard you'll spit up your own liver."

My knees wobble.

Out comes his hand and slaps my face. It knocks my head sideways. "More of that's waiting for you. But you keep your mouth shut, you got nothing to worry about." He looks meaner than ever, and I take a step back, hold my palm to my cheek, and feel tears by my nose.

"You got anything to say?" He stops, stares at me, and chews. But I know he doesn't really want me to answer. I've gotten in trouble for that before. "I better not hear you're thinking any different."

He stops chewing. "I can tell you right now who's gonna win out on this one, and it won't be you. Your mama would never believe you over me. Not about anything." He lights a cigarette, then picks a speck of tobacco off his bottom lip. "What's wrong? Cat got your tongue?"

I swallow hard. "Won't tell," is all I get out.

"You're not as dumb as you look. Now turn the TV back up and get out of my sight."

Someone else moved my feet to the television and twisted the dial. Someone heard him say, "Yeah, leave it there. One crappy show's good as another." Someone walked and didn't run to my bedroom. Then they spun in circles until they were so dizzy the room went by the same as if they were at the fair, riding the Tilt-O-Whirl. And when the room finally slowed, they flung out their arms and took to spinning again.

———

On Thursday, I watch to see if his truck is home. Sure enough, it's there again. But he's not in the house. Before he can come back, I run as fast as I can to the sitter's with my book satchel banging against my knees so hard it makes blue marks.

On Friday, his truck's there, but not him. Again, I race to Mrs. Middleton's, tripping and stumbling down the path in the woods, falling, and picking myself back up in my hurry to get to her house.

All that week, at bedtime, I hold Mr. Sand against my chest. Try as I might, I can't forget about Daddy's sleepwalking. Each night, I count the windows and doors. I lie on my right side, my left side, and back to the right. I curl up on my knees and say my Now I Lay Me Downs. They must be working. Daddy stays away.

But tomorrow is no-school Saturday. Mama will go to work and leave me here with Daddy all day.

There are crickets living in the field next to Mr. Hickory. As I toss and turn, they won't shut up. My heart beats the sound into my bones until I'm itching on the inside. I lay there in my bed, squirming and doubled over from my stomach hurting so bad I can't sleep. Those crickets won't stop. No matter what I do, they won't leave me alone.

Eight

On Saturday morning, I get up before the rooster that lives up the road can make a peep and am dressed and waiting on Mama when she comes into the kitchen. Daddy's still in bed asleep. "Can I go to work with you today? I'll be real good. I promise."

She takes her round compact out of her pocketbook and smooths on her lipstick. "Where in the world did you get that idea? Firestone is no place for a little girl, especially on Saturday, when every good ole boy and his uncle from Rockmart to Adairsville crowds into that store."

I pull on the sleeve of her dress. "But Daddy dropped me off at the store the time he got called into work."

She looks from the mirror to me and answers as she dabs at the corner of her lips with her pinkie. "That's different. It was less than an hour, at the end of the day."

I grab her around the waist. "Please, Mama. Please don't make me stay home." I burst out crying, and I don't even know why.

"What is the matter with you?" I tilt my head back to look up at her. She's staring at me like I have two heads. Then she lays her hand on my head and checks me for fever.

"I'll be good. You'll see." I get filled up with the feeling I have to get out of here. It's all I hear in my head. I have to get out of here. I have to get out of here. "Don't leave me!"

She pulls my arms away from her. "For heaven's sake, what's gotten into you?" Mama's always in a big hurry in the mornings, and she doesn't like it when I'm a cry-baby. This morning, her voice is all I-mean-business. "I don't have time for this. Watch cartoons and be glad you don't have to go to that nasty store."

I snatch her purse. "Then stay home with me."

"Mary Alice Lydell! What's gotten into you?" She pries her bag from me. "Stop your nonsense this very instant."

"But Mama …"

She interrupts me. "No 'buts.' I have to go to work. You have to stay here. I'll see you tonight." She looks down at me chewing on my thumb, and her face softens. "We'll play a game tonight. Just me and you. Your choice. Even Old Maid, though I'm sick to death of it."

She slips on her black work flats. I know she'll be gone in a minute. I have to think quick. "Can I go to Aunt Jean's?"

"No. I don't have time to take you all the way over there, and you were just there last weekend." She heads to the kitchen counter to get her coffee mug.

"Can I go to Carolyn's?"

She spins her head towards me. "Stop it. You haven't even been invited."

"Can I play outside all day? On the swing set, where Daddy can see me?"

"No. Six-year-olds have to stay inside when nobody's home to watch them. You know that." Now her voice sounds sharp.

"But, Mama, you said yourself Daddy's home to watch me. I'll stay in sight." I know I'm sounding like a whiney baby now.

"Stop your back-talking. I know you go outside sometimes after school when Daddy's here, but you're not allowed outside all day unless I'm home. And that's that." She looks at her Timex watch and points at me. "You are making me late." She runs out the door, waving her hand behind her. "See you tonight."

I'm left standing in the kitchen listening to her crank the car. What if I go outside anyway? But I know Daddy will skin my hide. I wish he'd go away and never come back.

The only thing I can do is turn the TV on and hope he sleeps all day. I hate stay-at-home Saturdays, especially now Daddy has a secret about his job.

After four cartoon shows, Daddy shuffles into the kitchen wearing a pair of old work pants with a hole in the knee and a white T-shirt, no shoes, rubbing his eyes, and coughing. He pops a couple of pieces of bread into the toaster. His dark, greasy hair is flopped on his forehead over his monster-green eyes that look like somebody took a red crayon and drew circles around them. He has on his scratchy face.

I don't think it's a good idea to bother him, but I know if I don't go and help, he'll snap at me, "Get off your lazy ass."

Used to, if I offered to lend Daddy a hand, and he was feeling good, he'd pull up the stepstool so I could spread butter and pear preserves on the toast. He might even tell a funny joke. Those times, I craned my neck up at him while he made coffee. I liked seeing how tall Daddy was.

"Six foot three and counting," Mama always said when she hugged him around the waist with her head tilted way back, her wavy brown hair swinging below her shoulders.

Where he used to work at the plant, they called him String Bean because he's skinny and long. Except his arms are muscled-up from the heavy work he did there, and his hands are big and hard. "Work a man to death and then expect him to clock in from the grave."

When he talks to Mama about his job, she clicks her pink fingernails on the wooden arm of our couch and never says much.

So, even though he has on his scratchy face this morning, I go climb on the step stool, and he doesn't swat at me like a buzzing fly or make wisecracks. We just make the toast, and nobody says nothing. I pick at mine while Daddy eats his standing at the sink, slurping from his coffee mug. He spits a green glob into the kitchen sink and drops his cup in. "I've earned a little dessert after my breakfast this morning."

I never heard of such a thing as dessert after breakfast, but I'm hoping for a slice of Mama's pineapple upside-down cake she made last night.

Daddy opens the refrigerator and pulls out a beer. He's lying again. That's not dessert.

As he walks to the sofa, he makes little grunting noises before plopping down on it, his head resting on one of its arms and his feet crossed at the ankles on the other one. He pulls a magazine from his back pocket and reads with it turned so I can't see it. I bet it's one of those "dirty books" I've heard Mama tell him not to bring in here.

I don't know why he's taking up the whole couch, knowing I'm not allowed to use his recliner. He does it all the time, too. I go stand at the front window and watch the big girl from down our road jumping her bicycle over a ramp she made from a rock and a piece of wood.

In no time, I hear Daddy. "Mary Alice, bring me another beer."

As I go get the beer, I see Mama's iron on the counter and remember the time I told on him to Mama.

"Daddy was drinking beer all day." Since she'd been at work, I thought she'd be mad.

But she hadn't even glanced up from ironing. "Daddy likes to relax on Saturdays."

"Aunt Jean says drinking's a sin."

Mama had lifted her eyes. "You're not to discuss our family business with Aunt Jean. We don't see eye-to-eye on drinking. Beer's just beer. Not a sin." She misted the shirt and went back to ironing.

"But he was mean to me."

Mama slammed the iron down so hard the ironing board shook on its skinny legs. "I'm bone tired and not listening to this nonsense. Daddy said you aggravated him all day long. When my daddy told me to do something, I didn't argue. If he said, 'Jump!' I asked how high! Do what your daddy says, and you'll stay out of trouble."

"But, Mama …"

She wouldn't let me finish. "This is our home, and we'll do as we please here. Do you understand me?"

When I trot over with Daddy's beer, he slips the magazine down between the couch cushions. I keep my eyes on the linoleum with the beer held out towards him. "Same bullshit every Saturday morning … nothing on TV." He jerks the can from my outstretched hand. "You damned kids these days. Spoon fed!" He guzzles half the beer. "Think you're royalty, don't you? But you're just a fucking retard." He makes a fist and knocks it against the side of my head three times. It doesn't hurt too bad. I stand perfectly still. Don't want to rile him up.

"Your mama and Aunt Jean spoil you rotten. Don't ever forget you're nothing but a snot-nosed brat." He shakes his head, and his right foot bounces up and down. "When I was a boy, I would've been cleaning out stalls in the barn Saturday mornings. Shoveling shit." He points at me with his long, skinny arm. The tip of his middle finger almost pokes my nose. "Been shoveling shit my entire damn life! Well, you ain't no princess. You hear me?"

"Yes, Sir." I nod fast.

My friend Carolyn's daddy calls her "his little princess," and when he does, I want to scratch her face. But then I hear Aunt Jean's voice in my head telling me, "Jealousy's a sin. 'Thou shalt not covet' is one of the Ten Commandments. That's the Lord's rules." Seems like I'm always in trouble with one of those Commandments.

Daddy waves me away. "You get outta my face and keep your nose away from that window before the neighbors see you acting like an idgit."

My coloring book and crayons are on the counter. I take them to the table. I haven't even finished coloring my Alice in Wonderland picture when I hear Daddy crunch his beer can and get up.

"Stay out of trouble while I lay down and take a nap. And keep that TV turned down low or you can turn it off." He gets another beer and slams the fridge door.

I turn my head towards him. "Yes, sir."

He mutters going down the hall, "Some kinda weekend this is."

I let out the part of my breath I hold in tight whenever Daddy's in the room. Curling up on the couch to watch TV, I pull my yellow nightgown over my knees and chew on my fingernails. I like biting down so hard my teeth hurt, but my top two teeth are so loose now I have to use my back teeth, and they don't hurt as bad as front teeth do. Instead, I just push real hard against my bottom front teeth with my pointer finger, and then wiggle, wiggle, wiggle the two loose ones with my tongue.

Top Cat is just going off when I hear Daddy's bedroom door open. That wasn't a very long nap. I spring up and go back to color at the kitchen table.

Daddy comes in, rocking his head side to side and making a "pfff" sound. When he gets another beer, he turns to me with his forehead wrinkled up like the sheets on my bed. "Cut that infernal racket off, right this second."

Up I go, and over to pop the knob. He sits on the couch and lights a cigarette, blows the smoke out with a "whew," and tosses the match into the ashtray on the coffee table. His right leg jiggles. He pulls a flat, shiny bottle from his back pocket, unscrews the lid, takes a gulp, and slides it back into his pocket. Then he takes a gulp of beer.

I keep my eyes to the floor and try to slip out of the room. That bottle can mean Daddy's happy, but most of the time, it's like a black cloud telling me to get away before the thunder and lightning starts. When I see it sparkling, I get a bad stomachache.

"Where you think you're going?" His heel thumping the floor sounds the same as Mama's washing machine loaded to the top with towels.

"To look at a book." I hold my breath, hoping he'll tell me to get out of his sight. My ears feel the way they do when I hold my nose and my breath and blow.

"Did I tell you to go anywhere?" His top lip puckers as if he smelled something stinky.

"No, sir." I look at the floor.

"You're the rope round my neck, so you're gonna stay in here where I can watch you." He turns up the beer can again. I count five gulps before he crunches it with one hand and holds the crushed can out to me. "Get me another one."

"Yes, sir." My hand pulls back like a turtle's head. I shake it free and make it reach out to take the can.

When I bring him the cold beer, he stubs out his cigarette, takes the can, pops the tab, and, this time, gulps to the count of three before stopping.

"Come over here." Daddy pats his knee, the one with a big hole in his pants so his knee pokes through.

I look at the hand on his pants leg. It's covered with black hair and the end of his pinkie's missing from the time he shut the car door on it.

"I said get over here." The hand wiggles like the tarantula I saw at school one time. My feet take off on their own, and I step, step, step to him, chewing one thumb nail and plucking at my nightgown.

He reaches for another cigarette, lights it, plants it between his teeth, takes both hands around my waist, and lifts me onto his knees. He talks from behind the Pall Mall, and I cough from the smoke.

"Lord, you're getting heavy. Pretty soon you'll be too big for this." He leans forward to put the cigarette in the ashtray, and his stained white T-shirt comes towards my face smelling of ashes, lemons, and the mop bucket.

We've been playing Ride a Little Horsy since I was a baby, but only when Mama's here or one of my aunts or uncles are over to see what a good daddy he is. Those times, Daddy bounces me on his knees, and both Mama and he smile. And when the game's finished, I'm in his lap for a couple more minutes and can lay my head against his chest and feel his heart thumping. Smell his Old Spice shaving lotion and play that he's giving me a hug. I used to like it, until Daddy's hands got mean.

Lately, when Aunt Jean watches, she throws her head back and laughs. "Mary Alice is getting too long in the stride for Ride a Little Horsy. Her legs are clear to the ground and could stop that horse dead in its tracks if she just put her feet down!" She thinks it's just a game, because Daddy's hands act different when other people are not here.

Now, he's got me balanced with my legs dangling on either side of his knees and my nightie bunched up at the top of my thighs. I could touch the floor if I wanted, and if he'd let me. What would he do if I just got down and ran to my room? I tell my feet to move, but they think I'm playing freeze tag.

His hands move up and down my bare legs. I look at his big red-ringed green eyes. Under his eyes are half-moons dark as rubbed-in dirt. He's smiling the way Skip, one of those nasty little boys at Mrs. Middleton's, does, when he's trying to sneak a bug in my hair.

He starts bouncing his knees, but the only part he says is, "Don't fall down." His knees open. They open too wide. I drop through and my tail bone whacks the floor hard. I bite my tongue.

My eyes burn. It tastes like I licked the bathtub faucet.

"Fooled with the wrong horse, didn't ya?" Grinning, he cups his big hands under my armpits and lifts me to my feet. Pats his knee again. "Gotta get right back on the horse that threw ya."

I step back.

He grabs my wrists with both hands and yanks. "Come on, you scaredy cat. I'm just playing with you."

Then I'm on top of his knees facing him again, but he's lifting my legs and pulling me forward. I try to pull away, but it doesn't help.

What is he doing? I'm too big to lie down in his lap for riding horsy anymore.

"Be still."

I try to push away from him by using the bottoms of my feet on the cushions.

"I said be still and you better believe I mean it!" He lets go of my legs, uses both hands to circle around my waist, and jerks my butt up towards his lap. My head drops back onto his bony knees. I make myself into a freeze tag statue.

"Now you won't get hurt." His kneecaps feel as hard as concrete on the back of my head.

"Ride a little horse, going downtown. Watch out horse. Don't you fall down." He repeats the ditty in a singsong voice, over and over, until he's only humming the tune. One hand is locked tight around both my wrists. My hands can't even wiggle, and my wrists feel like they're breaking. My nightie's up around my waist, and he's rubbing one hand up and down my leg again. He bounces so fast my head starts banging his knees. I see double.

He pulls me even closer to him. My hurting arms drop free and dangle by my sides.

He starts rocking us back and forth. He's pulled me so close to him my head's on the top of his legs. At least my skull's not cracking against his knees anymore. But my legs are on either side of his waist, my pink rosebud panties tight against his stomach, and I wish I could pull my gown down to cover them. There's his zipper and a hard lump pressing hard against me, between my legs.

As he rocks us, he pushes my gown up under my arms. I picture myself outside spinning my rope and counting the jumps. Using his middle finger, he rubs back and forth across my flat boobie, then taps it. Chills bumps rise.

I know he's not supposed to be looking under my gown like this. He's not supposed to be touching me this way. I want to cover my eyes, but I'm too scared to blink. He's staring at my chest and rocking. In my head, I'm spinning circles in the backyard.

With one hand, he starts pulling at my panties; edging the elastic band down. I shake my head, but he doesn't look at me. My arms won't move. Daddy's looking at my panties as he pulls them down.

With the other hand, his pointer finger traces the line of fine hair that runs from my belly button all the way to my front fanny. Then he does look at me, and he has a scary grin on his face.

I want him to stop it. My face is so hot I think I'll catch on fire. I want to pull my panties back up, but I don't dare move. I want my mama.

We're so close to each other my panties won't go down any further unless he moves me away from him. He leaves them the way they are and pinches the elastic away from the inside to uncover where I go tee tee. He holds open my panties and his dirty fingers touch me. It tingles. He wiggles his fingers on me and sparks shoot all the way up into my belly. He's grinning and looking at my privates, and then he pushes his fingers in and it burns.

He lunges forward with his eyes shut tight, his face all screwed up, and pulls his breath in through clenched teeth. It makes a backward whistle. Then he grunts and stops moving all of a sudden.

I lie there with my breath still not going in right. All the air in the house has been sucked away. Daddy's head slumps back on the top of the couch with his eyes still closed. Between my legs feels like soap bubbles bursting but his fingers are pinching me. It stings, too. I want to disappear like the air.

Daddy jerks. Opens his eyes. Acts all surprised to see me lying there on his legs.

"What the hell do you think you're doing?" He slings my legs over and gives me a push. "Don't you know better? You're too old to play baby games."

I tumble to the floor, pulling up my panties as fast as I can.

"You must be crazy. You better not tell anybody what you did. They'd send you away and lock you in the loony bin." He takes my face in one hand, squeezes tight, and leans in close. His monster eyes put a spell on me. "Then you would never see your mama or Aunt Jean ever again. Anyway, they'd never want to see a nasty little girl who does dirty things like you." He lets go of my face and gives me a push in the middle of my chest.

"Get out of here. Right now. Take them colors to your room outta my sight and don't come back." He doesn't look at me. Just lights another cigarette, swallows beer, and stares at the blank TV screen.

I feel as if I'm still outside spinning. My feet move in slow motion.

The table and my crayons come a little closer, inch by inch. The tip of my tail bone burns like the red end of Daddy's matches. I gulp back something rising in my throat, so I don't yuk up right here on the den floor.

Then I'm in my bedroom. I closed my eyes in the kitchen and opened them sitting on my bed. Like a time machine.

My bottom smarts, but not as sore as my red wrists. And my head aches so bad it makes my eyes squint.

I strain to see the black outlines on my coloring book page and use my eyes to trace them around and around Alice in Wonderland's white apron, counting from one to four over and over and over again. It doesn't take long until I sink into the white pages and disappear. As I disappear, I disappear Daddy, too.

Nine

It was morning when I came in here. Now, I'm on the bed playing with my Snap cards, but the light outside has faded so much the room is getting dark. The time machine sent us into the future again. I button up Buzzy's little blue jacket. "You know you can't go outside without your coat. We're gonna climb all the way to the top of the hickory tree and live in your nest."

I search the deck for my other friend, the organ grinder's monkey with his blue and yellow drum hat, but instead I see the sleeping bear. Except she seems dead today. I turn her over, face down. The tiger, lion, and crocodile cards look like they could eat me alive. I flip them over, too. They used to be my friends. Nobody likes me anymore.

The bedroom door opens. I lay my body over all the cards to protect them. But it's not Daddy. "Mama!" I run and jump straight up into her arms.

"My goodness. What a welcome! But you'll wrench my back." Fitting one hand around my waist, she flips my overhead light on and sits down on my bed with me. "I see you have the cards ready and waiting. Staying home wasn't so bad, now, was it?"

She's smiling down at me. I don't remember why it was awful bad. I just know it was. I feel funny, like another little girl is talking inside my head.

But Mama's home now. I press my ear against her lap. She runs her fingers through my hair, catching them in the tangles, but I don't care.

"I can't believe I forgot to brush your hair this morning, and I see you haven't touched a comb to it." Her touch feels heavenly. "Let me get a brush."

When I lift my head, it's as heavy as Daddy's bowling ball. She gets up and leaves the room. I'm so tired I lay the side of my face back on the bedspread.

Mama comes back with her blue brush. "Sit up. What are you moping around for? That's not like you."

I get up and try to look happy, for Mama. As she brushes, I close my eyes and feel every pull from the roots to the tips of each strand. Even when she tugs the knots out, I don't want it to stop.

"I don't know when I've ever seen you this quiet." She lays her hand on my forehead again. "Nope. No fever. But I think you're coming down with something."

Leaning against her shoulder, I stare at the mirror on my wall and see a woman and a girl sitting on a lavender bedspread. The woman is Mama and the girl is Alice, that girl in the book, who lives in mirrors and other worlds. I must be her now. Or maybe I'm both of us, with me behind my eyes and Alice on the outside. I like the fuzzy way it feels on the inside.

Alice raises her hand and curls it around Mama's thumb. I can feel everything she does, but I'm down the rabbit hole. I always thought it would be scary, but it's not. It's nice and dark and I can float. I'll stay down here and let that Alice girl be me. It's not that I'm her now. It's that she's become me.

Alice looks at Mama, and Mama squeezes her hand. Mama can't tell the difference. I'm safe down here. No one will ever know.

Mama leaves to fix dinner. The sound of Alice's voice inside my head, between my ears, surprises me. Her voice is the same as mine, only prettier. Alice says, *stay in your room, away from Daddy.* I guess she's not just on the outside, but inside, too.

I lie on my bed and float. From a long way off, I hear music. It's Mama in the kitchen banging pots and pans. "Mary Alice, dinner's ready!"

On the outside, Alice doesn't move. She can't move. Inside, I'm falling.

When Alice doesn't come, Mama shows up at my door with her worried face. "I thought you weren't feeling good. Think you can eat something?" From where I am, behind my eyes, I look at her. When I don't answer, she asks, "Want me to bring your food in here?"

Without taking her head off the pillow, Alice nods yes.

Mama leaves and comes back with a bowl of chicken noodle soup, a cup of applesauce, and a glass of Sprite on a rusty metal TV tray. "Sit up."

Alice lifts herself, and Mama rests on the edge of my bed and spoons broth into Alice's open mouth, the same as when I was little. Open. Spoonful. Swallow. The clink of metal against my teeth. The soup makes a warm spot behind my heart. Mama hands Alice my drink. While Alice sips, Mama straightens my bed covers and smooths down my hair. Alice gives her the cup and pulls at Mama's sleeve. Mama sits it on the floor by my bed and brings her palm to my cheek. Alice says, *Don't let Daddy come in here.*

Usually, Mama's face is drawn up in wrinkles around her eyes and mouth. Now, her skin is smooth and soft. "I know you'd rather be at your Aunt Jean's, but he's your daddy, and he loves you. You're being silly."

Alice plucks at Mama's blouse. "But he'll sleepwalk. He'll have a fit."

Mama pulls Alice's hand away, and the wrinkles are back. "Now, you're being ridiculous. I don't want to hear any more of this from you. I don't know how you get so confused."

I can't let that Alice girl open her big mouth again.

I rise up out of the rabbit hole and grip both of my hands around Mama's. "Your hands are freezing." She begins rubbing them between hers. When she looks at my hands, her head jerks up fast. "What in tarnation happened to your wrists!" I bring my eyes to them and see bruise bracelets circling each one.

Alice talks in my head, *that's what Daddy did.*

"You've been up in that tree again, haven't you?" She holds my hands gently, but her words are cross. "I made myself perfectly clear you were to stay inside. You went out anyway, didn't you?"

Had I been in the tree? I must have. How else did this happen?

You know better. Tell her what Daddy did. The lies that Alice girl tells.

"Answer me, Mary Alice." Mama brings her face close to mine.

"I guess so." I picture the rope hanging from Mr. Hickory, with my wrists wrapped up in it. I must have been playing pirates. "Walking the plank?" I say it, but I don't remember it.

"You stay out of that tree. You hear me? Next thing I know, you'll break your neck. I'll be right back with some lotion." She leaves my room.

Liar. You do too remember. Tell her about Daddy.

No, then Mama won't love me anymore.

But it was Daddy!

I think back to this morning and Daddy's face comes in clearly. "They'd send you away ... lock you in the loony bin." If I tell, I'd never see Mama or Aunt Jean again. That's what he said.

See! You know. Why would he say something like that about you climbing a tree?

Never mind why. I'll never tell. The words echo in my mind. Never tell.

Mama comes back in and rubs lotion on my wrists. I don't feel a thing. "I won't climb again, Mama. And I'll stay inside. Please don't be mad."

"I'm not angry, you silly girl. I just love you and don't want to see you hurt. That's why you have to mind me. I know what's best for you." She kisses the soft spots at my wrists, my forehead, and the tip of my nose. I press my cheek against hers. In my whole life, I never wanted my mama to love me as much as I do right now.

Ten

Friday, when I turn my key and open the door, his snores fill up the empty house and boom out at me, jet plane strong. I stand still on the top step. The Alice-girl is loud in my ear, *I'm telling you, don't go in there.* But that would get us in big trouble. Nothing's worse than Saturday morning. My knees shake. I blur my eyes and count my breaths to make Saturday disappear.

If I'm very quiet, I can sneak into my room without waking him. Inching the door open a tiny bit at a time, I squeeze through and turn the doorknob without a sound.

Thirty-three steps to my bedroom. I wrinkle up my forehead and walk heel-to-toe as slow as Mrs. Littlejohn, who uses a walker at Aunt Jean's church. Counting the steps, I cross the kitchen and into the den. When I pass by his recliner, his head is dropped back, eyes closed. With each snore, his lips move in strange flutters. I turn around to walk backwards where I can still see him, but I can't figure out how to tiptoe that way.

Daddy lets out an extra-loud noise and his hand jerks up. It scares me so bad I drop my book satchel. The metal buckles hit the linoleum with a loud clang. I press my eyes shut and hear Daddy moving in his chair.

"Jesus Christ!" When I pop open my eyes, he's wide awake and glaring at me. "Can't I get one minute of goddamn sleep, you little shit?" His hair is greasy. His eyes have darker circles than ever. His stained T-shirt has food stuck to it.

I reach down to get my satchel. The sound of his footrest snapping shut freezes me in place. I round my shoulders in and duck my head at the flap of his bare feet on the floor.

He grabs me. Lifts me in one move. Up against his chest. My feet dangling. I try to hide behind my eyes, but it won't work. That Alice girl won't come out. See for yourself, she tells me.

Dropping his head over my shoulder, he mumbles. "Daddy's sorry and don't mean it. He just don't know what to do. Ain't no jobs out there. Ya gotta know. I tried."

He's got me squeezed in a lock like the wrestlers he watches on TV. I look out the back window at the sun shining on our crape myrtle tree and count the branches and wait.

Daddy's chest starts to jerk, and he almost drops me. I wrap my legs around his waist, so I don't fall. Something wet's dripping on my neck. He can't be crying. Boys don't cry. He pulls me closer and lays his cheek on the side of my head. He sounds afraid.

I pat his back the way Aunt Jean would. "There, there. It'll be okay."

He stumbles with me to the chair and drops down, catching my foot between him and the cushion. While he wraps me in both arms and cries out loud, I jiggle my shoe, trying to get it free. I pull air in sharp against my teeth and start to cry myself. He reaches in his pocket, pulls out a handkerchief and honks into it. "Don't worry. Daddy's fine." I yank my foot. It comes loose, leaving the shoe behind.

"Daddy needs another beer." He sets me down, facing away from him, and stands up. "You go play. Stay inside." His voice catches. "Leave Daddy alone." I peer over my shoulder at him. He doesn't look at me.

I grab my shoe and satchel but can't help staring into the kitchen. Daddy's leaned into the refrigerator with his hands over his face. I don't want to feel sorry for him. But I do.

Limping into my room with one shoe on, I wonder if Daddy has someone else inside who comes out sometimes. If he does, which one is really him?

In my bedroom, I look for the Bible Aunt Jean gave me. I can't find it, but when I put my shoes in the closet, I see it lying in there, on the floor. It's shiny white and new, with a gold zipper. I lift it, take it to my bed, and flip through the pages. No pictures. Just some maps and red letters in the back half. Nothing to make things better.

At the end of the zipper is a tiny gold cross. I pinch it between my fingers and pull the zipper back and forth. It sounds like it's saying,

"Help me. Help me." But the longer I zip and unzip, it changes to, "Can't do-it. Can't do-it." I poke the bottom of the cross under my thumbnail until it hurts, then I feel better.

———

For the next two weeks, Mama takes me to Aunt Jean's on Saturday. I don't know why, and I don't ask. But, every school day, he's home when I get off the bus. He hasn't cried, and he hasn't yelled. When Mama gets home late and asks him how work was, he grunts, as usual.

Today, when I open the door and walk on soft feet towards my room, he doesn't even look at me. "Stay in your room." That's all he says, with his eyes set straight ahead on The Match Game. It's one of my favorite shows at the babysitter's. I see the blue-striped pajamas he still has on, his red face and the beer in his hand, and don't ask to watch it with him.

Earlier this morning, I put my Snap cards under Mr. Sand. Buzzy thinks it's nice and dark and safe under there. I've been keeping my Bible there, too, thinking maybe it will work some kind of invisible magic.

I pull out the deck and lie across the bed on my stomach. I used to be bored at the Middleton's. But nothing is worse than being locked in the house with Daddy. Nobody to play with. No TV. Nothing to do. Scared to cross the hall to go to the bathroom. Afraid to go get a drink of grape Kool-Aid.

I spread my Snap cards on the bed, pluck up Buzzy, turn onto my back, and prop him against my pillow so we can talk. "Let's play Jungle. I'm Tarzan. You can be Jane. I'll get Cheetah." I turn for the monkey card.

"What the hell are you doing home in your pajamas knocking back beers and sitting on your ass?" I hear Mama all the way down the hall, even in my room with the door shut.

Daddy screams something back at her, but I can't make out anything except a roar. I inch my door open and put my ear to the opening.

Mama comes in loud and clear again. "Don't lie to me. I stopped by Sandy Middleton's first. She said Mary Alice hasn't been there in weeks. And now I see the babysitting money's been going for beer. Don't tell me. You've lost another damn job."

I open my door all the way and step into the hall.

He yells back. "Get off my back. Got laid off. Figure to be back in a week or so."

"Laid off, my ass! You think I wouldn't have heard if the plant had a layoff?"

Their voices get louder and louder. I run with my fingers in my ears across the hall to the bathroom, stuff toilet paper in my ears, and hurry back to crawl into the closet. With my back pressed against the corner of the closet, I hum *Red River Valley*. I only hear music and a sound like thunder a long way off.

But the thunder doesn't stop the way it usually does. I creep out in my sock feet and edge along with my back against the wall, down to the den. I hear every word, even with the TP in my ears. There's a big mirror hanging over the couch. I can see them without them seeing me.

Daddy's sitting in his recliner. His eyes are almost swelled shut, and his red nose looks like Bozo the Clown's.

Mama's yelling over him, her dark hair loose from where she had it pulled back. She has one of Daddy's girlie magazines in her hand, the ones he looks at every day and thinks nobody knows about.

Daddy's saying loony things to Mama. "Come on over here, over my knee." He winks at Mama and slaps his knee. "Stop your bitching or I'm gonna have to spank you."

He's really gone crazy. He's gonna spank my mama.

"You sonofabitch! Gonna spank me, my ass!" Mama bats at a cereal bowl from breakfast, still sitting on the end table. She screws up her face and lets loose. "I can't believe you've been here staring at girlie books in broad daylight, with Mary Alice in the other room, when you should be out looking for a damn job."

"Come on, now. I been looking for work. Honey, if I was lying, I'd tell you the truth." He holds his hands out toward her and puts that sweet look on like when he wants smooches.

"Well, now. There's the truth if I ever did hear it. I swear to God, I put up with enough of your shit day in and day out." Mama marches back and forth in between his chair and the TV, her arms swinging. "I've had it. Told you if you lost another job, you'd be leaving for Bobby's house so fast, your head'd spin sideways."

"Now, Baby. I was gonna tell you after I found one, so you wouldn't have to worry."

"Jesus Christ! Get that filth out of here." Mama drops the girlie book and kicks it clear across the room.

Daddy looks mean at Mama. "You don't tell me what to do. I got a man's rights. Conversation closed. Now get down off your high horse and fix us some dinner." He jabs his finger at her. "I tried to be nice to you!" He turns back to the TV. Match Game's gone off and now it's wrestling.

But Mama doesn't go into the kitchen. "You ain't no use to me or Mary Alice anymore. Time's come when we'd be better off without you."

Daddy doesn't look at Mama but starts his chewing thing.

"I ain't living with a man who can't keep a job, won't lift a finger around the house, and expects me to work my ass off every day while he looks at dirty pictures." She points at the TV. "And turn off that damn wrestling show."

Daddy jerks his head towards Mama. "Shut your damn mouth." His whole face is as red as his nose. "Push your luck and I swear, Marva, I won't be responsible. I'm warning you."

Mama goes into the kitchen, but she doesn't fix dinner. She comes back with her arms full of beer and another magazine on top. "Cherry Poppers! You popped your last cherry seven years ago, you dumbass! And I was out of my mind when I let you do it!" She opens the front door and dumps the Schlitz on the stoop. Beer cans clunk and hiss. "Now get the hell out of my house."

"You bitch!" Daddy stumbles out of his chair as Mama comes towards him. "Your house? I'll show you whose house."

Before I can blink, Daddy knocks Mama in the side of the head. She almost falls down. I yell, "Mama!"

He grabs her arm and twists it behind her. Mama cries out and doubles over. "Now get my beer." He uses both arms to hook her around the waist and drag her to the front door. "Then you'll fix my supper, way I said."

She tries to pull away. He grabs her hair. Mama's arms and legs kick and punch, but Daddy's too big.

I have to help her. I run and grab Daddy's arm. He pushes me. I hit the door. Mama screams and jumps at him.

Both of them hit at the same time. Him with a punch to her face. Her with a knee between his legs. He falls backwards, grabs himself, and lands on the porch, on top of the beer. The back of his head whacks against the metal porch railing.

"Sonofabitch!" Daddy's on his back, holding himself between his legs. Mama rolls away, pushes up on her hands and knees, jumps up, and slams the door behind her. The lock pops into place.

She scoops me up in one arm, on a run to the kitchen, double-checks that the back door's locked, and sets me down hard on the floor. I hang on to her leg and won't let go.

Daddy's outside on the front porch, pounding on the door.

She drags me with her the three steps to the phone and dials zero. "This is Marva Lydell. 57 Miller Mountain Road. Get the police. It's an emergency. Please, God, hurry!" She hangs up, snatches a knife from the wooden block, and sinks down with her back against the corner, next to the refrigerator. I climb in her lap and press my head against her chest. She stretches one hand out, away from us, the blade shining. Her heart hammers against my ear.

"Let me in!" Daddy bangs and bangs. The noise makes me want to crawl into the cabinet and hide behind the dish detergent, but I hold on to Mama.

She whispers into my ear, but the sound comes out as a hiss. "Sssshhhhh."

Glass breaks. A siren's whoo-oooo makes my eyes un-focus. I count that one-two sound coming towards us, over and over, and my fog comes in.

Then Mama's standing above me, saying, "Hushpuppy, come on. It's gonna be okay." But her voice sounds like someone's standing on her foot. She puts the knife back and tries to pick me up the way she did when I was little. But the arm Daddy yanked hurts too bad, so she grabs my hand and pulls me along with her.

A loud knocking on the front door drills into my head. I wrap my arms around Mama's leg and hide my face. She pulls me into the den and reaches for the doorknob.

I just know Daddy will come in and get us. "No, Mama, don't." But she opens the door.

I peek up. It isn't Daddy. It's a policeman. He's going to put all of us in jail. I hold Mama's leg in the biggest bear hug ever.

"Marva, who started this?" He sounds mad at Mama. I turn my head to steal a look outside. Another policeman pulls Daddy away, in handcuffs, to the car in the driveway, with its blue lights flashing. Daddy's shouting bad words, even at the policeman.

"I asked you what's going on here." The policeman at the door raps his hand on the doorframe. I grip Mama's shirt with both hands.

"Randy, I got home, and Carl must have been drinking heavy all day. We started fighting, and he got out of hand."

"That's Officer Scroggins to you, Marva." The policeman's long nose twitches.

Mama draws her breath in fast. "No disrespect intended." Mama wraps her good arm around my shoulders and shifts foot to foot. "He came at me swinging."

"What is it you want us to do?" The policeman's voice sounds the same as the school principal talking to a kid in trouble. "Really want us involved in your little tussle?" Mama doesn't answer.

I stare at Daddy ducking his head to get into the back seat of the police car. Our neighbors are out on their lawns, watching. The teenager from four doors down has a Kodak Instamatic and snaps pictures of my Daddy sitting in the back of the car in his pajama drawers, with his legs sticking out of the open door.

"I advise you to take care of your problems. We'll talk to him, calm him down." The policeman steps away, over the broken glass and beer cans. He doesn't even turn back to look at Mama when he says, "And clean up this mess before someone gets hurt."

Mama pushes the door shut with her foot. I pluck the toilet paper out of my ears so I can hear better, in case my mama needs me. Because that policeman is like my Daddy. He won't help us one bit.

Eleven

The blue police lights flash through our curtains and bounce off the big mirror on the wall. Mama walks fast through the house, with me clinging onto her shirt like a baby monkey. When we get inside my bedroom, she motions for me to sit on the bed, but I won't let go.

"Turn loose. We have to hurry." I hold tight. Mama pulls me loose. "Let go!" I drop to the bed with a bounce and bury my head in Mr. Sand.

Mama leans down and turns my face towards her. "Listen. We have to go. Now. Before the nice policemen leave. Daddy's lost his mind. We're going to Aunt Jean's."

Aunt Jean's? I grab Mr. Sand and follow behind Mama, sucking my thumb, while she fills a pillowcase with a handful of my undies, shirts, and skirts.

Mama scoots across the hall to her bedroom and packs some of her clothes in her travel case. Then down the hall we go, with her carrying the case and my pillowcase in one hand. She's holding her other arm funny and won't give me that hand. I'm holding Mr. Sand and Mama's shirt. I have to step double-time to keep up with her.

In the kitchen, Mama grabs for her purse and groans, "My arm." She races us out the door and to the car. It's starting to get dark, but the minute we step foot on the carport, I see Daddy. He's coming up the driveway towards the house, with a policeman on either side of him.

I lower my head fast, so I don't have to look at him. Mama hustles me to the car, opens the driver's door, and shoves me and our bags in.

"Where the hell you going?" Daddy yells.

Mama's head pops into the car for a second. "Be right back." Leaving the car door open, she dashes behind the car.

"Mama!" I moan loud into my hands. "Don't leave me." But I have to see. I kneel on the front seat and look out the back window.

Mama's walking towards Daddy and the mean policemen. I hear her through the open car door. "Officer Scroggins. Sir, could you three please stand on the porch while I back out and get my little girl over to my sister Jean's?"

Daddy lunges towards Mama. The officers grip his arms and hold him back. "The fuck you say. You ain't going nowhere," he screams.

One policeman yanks Daddy backwards with both hands. "Ease up, Carl. Best you two spend the night apart. Sleep it off."

Daddy doesn't stop. "I'm taking care of that bitch right here, right now."

Both officers slam Daddy against the carport wall and pin him there. "No. You're doing it our way. Or we're taking you in. Got it?"

Daddy doesn't answer. Mama flashes by the back window and is in the car before I can turn my head. She slams the door and backs out fast, with me still kneeling on the seat. As we fly by in reverse, Daddy head-butts one of the policemen. They start punching him.

We go over the hump at the end of the drive. Sparks fly. Tires squeal. I fall back into the seat and see Mr. Sand in the floorboard, lean far down to scoop him up. Draw my feet onto the front seat, hug my knees in tight with my face pressed into Mr. Sand's belly. Mama doesn't say anything, just drives. I breathe in and out. I wish Daddy would go away forever. I wish the police would kill him dead.

After a long time, the car stops. Mama reaches over and puts her hand on top of my head. "Honey, we're at Aunt Jean's. Come on, now. Tell Mr. Sand we're here."

I peek up at Mama and swipe at my snotty face. Mr. Sand's all wet. Mama wipes my face with her bare hand and rubs them off on her pants. "Ah, shit, Honey. I'm sorry. But we're safe now."

"Promise?"

"Little Hushpuppy, I promise." The tears in Mama's eyes sparkle in the light from the streetlamp.

I sit up straight. "Buzzy! We have to go back and get him."

Mama shakes her head. "No. We can't." She gets out of the car.

How could I forget Buzzy? He'll be so afraid. Mama swings my door open. I slide out with Mr. Sand. A rainy mist comes down wet on my hair. Aunt Jean's bedroom window shines yellow in the darkness. I move my feet and run past Mama. Aunt Jean will know what to do.

Twelve

That night, I sleep with Aunt Jean. Mama sleeps on the living room couch. When I wake up, Mama has already left for work, and Aunt Jean sits with her Bible at the kitchen table.

I know Aunt Jean's schedule like the freckles on the back of my hand. "What's the Bible verse this morning?"

"Beatitudes, Matthew Five. Now there's one you know. Remember?" Aunt Jean lays her palm on the top of my thinking cap. "Blessed are …"

As I nod yes, her bony fingers move with my head. I'm one of those doggies in the back car window with its neck moving up and down. I wag my butt back and forth, like that doggie and recite, "Blessed are the weak, for they hear the Earth. Blessed are the hungry and thirsty, until they're full."

Aunt Jean laughs her biggest laugh. "You and me'll have to practice that one some more. You're a first grader now, and I'll be expecting you to recite verses along side me." She winks. "Then, I'll be 'specting you'll read the Bible to me. Give my old eyes a rest, for a change." She takes her hand from my head. I make whining puppy noises as she brings over a cookie sheet and lines up three bread slices on it. "Sit still, Miss Priss. We'll get this ready in two shakes of a lamb's tail."

She opens the fridge and hands me her clear butter dish with a pineapple drawn into the lid. Grabbing the egg carton, she takes it to the stove and breaks eggs into a pan.

I dab margarine with a dull knife. "Let's make cinnamon toast."

"What a good idea!" She brings me the sugar bowl and the red-and-white can of cinnamon. I pick up pinches of sugar and sprinkle it on top, followed by eight shakes of cinnamon on each piece, while she beats the eggs.

"What's wrong with my daddy?" I make a point not to look at Aunt Jean when I ask. Maybe she'll answer me.

"Nothing the good Lord can't make right." Aunt Jean turns to light the gas oven. "And nothing for you to worry your pretty head over. That's grown-up business for your mama and daddy to handle." She takes the pan from me and slides it into the oven.

I toss my ponytail. I didn't figure anyone would tell me what's going on. Noone ever tells me anything, but that doesn't keep me from knowing something's bad wrong. "I don't want any eggs."

"If you want the toast, you do." Aunt Jean goes to the window and looks at the house next door.

"Why?" Nobody ever lets me eat what I want.

"Eggs build your bones. Looks like Mr. Bledsoe's putting some tomato plants in the backyard again. Hope his crop's as good as last year. He gave me half after I canned all of them." She comes away from the window and sits down at the table. "Now drink your milk."

———

After breakfast, Aunt Jean pulls out a new jigsaw puzzle. I begin sorting the border pieces on the kitchen table. She sits down next to me. Her chest heaves up and down with each breath. I wish I had a friend to help me with the puzzle, then Aunt Jean could go lie down.

"Aunt Jean?" She nods at me. "Were you ever married?"

"No. You know that." She flicks a corner piece over to me.

"I forgot." The one I'm working with won't fit. I pick up another. "Why didn't you ever have a baby?"

She looks up at me and frowns. "You know only married people have babies."

I run my finger over the rounded edge. "Didn't you ever want a little girl like me? Then I'd have a friend to play with."

She slaps her hands down and the puzzle pieces jiggle on the table. "Didn't you hear me? I never married." Her face is all pink.

"But you could have had a sweet little baby if you'd got married."

Aunt Jean stands straight up. Her chair falls over and hits the floor with a crack. "That's enough! You're being sassy, and I won't have it."

As she walks out the door, her feet make loud booms on the floor, then I'm alone. The bathroom door slams. What did I say wrong?

I prop the jigsaw's box top up against the Popsicle stick napkin holder I made for Aunt Jean at Vacation Bible School last year. When I come to visit, we usually take the bus downtown, and Aunt Jean lets me pick out a toy at Kessler's 5 & 10, then we go get books at the library. Last week, I got this puzzle. It looks like a picture postcard of a waterfall with bright red flowers shooting out beside it. I trace the waterfall over and over with my finger. Inside my head, I hear the sound it would make, like a big faucet turned on and pouring into a giant tub. That'd be a fun way to take a bath.

My two favorite things about putting together puzzles with Aunt Jean is first getting to sit and talk with Aunt Jean at the kitchen table. The second is the way the pieces fit together. I especially like putting all the edge pieces together. When I snap the last of those pieces in place, I feel a click in my head, like playing marbles when the shooter hits an aggie out of the ring.

I've almost finished with the edges when a quick tap-tap comes at the front door, and Mama's voice fills the house. "Hey. It's me."

The dreamy feeling goes away. What's Mama doing home from work so soon? Bringing both hands down hard against the table, I whisper, "No. Not ever going home again." I go back to the puzzle and concentrate on fitting pieces together. But I hear Aunt Jean's and Mama's voices and want to hear what they're talking about. I walk quietly to the living room door.

Mama's sitting next to Aunt Jean, and they're talking in quiet voices. Mama's hair's messed up. Her eyes are red and squished, and her left arm is wrapped in a piece of cloth tied at her neck like one of Aunt Jean's hair scarves, but jumbo. She's saying, "They have him for assault on an officer. I don't know how long they'll keep him. I just know I'm not bailing him out." I walk into the room and they both look up.

"Mama, your arm!" I run to her and start to throw my arms around her but stop myself because I'm afraid it'll hurt her worse. I pat her hand. "Poor Mama." Daddy's mean. I hope Mama and those police never let him get away.

Mama and Aunt Jean look at each other. Mama says, "It's just sprained, not broken. Now you run get your things."

I look from one of them to the other. "Why aren't you at work? Can't I stay a little while longer? Please. Pretty please." I fold my hands together under my chin like a prayer. It isn't fair. I've just got to Aunt Jean's. I think about going home and start feeling like something's scratching me all over from the inside.

Mama shakes her head "I didn't work today. Now I got to get home and clean up that mess and lay down. I didn't sleep a wink last night."

"But me and Aunt Jean just got started putting a puzzle together." I look for Aunt Jean to rescue me.

"You mind your mother. Go get your things. I'll move that puzzle to the end of the table. Next time you're here, it'll be right where you left it." Aunt Jean waves at me to go on.

"All right." I kick at the couch and run from the room, but tiptoe back to lie down low outside the door with one eye spying around the baseboard.

"You've been through the mill with him. No one would say different, not even the Lord Himself. But you've got Mary Alice to think of." Aunt Jean's sitting tall, the same as she does on the church pew.

"You don't know what it's like." Mama glares at Aunt Jean. I can't get over how different they are. Aunt Jean's a lot older than Mama. She looks like a grandma, with her grey hair, missing tooth, and old-fashioned clothes. Mama has on a pretty yellow blouse and bright red lipstick. Even with her messed up hair, she's still pretty.

"I got a rusted-out Mustang in the backyard next to Mary Alice's swing set, all because one day he's gonna fix it." Mama lays her head on the back of the couch cushion. "I got him losing job after job and promising the next one'll be different. I got one drinking jag after another. My life's busted up with all his one-days." She turns her neck side-to-side. "One-day's never gonna show up, Jean."

Aunt Jean taps her fingertips together like "here's the church, here's the steeple." "There's nothing here the Lord can't make right."

Mama rolls her eyes and sighs, but Aunt Jean puts her hand in the air.

"No. Hear me out. You were brought up under the Lord, and you can come back to Him. Carl, too. God can turn his heart. Make you a family. Worse men than him have found Jesus." Her hands lace together in her lap, like she's praying.

Mama raises her hurt arm. "No. Last night was it. I can't take no more." She snaps her head up. "He told the police I attacked him. That he couldn't allow no woman to lift a hand to him and live to tell about it. You weren't there, Jean. That man's gone round the bend. He could have killed me."

My eyes open wide. I saw them. He could have.

Aunt Jean lays her hand soft against Mama's big bandage and stares at it. "You know I don't want you living like that. But are you sure this is the right thing?" Her eyes lift to Mama's face. "Marriage is sacred, Marva. You took a vow before the Lord. And like it or not, he's Mary Alice's daddy."

Mama juts her chin out. She takes Aunt Jean's hand and pushes it away. "I know you mean well. But, of all people, you should know sometimes a person has to make a hard choice."

Aunt Jean pulls her hands back into her lap and looks at them. "You think I don't spend every day wondering where she is?" Looking like she might cry, she raises her head and stares straight at Mama. "More reason for you to think this thing out, so you don't spend the rest of your life agonizing over the wrong decision." Who's she talking about?

"Ah, Jean, I didn't mean to bring it up. I'm sorry. I'm half out of my mind." Mama rubs hard circles on her forehead with the heel of her hand, leaving a red mark on top of her nose. "You're right about me having Mary Alice to think about. But that's even more of a reason. He's too rough on her."

Aunt Jean leans forward. "What do you mean?"

"He's on her like a whip on a mule. Rides that child non-stop." Mama drops her chin. "When I saw him yesterday, it made me sick to my stomach she's been there alone with him after school for weeks. But I didn't know she wasn't at the sitter's." A tear runs down her nose. "That man was so drunk, he was in no condition to watch after himself, much less my baby."

Aunt Jean sucks hard on her teeth and runs her tongue over them. "She told me he was mean, but you know how children talk." She points at Birdhouse Jesus. "That's why she took the crucifix."

Do they understand about Daddy? I clamp my hand over my mouth and hold my breath.

"I need you to back me on this. I wouldn't do it if I had any other choice." Mama stands and Aunt Jean does, too. Mama takes one of Aunt Jean's hands. "You're gonna have to help me take care of Mary Alice."

Aunt Jean pulls Mama into a hug but keeps Mama's hurt shoulder held away from her. "I'm none too happy about it, but you can count on me. You know how much I love that little girl in there. This will be hard on her."

Mama squeezes her eyes shut. Then she pulls loose. "My God, Jean, you never stop hugging first. Never. It's what I remember most from when I was just a kid."

Aunt Jean laughs. "Honey, I reckon you've always needed as many hugs as you could get. When you were seven, I was twenty, and you'd tease me. Perch your hands on your hips and tell me, 'When I get growed up, you better bet I'll be out having a good time 'stead of hanging around here helping Mama cook, Miss Goody-Goody!'"

Mama finally looks happy. "Even then, you'd fix me with one of your stares, wrap your arms around me and not let go."

Aunt Jean leans her head down to Mama's until their foreheads touch.

"I love you, Jean." I barely hear her say it. Then she pulls back after a few seconds, wipes at the corners of her eyes, and looks toward the door. "Now where in tarnation is that child?" She yells, "Mary Alice! Get in here. I said we have to go."

I bite my bottom lip and edge away like a snake crawling backward. Stomping into the kitchen, I think about what Mama and Aunt Jean said, but it don't make sense.

My favorite song is *He's Got the Whole World in His Hands*. When I hear it, I imagine giant hands filled with people—no body, just two hands.

I can't even imagine how big those hands have to be to hold everybody in them. I bet Heaven has a great big waterfall for them hands to wash in. Then what happens to the people? I bet the hands set the people down for a day and that's when trouble sets in. Like with Daddy.

I hear that Alice-girl. *I hope those hands drop Daddy from so far way high up that he never comes down.* I push that thought into a hole in my head and cover it up.

Mama and Aunt Jean's voices come closer. I pick up the puzzle's last edge piece, kiss it quick, and put it in place so I can go get my things. But this time, when I snap it in, there isn't any click in my brain that sounds like my marbles. It doesn't make any noise at all.

Thirteen

When we get home, Daddy's not there. Mama tells me to go play. On the driveway, I squat down and make a hopscotch board using a broken piece of rock, because I don't have any chalk.

With the squares finished, I draw in the numbers and sing, "One is for one box of candy. Two is for two boxes. Three is for three. Four is for four. What for? For four. Five golden rings." Pointing my face to the sky, I hold that last note as long as I can. While filling in the rest, I recite, "Six growling birds. Seven lives in heaven. Eight goes round and round and round and round, down and back, down and back." I trace the number eight—outline it eight times—because it's my lucky number. "Nine brown mice, cut off their tails with a carving knife. Ten. I win." Standing up, I step back and tilt my head to get a good look at the whole thing. Not quite finished.

I draw in a five-pointed star in the number ten box and use a sliver of black crayon to shade its lines in as dark as Frick's Cave. Then I search around the yard for two rocks with different shapes. Hop, hop, hop, I play against myself, taking a turn as Black Beauty with a rock that looks like black coal and leaves smudges on my fingers. Then, it's Star Girl's turn. Her stone has shiny speckles. When I'm Black Beauty, I pull my shirt tail up, hook my left elbow in it, and hold that arm close to my chest, like it's in a sling.

Star Girl's almost made it to ten when Mama calls me in for supper. I hip-hop-tromp up the front steps and run in to wash my hands. When I get to the table, it's set with two places instead of three. "Where's Daddy?"

Mama's at the counter, pouring a glass of milk, and answers with her back to me. "You know good and well your daddy's not here."

"I forgot." I was hoping she'd tell me where he is. Because I've already decided. If he's coming back, I'm running away to Aunt Jean's before he gets here.

Mama sets the milk in front of me and a glass of red wine at her place.

I point to her glass. "Why've you got wine for dinner?"

"Mary Alice! Why do you ask so many questions? And how many times have I told you it's rude to point?" Mama's voice comes out loud and squeaky. She clears her throat and breathes in deep before talking again. "What I meant to say is Mama can have wine with dinner without it being anything special. Okay?"

I nod and use my fork to cut my hamburger steak into pieces, but keep peeking at Mama to check out what's happening. That voice means I'd be better off not saying anything.

First, I cut my steak in half, then the two halves in half, then each half in half, and on and on until I have thirty-two pieces. I reach for the little round container in the middle of the table and shake a toothpick out through the tiny holes on top, then use it to spear a piece of meat and dip it into ketchup. I chew it eight times.

After several pieces, I notice Mama's frowning and not eating. I lay my toothpick down. "What's the matter, Mama?"

She raises her glass and swallows all the wine down. "I don't want you to get upset, but your daddy's not going to live here anymore. And he's probably going away for a while. I don't know when you'll see him again."

My heart feels so happy I almost can't believe her. But what if she finds out I wished him away? I pick up my toothpick and drop my hands in my lap so I can poke it under my fingernails. "What?"

"Mary Alice, I know you understand me. You know the police were here. Your daddy's in big trouble. Plus, you know him and me haven't been getting along for quite a while." Mama tries to take another drink from the empty glass, then glares at it, sits it down hard, and turns back to me. "The truth is, I'm going to file for a divorce, and you can't be surprised."

I poke harder with the toothpick. "I don't understand." Tiny drops of blood seep onto my cut-off jean shorts. Divorced? It's all my fault. That Alice-girl says, *Who cares if we made him go away? Just don't let Mama find out. You'll get in so much trouble. I bet they put little girls like that in jail, too.* That scares me bad. I start to cry.

Mama sets her fork on her plate. "Mary Alice! Don't pull that Mopey Mary act on me. I've got enough on my mind without having to worry myself sick over you." She pushes her chair back hard with a loud scraping noise, gets up, pours herself another glass of wine, and gulps it down.

Alice hisses in my ear, *See.*

Mama rubs her forehead. "That didn't come out right. Mama's sorry, Honey." She pours another and drinks as she leans against the counter. "What I mean is, you don't have to worry about any of this. Everything will be fine. You hear me? Fine." She takes another sip and raises the glass towards me. "Better than fine. It's going to be better, Mary Alice. You wait and see." She smiles big and wide, and it reminds me of a few times Daddy dropped me off at Firestone on his way to "a night with the guys." I'd sit on the tall stool behind the counter and color in my coloring book while Mama finished closing the store. Mama's smile now is the one she gives a customer who's irritating her at the end of a long day.

There's a drop of red wine on Mama's white blouse. It looks like a red-light saying Stop. Mama's blue eyes are bright and shiny. They say Go. I move my eyes back and forth between the two. Stop. Go. The third time around, I see Mama has stopped smiling and is twirling the wineglass by its stem and staring out the window.

"Mama?" My voice is low. She must be looking at that crepe myrtle she likes. She probably wants to look at anything but me. I bet she knows I've done something wrong. I clear my throat and say it louder. "Mama?"

She turns towards me as slow as Papa Lydell's hound dog. "Huh?"

"Mama, You don't have to worry. I'll be good. I promise."

Mama's smile-for-the-customer comes back. "Oh, Honey. I'm not worried. Of course, you'll be good. You're always a good girl. Now, aren't you?"

"Uh, huh." Mama sounds happy, but one of her eyes keeps blinking and her hand is shaking. Wine sloshes in the glass. Alice pokes at me. *I told you. Don't you dare let her find out you sent Daddy away.* She's right. Then Mama would find out what a really bad girl I am, and she wouldn't love me anymore. Just like Daddy said. Aunt Jean too! Oh, no! Aunt Jean can't find out what I've done.

I poke the toothpick extra hard under my thumbnail. The sharp point goes deep into my skin, and I feel better. Alice and I won't tell nobody. That Alice girl is right. Mama and Aunt Jean can't ever find out about anything that happened. Not ever.

Part II

Down the Rabbit Hole
Thirteen Years Old—1974

Fourteen

Life was good. My best friend, Carolyn, waved at me from the bleachers. Two weeks ago, we started eighth grade at the high school. Today, we stayed after school for a huge meeting in the gym to learn about clubs we could join. After that, we were going to our first Junior Honor Society meeting. Her mother would pick us up at six o'clock. It was a really big deal.

Carolyn was up and grabbing my arm. "Come on! I got a front seat." We didn't want to climb the steps in our miniskirts, which was impossible to do with an armful of books. We needed one hand to sneak around to our backsides and hold the fabric under our tushes. There were always a bunch of boys sitting down below, waiting for a view.

Mrs. Snow, the guidance counselor, was a thin, pale woman with brown hair hanging down straight in front of each ear, but with the bottom cut ragged across each side, like somebody'd taken to her with pinking shears. Mrs. Snow yelled out, "If you can hear me clap once." She clapped once. Only a few kids clapped. "If you can hear me, clap twice." She clapped twice. I started to clap, but Carolyn grabbed my hands and shook her head. Hardly anyone paid attention to her and all the noise the kids made echoed off the walls.

A big man, over six feet tall, and as wide and square as the chest of drawers in my bedroom, stood up from the front row and pivoted military style to face the crowd. He took two precise steps backwards, raised one hand, and boomed out, "Young ladies. Young gentlemen." The noise ratcheted down by half. In the bright gymnasium lights, his scalp shone beneath his crew cut. "Shut your rat traps this instant." The entire group shushed. "You will give Mrs. Snow your undivided attention now." We heard the squeak of his shoes as he turned to Mrs. Snow and saluted. She sort of waved her hand at him and cleared her throat.

Carolyn whispered in my ear, "That's Mr. Green. Honest to God, they say he was a Green Beret in the war. I bet he salutes his own toilet." I started to giggle, and she pinched the underside of my elbow. "Don't you dare. He'll come behead you or something."

At the meeting, we learned a ton about all the clubs we could join. There was the FFA, Future Farmers of America. Nobody but the greasers joined it. The FHA, Future Homemakers of America. Most of the girls—the good girls—joined it. I nudged Carolyn, but she bobbed her chin, telling me to wait and see. FBLA, Future Business Leaders of America. We turned to each other and snorted. Library Club, Pep Club, Art Club, Chess Club, Science Club, Spanish Club, Christian Council, Black Alliance, and S.A.G.E., Student Action for Georgia Education. We both shook our heads no fast and hard for each of those. Drama Club. Her eyebrows raised. FTA, Future Teachers of America. I grabbed Carolyn's knee and she quickly nodded yes. Then Mrs. Snow talked about sports, cheerleading, and the annual staff. Carolyn whispered, "They never let anyone in eighth grade onto the annual staff, but maybe one year. What do you think about softball, in the meantime?" I nodded. We both knew how we felt about cheerleaders. They weren't worth a mention.

As soon as we walked into the cafeteria and sat down, a boy from my homeroom class smiled at me. His wavy, sandy-colored hair curled around his ears. He wore jeans slung down low on his hips with a wide, leather-tooled belt and a belt-buckle in the shape of a guitar neck. Carolyn leaned over to me. "Who's that?"

I felt my cheeks turn red. "Jeff Davis. In my homeroom. Came from another school." He was cute, but I was too shy to talk to him.

"He likes you." She poked me in the ribs.

"As if." I muttered at her and kept my face pointing toward the front, where the faculty advisor was talking about our accomplishments.

When the meeting ended, we piled out. The juniors and seniors headed to the student parking lot, while us sophomores, freshmen, and pre-fresh either started walking, if we lived close by, or looked for our parents' cars. Jeff waved at me, and I threw my hand up. Carolyn elbowed me. "Told ya." I didn't say anything. She wouldn't understand. Boys scared me.

I saw Mrs. Townsend's Chrysler LeBaron near the front of the line. Carolyn and I hopped into the back seat, both talking a mile a minute. "Everybody in the whole school was there."

"We're going to join FTA and try out for softball." I bounced on the back seat as I talked.

She threw her arm around my shoulder. "Going to be the best year ever!"

We chattered the whole way home. When we turned into my driveway, the sky was growing dim and every window in my house was dark. Mrs. Townsend spoke to me over the bench seat. "Isn't your mother home?"

"No, ma'am. She has to close the store." I rummaged in my handbag for the key and opened the car door. The interior light came on, and I could see Mrs. Townsend was frowning.

"Are you sure? You could come home with us."

Carolyn didn't wait a second to chime in. "Oh, do! We'll have more time to talk about school … and him." She winked.

Mrs. Townsend added, "I have a roast chicken in the oven, corn on the cob, and scalloped potatoes. You like peach cobbler?"

I didn't know what scalloped potatoes were, but they sounded delicious. Before I fainted from hunger, I got out of the car and turned on my heel to face them. "Mama will be home any time now. The store closes at seven. I wouldn't want her to have to eat alone." I swung the door closed. It was too embarrassing for them to know how different it was at my house.

"See you tomorrow!" Carolyn yelled.

Mrs. Townsend rolled her window down. "Maybe next time. Ask your mama if you can't stay to dinner with us sometime, okay?" She shouted as I ran to the carport. "I'm not leaving until you're safe inside."

"Yes'm!" Her headlights lit up the door, and I quickly unlocked it and let myself into the empty house. She tooted the horn as they backed out and scraped across the hump at the end of the drive.

I flicked the lights on. Mama worked from seven in the morning until seven at night, Monday through Saturday. Most of the time, when she did get home on Saturdays, it was just long enough to change clothes and head out to her friend Lucille's. Up until a couple of years ago, I'd go with her. But Lucille's little boy was a lot younger than me, and I just ended up babysitting. I'd rather stay home. But there was just so much TV to watch, homework to do, and books to read, before I was sick to death of myself and wanted a little company.

The metal legs on our rooster-shaped wall clock pointed to seven forty-eight when Mama finally pulled into the carport that night and stumbled in the door. I was lying sideways in our old recliner with my American History book in my lap, studying for the test Mr. Blalock promised we'd have at the end of the week.

Starving, I slammed the cover shut. "Did you bring something home for dinner?"

"Hello-and-how-was-your-day to you, too." Mama flopped her satchel-size purse onto the table.

Behind me, I heard the fridge door open and her rustling around and muttering. "I should have gone by Piggly Wiggly on the way home. Damn food bills are breaking the bank." Then louder. "Mary Alice, what happened to the leftover pot roast from Sunday?"

I craned my neck over the top of my chair. "We took Aunt Jean some of it, remember? Yesterday, when you left me here all alone, I ate the rest."

"Then I don't know what we're going to eat." She pushed the door shut with much more force than necessary. Condiment bottles rattled. She held an open can of Budweiser. "You were invited to eat at Lucille's with us yesterday. We've been over this before. Scotty's only six and in bed by seven-thirty. It ain't like she can leave him there all alone." She tilted the can up. There was something about the way light glinted off a beer can always made my stomach hurt.

"And, God knows, you can't just stay home with me," I mumbled.

"When you were little, I stayed home more nights than I can count. Now you can take care of yourself, this is all the thanks I get for not dragging you along behind me." She turned her back, finished the beer, and opened the fridge again. "Think whatever you want. I deserve time of my own. If you had a lick of sense, you'd get your nose out of those books and go off with your friends, like any other teenager."

"I do things with my friends. Any other mother would be glad I get all A's."

"Name me one friend of yours who isn't named Carolyn." She talked as she pulled out mayonnaise, a stick of margarine, an almost empty pack of Kraft American cheese, and another beer.

"Grilled cheese! I could have made that myself." I thought about Carolyn's roast chicken dinner.

"Then why didn't you!" Mama set the skillet down with a clatter on the stove's eye, cut off a hunk of margarine, and got it melting. "And make one for me while you were at it? I've had a rough day. You're old enough to fix supper. Don't start in with me."

"All you ever talk about is your day. Never think that I have a lot of work, too. All the algebra homework I have every single night, and Mrs. Gibson slamming us with another crummy old two-page paper on some nineteenth-century scientist nobody cares about." I took the loaf of white bread out of our wooden bread box, handed it to her, and hefted myself up to sit on the counter.

"You better poke that bottom lip back in before you step on it or won't nobody ever want to kiss you."

"Kiss me? Nobody's ever gonna want to kiss me." I muttered loud enough she could hear.

"Come down off your cross. You get that shit from Jean." She spread both slices of each sandwich with a heavy layer of mayo, unwrapped the cellophane wrappers from the last two pieces of cheese, dropped the sandwiches into the pan, and twisted the stove's eye up before gulping on her beer.

Mama carried two plates to the table and slammed them down. When she lifted the top plate, the one on the bottom had broken in half. She held a piece out to me. "Now see what you made me do."

"I made you do? I don't have anything to do with your foul temper." When she snatched up the other half and strode towards me, it was all I could do to stand my ground and keep my chin up.

"You are the most selfish child I ever saw in my entire life. Never think of anyone but yourself. Do you ever once think about what I might be going through?" She dumped the broken plate into the garbage, along with the empty beer can. "It's a damn good thing we don't have matching china in this house."

"You're the one's selfish." I kicked my heels against the cabinet. "Carolyn's mother has dinner ready for her at five o'clock every night—meat and vegetables and homemade peach cobbler."

"Then you better scurry on over there and see if she's willing to take you in. I don't have the luxury of sitting at home all day flipping through a Betty Crocker cookbook to pick out the dish of the day." Mama turned to the stove and tossed the sandwiches over. They were burned to a crisp on one side. "Nope. Ain't throwing these out." She whacked the spatula against the pan. "We'll just have to scrape the black off and eat 'em. It's all we got."

"You are the worst mother in the whole world—in the entire universe." I vaulted myself off the counter, ran to my bedroom, and slammed the door. She'd be happy if I lived somewhere else. She could go off having the good time she deserved from now to eternity.

I was face down on my bed with the phone in my hand, getting ready to call Carolyn, when Mama stormed into my room.

"I'm not putting up with you sitting on your duff the way your daddy used to do, while I'm on my feet all day, convincing goons that Firestone's not the one drove their junk heaps into the ground, and we can't work miracles for $16.95."

"I am not anything like him." As furious as I was that she'd compared me to him, I was more shocked she mentioned him at all.

"You will show me the respect I've earned. I work hard to put this roof over your head." Mama jerked the receiver out of my hand and slammed it onto the base. "Do you think princess phones in your bedroom for Christmas come cheap? You're past old enough to help me out. Sweep the floor. Put a load in the washer." She stopped. Her eyes widened, and her mouth opened.

I wanted to ask what she was thinking but didn't dare.

When she spoke again, her voice was lower. "I am not my mama. But I've been too lax on you. Gave you too much. Wanted you to have a little fun growing up. My mama thought I was her personal slave, or so I thought back then."

She stared off at the ceiling. "Now, I'm not sure. Seems like she was asking the same of me that I'm asking of you. Only now, it don't seem so unreasonable. I'd give my right arm for the chance to mop my Mama's kitchen floor again." And then Mama busted out crying.

A dancing bear could have come in here and waltzed off with her, and I wouldn't have been more surprised. My mama did not cry.

Her shoulders trembled and a groan escaped her throat. I looked at my green shag carpet. My feet wouldn't move. I drew in a breath, made my toes push off, and went to her.

The heels of her fists were pressed into her eyes, and she shook with sobs, but no sound. I bit my lip. I wanted to throw both arms around her and pull her head into my chest, pat her back, and say, "There, there." That's what Aunt Jean would have done if she were here. But Mama never hugged anybody, except Aunt Jean.

I inched one arm out to her back, opened my clenched hand, and held it there six inches from her back for a count of eight before placing it spider-like between her shoulder blades.

She jerked away with such force she knocked backwards into my closet door with a loud thwack. "What do you want?"

She looked mad enough to hit me. Her eyes looked as if somebody said her puppy had died and it was me who poisoned it. A chill went down my arms and spine. Why in the world was she so mad at me? The Little Girl inside me hid down low. Alice threatened to come out and make things worse, *Ask her who was there to teach us to cook.* I pushed her away.

"I do not need your sympathy." She pointed at me. "Things are going to change. You have to grow up." She swept me aside and rushed out of my room.

I sank to the floor, my back against the louvered closet door, with each slat bearing into my backbone. Pulling my knees up to my chest, I hugged myself, trying to warm up on the inside, and sat there thinking about Mama and me. Seemed like we were constantly at each other's throats. We always made up, but then things would blow up again, especially when she was tired, which was most of the time. If she didn't have to work such long hours, it might have been different.

Alice's voice filled my head. *Your daddy's to blame. Even before he went to jail, your mama was the one who kept us going.*

I rose and changed into the over-sized men's chambray shirt I liked to sleep in. Dropping to my bed, I stared at the ceiling. Soon after Daddy went to prison, I overheard Mama talking to Lucille. "Judge threw the book at that sorry bastard for hitting a cop and the two of us are living hand to mouth. Be better off with him dead. Least then we'd get Social Security." But in the seven years he'd been gone, I didn't remember Mama ever mentioning Daddy again. That was her way. She was stubborn. I loved that about her, and it made me want to scream.

Anyway, I never wanted to hear another word about him. Just thinking about him made me feel like my bedroom walls were closing in and Alice was about to take over. Once, on a sleepover, Carolyn and I were lying in the dark, and she asked me if I missed him. "Not for a damn second. Don't ask me about him. Not ever." She never asked again.

My feet hit the floor and I paced back and forth on the old blue and yellow rag rug by my bed. I didn't want to fight with Mama. All I wanted was her home with me more. How come we always pushed each other away?

I inched my door open. The light in the den was on, and the theme song from Hawaii Five-O drifted towards me. If I went in there and she hadn't had enough time to cool down, we'd just start again. I turned into the bathroom and brushed my teeth. Maybe she'd hear me and come say good night. Then I could tell her to stop by the store on the way home tomorrow and get us a box of Chef Boyardee pizza. We always had a good time mixing the dough and sprinkling on pepperoni and extra mozzarella cheese.

I kept the water going a long time and flushed the toilet twice. Either she didn't hear me or was still mad. Standing in the hall, I couldn't decide whether to head to bed or go tell her good night. I thought about those sandwiches she'd made and wondered if she'd eaten.

Mama said I needed to grow up. I decided to go tell her good night. When I reached the den doorway, I saw her lying curled on her side on the couch, fast asleep, her work clothes still on. Her knee-hi hose were balled up inside her flat, navy-blue loafers on the floor. On the coffee table, a half-eaten grilled cheese lay on a plate, alongside a crumpled beer can. I crouched down and watched her. She'd unbuckled her narrow belt but hadn't taken it off. Her white blouse was halfway un-tucked. Her only movement was the steady rise and fall of her chest and an occasional twitch of her bare toes.

I went into her bedroom, took a quilt out of the hope chest at the foot of her bed, and carried it into the den. As I laid it over her, she didn't stir. After turning the TV down a hair—I thought she'd wake if I turned it all the way off—I quietly gathered the remains of her dinner and made my way to the kitchen. When I tossed the trash in the garbage can and set the plate in the sink, I saw my soggy sandwich she'd laid out for me and took two bites before throwing the rest of it out. I poured myself half a glass of milk and turned out the lights. Mama never roused. In the flickering pattern of TV light beaming across her face, she looked like a scene from a movie.

I wondered about what she'd said about her mother, who'd died before I was born. I never considered Mama might miss her. What would it be like to not have my mama? The very idea was impossible. I refused to think it. Instead, I vowed to myself I'd surprise her and learn to cook. Maybe Mrs. Townsend could show me.

I grabbed an apple and my history book and went to my room to study. Both Mama and Aunt Jean thought book learning wouldn't get you too far in the world. Mama was convinced I should learn a trade, like stenography or nursing. Aunt Jean had the crazy idea I'd grow up and go save the natives in the jungle or something. They were so old-fashioned. I wasn't going to be an old, dull secretary or missionary. I loved reading and English. I was going to be a teacher and get to read all the time and have kids in the class who liked me. Chomping into my apple, I opened my textbook and got to work.

Fifteen

That fall, I learned to cook Hamburger Helper by reading the directions on the box. For spaghetti, I watched Mama sauté onions, brown hamburger meat, and drain the excess fat into an empty can she kept by the sink. "You can open those for the sauce." She pointed to a tiny can of store-bought tomato paste and a big jar of tomatoes Aunt Jean had canned.

She'd pre-heated the oven to 350°. I slid in a pan of garlic bread, and dinner was done in five minutes. It was easy. From then on, I made Hamburger Helper one week and spaghetti the next. The batches always lasted for two dinners for both of us and even two lunches for Mama.

I had good intentions to learn how to cook some real suppers from Mrs. Townsend, but Mama didn't let me go over there very often. "I don't want you imposing on the Townsends. You'll wear out your welcome."

About once a week, I did get to go over. Then, Carolyn and I had so much fun I ended up laughing and talking instead of standing by Mrs. Townsend at the stove. All through September and into the first of October, Carolyn and I talked about school and our plans to play softball on the Junior League team. She also yammered on about boys. I kept quiet on that subject. Even though I wished I could tell her about Jeff, the boy in my homeroom class. He didn't seem like the other guys, and we'd started talking every morning. He even walked me to my first class.

Unzipping her yellow plastic pocketbook, Carolyn pulled out a book and slid it over to me. "Ever read this?"

Go Ask Alice. "Never heard of it. Any good?"

She nodded. "To the max." She whispered, "But don't let your mother catch you with it."

"Why not?" The front cover was seriously scary, with a chick's spooky eye glaring at me.

"Not unless you want her searching your room for drugs and stuff, you know." She put on our decrepit librarian's syrupy voice and tilted her nose up. "'That book, and I use the term loosely, is simply scandalous.'"

"Heck, I didn't know the old biddy allowed students in her library. I ride in with Mama some Saturdays and spend all day at the library downtown." I flipped the pages. "What's so degenerate about it?"

Carolyn grabbed it out of my hands. "No reading ahead! Here, put it in your bag, and let me know when you get to the juicy parts."

I started to open my mouth to tell her about a good one I read, *I Never Promised You a Rose Garden*. But sometimes I wondered if I was crazy like that girl, Deborah, in the book, so I stopped. A person who talked to herself and had crazy thoughts was deranged. I knew having the Little Girl inside me, much less Alice girl, was enough to make me "certifiably insane," as Mama called some of the Firestone customers.

Barely listening as Carolyn talked on and on about the cute guy in her math class, I chewed on my thumbnail and nodded at the right moments. By the time Carolyn quit yakking and took a pee break, I'd chewed my nail down to the quick. Blood welled to the surface, and I had to hold it upright and squeeze it with my other thumb and forefinger to make the bleeding quit.

The Alice girl in my head said, *That's the kind of thing crazy people do.* I stopped her by running my finger along each piece of fringe on my purse and counting them. As I forced my mind into thinking about something else, the softball team stood out bright and solid. I could see Carolyn and me out on the ball field with the sun shining down on us in those cute black and gold shorts and jerseys.

Carolyn popped back into the room. I stood and spoke fast, before she started in again. "Listen! We don't have to wait for spring try-outs to get ready for softball. If we started practicing now, we'd be a shoo-in come March."

"Great idea!" She snapped her fingers. "Where can we practice?"

I looked out the window at the field next to her house and jerked my thumb in that direction. "There! Me and you could clear that field of the biggest rocks. It'd be perfect."

"We could do it right after school. Maybe a couple of the girls from our bus would come over, too. Then we could practice batting." Carolyn did a little twisty dance. "Oh! I bet your mama would let you come over a couple times a week if you had to practice ball. We could see each other a whole bunch then!"

When I got home, I called Aunt Jean. "Guess what?"

"Tell me." Her quarter-time breathing was loud on the phone. "Not up to guessing games."

I told her all about Carolyn and me going to be softball players.

"Got it all planned out, huh?" She coughed and cleared her throat.

"And guess what else?" I didn't wait for her to say anything but kept on talking. "We've been reading *The Rime of the Ancient Mariner*. Everyone in Lit class takes turns learning different verses. It's horrible long and mostly boring." As I talked, I went to the refrigerator for a snack. Tucking the receiver between my shoulder and ear, I carried the jar of mayonnaise and a pack of pickle loaf to the counter. The phone cord strung out behind me, quivering. "It says, 'O happy living things.'" I paused so it could sink in. "Isn't that one of the most beautiful things you ever heard?"

"If you say so." She loved to tease me.

"Oh, Aunt Jean. I'm serious." I huffed into the phone and twirled the cord around my finger.

"Don't get in a tizzy." The line was quiet, except for the rasp of her breath. "What about it?"

"I got to read the best line: 'A spring of love gushed from my heart, And I blessed them unaware.' Aunt Jean, it's the prayer that makes the gross albatross finally fall from his neck! See! Outta sight, huh? I thought you'd like the prayer part." I grabbed a round tin of Pringle potato chips from the cabinet.

"What's out of sight?" She sounded confused. "The albatross?"

"No!" My Aunt Jean was the un-coolest person on the planet. I giggled into the phone. "'Outta sight' means groovy, you know."

"Oh, I know." She was laughing at me again. "I surely do know."

"Aunt Jean, you shouldn't mock people. This boy in class got made fun of today."

Larry, the guy who sat behind me, was supposed to read, "That slid into my soul." Instead, he accidentally said, "That slid into my hole." But I couldn't tell Aunt Jean that.

"All the guys burst out laughing at him, and he turned twenty-two shades of purple. I bet he's so embarrassed he won't ever be able to come back to school again." I layered a few of the chips on top of my sandwich meat.

"Twenty-two. So specific." She drew in a deep breath. "Honey, your friend will be back tomorrow. Whatever happened can't be that bad."

"He's not my friend. Just a guy sits behind me in English. I wouldn't want people thinking I like him or anything. Don't be telling anyone what I told you."

"Who exactly is it you think I'd tell?" There was a grin in her voice.

"I don't know, but don't tell anybody. Okay?" When I pushed on the top slice of bread, my sandwich crunched.

"I promise not to tell a soul." She sounded serious.

"Good. Gotta go study. Talk to you later. I love you the mostest."

"Oh, no. I love you the mostest, forever and ever and a day." She always said that. My Aunt Jean may not have been cool, but she was the best.

Sixteen

Carolyn's and my great plans to be part of the softball team were on the way to coming true. In October and November, a bunch of us girls practiced in the field next to her house twice a week. Mama even let me get off the bus at her stop on those days, as long as Mrs. Townsend drove me home before dark. I never mentioned the snack Mrs. Townsend always had ready for us when we got there. One day, it'd be homemade pimento cheese sandwiches and fresh-baked chocolate chip cookies. Another day, it might be a scoop of tuna salad with Ritz crackers and carrot sticks. I would have gone for the food, much less the fun.

When we realized it would be too cold to play outside most of December and January, Carolyn came up with the perfect idea.

Mrs. Townsend had a big pot of vegetable soup and cornbread waiting for us when we ran through the pouring rain and stomped up the front steps. We were chowing down in her breakfast nook—that's what they called it, though it was just a part of the laundry room with a little round table and two chairs. Her mother was getting ready to go to GA's, Girls in Action, she led every Wednesday night at the New Prospect Baptist Church.

When her mother went to change clothes, Carolyn sat her spoon down. "You know, we were GA's from first grade, up until sixth."

I answered with my mouth full, "So?"

"What if we offered to be GA Teen Leaders, Acteens? Then, you could come over every Wednesday. Heck, we'd have an excuse other days, too. We'd need to plan out activities." She leaned back on her chair's two back legs and held her hand up for me to slap.

"Yeah, we know all about Annie Armstrong, Lottie Moon, and everything." I drew my hand up into a claw. "My hand still cramps up on Wednesday nights from all the letters we wrote to the poor mountain kids."

"I could make a mission box in my sleep." Carolyn cut herself another triangle of cornbread and slathered it with soft Parkay.

"Me, too! Decorating them was the best part." I eyed the brownies cooling on the counter. It would be rude to ask for one before Carolyn finished eating. I turned back to her. "You think they'll let us?"

She licked margarine off her top lip and grinned. "Who's gonna discourage us from helping little kids with the missions?"

I slapped her upper arm. "Oooooh, you are so bad."

Carolyn scooped her final bit of soup up with the last hunk of bread and sat back, chewing. "There's nothing wrong with us figuring out how to spend more time together. No way will your mama think you're imposing, and it would be fun. Think about it, we really do know how to lead the group."

"We could make our own word search puzzles and show them how to bead cross necklaces and teach them songs for singing at the nursing home." It was starting to sound like a good time.

"What about baking cakes and taking them to thank the policemen and firemen? We did it every year." Carolyn took her bowl to the sink and came back with the brownies. "The little girls would get a kick out of visiting the stations and sitting on the fire engine."

"And car washes! To raise money for food drives. Those were a blast in the summer!" I waited for Carolyn to set the plate down before grabbing two chocolate squares and laying them on my napkin. "Remember the motto?"

We both threw our fists out and shouted it together, "Go forward!"

———

By the time February came around, I was having more fun than I'd ever had in my entire life. Carolyn's breakfast nook stayed covered with projects from school and GA's.

The weather turned out warmer than usual. We let the other girls know we were back to having softball practice on Tuesdays, Thursdays, and Saturdays. Softball try-outs were scheduled for March first.

Mid-February, Carolyn had a dentist appointment. I rode the bus home alone and thought about that guy, Jeff, in my homeroom. He rode an early bus, same as me. Often, we were the first kids in class. Sometimes, he came over and pulled a desk up next to mine. At first, I didn't know what to say or how to act. But he wasn't the type who had to be talking all the time. Sometimes, he just sat next to me flipping through a magazine. He didn't read typical teen stuff or even Sports Illustrated, which I hated since Daddy had always read it. Jeff's choices were more like Time or Analog Science Fact & Fiction. When we did talk, he asked me questions and listened to my answers. I liked all those things about him. But the thought of actually having a boyfriend made my bones shake. Alice's voice whispered, *You know why*. But I didn't know why.

Mr. Lancaster, the bus driver, woke me from my daydreams, "Mary Alice! You riding around again, or what?" I scurried off, to the sound of kids making fun of me, singing, *Wake up, Little Susie*.

The sky that day had lost its dank gray and was a shade of Carolina blue, with the sun going in and out of a line of layered clouds. I threw my coat across my shoulder and trotted up the driveway. The heat, after winter's cold, made me feel warm inside and out. Sally, the neighbor's basset hound, wobbled over on her short legs with her tail wagging for her usual back scratch. "That a girl. Feels good, huh?" When I hit the spot right at the base of her tail, she started kicking out her left leg and flipped onto her back so I could rub her belly. "Silly old dog. There you go, one belly rub. Now, go home." I gave her one last scratch behind her long ears and sent her on her way.

As soon as I walked in the house, I tossed my bag and jacket on the kitchen table and called Aunt Jean, but her line was busy.

The first thing I wanted out of the way was studying for my science test. I poured myself a glass of Fanta Orange and curled up in the recliner. Atoms, neutrons, electrons, croutons. Give me English any day. I dug through the chapter and quizzed myself on the review section at the back. That would do.

My grades were already good enough. What I really wanted was to make the softball team. Besides, today wasn't made for staying indoors. It felt like spring out there.

After changing into a navy-blue t-shirt and a pair of orange short shorts, I grabbed my softball and glove from my closet. Even if Carolyn and the girls weren't here, I could at least toss the ball against the house.

I walked into the den. My ball and glove dropped from my hands. It was Daddy. Standing in the kitchen, by the carport door.

"I see your mama never got around to fixing that weak lock. She should've done something about it. Anybody with a mind to could just waltz right in here." The sound of his voice was torture.

He stood there, swaying on his feet and looking me up and down. "Look at you. All filled out." His gaze lingered on my breasts. I wrapped my arms around them. "Close to being a woman. So grown, I reckon you think you're too good for me."

As he talked, I couldn't move. My mind turned to a cloud of buzzing mosquitoes that settled between my brain and eyes. My sight blurred the way it used to when I lived with him. I was Alice girl again, but even she couldn't make a sound. Somebody looked out, only as tall as a first grader, with tiny feet—Little Girl inside.

He took three long steps towards me. "Think you're too good to speak to your own daddy!" The smell of booze and sweat enveloped me. It all happened so fast I must have faded away between the time he moved to when he grabbed my arms. Alice finally spoke up. *We have to get out of here.* When she said it, the room started coming into focus. Daddy's familiar red-ringed, green eyes tuned in, but his leathery skin and the purple broken veins all around his swollen, broken nose were new. His hair was shaved to stubs all over his head and an ugly scar ran from the top of this head down the side of his face and to the corner of his mouth.

His fingernails dug into the skin above my elbow. "Goddamn you and that bitch to hell. The two of you's ruint me. You have any idea what the guards pay prisoners to do to inmates who hit cops?" He stumbled to the refrigerator, dragging me in tow. With each step, he lurched to the right. Something was bad wrong with his leg.

"Mouth's dry as an old whore." Mama had Bud in there. He grabbed the whole six-pack and jerked me over to the couch. My butt hit the cushion and half-bounced. When he moved to sit, I tried to stand. He pushed me back down by slamming his arm out. "Oh, no you don't."

Holding me in place by gripping the back of my neck, he passed me a beer with his free hand. "Open it."

The cold beer in my hand. Daddy and me on this couch. All the buzzing in my head swirled up the way a tornado spins, then crashes down. I remembered. Something bad. This couch. Something wrong. Ride a Little Horsey?

Daddy slapped me across my face. "I said to open it!" I popped the top and handed it to him in slow motion. He stared at my legs, the same look as the boys at school. He took a gulp.

I lunged up, out of his grasp, towards the door. Behind me, I heard the slap of his soles against the linoleum. My hand touched the doorknob. He twirled me around, slammed me against the wall and stared at my chest. I squeezed my eyes shut to block out that sight. His body pinned me against the wall, with my hands caught between us.

I tried to push him away. No use. I was trapped.

"Let me go." Little girl's voice sounded small and far away. His hands cupped my butt cheeks.

"Those are some mighty fine hot pants you put on for your old man. I always knew you were a little whore." He laughed and pulled me in so close the tips of my tennis shoes barely touched the floor. I opened my eyes. He leaned his head in closer. "You're the one thing that's mine in this shit world." Using his hands to pull my hips toward him, he thrust against me. "Mine."

A sudden need to sleep came over me. My head rocked back and hit the wall. An image came to me of the nasty Boston terrier down the street wrapping his front paws around my calf and humping until I flung him off.

Daddy's hands crept up my ribs. His thumbs and index fingers reached the underside of my breasts. The shock roused me. Frantically, I pushed my captured hands down against his, down against his, down against his. But movement was nearly impossible.

"Stop it." I whimpered. His hands moved up to my breasts. I saw the girl I would have been float away from me like she was filled with helium. Forever gone.

His eyes were crazed. His breath came in spurts matching each surge of his hips.

I closed my eyes and tried to disappear. Instead, something snapped, and a slide show filmed seven years ago played at breakneck speed through my mind. Daddy hunching on me in my bed. Daddy's truck and him putting his hands up my dress. Ride-a-Little-Horsy and Daddy touching under my shirt and panties. It all came gushing up at me.

When the memories spewed out in my head, it was like every cell in my body began to smolder. What had been buried would not slide back into the darkness. Until then, I'd made all the times he touched me disappear. I had no conscious memory of it ever happening. I guess it sounds weird to anyone with a normal father, but that's how it was.

The Alice part of me—she knew all along. She's another thing I can't explain. It's like there's three parts of me. First, there's just me. Second, there's a little girl hiding down inside. Little Girl never says a word, just stows away in the dark. But Little Girl is gone now. Third, there's Alice. She talks to me and is good for coming out when there's trouble. When I was little, I thought Alice emerged from the looking glass to take care of me. Since I got to be a teenager, I've wondered if having Alice and Little Girl means I'm bonkers. Crazy or not, until then, Alice was the only scrap of me that knew what happened with Daddy.

Remembering what he did to Little Girl filled me with rage. "Stop!" I said it loud, and spit dappled his cheeks.

But he didn't stop. His hands moved down to the place between my legs. I smelled English Leather, soured milk, beer, and whiskey.

My body twisted, trying to escape him.

"You let boys do this," he accused. I gasped.

"If you don't stop, I'll tell Mama." The voice I heard coming from me sounded like a sniveling brat. Pathetic.

Even so, it was the kick of a gun. He shoved me away. "She'd never believe you."

I nodded deliberately. "Yes. She would."

He gripped me around the throat, throttling me. I coughed and choked and clawed at his hands. He let go, but pushed me towards the door, half-lifting me as he pulled us both outside. "Get out there."

I tried to yank away, but he wrapped his hand around the back of my neck, brought his face right in front of mine, and said, "You do what I say, or I hurt you bad. Now! Gonna show you what to believe."

As he dragged me to his car, I frantically looked around, but no one was outside the few houses near us. All I saw was Sally loping toward us.

He opened the driver's door, reached under the seat, and pulled out a handgun. Every cell in my body froze.

Pointing it at me, he said, "You believe this? Huh? Answer me."

I had to swallow twice before I could get the word out, "Yes."

"You ever tell your mother or anybody, I'll be back. You'll watch me shoot her. Then you get to live, knowing you killed her." And before I could do anything, he jerked the barrel to the left and shot Sally in the head. I screamed as she fell over dead.

He pressed his stinking hand over my mouth. "Shut the fuck up or I'll shut you up." I tried gulping in mouthfuls of air. Everything turned two shades darker.

The next thing I knew, he had a trash bag, and we were standing over Sally. "Put it in the bag. Now!"

As I stooped to lift her, I passed my hand over her fur one last time. Then I slid her into the bag with my ice-cold, bloody hands.

He nudged me. "Dump it in the woods."

I lifted her in both arms and Alice moved my feet as he walked with me into the woods behind my house. The feeling in my head was so light I thought I would float away where Little Girl went, but each heavy step let me know I'd never have it that easy.

When we'd gone a piece into the woods, he stopped and pointed the gun at me again. "You believe what I told you?"

I nodded my head yes, like bobbing a balloon on a string.

"You best remember I'd just as soon kill that bitch as not. You got that?" His face swelled up in front of me. I nodded yes. "Good." He turned and walked away with me clutching Sally to my chest.

I don't know how long I stayed there until I sat Sally down by a pine tree and trudged home. Back inside, I locked the back door and collapsed onto the kitchen floor. I breathed, but the air was poison. Lights seemed to pop and flicker. The pain was nowhere and everywhere. My bladder released, and I smelled piss.

When I could heave myself up, I cleaned the pee and put the rest of the six-pack back into the refrigerator, cleaned up the beer he'd dropped, stumbled to my room, and crawled into my closet, where I used to go when I was little. It had seemed so much bigger then. When my eyes adjusted to the dark, I saw something stuck down where the baseboard pulled away from the floor. I reached for it, and my hand came back with a playing card from my old Snap deck. I turned it over. It was Buzzy.

"Oh, Buzzy." I clutched him to my chest, curled up on my side, facing the back wall, and held my breath until sparks danced before my eyes. I willed myself to die, but my lungs demanded air. Hitching in huge, gasping mouthfuls, I rocked back and forth with dry, unblinking eyes shifted out of focus. Just like my foot going to sleep, numbness moved in waves from my toes, up past my knees, hips, stomach, chest, lips, and eyes.

Hours later, I woke up in bed, in my pajamas. It was the time machine I used to believe in when I was little, and now I couldn't believe how stupid I had been.

The clothes I'd been wearing were lying in a heap next to my dresser. I stumbled out of bed, kicked them in my closet, slammed the door, and crawled back under the covers. How could I have forgotten all those things he did?

When Mama got home, she came into my room. "What are you doing in bed?" It was just like the Ride-a-Little-Horsy day.

"I'm sick." I pinched the inside of my wrist and held the skin tightly between my thumb and index finger, to keep myself from blurting out everything.

"Fever?" She laid her hand on my head. I wanted to grab it and never let go. "You're not warm. Cramps?"

I couldn't look her in the face. "Leave me alone." It came out much louder than I meant it to.

"For heaven's sake, what's wrong with you?" She took a step backwards.

"Go away." I turned from her and crushed my old pillow, Mr. Sand, to my chest.

"You don't have to get snippy with me, just because you feel bad." I kept my back to her. "Well, have it your way. Cut off your own nose to spite your face." The click of my door closing was thunderous. I wanted to yell, Don't go! I wanted to tell her everything.

It wasn't long before she returned with Sprite, soda crackers, and Midol. "Come on. Sit up and take this. Eat a couple of crackers to coat your stomach before this medicine upsets it more." Without a word, I did as she said.

"That's a girl. Now you curl up and get some sleep. Best thing for you." She tucked the sheet around my shoulders.

Alice spoke up, but she sounded scared and unsure. *Tell her.* A hole under my bed promised to suck me down into an abyss if I dared open my mouth. No, I couldn't tell. Not ever. Mama's life was in my hands.

Seventeen

I thought I'd be awake all night, but I fell into a deep, quicksand sleep—a dark smothering oozed and sucked me into its depths. The next morning, my 6:30 alarm went off from somewhere miles above me. The droning continued until Mama came in all dressed for work and turned off the buzzer. She shook my shoulder, but I was so far down inside myself I could not move or speak. All I could do was direct my attention to Alice, but even she sagged lifeless in the mire.

"Mary Alice. You getting up?" Mama said it softly. The words echoed down the bottomless rabbit hole.

Later that morning, a phone rang in the distance, three different times. Part of me recognized the sound but, down in the sludge, it held no meaning.

There came a time when the pressure on my bladder forced me to move up through the weight bearing down on me. I hefted myself from the mattress a little after one o'clock. Making my way to the bathroom was like wading across the Cave Spring swimming pool, with only my head above water. I gave in to the feeling, and let it flow through me while I drew a bath and sunk into water as scalding hot as I could stand. The phone rang again and kept ringing for what must have been thirty times. I laid a wet washcloth over my forehead and eyes and submerged my ears, with only my nose sticking out.

I don't know how long I'd been floating when I heard the back door slam and Mama yelling my name. She skidded into the bathroom as I pulled the rag off my face. "God damn it! Why didn't you answer the phone?" Her voice reverberated off the tile walls. "Left me thinking something's bad wrong, and you in here lazing in the tub."

I opened my mouth, but my mind was blank, the same as a phone line that's been cut. Her breathing slowed, and her eyes widened. "You're white as Death himself." She jerked open the linen closet and pulled out one of our worn-out yellow towels. "Stand up. Come on." I stood, the way I'd done hundreds of times as Little Girl. Mama wrapped me in the towel and pulled me in close. "What's wrong? Tell Mama."

I started shaking all over and couldn't stop. Mama dried me off and put her arm around my shoulders. She walked me to my room, took my long daisy-print robe off a hanger in the closet, threaded my arms through, and tied the sash. I lay down on the bed facing the wall and pulled up my knees. My teeth chattered with the cold and the bed vibrated with my fierce shuddering. She used the spread to rub me all over in fast circular movements. Slowly, the ice broke free.

"Good Lord, it's like you've been out in the snow." She leaned over me to snatch up my extra pillow, yank its case off, and use it to wring out my long hair. Her fingernails gently traced from my forehead over my crown. My body calmed. "Talk to me. Do you hurt anywhere?"

I shook my head no. She tried to turn me, but I wouldn't face her. "Come on now, Mary Alice. You have to tell me what's wrong."

I couldn't tell. "I don't know."

"This is me you're talking to. I know you like the back of my hand." Her tone shifted a little, still tender, but with an edge. "Are you sick? Hurt? What's wrong?"

"I don't know." Pressure mounted between my temples. I clamped the heels of my fists against those hollowed-out spots and pressed in as hard as I could.

Mama caught my hands in hers. "Stop that."

I mashed my face into my pillow and wailed over and over and over, "I don't know. I don't know. I don't know."

Mama covered me with her body and slid her right arm underneath me. "Shhhh, it's okay. Shhhh …" She curled in so snug her knees fit beneath my buttocks and her chest molded to the curve of my back. Her left arm encircled my body. Then she was quiet and still. Her face pressed against my neck and the whoosh of each out-breath tickled my earlobe. Slowly, her warmth eased its way into me and became mine.

I ran down, the same as a wind-up toy, and she whispered, "Hush, now. I'll leave you be." She sat up and laid her palm on the small of my back. "That what you want?"

With my head still buried, I nodded yes.

"It's okay. I'm here if you need me." She stood, left my door open, went into the kitchen, and dialed the phone. "Fred, it's Marva. Yes, yes, she's okay, but she is sick. I need to stay here." And that was the last I heard before falling back into a quicksand sleep, where nothing stirred under the inky bog, and I could sink.

—

When I woke, morning illuminated my windows. Rising through the oozing shadows, my muscles ached all over like I had the flu. I stretched and flexed to get relief. I blinked my eyes open. Mama sat next to my bed in a chair she'd brought in from the kitchen table.

"Good morning, Sleeping Beauty." She laid down her Reader's Digest. From the light coming through my curtains, I saw she was late to work. "How're you feeling?"

My mouth was bone dry. Each beat of my heart caused an electric pulse to jag between my eyes. "Fine."

"You had a rough day yesterday." She leaned forward, with her hands flat on her knees.

"I don't know." The words were out of my mouth before I even thought.

Mama pounced at me, laughing, and sat at my feet. "Don't start that again. What you don't know must fill the bucket to overflowing." She ruffled my hair, and I had to smile. "How about some breakfast?"

My stomach clenched and growled. "I'm starving."

"I bet you are. Didn't eat a bite yesterday." She laced her fingers through mine. "What would you like?"

"Hmmm," I rolled it around in my pounding head. "Scrambled egg sandwich."

"You got it." She grazed her lips across my forehead. I knew from experience she was checking me for fever. I must have passed her test because she went into the kitchen and came back with food instead of a thermometer.

After finishing the sandwich off in no time flat, I sipped on the milk she'd brought. She perched on her chair again. "You can go to work. I'll be okay."

"I don't think so." Two lines wrinkled above her nose.

I wanted to be alone. I needed time by myself the same as my lungs needed air. "Really, Mama. I feel a lot better."

Those two lines on her forehead relaxed into one. "Let me see how you're doing at lunchtime. If you're still good, I'll go in for half a day."

The thought of her sitting in that chair watching me all day made the pressure in my head threaten to build again. "Okay, I'll get my bath, then."

"A hot soak will do you a world of good." She gripped the chair under its top slat to lift it. "You think the Firestone gods will strike me dead if I go watch some TV?"

"Come on, Mama, live a little." I forced myself to get out of bed and scooped up a pair of undies, jeans, and a T-shirt from my chest of drawers.

"I will, if you promise not to stay in there so long you freeze up like a giant Popsicle again." She hugged me around the waist and took her chair into the kitchen.

After my bath, I wrapped up in my robe and the two of us sat side-by-side to watch Jeopardy. She shouted out the answers and looked to see what I thought about her. At first, she got most of them right. Then Alex read, "It completes Shakespeare's line, 'Shall I compare thee to …'"

"What are witches' warts!" She hollered and looked at me from the corner of her eye to confirm I was laughing. I couldn't help giggling at her. "On their tits!"

I doubled over, "Mama! That's bad!"

Alex continued, "This Frenchman lent his name to an early form of photography."

"Who is Sir Cheese?" She laid her palm over her heart as she said it.

"Now you're just being silly." I shoved her shoulder with mine.

"And what's wrong with that?" She pursed her lips and looked me straight in the eyes.

"Nothing, I guess." I lowered my eyelids and picked at fuzz on my housecoat.

Mama sighed. "Should I be worried about you?" She brought her face around in front of me and lifted my chin, so I had to look at her.

Eye-to-eye, I almost blurted it out. Alice jerked me back to reality by sending me an image of Sally Dog shot through the head. *Shut up, before you get her killed!* I held her gaze and shook my head no, while tracing figure eights on the side of my leg.

"Honey, I have to ask, do you have a boy causing you trouble?" She actually looked upset.

I reached out, squeezed her knee, and shook my head an emphatic no. "No, Mama. God, no."

"Mary Alice …" Her breath whished out her nose. "I know that something's …"

I cut her off and talked fast. "Nothing's wrong, Mama. I don't know what got into me." I made sure to look full-on at her. "Must be my period. They can get bad, you know. Or maybe I caught a bug. I don't know. I really don't, Mama. But I'm okay now. You have enough to worry about."

She looked at me with such a strange expression, her forehead brought down low, and her eyes squinted, I felt like she thought something was fishy.

"I'm not saying I feel real good. My head still hurts something horrible, and my stomach keeps turning over like I'm gonna barf." I crossed my arms across my middle. At least that part was the truth. "But I do feel better. You go on to work. Anyway, you won't be gone that long."

Mama bit her lower lip, and I could tell she was thinking about it. Then she shook her head, as if to clear her thoughts. "Well, if you're sure." Right away, I nodded yes. "Okay, then." She tilted her head and shook her index finger at me. "But you're to call me if you get worse or if you need anything. You hear?"

"Yes, Mama. I will." It'd been at least three years since she'd worried about me being sick and home alone. A lump rose in my throat. I leapt forward, hugged her, and spoke directly into her ear, "I promise."

She let go before I quit hugging and that lump came back. "Let me fix you some lunch before I go."

My arms hung at my sides. "I'm just not hungry right now. I can open a can of soup later."

She hopped up. "Then I think I'll have a peanut butter and banana sandwich."

I grimaced. "Yuck. You trying to make me sicker?"

She laughed and strode into the kitchen. All Mama-like again.

Twenty minutes later, her car grated across the hump at the end of the driveway, and I remembered what Daddy had said about the door lock. Until that moment, I'd been too out of it to think he might come back. I grabbed a kitchen chair and propped it under the doorknob. Would it hold? Alice answered. *He'll get in if he wants to. All he's got to do is break a window.* I spun around in the middle of the floor. So many windows. So many ways he could get in, could get to me. Nowhere's safe. You might as well get used to it. It's not just here. He could be anywhere.

That thought filled me with a burning running from my tail bone up my spine to sizzle in the back of my eyes. I pounded my way down the hall to my bedroom, threw open my closet, and snatched up the orange short shorts, top, and underwear I'd been wearing when Daddy busted in. Back in the kitchen, I yanked the junk drawer open and grabbed the good scissors. As the fabric rent beneath the shears, I let loose. All the tears I'd been holding inside ripped out of me. Scraps flew in the air and dropped like confetti. I threw the shorts on the floor and stabbed them repeatedly.

I cut every piece of clothing into ribbons and buried them at the bottom of the trash can. Cramming the ruined clothes underneath the stinking coffee grinds, I imagined stuffing Daddy in there with them. Slamming the scissors on the counter, I jerked the trash bag out of the trash can, twisted the top, and tromped out the door. At our metal can,

I snapped up the silver lid, jammed the plastic bag in, and clanged the lid down. My eye caught movement in the woods. A big, black crow flew out of the tree line like death coming at Mama and me straight from Sally Dog. I grabbed the metal lid and crashed it down over and over but barely heard the racket over my hoarse screams.

A wind kicked up and flipped the back of my hair, making me think someone had snuck behind me. I spun around, armed with my metal shield, my heart hammering away. No one there. I looked up and down my street. Not a soul in sight. Not even a car at Shorty's store. I let the lid drop.

The blazing flash that propelled me died instantly. My breath caught at the base of my throat and all the energy drained from me as surely as if a vortex whisked it down. The fire that had felt so powerful was extinguished.... Now I just felt like a fool.

It was hopeless. He could come back whenever he liked and pitching a fit wouldn't stop him. I trudged back into the house and poured a glass of tap water. As I gulped, my eyes lit on the pattern of holes I'd made on the linoleum with the scissors. One more thing ruined because of me. That's what I got for carrying on like Daddy. I stumbled down the hall and went back to bed.

The rest of the week, I stayed home, breaking my perfect attendance record from the last four years. Mama seemed puzzled but didn't press me to go. Every one of those days, I spent sleeping down in the rabbit hole, where I couldn't feel Daddy's hands on me or see the bloody mess that had been Sally's little face ... couldn't see it transform into Mama's bloody head.

Carolyn called. I told her my throat was so sore I couldn't talk. Aunt Jean called. I wasn't lying when I said my head ached and I needed to be quiet.

But sleeping didn't help. Staying away from everyone didn't help. I prayed every day. Nothing helped. By Friday, my head felt as if it would split wide open with its slideshow of horrible images flashing in an endless loop. I couldn't go on like this. Alice got louder and louder and all she'd say was *Tell Mama*. So, I decided to tell her that night.

I planned on being ready when she got home at 7:30. I would bathe and do my hair before she got here. Then, I'd look normal when I told her, and she wouldn't think I was crazy. I'd start with, "Mama, I have something I have to tell you. I need you to listen." Or, "You asked me what was wrong. Something is bad wrong, and I need to tell you." I couldn't get past the beginning, so I just kept practicing it.

I paced back and forth across my bedroom floor, trying to get the words to come. The harder I tried, the sicker I got. The words stuck in my throat and gagged me. I changed the opening twenty times and ran to the bathroom twice to throw up.

Around five o'clock, I heard the carport door open, and I almost passed out. Little black dots swarmed in front of my eyes. I forced myself to run look and planned to escape out my bedroom window if it was him.

It was Mama. Fright made the room wobble. I steadied myself by pressing my hands to my knees, leaning forward, and repeating, "Not him."

Mama came into my room and grabbed me from behind. "Honey, come here." She hugged me tightly from behind. Hugged me so long I knew something was wrong.

I must have felt like a limp rag doll as my arms hung down by my sides, but she couldn't have noticed. Instead, she rubbed the small of my back and whispered in my ear, "I have something I have to tell you. I wish I didn't have to say this now when you've been sick." She paused and took a breath. "I'm so sorry to tell you. Your daddy died."

She let go of me and stepped back. I turned to face her. I know I blinked. I'm sure I blinked.

She went on, "He died in prison of pneumonia."

I looked at her. I'm sure I looked at her. At least, I had to have stared at her mouth as it said those unbelievable words.

She had her hands on my shoulders and after a minute or two, she jostled me. She shook me, just a little. And I started laughing. It burst out. I laughed and laughed, then I started crying and sobbing and shaking and rocking, and I don't know when it ended, but when it did, Mama was staring at me like I had lost my mind. And I had.

I was insane with a feeling I'd never known, not in my entire life. Relief. Pure and simple. Relief. I would never have to see him again. Never. Now I would never have to tell Mama. Never.

I had thought Aunt Jean's love was the best feeling in the world. But this sense of weightlessness ... was this what other people felt?

It should have set me free, and I knew it. That relief allowed me to breathe like I'd never imagined possible. Do other people really breathe this deeply?

But hand-in-hand with that incredible sense of relief, I felt the hole, the irreparable damage nothing could ever heal. Daddy was gone. He could never hurt me again. Yet, I knew I'd never get over what he'd done. This would save Mama, but it couldn't save me.

I wanted to be happy for her. I wanted to savor the lightness that almost lifted me clear off the ground. But the shame of what he'd done, and what people would think of me if they knew, would be with me for the rest of my life. Even his death wouldn't free me.

I stared at Mama with wild eyes and trembling hands. My legs gave way and I crashed to the floor in a heap. She sat on the linoleum and tried her best to hold me. I was stone. I was the Petrified Forest.

Eighteen

There came a time later that night when I remember Mama sitting on the side of my bed, asking me if I wanted to go to the funeral on Saturday. I could not speak. Alice could not speak. How could Mama be asking us this?

We could only stare at the wall as it receded ... always receding, farther and farther away. We could not bear looking at Mama because she would have faded further away, too, and maybe never come back. There was nothing to hold onto. So we floated, and Mama went away.

On Sunday morning, the world began to come back. When I woke up, there were colors in my room, and I wondered at how beautiful they were. Birds chirped outside. They lured me to the window, and when I pulled the curtains open, a scarlet cardinal sang on an elm branch. He sang and sang and was the most beautiful thing I'd ever seen.

I walked down the hall and felt the most glorious sense of freedom. I snuck up behind Mama in the kitchen and placed my chin on her right shoulder, wrapped my arms around her waist, and would not let go. Not even when she said I was hurting her. Not even when she tried to pull me away from her.

I sat at the table eating my pancakes and stared at the carport door, knowing he would never come through it again. As I watched the door, I held the plate to my lips and licked it clean of sweet maple syrup.

She stayed home with me all day. We curled up on the couch under worn-soft quilts and watched old movies all afternoon. *It Happened One Night*, with Clark Gable, was Mama's favorite. *Harvey*, with James Stewart, was mine, though the invisible rabbit reminded me of Alice. I told myself seeing something on the outside had to be different from hearing something inside your head. And I kept looking at the carport door, unable to believe Daddy would never come back. He was gone forever, even if the rabbit hole would always be inside me.

At dinner, Mama set our plates on the table, wrapped her arms around my shoulders, and gave me a quick squeeze. As she took her chair, before she lifted her fork, she piped up, "What say I drive you in tomorrow?"

The only time she ever took me to school was when I had a doctor's appointment. "What's the special occasion?" I knew it would make her late to work.

"You seem to need a little cheering up. I've got Frank opening for me. It'll be my little treat." She scooped up rice and black-eyed peas.

I'd been dreading the bus ride. Carolyn would be chirping away, without a problem in the world. "Gee, thanks, Mama. That'd be great." Sometimes, my mama had a way of doing just what a body needed. I guess wishing she was this way all the time would have been greedy.

I lay in bed that night and the quicksand wouldn't come. Daddy had left, but so had sleep. No matter how I plumped my pillow and stared down the hall at the now safe door, the witch fingernails of my childhood scratched at the windows and the minutes passed like hours, the hours like days, until the weak light of dawn told me it was time.

—

That Monday morning, I slipped the only ankle-length granny dress I owned over my head. It was dove gray, covered in tiny white flowers, with a high neck. Aunt Jean had given me a bulky black cardigan sweater I'd never worn. I found it on the closet floor. Shaking it out, I laid it by my winter coat and pile of books.

Mama came to tell me breakfast was ready. She glanced at my things, then looked hard at me. "It's going to be pretty warm today. You probably don't need a coat and a sweater."

I squeezed my arms around me. "I'm really hungry. Let's eat."

Not riding the school bus gave me an extra forty minutes, so we dawdled over breakfast. Both of us giggled when the bus's air brakes squealed down the street. "Feel good to play hooky?" Mama twirled her coffee cup on the table. I smiled wide and nodded.

We left half an hour later, and I still got to school before the bus riders. The assistant monitor was just opening my homeroom door when I walked down the hall. Jeff was sunk down on the floor, waiting to get in. When I saw him, I shifted the books in my arms and slowed my step.

He saw me, jumped up, and dusted off the backside of his jeans. "Hey!" His hand sprung up above his head. His voice boomed, "We missed you last week."

I dropped my head, trudged the length of the hall to my door, and went straight to my desk without responding. He pulled his desk over next to mine. Every morning, he smelled like oranges. "Were you sick? Looks like you still feel bad." Out of the corner of my eye, I saw he'd taken off his jacket and had on a short-sleeved T-shirt. I'd never noticed before that his arms were covered with dark hair, like Daddy's.

I refused to look at his face. "I got a lot of homework to catch up on." I pulled out my math book.

"Yeah, I bet you do. Want some help?" I heard him rustle around in the green military pack he always carried. He'd covered it in drawings of peace signs and Volkswagen Beetles. "I could quiz you for the algebra test you missed."

I closed my eyes and turned my head away from him. "I need to study," I mumbled.

"What?" I heard the question in his voice.

There were fourteen intersecting circles on the front of my algebra book. Keeping my chin to my chest, I pulled my sweater around me and drew myself in. "Just leave me alone." I said it so loudly I jumped.

He drew in his breath and got up so fast his desk clattered. With my head bowed, I watched from the corner of my eye as he picked it up with both hands and carried it to his spot two rows from mine. He pulled one of his magazines from his pack without looking my way. His face slowly faded from bright red back to his natural complexion.

At least five minutes before the bell rang, he had his things ready. When it buzzed, he was up and out of the room. The side of his face passed me without a turn or a twitch.

It was exactly what I wanted. Acid rose in my throat. My chest burned empty.

———

That day, I avoided everyone by keeping my head bent. Class after class, it felt as if I had a stain smeared across my face everyone could see and smell.

Right before lunch, I had Home Economics. My teacher, Ms. Miller, paced the front of the room in her burnt orange polyester pantsuit, the pants rising a full two inches from the tops of her white Keds, with white bobby socks gleaming in the gap. Her permed, gray frizz sprung all over her head as she lectured. "Girls, you must use a measuring stick when considering who you want to get involved with. Size them up."

She whisked a yardstick from its hook by the blackboard and held it between her palms. "Be logical. Weigh all risks. And never ..." she paused and looked over all of us, "... never, ever date someone you wouldn't want to marry. You cannot let yourself be swept away by a silly schoolgirl crush. It's up to you girls to be strong. Boys will try anything you let them get by with. You have to be the ones to say no." On the word "no," she whacked the yardstick against her desk.

The bang caused three-fourths of the class to jump and smash their knees against the underside of their seats. I wasn't one of them. After what Daddy did, I couldn't bear the thought of being around a boy, much less dating one, being alone with one, having one touch me. My stomach lurched. I clamped my hand over my mouth and dashed to the girls' room to puke.

I spent lunch in the bathroom stall, with my feet propped up on the toilet seat. Until we got on the school bus, I even managed to evade Carolyn.

We'd barely sat down when she started in. "Feeling better?"

I grunted.

"Man, that must have been some sore throat. You were gone all week, and you never miss a day of school." She lowered her voice, "Hey, your Mama told my mother about your dad." I jerked my head around, my face in a black glare, and before I could say anything, she quickly adjusted, "Sorry. Really. I am. I'm just stupid. Forget I said anything. Okay?" I nodded.

She snapped open her three-ring binder, pulled out a blank sheet of notebook paper, and clamped it shut. "Let's list everyone we want on the softball team and post it on both of our refrigerators. It'll be a kind of voodoo, but not the evil kind."

I looked out the window at Lambert's Pharmacy passing by and decided it was better to get it over with. "I decided not to play."

"You're joking … right?" She punched my arm playfully. "You're such a kidder."

I raised my eyes and looked at her. She had the bluest eyes, unless she was upset. They were hazel now. I sighed. "I'm not joking."

"What are you saying?" Carolyn's high-pitched voice rose, and a couple of kids turned around to see what was wrong. "We have it all planned."

"You can do it without me." I knew it wouldn't be the same for her, but I couldn't bear having all those people looking at me.

"Why not?" She pulled her chin up and glared. "What changed?"

"I'm not good enough. Won't make the team anyway." My voice petered off.

"You don't even try? That's crazy!" She was so loud Mr. Lancaster adjusted his rear-view mirror to check out the commotion.

My eyes filled with tears. "Carolyn, please. I thought it out. I can't do it. Okay?"

She drummed her pen on the piece of paper, then balled it up and tossed it to the metal floorboard. "Whatever. Fine. I get the message." Flipping her waterfall of blonde hair, she tapped the girl in front of us, Deborah Maynard from our lit class, who'd been practicing with us.

I sunk lower in the seat and sagged my head against the bus window. Rain spit on the glass.

The two of them babbled about David Cassidy. "Get real. David is way cuter than Donny Osmond." Carolyn had photos of David Cassidy thumb-tacked all over her bedroom walls. If I tried that, Mama would have had a duck.

"Dream on. Donny's singing makes David sound like a sick cow." Deborah held up the front cover of the latest Tiger Beat. "Do you see David anywhere? I don't think so. Donny is the new fab."

"Donny Osmond is a bogus turkey. Who sings with their sister?"

Deborah better watch her step. Knowing Carolyn, she'd rip the magazine out of her hands and bop her over the head with it. She was serious about her David.

"David's so dorky he sings with his mother." I waited for the fireworks.

"No, duh. Don't be such a spaz. She's not his real mother. She's an actress. It's a TV show. But Marie is Donny's honest-to-God sister. What a loser." Zing! Carolyn got them every time.

She swung her head toward me. "Tell her, Malice." Using that joke of a nickname told me she'd already gotten over me not playing softball.

Had to love her. I dropped my mouth open in disbelief at Deborah and rolled my eyes. "Everyone knows Donny's a phony."

The bus stopped at Carolyn's house. She hugged her books to her chest, stood, and turned back to me. "We're still doing GA's together and FTA, right?"

I hadn't decided about those, but she looked so hopeful, with her eyes wide and mouth in a half-smile. "Sure thing."

"Good!" She smirked at Deborah all the way up the aisle, then stood by her mailbox, shooting me a peace sign. Deborah turned her back to me for the rest of the ride to my house.

I found myself counting the stitches running along the top of the seat in front of me. When I realized what I was doing, and how insane it was, I slammed the side of my head hard against the window. It made a bang. Now kids really were swiveling their heads around at me.

I grinned big and rubbed the side of my head. "Youch! Attack windows. Better keep your eye out for them."

The smaller kids laughed, though some moved farther away from their window and gave it a wary eye. Most of the older ones cast a look on me that screamed, "Freak!"

When we stopped at my house, I lifted my head and walked with my eyes straight forward. Halfway to the front—the section we called Middle Murder because all the boys sat there and stuck their feet out to trip girls—I had sense enough to glance down. Sure enough, Bobby Thompson had near about his entire leg set as a trap. It flew all over me, like the whole world was against me. I reared back and gave his ankle such a vicious kick he screamed, and all the boys were so busy calling him a wuss I made it off the bus without any more of them bothering me.

That first day back at school was over. I held it together until I was halfway up the drive. Then I thought of Sally Dog.

I heard the bus gears grating as it pulled away, and I raced the rest of the way to the house, half-stumbling over my own feet, my hands trembling badly. I could barely get the key in the lock. There was something horribly wrong with me. Daddy proved it. No one would do that to his own daughter unless she was bad to start with. And Sally Dog was dead because of me.

I couldn't stand the feeling inside me, like a sheet being split ragged in two. High tailing it to the bathroom, I doused my face and neck with water and worked to slow my pumping heart and lungs. The girl scowling back at me in the medicine chest mirror was an ugly, nasty thing. I wanted to kill her.

Alice's voice spoke clearly in my head. *No, there ain't nothing wrong with you. What's wrong was your daddy.*

I pushed her back and screamed out loud, "You're living proof I'm crazy!" My voice repeated in my head. Now I was talking to myself inside and out. Daddy's words came back to me, from that horrible Saturday when I was six: "They'll lock you up in the looney bin."

Maybe I was nuts. Alice snuck around me and chimed in loud and clear. *Even so, you can't let anybody find out you're crazy. Then they would put you away.*

She was right. If it was mental to listen to Alice, I didn't care anymore. She had always been my best shield against the outside. I had to get my act together. I shoved the thought of Daddy way down, into the bottom of my rabbit hole. It was almost like before, when Alice remembered, and I didn't. Except, this time, we both knew he wasn't really dead but just rotting inside of me.

Picking up my brush, I flipped my head forward and ran the bristles through my long hair. When I lifted my crown, hair covered my face. Stupid, you can't wear it that way. I parted the strands in the middle like a curtain, the way Aunt Jean used to do many years ago. But it was no game. To keep going, I had to hide my face so no one could see the real me.

I practiced. I smiled big and wide. I looked in the mirror, directly into my own eyes, and said, "You don't say so!" "That's soooo funny!" "Thank you for asking but I can't." "No, no I appreciate you thinking of me, but I'm busy." "I have studying to do."

Daddy was dead and couldn't hurt Mama. I would study hard and make all A's and go to college and be a teacher and no one would ever find out how bad I was. It wasn't hopeless after all. I could make sure no one ever found out what he did to me. Then, everything would be perfect.

Part III

At Seventeen
1978

Nineteen

At the stove, whipping up scrambled eggs, I swung my hips as the Bee Gees belted out *Staying Alive* on my transistor radio. Mama rushed into the den with her shoes in one hand and a shiny black plastic necklace in the other. It was unusual for me to be out of bed, much less dressed, before she left for work. But Carolyn was picking me up in a few minutes for a seven-thirty officer's meeting of the Senior Honor Society held on the second Wednesday of each month.

Mama stopped and stared as she slipped on her black patent flats. "What in God's name do you have on? Something snitched from the locker room?"

"What?" I looked down at my baggy jeans and the forest green men's polo I'd bought at Sears. The shirt reached mid-thigh, and I had on my brown leather moccasins with no socks. "I love this outfit. It's comfortable."

"Why can't you dress nice, the way you used to?" Mama handed me the necklace. "Fasten this, would you? I cut my finger on our old cash register yesterday." She held up her bandaged index finger. I turned off the stove eye and hooked her clasp. "Thanks." She grabbed her lunch bag from the fridge. "Spring's coming in a few weeks. Put on something that shows off your figure for a change."

She had on flaming tangerine lipstick, dangling black earrings, and a shirt-waist dress covered in orange and black squares, with two more buttons unfastened at the neck than I thought necessary. I hugged my shirt around me.

"I kept hoping this was a phase you were going through. But it's been years of you dressing like a waif. Enough is enough already." After studying the freezer, she moved a frozen pack of hamburger meat into the fridge to defrost. "It beats me how somebody who organizes the refrigerator door and alphabetizes canned goods can't straighten herself out."

"You care about clothes. I don't." I was sick of hearing it. The idea of walking around exposed made my throat close up.

"Have you seen my keys?" She sat her lunch on the table and dug inside her monster purse.

"Let's talk about that pocketbook of yours." I poked my finger at her, and used a la-de-da voice, "Small purses are all the rage this season. Anyone seen with a giant, hulking bag will be ostracized from her own home."

Mama's lips puckered up, but she didn't laugh. "Leave my purse out of this. You used to look so pretty. Sometimes I think you want to look horrible. You're seventeen years old. It's high time you acted like a young lady instead of a ..." She gestured at me and seemed to be struggling to find the right word. "... hobo. For God's sake, I grew up during the Depression, when people didn't have decent clothes. I'm ashamed to be seen with you." Her hand came out of her bag with the enormous ring of house, car, and Firestone keys she always carried around.

I scraped the eggs onto my plate and slammed the skillet into the sink. "It's always about what other people think, isn't it?" She ignored me and stuck two slices of bread in the toaster.

I held strawberry preserves out towards her, but she waved them away and flicked my long bangs. "Can't even see your eyes for that mop." I jerked my head away and turned from her. "A little make-up would do you a world of good, too." Our toast popped. She snatched it, flipped one piece onto my plate, and poked me between the shoulder blades. "For God's sake, stand up straight. You've slumped around here for so long, your spine's getting as curved as your Aunt Jean's."

"You've had your say, Mama." I stared out the window and a tear trickled from the corner of my eye.

As she went out the door, she had to have the last word. "I'm telling you this for your own good."

"Yeah, right." After eating my breakfast, I went into the bathroom and looked at myself in the full-length mirror Mama had nailed to the back of the door. Shoving bangs off my forehead, I glared at pimples, a big nose, and squinty eyes. I was horrendous, pure and simple. I let my hair fall back over my eyebrows. Better.

Turning to the side, my big clothes created a rectangle-shaped profile … the way I wanted. Too bad if Mama had other ideas. Anyway, I didn't care how I looked. *Yes, you do.* The Alice-voice again. I used to think those thoughts meant I was crazy, but I'd read a book on psychology, and it said everyone had different aspects of themselves. My Alice aspect was loud and opinionated. She might want to look pretty, but it wasn't safe.

I grabbed the sapphire-colored jar of Noxzema from the counter, slathered my face with the cream, and scrubbed. The astringent stung my blemishes. When I heard Carolyn beeping her horn, I left the bathroom smelling of menthol and camphor.

Climbing into Carolyn's lemon-yellow VW, I pulled on the door twice before it would shut. "Hey." Carolyn greeted me while staring into the rearview mirror, plucking her eyebrows.

I yawned wide and covered my mouth with my hand. "Morning."

"Am I that boring?" She put her tweezers into a zippered cosmetic bag, pulled out a thin vial, and applied salmon-colored lip gloss to her pursed mouth.

"Yeah, you are. While you primp, I'm losing brain cells over here." I leaned my head against the window and let out a couple of snores.

"Don't guess you'd like to freshen your bitchy little egghead face?" She smirked and tossed the make-up bag onto my lap.

I shoved it back into her pocketbook, on the floorboard by my feet. "I prefer the natural look." I tucked my long hair behind my ears. "Living free."

She grabbed the gearshift with both hands and jerked it into reverse. "Mascara's not really a mortal threat to women's lib." As we backed over the hump at the end of the drive, my knees bounced up so far, I had to hold on to the handle above the door. "Consider it my right to wear what I please."

"You do your thing. I'll do mine." Unzipping my brown macramé purse, I pulled out a tube of ChapStick and smeared it over my lips.

"All right, Nature Girl." She zoomed down Cedartown Highway and turned onto Booze Mountain Road, taking the curves at forty miles an hour. We passed the old Gone-with-the-Wind house. Its massive white columns, second-story balcony, and gigantic oak and magnolia trees never failed to amaze me.

I rolled my window all the way down. Fresh air and pine scent filled the car and blew through my hair. "Can we talk about something else?"

"Yep. Guess what I have planned for this weekend." She had her Carolyn grin. It meant trouble.

"Overthrowing Cuba." I said it with a straight face.

"You think you're funny. But you're not." She glanced at me. "You are close, though. College applications! We're overthrowing the world!" Carolyn always made me laugh. "I sent off to schools from Atlanta to New York. Been saving up the brochures, and I've got a whole stack."

"Oh my God, where do you want to go?" I'd been looking in town, at Berry. Everybody called it the "cow college" because of its animal science program. But it had a good education department.

"Not me. Where are *we* going?" She knocked her fist against my thigh and banked the car over the rise that crossed the ridge. The green valley shone below in the morning sunlight. "I don't know where. That's why it's exciting." Her eyes grew wide. "But William and Mary or Vanderbilt seem the best to me. Wait until you see pictures of those two campuses!"

I groaned. "Berry's one of the prettiest places on Earth. And, if we go there, I can live at home."

"Live at home!" She screeched the car to a halt off the side of the road and a plume of dust surrounded us. "The whole point's to get out of here."

I coughed and rolled my window up. "I keep telling you, I can't afford room and board."

She bit her bottom lip. "We'll see. In the meantime, it won't kill you to apply. Now, will it?"

"Guess not." Carolyn's mother had gone to Shorter and was all excited about Carolyn going away to school. I didn't want her knowing what Mama had to say about me and college.

A few months ago, while Mama and I were fixing dinner, I mentioned it. "I've decided I want to teach English in high school. I'm looking at Berry. My guidance counselor, Mrs. Snow, said I could probably get a scholarship and financial aid."

She'd turned from slicing an onion and shook her head. "Forget it. With what they charge, any money you got would be a drop in the bucket. You're not some high class, rich girl."

"But, Mama …"

"Don't 'but Mama' me. I can't stand by while you fill your head with pretty dreams." She rocked the knife over the Vidalia. "You need a job and night classes at Coosa Valley Tech to learn a trade. Want ads aren't overrun with jobs for English majors. I've been holding down the fort since you were born. You want to keep going to school, you'll have to support yourself."

A school bus rumbled by Carolyn's tiny car, causing it to rattle all over. "Shit! It's fifteen after. We gotta hurry." Carolyn pulled her bug back onto the road. "Come over Saturday morning and we'll go through the packets. Just think about it … we can even room together and decorate any way we want."

It was like she couldn't understand plain English. "I'll look at your brochures. But money's not falling from the clouds."

"Well then, we'll work this summer." She jutted her chin out. "And the next."

That was a good idea. "You know, after working layaway and gift wrap over Christmas, the Penney's manager said for me to come see him if I wanted a summer job. I bet he'd hire me in a heartbeat. Wonder if he'd let me work weekends through my senior year?" Maybe nobody else in the family had ever been to college, but Mama was wrong this time. Whatever it took, I was going to be the first.

"Now, you're talking!" Carolyn zipped into the Pepperell parking lot. We both hopped out of the car and hustled to our meeting as fast as she could in her wrap-around skirt and wooden clogs.

—

On Wednesdays, during sixth period, I was a teacher's assistant at the elementary school one block from the high school. I'd walk over and help Mrs. Owen, one of the first-grade teachers. At the beginning of the year, she'd assigned me to a little boy named Bobby, who needed extra help with his reading. He was a small boy with lank, blonde hair falling in his eyes. A long, narrow belt wrapped through his belt loops held his pants up. Someone had tooled in extra holes and when it was fastened tight enough for his slight frame, his trousers bunched up around his waistband and a good eight inches of the belt flopped out of the buckle.

He wouldn't look at me at the start of the year. Mrs. Fisher had pulled me aside and told me, "Remember, you're not just teaching reading, you're inspiring Bobby to hold his head up so he can see his future."

We'd been working all year, but he'd just learned his alphabet and was still struggling to read a sentence. On that day, I walked into the room and all the kids chimed, "Hello, Miss Lydell." Nothing else in my life had the power their voices did to make me hold my head up.

I held my index finger to my lips to shush them and shook my head, so they'd go back to their work. As I crossed over to the long table in the corner, Bobby was already there, waiting for me with his reading book. I sat next to him in a chair the same size as his. He gave me one of the grins that made my heart leap … lips pressed together, eyes held wide, and right knee pivoting back and forth. I wanted to hug him up close, but after seven months of working with him, I knew he still wasn't ready for that. Instead, I squeezed his shoulder, and he leaned his head toward my hand and smiled up at me, meeting my eye.

I turned his book to the day's lesson and talked low. "Look, today we have a new story. You know these words, and it's a short page. I bet you can read this all by yourself."

He pulled the book to him, studied the page for a minute, and slowly sounded out each word. When he read the last one, I felt a click in my brain, the same as I'd always felt when puzzle pieces snapped in place. "You did it!" I held up my hand in a high five, and Bobby slapped it, his head held high, grinning from ear to ear. That day, I knew I had to make my dream of being a teacher a reality, for the kids and for my future.

Twenty

Lying on my bed in nightshirt and panties, reading *The Bell Jar*, I jumped when Carolyn flung the door open. "Hey! Why aren't you dressed?"

"This your April Fool's trick? Dressed for what?" I folded a page back to mark my spot, swung my legs around, and sat up.

"April Fool's tomorrow. Tonight's Friday fun and French fries, you freak!" She laughed at herself. "Hear that. I'm a poet. Bet ya didn't know it."

I couldn't help laughing but I shook my head. "Don't think I'm up to it."

"As if you ever are!" She crossed her arms over her chest. "You're not leaving me on my own again. Nope. Get up!"

"No, really ...."

"Yes, really. It'll be a blast." Carolyn tugged my arm. "Everybody thinks you're stuck-up. Want them thinking you're a snob, huh? That you're too good to ride around with the rest of us?"

"You know better." It made me furious that people thought I was a snob, when really, I was just shy. "Why would I want to hang out with people who feel that way about me, anyway?"

Carolyn grabbed both of my hands and pulled me to my feet. "C'mon. I'll help you. Whatcha wanna wear?" She flipped through the clothes in my closet. "Ooooh, this is cute. When'd you get this?" She held out a blue jean jacket with embroidery lining the pockets, lapels, and back seaming.

I curled up my lip. "It's the old jacket you didn't want. I stitched flowers all over it. Cool, huh?"

She tossed the jacket onto my bed. "Way cool. I can't believe you. Flower Power Chick and all. And nobody'd think it, 'cause you live like a hermit."

"You got that right." We both turned to Mama, who leaned against the doorjamb. "See if you can whip some fun into her. She mopes around here as if the world's coming to an end, reading books about crazy people." Mama waved her hand at the bedroom. "You never would've seen me at home on a Friday night when I was her age."

There she went again. I rolled my eyes and plucked a pair of jeans, a bra, and a plain white T-shirt from my dresser drawer. "Okay, okay. Got it, you two. I'm going already. Out for some fun." I turned my back to them and slipped on the jeans. Without taking my night shirt off, I slipped my arms out of its sleeves, hooked my bra around my ribs, turned the band around, and pulled the straps over my arms.

Mama's voice behind me sounded like she was laughing. "Have you ever seen anybody so modest around their own mother and girlfriend?"

"Leave me alone." I huffed as I drew the nightshirt over my head and replaced it as quickly as possible with the T-shirt. "You're both always acting like something's wrong with me."

Carolyn chimed in, "Nothing's wrong with you, but you're missing a key element—boys."

I muttered under my breath, "As if. Not like any of them will give me a second look."

Carolyn rushed over to me and took me by the shoulders. "Well, they would if you'd fix yourself up and talk to them, instead of sitting in the corner as quiet as a dead mouse." She whipped the wide green headband off my head.

Mama approved. "Sic her, Carolyn!"

"Hey! Give that back." I lunged for it, but she back danced out of reach. "I've started growing out my bangs. They won't quite tuck behind my ears yet."

"It's better than them covering up her face." Mama interjected.

"Nope we're doing her hair tonight. No more crappy green headband, and I'll fix those bangs." She spun the spandex on her index finger and glowered at me. "No more pulling it back in a rubber band, either. I keep telling you it breaks your hair and gives you split ends."

Mama left the doorway, came back with a brush and hairspray, and tossed them to Carolyn. "See what you can do with her. I can't even get her to smear on a little lipstick. Says she's into the natural look." She gave us a little wave. "You two have fun. That's an order. I'm off to Lucille's for a game of cards." She spun on her heels and was gone.

"I can fix my own hair." I grabbed for the brush.

Carolyn knocked my hand away. "You can, but you aren't. I am. So, sit your bony butt down."

"Anything to shut you up." Sitting on the edge of my bed was torture while Carolyn primped on my hair. I couldn't stand this kind of attention. When everyone ignored me, I didn't have to worry about what they thought of me.

She stood, eyed the finished product, and patted the back of the brush against her open palm. "Not bad. Close your eyes and hold your breath." A cloud of hairspray filled the room. Still, she kept spraying.

Coughing, I pushed her away. "You're trying to kill me!"

Batting my hands away, she patted my hair in place. "No, just plastering those bangs over to the side." She stood back to look me over and nodded like she was proud of herself. "Now, for your face."

"My face is fine."

"Fine for nothing." Carolyn pulled me into the bathroom, opened the medicine cabinet, and quickly lined up Mama's blush, eye shadow, mascara, and lipstick on the counter. She closed the toilet lid and pointed from it to me. "Sit."

Could she really make me pretty? "All right. But not too much." I lowered myself to the seat.

"Tonight, I'm saying how much's enough." She swished the tiny brush across the peach-colored blush.

"I'll just wipe it off." I said with a grin.

"The hell you will." Carolyn aimed the end of the makeup brush at me. "You're too stubborn for your own good."

"You been talking to my mama?" I swore they were ganging up on me. "Did she call you and put you up to this?"

"Keep your face still. Nothing says we can't have a confab over you."

I knew it! "What if I sided with your mother?" If Mama wanted to stick her nose in my business, couldn't I at least have a best friend who took up for me?

"It's high time we got you out of your own way. Now shut up and don't move, or I'll end up poking your eye out with a mascara wand."

"First, give me that compact so I can see what you're doing." With my face reflected at me, I watched Carolyn sweep a spot of color across the apples of my cheeks. I had to close my eyes for her to dab eye shadow over my lids and then hold them wide as she swooshed on mascara. When she finished, what would I look like?

When she'd applied everything except the lipstick, she opened Mama's neon orange tube, and held it out to me, with a mock look of terror on her face. "Is this Bozo the Clown's?"

I died laughing. "Don't let her hear you. Thinks she's fab in it. Wears that color with black dresses hemmed two inches over her knee. I'm terrified her next step will be a pair of knee boots."

"Don't move. Be right back." When she left the room, I peered into the tiny, round mirror, but it was hard to see much of my face at once.

She returned with a tin of strawberry lip balm and dabbed it on my lips. I inhaled the scent of artificial berries as she leaned back and whistled. "Lookee. Lookee. Here comes Cookie."

"Let me see." My heart pulsed in my neck as I stood and turned to the wide mirror over the bathroom vanity. Carolyn and I floated side by side in the reflection. Her sleek, long blonde hair parted straight down the middle framed her wide, blue eyes—a counterpoint to my wavy brown hair, parted on the side, a seductive strand pulled down over one of my brown, almond-shaped eyes. Could that really be me? I lifted my shoulders and the girl in the mirror smiled. She looked as pretty as Carolyn, except for the crooked teeth. But the thought made me feel conceited and rattled me badly. I just wanted to go back and read my book.

Carolyn turned her head from side to side, looking at herself. She used both hands to adjust her strapless, sky-blue scarf-top, which kept inching down over her cleavage. I'd be terrified the whole thing would slide to my navel, but she looked so sure of herself.

She spoke up just as I started to chicken out. "Come on. I'd like to get there before the night's over. Grab your shoes and jacket and, by God, you are not wearing those fringed moccasins."

An hour later, sitting in a booth at McDonalds, I had to admit I was having fun. The Hewitt twins, Kim and Tim, went from table to table telling jokes. When my old heartthrob, Jeff Davis, nodded to me, my heart flip-flopped like a catfish in Wax Lake. Shortly after I brushed him off in eighth grade, he'd started going with another girl. They'd dated for years but had just broken up.

Outside, Carolyn leaned through the open window of David Anderson's Chevy in the drive-through lane. Every time a car moved up, Carolyn advanced with David's car, her elbows propped inside his window and her butt poked towards the sky.

I took a sip of my strawberry milkshake and felt someone slip in the booth next to me. Thinking Carolyn had come back, I swung around to say, "David ask you out?" It wasn't Carolyn, wasn't even Jeff.

It was a boy I didn't know, but thought I'd seen around. Long, wavy chestnut hair pulled back in a ponytail. Blue-green eyes with a carefree shine. Impossibly white teeth in a sun-brown face. My smile reeled back in, and I pulled my shoulders flush against the wall, away from him.

He took one of my French fries, popped it into his mouth, and seemed to be studying my face while he chewed. What kind of nerve did it take to sit there and eat my food?

"Needs salt." He reached across for the shaker, grazing his hand over mine. Tiny hairs crackled with electricity from my fingertips to my elbows, like a wool sweater on a winter day. My mouth dried up and the current running up my arms crossed down into my stomach.

"Who are you?" As I said it, I had a feeling I knew this guy, had known him all my life.

He gave a big belly-laugh, head thrown back, ponytail tossing. "Well, that's a fine how d'yado. Back at ya." He moved his head one tad closer to me and spoke in a soft voice I was sure only I could hear. "And who are you?"

My shoulders left the wall. I leaned in closer to him and mimicked his low voice, "Mary Alice." Then I raised my eyebrows to say, and you?

He leaned in. I moved nearer.

When he said, "Jimmy, but I do believe you'll be calling me Jim," I saw we were almost nose to nose. He'd taken my left hand in his so gently I hadn't noticed. By the time Carolyn came back, we were sitting there, his hand cradling mine, just looking at each other, grinning sloppy grins.

Even from the corner of my eye, I recognized the mother hen furrow on her forehead, and thought, you wanted me to meet someone ... here he is.

Carolyn scooted in on the other side of the booth. "What's going down, Malice?" She only used my nickname when she was teasing or deadly serious. I shot her a killer look that said, not in front of the new guy.

Jim rolled off a lazy smile for Carolyn. "What was that you called her, Barbie?"

She choked on her mouthful of Coke.

I pursed my lips and tried not to laugh. Carolyn hated it when people treated her like a bimbo instead of a girl who helped out in the nursery at church and swore she'd be a teacher one day.

But Carolyn should have known not to call me Malice in front of him. Vindication made me brave. "Carolyn, this is Jim. Jim, my best friend, Carolyn."

Carolyn ran her tongue over her top teeth and looked from me to Jim to our entwined fingers. "Hey Jim, you mind if I borrow my friend for a minute?" She smiled sweetly at Jim, then spoke directly to me. "I need to tell you something."

The feel of Jim's hip and leg aligned with my hip and leg distracted me. I sighed. "Uh huh."

Carolyn nodded her head towards the back of the restaurant. "Girl talk."

Jim chose that moment to lean his mouth inches from my ear. "This place is too loud. Let's talk in my car."

I turned to him and brought my fingertips up to my tingling earlobe. Without touching my skin, he brushed back the lock of hair Carolyn had combed over one of my eyes, took my hand, pulled us both to our feet, and addressed Carolyn, "I'll bring her right back for your girl talk."

I gave Carolyn a little wave.

She raised her voice, "Mary Alice, wait."

I stopped and looked at Jim, who stood by patiently while Carolyn scowled. Tilting my head at Carolyn, I raised both eyes, as if to say, not now. Out loud, I said, "We'll be right back."

I strolled out the door with Jim and into the front seat of his red Dodge Dart, giggling when he held the passenger door open for me and gestured wide with his free arm like your majesty.

Once inside, he flipped on the radio to WROM. An old song by the Carpenters, *Close to You*, drifted from the speakers. He leaned his back against the driver's door and crossed his arms behind his head. "Your friend doesn't like me."

"No, she just doesn't know you." I didn't want to talk about Carolyn.

Jim shot me a grin that made me feel like springtime and a heart-red cardinal rising in the wind. "You don't know me either."

This was the drop-dead truth but struck me as horribly funny. I doubled over laughing, and a bubbling coursed through my head, chest, and stomach.

Pure joy, hopped up on nerves, flowed through me. My heartbeat was a vibrating hummingbird. I was happier than I'd ever felt in my life.

I shook my head. "No, I don't know you. Why's it feel like I do?"

"Because we were cut from the same cloth," he said, with a glint.

"What's that mean?" All I saw was him. The easy way he sat back in his seat. The way his eyebrows grew in a perfect arc of tiny, curved hairs. The way he looked at me, like seeing me made him happy. I liked that thought, making someone happy.

"Don't you feel it?" He brought his arms down and reached towards me.

For a split-second, everything changed, like a shadow passing in front of a lit window. I was inside a dark car with a stranger, and I drew back. I had never really been able to relax in a front passenger seat. Not since Daddy. No, I couldn't listen to Alice, especially not now.

When he saw me hesitate, puzzlement crossed his face. I couldn't let him realize there was something wrong with me, so I moved fast and took his hands in mine. The pressure of his fingers sent voltage clear up to my ears.

"Yes. I feel it." The inside of his car was hot, so hot. Yet the nape of my neck was early morning frost. And the radio played another oldie, *This Magic Moment*. I knew it was a sign.

He leaned in, pressed his lips to mine, firm but light, long enough for lightning to snake down my spine, but over in a heartbeat. He squeezed my hands and jerked his head towards McDonald's. "Your friend-don't-like-me's 'bout to pop her top out there. Been pacing up and down, watching you like a hawk. I need to get moving." He gently released my hands, and the feeling was empty to the point of starvation. "What you say we go for a Saturday drive tomorrow? Two o'clock?"

All I could manage was a nod.

"Where do you live?"

"Off Cedartown Highway."

He smiled. "Yeah, and then where?"

"Oh! Miller Mountain Road, the yellow house on the left, before you get to Booger Hollow Road." I smiled back.

"Tomorrow. Two o'clock." He cupped his hand on the curve of my jaw. "Now don't go letting anyone say bad things about me. You hear?"

I keened my cheek into his palm and nodded yes. He was out the door and opening mine before the tart smell of his hand faded.

"I'll see you tomorrow." He held open my door and waited for me to skip across the line of circling cars, then vaulted himself feet first through his open driver's window, beeped the horn, waved, and drove away.

Carolyn was beside herself, tugging at my arm, "Why didn't you listen to me?"

I ignored her and sighed as Jim's taillights disappeared. I'd heard people say they were walking on clouds, but it had never happened to me before. I was floating, buoyant, alive. Before, I'd just been breathing in and out. Now, blood coursed through my body. The night sky gleamed a magical indigo color.

"Mary Alice!" Carolyn's voice broke through the moment.

"Did you see him? Did you?" I linked my arm through Carolyn's and pulled her close. "Oh, my God! He's a stone fox."

"Yes, I saw him. That was Jimmy Ledbetter." She looked royally pissed off and yanked her arm away.

"So?" I couldn't keep the irritation out of my voice. Didn't she see what had happened? To me! All the girls here tonight, and he sat down next to me. He kissed me. I still felt his lips on mine, his hand on my face. I raised my hand to that cheek and stroked it.

Carolyn shook her head, "He's old. Must be twenty-something. And he's got a reputation."

I snorted. "He said you didn't like him." But a flag went up. Tomorrow, I was going out with a guy I didn't know. I told myself not to be such a worrywart. The girls at school went on blind dates all the time, and it wasn't like a stranger was showing up at my door. With Jim, it felt like I'd found a comfortable blanket I didn't remember losing.

"Don't like him? I don't even know him." A car engine revved behind us, and two shrill voices shouted in unison, "Carolyn!" But neither of us turned.

"Then why're you against him? He said you'd say bad things about him." I set my lips in a straight line. "Well, I'm not listening." I didn't care what she had to say.

"What?" Carolyn flipped her hair back behind her ears. "I'm just trying to warn you."

"Warn me." I narrowed my eyes at her. "About what?"

"That he's trouble. That he's had lots of girls."

"And you think he wouldn't want somebody like me!" I drew my chin up and shoulders back. The yellow neon light shining in Carolyn's eyes turned them from blue to green.

I saw what this was about. It had nothing to do with Jim. She was jealous. All these years, she must have been my friend because she could look even prettier next to me.

"Nope. I think maybe you don't want somebody like him." Carolyn's tone had a sharp edge.

I tapped my foot and spoke in a flat tone. "You're not ruining this for me. Don't even try." I charged away from her but wheeled back around. "I'll find myself another ride home."

From the look on her face, I might as well have slapped her. I almost went to her then. Except, I'd never felt so much in my life, so ecstatic about Jim and so furious with her. Instead, I pushed my way through the crowd, back into McDonald's.

Twenty-One

When I got home from McDonald's, Mama wasn't back from Lucille's. I grabbed a Coke from the fridge, boogied to my room, and flipped on the black light rod propped on top of my portable television. My jeans gleamed and the walls pulsated from my fluorescent posters of poppies and zigzag patterns. I sprawled onto my blue and white bedspread, the three-dimensional stripes rising from beneath me.

As I lay there with eyes wide open, I replayed the night's memories. Jim sitting down next to me. His hand touching mine. The moment our lips touched. I held my hand in front of my face and examined it: the fine pores, the feathering of tiny hairs, the red dot from an especially painful shot for cat scratch fever when I was seven. Nothing had changed about it, but it was an entirely different hand.

I pressed my mouth to the spot above my thumb where I felt his touch for the first time. My lips still prickled with the pressure of his lips—my first kiss.

Remembering his mouth on mine brought chill bumps down my arms and made my inner thighs, and the space between, tingle. The tingle changed to pain. Why did it hurt? *You know why.* Stupid Alice. I wasn't going to let those Daddy memories mess this up. I rammed my thumbnail into my wrist until the stinging took everything else away.

I opened my nightstand drawer and squeezed the red-faded-to-pink rubber ball I'd had since third grade. Tossing it up and down, catching it with one hand, and sending it a little higher each time, I tried to come as close to the ceiling as possible without touching it. As the ball circled, I contemplated what I knew about boys. Most of it came from Carolyn, or books. Boys were different from girls. They couldn't be trusted. They only wanted one thing. I switched up and batted the rubber ball back and forth between my fingers while I ruminated.

Old Mrs. Miller in eighth grade Home Economics had warned us about boys. What if Jim was one of those guys who cruised McDonalds every night looking for a new conquest?

Size him up, that's what Mrs. Miller had said. I took out a sheet of paper, drew a mark down the middle of it, and tried to figure Jim out on paper, to see if he added up like an algebraic equation. I penciled in a plus sign at the top of the left side of the paper and a minus sign on the right. First, I wrote under the minus sign. Carolyn says he's trouble. He drives a fast car. It's irrational to fall for a guy so quickly. How old is he?

The negatives sure seemed to add up to a big number. I didn't really know anything about him. My worries stuck like beggar lice.

He could be one of those guys Mama had warned me about since I started high school. "Baby, you watch out for them good-time guys, you hear me? They're nothing but trouble with a capital T." Mama had been scrambling eggs at the time, and her fork whipped so fast in the bowl I only saw a whir matching how fast Mama was talking. "Your damn daddy was an A1 troublemaker from the day I laid eyes on him, and being young and stupid as shit, I didn't recognize him for what he was."

What if Jim was a troublemaker? But he couldn't be. Under the plus sign on my list, my pen raced. He'd been a gentleman. Didn't try to touch me in the wrong places. Opened the door for me. Made a real date for tomorrow. At the bottom of the list, I added "My heart says yes" and sketched a five-pointed star next to it.

The hard, cold "numbers" under the minus sign looked puny compared to the weight of my heart. What did my dried-up, old teacher know about love anyway? What did Mama know? She hadn't cared about men for over ten years. Jim couldn't be like my daddy. No way anybody could be.

I scratched a giant X over everything on the negative side. On the positive side, I sketched in the words Jim & Mary Alice, and encircled them in a lopsided heart.

Then I had the worst thought of all. What if he didn't show up? I'd die. If he didn't come, my life was over. The thought of not seeing him again, of going back to my abandoned life, made me feel so worn out I took off my clothes and slid under the covers with nothing on but my panties. I fell asleep imagining his car in my driveway and him standing at my front door with his hands held out to me.

Twenty-Two

The next morning, I woke up before the sun. Mama still wasn't home. Ever since I turned fourteen, she slept over at Lucille's if she had too much to drink. Most of the time it bothered me when she didn't come home, but not today.

I couldn't go back to sleep and pulled a kitchen chair into my room and sat at the window, staring at the sky as it lightened from rose blush to bound-to-be blue. When a pair of cardinals arrived to flit about the branches of our crepe myrtle, I couldn't keep my eyes off the vivid male. The female seemed drab in comparison. His plumage overpowered her muted colors. But the longer I looked at her, the more I appreciated the blending of sandy brown and charcoal gray, and the airbrushed tone to her orange-tinted beak, wings, and tail feathers. It was the sign I'd been looking for. After being alone all my life, I was going to be part of a twosome.

I went to my closet and clicked through the hangers. Most girls would have probably pulled all their clothes out and took all morning trying on different outfits. Most girls would have called up their best friend and had her come over to help them decide. I wasn't like most girls. Most of the time, I succeeded in not thinking about Daddy. But I knew nobody's own father did things like mine had. Something was bad wrong with me for him to do that. If I didn't get too close to people, they wouldn't find out. So, I stayed here in my room most of the time. Alone.

Without Jim, it could have stayed that way forever. Jim changed it all. I didn't know what he saw in me, but whatever it was made him want me. I went into the bathroom, and my reflection in the mirror was lovely—straight from My Fair Lady. I saw myself the way I imagined he saw me, the color in my cheeks and sparkle in my eyes. Wasn't that what love was all about?

I showered, did my hair, and quickly decided to wear my favorite outfit—the frayed Levi's, tie-dyed T-shirt, and scuffed leather mocs. Carolyn wouldn't approve, but she wasn't here.

Opening my top dresser drawer, I chose pink bikini panties and the white bra with the most lace. "I'm gonna need new underwear." I said it aloud, then felt the tips of my ears grow hot. What was I thinking?

When I checked myself out in the mirror, I heard Mama's voice in my head. "Hobo!" Returning to my closet, I pulled out a white peasant blouse with cornflower blue flowers stitched around the scooped neck. Mama bought it for me, but I'd never worn it because I thought it was cut too low. I tugged off my old tee and slipped on the blouse. In the mirror, pure girl looked back at me. The top didn't show cleavage, just my collarbones. It was more exposure than I was comfortable with, but I'd wear it anyway. Jim would like it.

Years ago, Santa brought me a portable record player, and my older cousin gave me her used Beatles' 45's. Now, I put the stylus on *I Saw Her Standing There* and danced the twist as I sang along, substituting him for her, "… when I saw him standing there." As soon as the song ended, I set the needle back on the outermost groove and played it two more times in a row.

When one-thirty finally came, I'd been ready for over five hours. It'd been so long I'd read the entire book, *That Was Then, This Is Now*, with plenty of time for Beatles' records in-between.

At one-forty, I decided to put on mascara and lipstick. Following Carolyn's advice from the night before, I'd left my hair down, and it did look pretty, curled around my shoulders. My bangs, I plastered to the side the way Carolyn had, for luck. I also sprayed myself with Jean Naté and breathed in its lemon scent.

Ten 'til two. Any minute now, he'd be driving up. I crossed to the big plate-glass window in the den, pulled back Mama's drab olive-green drapes, and moved a chair over, facing the window. I'd be able to see when his car topped the rise past Shorty's Store.

Two o'clock. All morning, I hadn't allowed myself the thought he might not show up. As the minutes passed, I began jiggling my right leg and chewing on my fingernails.

Two 'o-five. He probably didn't realize how far out I lived. I opened the front door and gazed down the road. A car engine sounded in the distance. I held my breath until Old Man Crowley, who lived in the haunted house on Booger Hollow Road and drove a black Plymouth Valiant, came over the hill and pulled into Shorty's. I shut the door and resumed my post.

Ten after two. Had I given him good directions? I tried to run that part of the conversation back in my head, but it was a blur. Did he have my phone number? No, I couldn't remember saying the numbers. If anything had happened, he wouldn't even be able to call me. The number's in the phone book. Alice was always right. I had to face it. He wasn't coming. Maybe he had car trouble.

Fifteen after. Why did I ever think a guy like Jim would want me? He was probably having a good old laugh now. It was just an April Fool's trick. I laid my head on my knees and tried not to cry. With kneecaps boring into my forehead, I pinched the bridge of my nose, hard.

At that moment, I heard a car pull into the drive. With no hesitation and no thought of a purse, house key, or the dime-for-an-emergency-phone-call, I threw open the front door and sprinted towards him. Before he could get out, I opened the passenger door and peered in at him.

"Hey. I was afraid you couldn't find the house." I smiled wide, without being self-conscious of my two overlapping eye teeth.

He grinned back. "Started to come at one o'clock. But I was afraid I'd be sitting in a living room being cross-examined by your father while you finished getting ready."

"No need to worry about that. He don't live here. It's my mama you gotta watch, but she's not here, either." My laugh rang out. I scooted into the front seat and slammed the door. "Where we going?"

"I promised you a Saturday drive, didn't I?" He shifted into reverse. "If we knew where we were headed, it'd have to be a weekday."

"Sounds perfect." I couldn't take my eyes off of him. Long hair pulled back in a ponytail and tied with a leather cord. Plain red T-shirt, jeans, and brown suede boots. Long, thin, muscular arms.

Rod Stewart's Hot Legs blasted from the radio, and Jim's fingertips tapped along on the steering wheel. The song was so loud it vibrated in my chest, and I had to concentrate to hear Jim's words. "You a Braves fan?"

Guys loved that kind of stuff, so I didn't want him to know much I hated it. In my mind, Daddy and sports went together. The last time he showed up, I was getting ready to practice softball. After Daddy came back, I never played ball again. *This is not the time to think about Daddy.* Alice was right sometimes. She and I shoved Daddy into the rabbit hole and answered Jim with everything I knew about the Braves. "Hammerin' Hank broke the home run record when I was thirteen."

"Aaron was good. It's true. But Dale Murphy's a powerhouse hitter. Gonna have a helluva season. I'll bet he gives old Hank a run for his money one day. Be nice to see a regular guy take the record back, you know what I mean?" He winked, and I didn't like what I thought he was insinuating. But you could fill volumes with everything I didn't know about sports. I'd probably misunderstood.

As he drove, he propped his left arm on the open window and grasped the top of the doorframe. He steered with his right hand. His fingernails were clean and filed off into short curves. Even when he made a turn, he displayed his driving skills by only using his right hand to spin the wheel.

Reaching for the radio, he turned it down a notch. "What school you go to? Pepperell?"

"Yep. Eleventh grade. I've gone there my whole life." Immediately, I wished I hadn't told him what grade I was in. He'd probably like senior girls better.

"Those Pepperell Dragons. Know them well. Worked a little while at the cotton mill with all those damn lint heads." It didn't sound as if he liked Pepperell.

He braked at a four-way stop and turned to me. I'd been intent on listening and staring at him I hadn't paid any attention to the landscape. Now, I saw we were out on country back roads, with no other cars in sight.

"Which way?" He pointed straight ahead. "We could sit by Miller's Creek." Aiming his finger to the left, he said, "We could head back to town and get a bite to eat." Indicating the road to the right, "And that way, I could show you where my grandfather's buried."

I looked down the empty road. "A cemetery?"

"Nope. Not a graveyard." He gestured that way again. "Sounds like we're headed to Grandpa's resting place." He swung the car onto the road headed east. "Now tell me something about you I don't know."

I giggled. "That could be anything. 'Cause you don't know nothing about me."

Jim took his hand off the wheel and raised both arms into the air. "She's beautiful and brilliant!" The vehicle swerved across the middle line. He seemed in no hurry to adjust our course.

Without thinking, I reached across with my left hand, gripped the wheel, and brought the car back to our side of the road, then continued to steer while Jim leaned over and kissed the tip of my nose.

"We're coming to a curve." My voice rose into a tiny squeak. Still, he didn't take the wheel. "I can't drive this way!"

"You don't know what you can do." As he spoke, he accelerated.

Gluing my eyes to the road, I tightened my grip on the wheel. Gravel crunched as the car drifted a tad onto the right of way. "Jim!"

When I edged the wheel to the left, the car bumped back onto the road. Jim eased off on the gas, and the car came to a rolling stop.

He took my hands in his. "You think you can't do it, but you can. You think I'll put you in danger, but I won't." He raised my wrists to his lips and kissed the soft undersides of each. "I'll tell you something you don't know about me. You gotta trust me." Setting my hands back into my lap, he took control and drove off.

My thoughts ricocheted. He's wild. He's crazy. He's dangerous. He said I'm beautiful. Oh, my God, he said I'm beautiful.

Jim pulled off the blacktop onto a one-lane dirt road.

Where's he taking you? I wouldn't listen to Alice's unfounded suspicions. Jim said I could trust him.

Branches scraped across the sides of his car as we bounced down the ruts. "I'll tell you a story." I jumped at the sound of his voice. "My grandfather was a real pistol. They say he ran whiskey. I don't know. He was in the army in World War I and met a woman in Rome, Italy. Funny, huh? Town with the same name as ours."

We crested a rise, and a clearing opened up ahead.

Pulling onto the grassy area, Jim parked the car. "Her name was Maria, and they say the old man loved her like crazy. Talked her into marrying him and brought her back to America to live in his run-down farmhouse in Taylorsville." He laid a hand on my shoulder. "They had a baby, my father. My grandfather put bread on the table working as a pipefitter. Two years later, they had another baby." He squeezed my shoulder, just tight enough it pinched. Then he was out of the car and around to my side, opening my door. We walked hand-in-hand up an incline that ended in blue sky.

"Maria and the baby got sick." He faced me. "They both died."

"How terrible." I moved my hand up to his elbow and clutched it. His eyes looked so mournful, I almost gathered him into my arms.

"Yep. It was. My grandfather went out of his mind." Jim started walking again. I kept hold of his arm. "Watch your step."

We approached the edge of a gorge that could stretch across the width of Barron Stadium football field. It had to be two stories down to the black water, far below. "One day, right after she died, he carried my father, who was two years old then, to his mother's house, put him in her arms, and left, without saying a word. Drove up here in his old truck. Got to the clearing and gunned it. Right over the edge."

I gasped and stared at the side of his face as he continued to gaze intently at the water below.

"Far as I know, he's still down there in the cab. Course, he'd be all bones by now." He dropped his chin to his chest, as if paying respects. Then he peeked one eye up at me. "Think that's gruesome?"

"It's horrible. Awful." I pressed my fingertips against my mouth. "What happened to your father?"

"Raised by his grandmother. Don't think he ever got over it, though. Used to bring me here when I was a kid. Must have told me that story a hundred times. Always called himself a 'poor, abandoned orphan.'" His chest rose and fell with a heavy sigh. "My dad bragged about hanging around to raise me … if that's what you want to call it. He's a mean old bastard."

I nodded and let out my own deep sigh. Jim was right when he'd said we were cut from the same cloth.

"Mary Alice?" He said my name softly, the sound of a bell ringing.

"Jim?" When I heard my voice saying his name, it was like Claudette Colbert in *It Happened One Night* and embarrassed me so much I blushed.

He grinned. "You hungry?"

I nodded, but squinched up my eyes in puzzlement. We were a long way from town.

"Wait here." He jogged back to the car and returned with an old chenille bedspread and a Styrofoam cooler. "Thought we might have a picnic."

I waited a minute before speaking. "But you asked me about going into town for food." A doubt flickered in my mind. When I saw Jim drop his head and scuff his boot, I shushed my uncertainty.

"Hey, it's no set-up. I didn't take you for a go-into-town girl. So, I brought a picnic." He looked innocent. "I guessed right, didn't I?" He lifted those gorgeous turquoise eyes at me.

He was right about me preferring a picnic to a crowded diner. I knew so little about him. But he already understood me—better than anyone. Another sign.

A bird's cheerful warble sounded above my head. I tilted my neck back and shaded my eyes, searching for the little culprit, hoping it was a cardinal.

Twenty-Three

Jim's muscles flexed as he dropped the blanket and set the cooler under the low branches of a weeping willow, almost identical to the one in Aunt Jean's back yard. One sign after another.

I helped him spread the bedcover. It was yellow with the design of a peacock tufted in glaring aqua and powder pink. "My grandmother made it. She used to work in the chenille plant. They sewed in the design by hand, and the factory let her keep this one. When I was little, it was on my bed. Then I got old enough to realize it had girlie colors and wouldn't have nothing to do with it." Reaching in his back pocket, he pulled out two folded-up paper towels and laid them on the blanket. "I brought the best china." He winked at me.

I giggled. He opened the cooler and pulled out sandwiches wrapped in waxed paper, each one sealed by a ragged strip of masking tape. "Hope you like bologna and cheese. It's all we had." Two bruised apples, two cans of Seven Up, and two orange-wrapped Reese's cups followed the sandwiches onto his version of plates. "Madam finds it to her liking?"

Taking his outstretched hand, I lowered myself to the ground and sat on a corner of the spread. "I love it."

A blue jay squawked above our heads, and a breeze ruffled our groundcover. I breathed in deep and unwrapped my sandwich, all the while peeking at Jim and beyond the spindly tree to puffy white clouds in a pastel sky. "It's like a scene from a movie. How'd you think this up?" Biting into the gummy white bread, I wrinkled my nose at him.

He laid his lunch down and leaned toward me. "It was easy. I thought, now what would Mary Alice want to do? I know. She'd like walking in the rain under an umbrella. But the clouds wouldn't cooperate, and I figured anyone who liked rain would want a picnic." He waggled his eyebrows, Groucho Marx style, and lifted his can. "To rain, and picnics, and Mary Alice."

I raised mine and touched the aluminum edge to his. "To Saturday drives, and secret spots, and Jim." We sipped and munched, until our meal was nothing but crumbs. "Did you go to Pepperell, too? What year did you graduate?"

Jim straightened up. "That's a sore subject."

"Why?"

"Let's just say me and educational institutions don't see eye-to-eye." He wadded up our sandwich wrappings and tossed them into the cooler.

"Oh." I didn't dare tell him I loved school. This made me really wonder how old he was. Twenty? Older? He didn't look old. Or did he? Gauging by his face, I couldn't tell.

He gave me a wary look, his head cocked to one side. "Why you care? You sizing me up or something?" His voice turned a shade of gray and jarred me from my reflections.

I shook my head emphatically. "No. Of course not. Nothing like that."

"Well, I can tell you right now, if you're looking for a college boy or a bank president, I ain't your man. I reckon we can sit and have this picnic—that I did plan out for you whether I was valuh-fucking-dictorian of my class or not—or we could pack it in. I'll take you home to wait for somebody in penny loafers to pick you up in their damn daddy's new sedan."

I couldn't breathe. He didn't appear angry, though he sounded it. His face was clear of emotion, and he sat back on his heels, with his hands curled gently on his thighs, as if waiting on me to pick which one had a pebble in it. No indication he was mad or upset, like I used to see with Daddy. No twitch in his cheek. No clenched fingers. No grinding teeth. But his words shook a fist at me. Even Alice was speechless.

"I'm sorry." I dropped my head and sucked at tears forming, so he couldn't see them. "I didn't mean ..." But the words hit a dam in my throat and went no farther.

"You'll have to speak up. I can't hear nothing but mumbling." I jerked my head to look at him. Again, the words seemed to be saying something his face didn't mean.

I knew I had to act fast, or I was going to lose him. Gulping air, I sputtered, "I'm sorry. It didn't come out the right way. I didn't mean it."

He patted my hand. "I know you didn't. It's okay." Sweeping the rest of the picnic debris aside, he rose up on his knees, twisted his body to sit next to me, and swung his arm over my shoulders. "But you have to watch what you say. You don't want to be one of them ball-busting girls who are too smart for their own good and think they're smarter than their man."

My stomach churned. I tried to think back over what I'd said. How I'd messed up. There was a pulse I couldn't find, but I knew it had to be there. I buried my face into his shoulder.

"Oh, come on. I'm not mad." He stroked my long hair from the crown of my head to the spot between my shoulder blades, then ran his fingers up the nape of my neck, as he murmured, "My God, you're a beauty."

He moved his hands to my waist. Electricity whizzed down to my pubic bone. "We need to come to an understanding. What's the use of talking about past nonsense? It's just you and me now." He kissed me on my right cheek. "Me." Kissed my left cheek. "And you." His lips found mine.

He eased us both back onto the pallet. For a split second, I was six years old and back in my bed with Daddy pushed up against me. Panic closed in.

Closing my eyes, I imagined a metronome ticking back and forth, making a rhythmic noise, "Here. Now. Here. Now." That calmed me down.

Jim bent over me. "Raise your head." I wondered what he was doing, but lifted my head and tried not to let him see the cringe I couldn't control. He used both hands to spread my hair out over the peacock plumes beneath me. Over and over, he combed my hair, the flick of his nails starting at my scalp and running through to the ends of each strand, with him humming in my ear, "Me and you." He leaned to kiss the soft spot behind each of my earlobes. "Lie still."

Daddy's gruff voice bubbled to the surface: "Be still." *Calm down. This isn't him.* Alice spoke clearly and calmly in my ear. I counted three breaths as Jim kissed my forehead and each closed eye. The ground beneath the fabric was soft under my back, but pebbles ground into my right hip.

"Relax. You're wound up tight as a drum." I didn't move as his hands smoothed down my bare arms. I stayed still as he slid off my shoes and stroked his fingers over the soles of my feet. It didn't tickle. It was just oh-so-sensuous. My blood thickened to mystic mud and oozed through my body, except for my head, where it zinged from ear to ear and buzzed so loudly, I couldn't think.

And then he was face-to-face with me and the lips I'd dreamt of all night were on the indentation at the tip of my chin and the hollow at the base of my throat. All thoughts of Daddy vanished in that bliss. I moved to clasp him, but he whispered, "Be still," and lowered his clothed body over mine. His groin pressed against me, causing a heat to swell through my pelvis. It tingled between my legs, mixed with the same pain I'd felt that morning and didn't understand.

"I could lay here with you like this forever." His fingertips grazed the baby-fine hair at my temples, and my breath came fast and shallow. "See how this feels?"

My chest quivered. I nodded. I didn't trust myself to speak, for fear I'd shed the tears so close to surfacing, and whose meaning I couldn't comprehend.

"You haven't done this before, have you?" His eyes were dreamtime.

I shook my head

"Didn't think so. We'll go slow." Beginning at my left collarbone, he ran his index finger along the skin above my peasant top's elastic. From right to left. He slid the puffed sleeve down to expose my left shoulder. I startled.

Making shushing noises, he touched the pad of his middle finger against my pursed lips. I kissed it. He lowered his head to kiss my bare shoulder.

A moan left my lips as he drew his nails across the swell of my breasts with a pressure scarcely making contact. Again, he nuzzled my throat, and sparks ran a dotted line from my heart to the spot between my legs.

The tiniest tip of his tongue flicked across my top lip as his hand moved to cup the tingling place between my legs. Fast as fire, the panic came back. I tried to sit up, my hand reaching to shove his away.

"Shhhh." He moved his fingers. "It's okay." He slowly nodded his head and pressed his palm against my cheek. "I won't hurt you."

With trembling arms, I relaxed my body back to the spread. His hand was back in place before my shoulder blades touched the blanket. Now, with his hand pressed down and moving in small circles, my whole body rose to him.

"Oh." A small sound for me. A wide smile for him. He withdrew his hand. I wanted to tell him to put it back, but embarrassment held me back. Taking my hand, he placed it against the fly of his pants.

"Just a little," he said while he unbuttoned and unzipped his pants fast and smooth, I didn't have time to react. "Here, I'll show you." Placing his hand over mine, he slid both down beneath the gaping zipper.

I couldn't hold back a gasp as I felt skin, soft fuzzy hair, and a smooth shaft. I expected underwear, but he wasn't wearing any. I closed my eyes tightly as his hand guided mine down then up. I didn't know if I liked this or not. Again, the hardness beneath Daddy's pants flashed across my mind before I could push the thought away. My stomach clenched. I started shivering all over.

"Open your eyes." Jim didn't stop our hands moving. "Look at me."

I fluttered them and saw those curled lashes, finely fanned brows, and a smoldering expression I knew was for me. Seeing his reaction to me, I felt jubilant. Our hands moved faster.

In a swift movement, his other hand pulled my top completely down on one side, leaving my bra open to his view. He lunged forward and melded his mouth onto the lacy tip of my breast at the same moment he heaved forward and groaned. Our hands shuddered. Wetness spread beneath them. His weight crushed onto me, and he laid his head on my shoulder while drawing in gulps of air.

I wrapped my arms around his back and melted into the feel of him. We lay that way while, overhead, a line of ants marched down the willow's branch.

Jim eased up on an elbow and kissed me once. "See. Me and you. Didn't take us long to figure that out, huh?"

My skin burned, and I plucked my blouse back up. Inside me, a whirlwind swirled clockwise through my body and threatened to blow me away, the wide vertex of the funnel at my heart, the powerful pointed tip between my legs.

Jim showed his teeth in the cavalier smile which had drawn me to him and waggled those Groucho-Marx-eyebrows again. "I like that top. You need to wear it every time we see each other."

Twenty-Four

On Monday following our first date, Carolyn tried to talk to me about Jim in fifth period algebra class. Our desks were side-by-side in the back, against the far wall. She passed me a note that read, "I need to talk to you about Jim. It's important."

"Mind your own business." I spoke out of the corner of my mouth, without looking at her, and acted intensely interested in my math book.

Her next note read, "You're gonna get hurt."

I scribbled out my own note and tossed it onto her desk. "Stay out of this." Then I gathered my things and moved to an empty desk at the front of the room.

Our teacher, Mrs. Sitz, addressed me before my butt settled into the new desk. "Miss Lydell, would you mind explaining why you're disrupting the entire class?"

"Yes, ma'am. There's a pest bothering me back there."

"Indeed. What kind of pest would that be?" Mrs. Sitz ambled over to stand next to me.

"The stinging kind gets under your skin and won't leave you alone, ma'am." I sat with my back ramrod straight, even when the class snickered, and I heard Carolyn's sharp intake of breath.

"I will not tolerate petty quarrels being played out like Greek theater in my classroom. Do you understand me, Miss Lydell?" She raked me over the tops of her red-rimmed glasses.

"Yes, ma'am."

"And that goes for you too, Miss Townsend." Mrs. Sitz swiveled to face Carolyn.

"Oh, you won't hear another word from me, Mrs. Sitz. You can be sure of that."

On the bus, I sat by myself in the front row and watched Carolyn's bright yellow VW as it left the parking lot.

———

I'd spent Sunday in agony, waiting for Jim to call, and was sure that Monday would pass the same way. I was wrong. The phone rang at ten o'clock, and we made plans to meet the next day.

The second the sixth period bell rang on Tuesday, I grabbed my books and dashed off four blocks up the street to McMillin's Feed Store, where Jim waited. I tossed my books in his back seat. He gunned the engine and squealed off.

"Want to go back to the gorge?" His T-shirt was royal blue today, which made his eyes aquamarine.

I ducked my head. "Sure."

"Come over here." He patted the seat. As I slid next to him, I felt sick in the pit of my stomach. His arm around me seemed crushing and a memory flitted across my mind. Sitting next to Daddy in the front seat of his truck. A thought I couldn't allow.

"How's my little schoolgirl?" I shook my head, dizzy to the point of nausea.

He frowned. "Don't let those eggheads get you down. You're with me now, shackle-free. Take your mind off that bullshit and give me those gorgeous lips of yours." He leaned down, one eye on the road, and waited for me to kiss him.

I swallowed hard, curved into him, and gave him the sexiest kiss I knew how.

"I hear that!" He pulled the car off the road into the Lindale First Baptist parking lot, over by the Girl Scout Hut. He kissed me for what must have been five minutes, with his hands moving up and down my back. "Now, that's a welcome!"

I put on a grin. I'd kissed him back, but my throat was dry and stomach queasy. I glanced around to see if anyone could see us.

"You want somewhere a little more private, huh?" He started the engine. All the way to the gorge, I sat next to him with part of me floating away, wondering what he thought I was asking for.

———

Under the willow tree, spread out on the peacock spread, I wasn't sure what was going to happen. A silver necklace slipped from his shirt and dangled over my face.

I caught it between my fingers. "What's this?"

"St. Christopher. Came all the way from Italy. Same city where my grandmother was from." He flattened his body against mine.

"Can we still take it slow?" He shook his head at me. I wasn't ready for his answer.

"I'm never going to do anything you don't want me to do. What kind of guy do ya take me for?" I must have offended him.

"Sorry." I felt idiotic. "Guess I'm scared."

He kissed my left ear. "Did you want me to do that?" His voice tickled my earlobe.

"Uh hmm."

He nibbled at my right ear. "How about that?"

Giggling, I threw my arms around his neck, pulled his head down to me, and kissed him long and hard.

When he lifted his head, he was laughing and batting his eyes. "I wasn't ready for that." He delivered his spiel in a high-pitched voice, with his knuckles pressing into his forehead.

I grabbed both of his arms, loving how his muscles felt. "Don't you make fun of me, you rascal."

"You are the most incredible girl I've ever known." His words made my heart shine. He nuzzled all along my neck. Chills coursed through me as I lolled my head back. "You want that?"

"Oh, yes." I murmured.

When his hands undid my bra, it was so fast I couldn't say no.

His skin touched my bare breast, and a tear flowed from the corner of my eye. I did the thing where my vision blurred.

"Sssh, Just a little," was all he said. His kiss was gentle on the apple of my cheek.

———

On Wednesday, when I came out of school, it was raining buckets. I stood on the stoop, trying to figure out how to get to our meeting spot at McMillan's. Kim and Tim, the twins, bumped up behind me, and I turned around.

"Need a ride?" I could never believe how identical they were, down to their droll little smiles. I was about to ask them to take me to the feed store when I heard my name.

"Mary Alice!" Jim's car sat in front of the school steps; the passenger window rolled down.

"Hey!" I waved at him and swiveled my head back to the Hewitts. "Thanks, but I have one."

I skipped down the stairs and into Jim's car. He peeled off while I wiped water off the soaked seat. When we got a ways down Lindale Highway, he pulled into JZ's parking lot—I wondered what he needed from the store—and snapped, "Who were you talking to?"

"Who? The twins?" Rain was beating against the roof of the car.

"Who the hell you think I'm talking about? Your mother?" He hit the dashboard with the heel of his right hand. "I asked who those two guys were."

I felt my shoulders draw in. "They're in my class and asked if I needed a ride."

"Oh, I bet they did." He had an ugly sneer on his face.

"Jim, I've known them a long time. They didn't mean anything by it. They're nice guys and offered to help me." I reached to squeeze his upper arm, and he jerked away.

"Hell will freeze over before I put up with a girl of mine flirting with every Tom, Dick, and Harry who comes along. Like bees to honey." He started the car's engine and revved the motor. "Well, I won't stand for a little twat making a fool of me. Make up your mind right now. You want to be my girl or not?"

I didn't want him calling me names, but I was afraid of losing him. It was just a stupid misunderstanding. "I don't have to make up my mind. Of course, I want you." I drew my books up to my chest. My leg started jiggling.

"Then swear to me that you won't talk to other guys." He turned the key in the ignition.

I dipped my head and told him what he wanted to hear. "I won't talk to other guys." Not talk to which guys? All guys? This was ridiculous. I didn't do anything wrong.

"Damn right, you won't." He put the car in reverse and drove us to the old Spillman Store that had been deserted for years out in the middle of the country and surrounded on three sides by woods. All the way there, I stared out of the window. The trees and house flew by as fast as my breath.

We parked in the back, where no one could see the car from the road.

"Hey, I'm sorry for what happened back there." He ran his thumb along my jawline, and I flinched. "I saw you with those guys, and it flew all over me. I couldn't bear it if I found out you weren't true to me, you know?"

I blurred my eyes and stared at my knees.

"Ah, baby. I didn't mean to act like such an asshole. Can't you forgive me?" He lifted my chin and gave me deer eyes. "I mean, how can you blame me for getting a little Looney Tunes, when I'm so crazy about you? It won't happen again. Kiss and make up?" He leaned in, gave me the sweetest kiss, and cradled my head.

What could I say to that? I'd been terrified he didn't feel the way I did. It was everything I'd been longing to hear. He was crazy about me.

—

Thursday, he took me to a spot on Cedar Creek. True to his word, he was gentle, and we only went a little bit farther each time.

He couldn't see me on Friday. Carolyn had avoided me all week. At first, I was glad. But after five days it felt weird. We'd never been mad at each other this long. I'd planned on catching her in the hall on the way to fifth period, but she never showed up.

I rode the bus home alone, thinking about Jim, and sketching hearts and flowers in my World History composition book.

Saturday morning, my room reverberated with more Beatles, *I Want To Hold Your Hand*. The song said it all. I felt so happy inside.

I wished Jim would call. I hadn't heard from him since Thursday when he dropped me off near my house. We were careful that he didn't actually pull into the drive, since Mama thought I rode the bus home.

The phone rang. I grabbed it before it could ring again.

"Hey. How's it hanging?" It was Carolyn.

"Home alone. Playing records." She didn't sound angry. I missed her.

"Want some company?" Her voice was hesitant, like she thought I'd blow her off.

"I'm down with that." What a relief. I couldn't wait to talk to her.

"Cool, be there in a few." The phone went dead, and I rushed around the room cleaning up the mess that had accumulated all week. After being gone for hours after school, homework was all I had time to fit in.

When the doorbell rang, I'd just cut up some cheese and apples and laid them on a paper plate, along with some Ritz crackers. Carolyn sprang through the door, her usual peppy self.

"All right. What's going on?" She flopped onto the couch.

"Where were you yesterday at fifth period?" I postponed the inevitable.

"Dentist appointment." She flashed her super-white teeth at me. Sometimes it was years between dentist visits for Mama and me. "You're not faking me out. Where were you the rest of the week?" Leaning forward, she seemed positively fiendish with her tight-lipped grin and the sheer look of anticipation on her face.

"You're not going to freak out on me?" I chewed my thumb nail.

She shook her head, with a decided snap both ways to emphasize her sincerity.

"And you won't tell a living soul?" I held my hand up, palm out, in the "You swear?" gesture.

"No. You know I won't, so stop the suspense and tell me already!" She leaned so far forward, I thought she'd topple over her own knees.

"I've been with Jim."

"I knew it!" Pulling her legs up, she kicked her feet up in the air. "Ignore what I said before. I sounded like your mother, or something. Tell me all."

I closed my eyes, and my smile was so big that my cheeks reached my temples.

"Oh, my God! I've never seen you this way. You're totally in love." Carolyn jumped up and was all over me, hugging and yapping.

"How did you know?" I really was in love. Carolyn could see it without me having to tell her.

"Duh. It's all over you, you dope!" I turned a kitchen chair and sat backwards in it, facing her. She was all questions. "So how old is he?"

I shrugged my shoulders.

"Is he in school?"

I pursed my lips and shook my head.

"Does he work?"

"I think so."

Now she wrinkled up her forehead. "Why don't you know anything about him? What do you talk about?"

Blood rose to my cheeks. "We don't talk that much."

Even she blushed. "Guess I asked for that."

There was an awkward silence. I felt I owed her some kind of information. "Okay, you want the skinny, I'll give it to you. He's so romantic and funny, and you saw how handsome he is. But the best thing is the way he looks at me ...."

We spent the rest of the afternoon talking and playing records. By the time she left, she must have been sick to death of hearing about Jim.

———

He didn't call me Saturday. By Sunday night, all I did was lie in bed with the TV on, staring into the moving images on the screen and wondering if I'd ever see him again.

In the middle of *All in the Family*, I grabbed the phone on the first ring.

"Mary Alice?"

"Hey. It's me." I held the phone up close to my ear, so I didn't miss a word.

"I'll pick you up tomorrow after school. All right?"

"Sure." Relief coursed through every muscle in my body.

"Can't wait to see you, baby." His tone was a little breathless and sexy.

"I can't, either." I tried not to sound too desperate.

———

On Monday afternoon, I was so excited that I started chattering from the time I got in the car. "It's not long until summer break, and I can't wait. I'm going to work at Penney's to earn some extra money."

"Hmm." He fiddled with the radio dial.

"I'm looking at colleges, too. One of my teachers thinks I can get a scholarship."

His head came up fast. "That right?"

"Carolyn and I want to be teachers. We were talking about it Saturday when she came over." I opened my purse and took out a pack of Dentyne. Then I remembered that he hated teachers.

His jaw was set, and he had his don't-mess-with-me look going. "You talking about that same Barbie girl from the night we met?"

"Yeah, Carolyn. My best friend."

"You want to explain why you think it's okay your best friend don't like me?" His eyes were slits in his head.

"But Jim, she and I talked on Saturday, and she understands now."

"What is it she understands?" He ran his hand over his mouth.

I wished I hadn't brought Carolyn up. "That we're seeing each other. She's happy for us."

"Oh, she is, is she?" He pulled the car into Girl Scout Hut parking lot again. "Didn't I tell you not to talk about me to anyone?" The tapping of his silver ankh ring on the steering wheel drilled into my head.

I ran through my mind, trying to see if I'd missed something. "I don't think so."

"I don't think so," he said in the high-pitched, mocking tone he used when he was really pissed off. "You're not to discuss our private business. That's between you and me. And let me tell you, we don't need trouble like that girl. Stay away from her." He pulled out a pack of Winstons and popped in the car's cigarette lighter.

"I didn't know you smoked." I couldn't keep the surprise out of my voice.

He didn't answer, stared straight ahead, lit the cigarette, pulled back onto the road, and accelerated the car to fifty.

We screeched around each two-lane curve, with the rear of the car fishtailing once. I clutched the edge of my seat. Two cigarettes later, we reached the gorge. He parked, flipped his cigarette butt out the window, and turned to me. "You going to be one of those self-righteous bitches harping at me all the damned day long? Because, if you are, I can take you home right now to your mommy."

I dropped my head and wondered if that wasn't exactly what I wanted.

But then he changed. Reached over and tipped my chin up with his thumb, then used his palm to cup my cheek, the way he had the night I met him. "You're not gonna let a few bad habits come between us, are you?" He kissed my forehead and moved his head in close to mine. His breath smelled. "I won't stand for anyone telling me what to do. You got that?"

I nodded.

"You know, sometimes it takes you a fucking long time to answer my questions. Let's try it again." He looked slightly amused. "Nobody, not nobody, tells me what to do. You got that?" He said it like he was jabbing his finger in my face with each word. He had that same ultra-casual expression about him that made me think of him as my own James Dean, though his tone was vicious.

"I got it." I said it quickly.

"You'd think a girl would like a man who calls his own shots." He stared at the car's headliner, as if deep in thought. "Yeah. Definitely. I want a girl like that. A girl who likes me the way I am." He turned to me expectantly.

I spoke fast. "You're the coolest guy I ever met. I don't care what you do, I like you just like you are. I do." I reached out to grab him. What had I done? How could he think I didn't like him? He drew back, and I clutched air.

"You sure about that?"

"I'm sure, more sure than I've ever been about anything in the world." *What are you doing?* I shut that Alice-voice away in a compartment in my brain and locked the vault.

He smiled. I loved it when he smiled.

"Well, that's more like it." He leaned in for a kiss. His breath stank of cigarettes. Holding my breath, I threw my arms around his neck and kissed him back for all I was worth.

"Uh huh. Now that's more like it." He unhooked his St. Christopher necklace. Holding the clasp between his thumbs and forefingers, he reached around my neck. "Lean over." I bent my head, so he could fasten it.

Lifting the oval pendant, I read the inscription, St. Christopher Protect Us. Baby Jesus rode piggyback on the shoulders of a man with a walking stick. "I love this."

Jim took the charm from me, lifted it to his lips, and kissed it. "This will guard you when I'm not here to keep you safe." He set it back, where it felt cool and magical against my skin.

The words popped out before I could stop myself. "I love you." I hadn't wanted to say it before he did.

But his mouth widened in that dashing smile of his. "I've been waiting to hear you say those words." His finger traced my skin, around the St. Christopher medallion lying at the hollow of my throat. He looked at me with his butter-melting eyes. "You hung the world, didn't you? The way I feel about you ... like the creek prizes the rain. You fill me up, all the way to the top."

He didn't say he loved me, but his words were poetry, and wasn't that what he meant? I breathed in the sound of him, the sight of him, the smell of him, and anchored myself so I didn't soar away. We practically ran to the willow tree with the peacock bedspread flying out behind us like Superman's cape.

—

By that Thursday, I was used to him smoking, but concerned by the quart of beer wrapped in a brown paper bag that he sipped from as we drove down the half-deserted country road in the rain, singing to his *Let It Be* eight-track tape. Two of us riding nowhere.

When we parked behind Spillman's store, he kissed me with beer breath. Like Daddy.

It was all I could do to keep my face smiling the way he liked. I rested one hand next to my left leg and drew the figure eight over and over on my jeans, until I could get used to the smell.

Half an hour later, I was curled up under his arm thinking I'd have to take a bath and wash my hair before Mama got home, or she'd think it was me smoking. It popped out, "What're we doing this weekend?"

He stiffened and took his arm away. It was so hard to tell what would set him off.

Taking me by the shoulders, he sat me away from him, the way a grown-up would do a kid. He scratched the side of his nose, tilted his head, and nodded. "This is a point needs to be crystal clear. You listening up, without your fingers in your ears like a dorky little girl?"

I nodded and said, "Yes," as soon as he finished speaking, and loud enough where he could hear me clearly.

"I ain't no little teenager playing school. I got a job and responsibilities. I'll let you know when I can see you, and I won't stand for you nagging at me all the time, 'When are you gonna see me, Jim? I haven't seen you in so long, Jim.' None of that. When I can see you, I will. When I can't, I won't. That good enough for you?"

"Yes." He hadn't seen me on the weekend since our first date.

"This is a man's world, not playacting. You sure you know what you're dealing with?"

"Yes, Jim." I nodded as if I understood.

—

The next two weeks went about like the first two. Jim picked me up three or four days a week after school, and we parked at the darnedest, most out-of-the-way places I'd ever seen for "just a little," though our favorite was still the gorge, under the willow tree.

In case Aunt Jean or Mama called the house, I told Mama I was going to the library after school or attending club meetings, and riding home with Carolyn. She was happy to hear about me spending more time with friends.

I stopped calling Aunt Jean as much as usual. Just the thought of her knowing what I'd been doing was seriously humiliating. She had radar and would be able to tell something was up, simply from my voice.

At school, I still talked to Carolyn, and the few times I rode home with her, it was like old times. I told her, "I don't want to talk about Jim. It takes away from the romance." Strangely, it was a relief to just talk to her about school and TV and girl stuff. But she seemed hurt that I was off with Jim most of the time. At school, we called it "gaga-itis" when girls were seeing so much of their boyfriends that their girlfriends were left hanging.

———

Jim and I had just made out on the chenille bedspread in his back seat. We were parked on an old dirt road in the woods near the power line off of Morgan Dairy Road. I couldn't believe how many of these remote areas he knew, and I wondered if he'd brought other girls to these make-out spots.

"How do you find all of these old roads so far off the blacktop?" I had my head leaned into the corner between the back passenger window and the seat. I made my voice light and curious, so he didn't sense that I was really suspicious.

"Hunting. Bet I know all the best sites in Floyd County." He sounded proud. I didn't know if I believed him or not.

Today, it was raining, and the windows were all fogged over. But I was always afraid someone would come up on us. Sitting there wearing nothing but my panties, I couldn't believe how quickly I'd not only gotten used to him seeing me half-naked, but how much I enjoyed him looking at me and how much I liked looking at his naked body. I'd drawn the line at my underpants. As long as they were on, I didn't worry about us going all the way. I pulled the chenille bedspread up around me.

"Ah, you're ruining my view." He ran his finger down the bridge of my nose, and I nipped at it. "You deserve better than us making out in my car all the time. We need to find somewhere more private, so I can give you the attention you deserve." It was amazing how many times Jim seemed to be reading my mind.

I was shy to ask, but questioned him anyway, "How about your house?"

"Nope. Won't work." He answered immediately, without explaining, then held up his index finger in a but-wait-a-minute gesture. "Good point. What about your house?"

I had never considered it. "What about Mama?"

"How's she gonna know? From what you tell me, she's at work all the time." He lit a cigarette and hugged his arm around me. "Sure would like to spend more time with you. Unless you think this is cozier?" He tugged a corner of the spread over him, and I snickered.

"But a neighbor might tell her." I chewed the side of my thumb.

"How will they know?" Laugh lines formed around his eyes. He was in a good mood.

"Your car, Silly." I pecked a kiss on his forehead, and the smoke rising from his cigarette stung inside my nose.

He sat up. "What say my car's parked off Booger Holler Road, and I walk in through the woods behind your house after your mother leaves in the morning? We could be curled up in bed all morning."

"When I was little, my babysitter lived over there. Every day, after school, I walked through those woods to get to her house."

"I bet you were the prettiest little girl in the world." He ran the backs of his fingertips from my chin up to the top of my cheekbone. His touch was so soft that the downy hair on my face prickled. "Why couldn't I have known you then? You would have been the girl I brought candy and Valentine Day cards, and then had to whup-ass all the boys in class who ragged me about it."

I mulled over his plan. It was risky but might work. "Maybe you could come to my house every once in a while. Except, I have to go to school."

"You don't need to go every day. You're one of them whiz kids from the look of that last test paper you showed me. A day here or there's not going to spoil your record or nothing." He furrowed his forehead. "Your mother leaves for work about six thirty every morning, right?"

"How'd you know that?" He was constantly surprising me with the things he noticed. Showed me he was paying more attention to me than I thought.

"I have my ways." He narrowed his eyes at me in a playful expression. "You don't have to be at school until eight-thirty." Back to his pondering ... but then I figured it out.

"You could come over about seven. If you drive me to school, instead of me riding with Carolyn, we'd have a whole hour!"

A frown flashed across his face and was replaced with a big smile. "Hey! Now, that's a great plan."

I beamed with pleasure. This would solve most of our problems. I couldn't believe I hadn't thought of it earlier. "You'd drive me to school?"

"Absolutely. Let's start tomorrow morning."

My voice caught in my throat. This was happening so fast.

"Changing your mind on me?" He raised his eyebrows but kept smiling.

I didn't want to disappoint him, and I didn't want to pass up the chance to see him more. "No, but my mama can't find out."

"She won't." His smile melted away. "That is, unless that Carolyn tells her."

I shook my head. "No, Carolyn wouldn't do that."

"We have to make sure she doesn't." His fingers encircled my wrists. "Thought I told you to stay away from that girl."

"I don't say anything about you." I stared at our hands in my lap. "She's my best friend."

"Mary Alice, you're smarter than that. It's the two of us now. We let other people get between us, it'll be over before we know what hit us." As he talked, he turned my palms facing up and ran his fingers over mine. "We've got a way worked out so we can spend real time together." He motioned at the car's interior. The rain still pattered against the roof. "I want to give you better than this. Understand?"

I nodded. "I do, but Carolyn's different."

He shook his head. "Sometimes, you're too sweet for your own good. That girl didn't want me seeing you from the start. What kind of friend is that? Huh?"

He was right. I thought back to the night I met him. Not only had Carolyn tried to warn me against him, but I'd found out that Mama and she had talked on the phone without me knowing, the two of them scheming behind my back for Carolyn to get me out of the house.

"She can't tell what she don't know. That's the only way your mama won't find out. You don't need her driving you around anyway. You've got me." He kissed my palms. "What could be better than me taking my girl to school every day and picking her up?"

"Really?" He nodded. I'd not only see him every day, but twice a day. I laid my head on his shoulder, and he pulled me in closer. "I'd like that."

"Then, it's a deal. Starting tomorrow, I'm your private chauffer and morning lover." He kissed my hair. "And you'll avoid that girl, so nobody suspects a thing. When you've got me, what do you want with a girlfriend, anyway? All we need is each other."

I plucked my shirt and bra from the floorboard and began to get dressed, keeping my face turned from him. If I had to choose between Jim and Carolyn, I knew who would win out. I just didn't want to have to make that kind of decision.

———

When I got home, I put off calling Carolyn until I couldn't delay it any longer, or Mama would be home and might overhear. She answered on the second ring.

"Hey, it's Mary Alice." I tossed my old red ball as I talked.

"Well, duh? You think I don't know your voice by now?" Her laugh rang out.

"I wanted to let you know I don't need a ride in the morning." I squeezed the ball and bit my fingernails into the rubber.

"Okay, you have an appointment or something?" I took a deep breath before answering her.

"No, it's just that Jim's going to drive me to school every morning." I could hear her television in the background.

"Well then, I'll see you in fifth period and on the way home."

I dropped the ball to the floor. "Um, he's going to pick me up, too."

This time, seconds ticked by without her saying anything. When her voice came on the line, it was the peppy one she used at school, around a group of kids. "Well, I'll see you fifth period, unless you're too busy for that. Listen, I gotta go. My show's coming on."

I opened my mouth to say bye, but the line had already gone dead.

Twenty-Five

I tossed and turned all night. Jim would be here at seven o'clock. If Mama caught me, I'd never be able to leave the house again. On top of that, he'd want to go all the way. He'd been patient. Was I ready? *No.* Alice always knew.

At 5:30, Mama's alarm went off and the shower came on. I hopped out of bed and sprinted to the kitchen. When Mama came in the kitchen, I handed her a cup of coffee in a to-go cup and a scrambled egg and cheese sandwich in a paper lunch bag. She saw what I had and dropped her purse to the floor. "Oh, my goodness." Her mouth dropped open, too. She lifted her eyes from the food to my face. "Thank you." One tear trickled down the left side of her face.

Flustered, I shifted from foot to foot. Feeling guilty, too. "It's not much, Mama. I'm sorry I haven't done more before."

Mama started as if from a dream. "Yes, it is much, and I appreciate you, little girl. This is wonderful."

"I'm making dinner, so don't be late." I grabbed her and squeezed.

She ran her hand down my right cheek. "I'll be here. Bye!" And she was off.

Six forty. He'd be here in twenty minutes. I dashed to the bathroom to wash my face and brush my teeth and hair. I left my hair down, over my shoulders, the way he liked it. Back in my room, I sat on the bed and looked at my pajamas. Plain blue gown. Not sexy at all. What else did I have? Rummaging in my drawer, I found a white, lacy gown that was a little better, so I put it on, opened my back window, and popped the screen out.

I pulled my desk chair over to the window and sat watching for him. My right leg jiggled so fast, it blurred. If I got caught. I couldn't even think what Mama would do! I stuck my head out of the window to look at the Middleton's house next door on the left and the Burkhalter's on the right. Nothing but woods behind. Not much chance anyone would see him come from the trees, but what if they did?

Then I saw him leaping over the chain length fence and loping to my window. Jim! My heart grew large. I loved him so much. He clambered in the window and dropped to the floor. I poked my head back out to see if anyone saw him, but no one was there.

He sat on the floor, gaping up at me. "You look exactly like an angel." He stood. As he did, he held the hem of my gown and pulled it up and over my head in one fell swoop. I covered myself with my hands. "Jim!" All I had on was my panties. He'd seen me only in panties, but it was somehow different here in my childhood bedroom.

But he gently took my hands and held me out to look at me. My face flamed red. "You are so beautiful. Just look at you." He drew me close and kissed me long and hard before lifting and placing me on my bed. "We've waited a long time for this day, my love."

My stomach turned over and over. I squeaked out, "Yes."

He lowered his body to mine and kissed my neck and earlobes. Fire burned down my spine and pubic bone. He moved his hands to my breasts and my body reacted violently on its own by jerking away. An image of Daddy lying in my bed intruded. "Wait!"

Jim stopped. "Hold on. You're fine. It's okay." But he kept his hands on my chest.

I started to feel dizzy and sick to my stomach. Jim moved his hands down and pulled my panties off. I gasped. He'd never taken my underpants off. He touched me down there and it felt so good. But it felt bad, too. Like when Daddy touched me there when I was six years old. I felt a wild animal inside me trying to get out and started trembling all over. "Wait!"

But he didn't wait. Instead, he pulled his pants off then climbed on top of me and kissed me hard as he guided himself into me. "Wait!" But he didn't wait, and it burned and hurt, and I completely froze. Jim started moving up and down inside me and the physical pain was nothing compared to the feeling of despair that rose up in me and clambered around in my brain. A buzzing noise filled my ears. I squished my eyes shut and went away in my head.

"Mary Alice, look at me." I heard Jim speak as if from a long tunnel in the distance. I frantically shook my head no. No. No. No.

Jim placed his hand under my chin and lifted my face to his. "Look at me." I opened my eyes. "It's me. Relax."

Relax. *He said to relax?* Alice was incredulous.

Jim began moving up and down again. I didn't know how much more I could take when he gave a final shove and collapsed on top of me panting like an old dog. Tears coursed down my cheeks as his weight pinned me to the bed. He was crushing me. I grunted and he rolled off and pulled me into his arms. The bed was wet beneath me, and my bottom hurt.

Alice was frantic. *Daddy never did this. He never did this.* Did he? Oh, God, no, I hope not. Well, no matter what, my virginity was gone. I couldn't stop crying. "I need to get ready for school." Snot dripped from my nose.

"Hey. What're the waterworks for?" Jim tucked a piece of hair behind my ear. "Shhhhhh, you're okay. The first time's the hardest. You're fine. Will be easier next time." He pulled me tighter. "Don't move an inch. No school today, Miss Whiz Kid. You can miss a day or two. I took the day off myself, so we'd have time. No harm. No foul. We have all day." His grin was infectious, but all I could see was Daddy's lewd grin when he touched me.

—

By the end of April, Jim had been coming to my house every day at seven o'clock for three weeks. I was surprised by how relaxed I could be in my own bed, instead of his back seat or outdoors on a bedspread thrown on the ground.

I kept my routine the same, so Mama wouldn't suspect anything. At night, I twisted the winding knob of my little round alarm clock. When I was little, I liked to pretend there was a robot fairy trapped inside. Every night, I kept her alive by spinning her metal wings that stuck out.

Now, setting it for six-thirty, I buried the dial under my covers, so Mama wouldn't hear it. So far, I had been so excited that I woke up around six every morning and cut it off, but I had to be careful.

Each morning I lay in bed until Mama left around six thirty. I used that time to stretch and make my plans. When Jim and I got married, he'd work while I went to school. I hadn't talked to him any more about college. I figured I should take it one step at a time. Next year, I'd finish high school and get everything lined up so Berry College would be paid for with scholarships and financial aid. Then, when the time was right, I'd tell Jim the good news. Every day, I hugged Mr. Sand to me and arranged the future in my mind, until it all lined up like dominoes.

Then, the minute I heard Mama shut the door and crank the car, I'd leap out of bed, take a quick shower, and brush my teeth and hair. We thought it best if Jim didn't come around to the front door. Smelling of Jean Naté, I'd open my bedroom window and watch the cardinals flit to the nest they'd built in the crepe myrtle's branches. Jim would emerge from the woods like a wild animal and come loping across the backyard. He'd hop on my windowsill and climb inside.

This morning, all I wore was my short robe covered in white hearts. The second he crawled through the window, I clasped my arms and legs around him. With both hands cupped around my bare bottom, he twirled me in circles. Dropping to the bed, I smothered kisses all over his face. He didn't smoke in the morning, so his citrus smell was divine.

"Did you know you're all I can think of?" I pulled his shirt off over his head and smoothed my hands up and down his back.

"That's just the way I want it." He stood up to unbutton and unzip his jeans. As he slid out of them, he looked around my room. "Our bedroom's not going to look like this, little girl." I glanced around at the neon posters on my wall and the shelf filled with stuffed animals. He lay back down next to me. "It'll be a place of our own. You'd like that, wouldn't you?"

"A place of our own." My head bloomed full of joy. I ran my palm across the soft down that framed his belly button. "I could see you all I wanted every day."

"You'd do more than see me every day." He untied the sash of my robe.

After making love, I kissed his shoulder. "Be right back." I always went to the bathroom afterwards and peed because I was worried about getting pregnant. Jim pulled out and said that made it safe, but I'd read differently. Then, there were the times he said it felt too good to pull out, and that concerned me the most. But I was counting the days of my cycle and being extra careful until I could go to the health clinic and get the pill.

Back in bed, he snuggled up against me. When he did it, I wasn't crazy about the way it felt, but I'd gotten used to it and could lie afterwards cuddling this way for hours.

"One day, I'll have you all to myself. We'll wait for you to finish high school next year. I don't know why that piece of paper's so important to you, but once you get it, we're running off to Alabama to tie the knot." He faced me, took off his ankh ring, and slid it onto my right-hand ring finger. "Will this hold my place 'til I get you the real thing?"

"Jim!" I flung myself on him and smooched all over his face. "I won't take it off for anything." It was way too big, but I could wrap a rubber band around it, the same as the girls at school did with their boyfriends' class rings.

"So, you'll promise to be mine?" His tousled hair fell over one gleaming eye, the color of denim against my carnation pink sheets. "All mine?"

I clasped both hands on his cheeks and kissed him long and hard. "I'm yours until the day I die. Our own house. Our own yellow kitchen, the color of sunshine." As I talked, Jim encircled his left arm around me, spooning me to him.

"Uh huh."

"A front porch with rocking chairs and a dog—a spaniel." I burrowed down under the covers and nestled my head onto his back. "And our own babies." I lay perfectly still, holding my breath, to see his reaction.

"Uh huh."

I gave a satisfied sigh and thought about boxing up my toys and saving them for our kids. Glancing around my room, I saw it the way he must have. I hadn't realized how childish my room was. My voice came out a low singsong, "A boy for you and a girl for me. I never even thought about having kids before you. You've changed everything." The sound of his breathing was low and steady. He was asleep. I whispered, "I'll have a real family, a real life." I snuggled up to him and closed my eyes.

When we both woke up, it was long past time for classes to start. Since he'd started coming to my house, I had missed a few days of school. Anyway, it was Friday, and the year would be over soon. "You stay right here, and I'll make you breakfast in bed." I'd always wanted to say those words. Breakfast in bed.

Pirouetting into the kitchen and to the cabinet, I searched for a bowl and saw that Mama had made a mess of the dishes again. I liked the dinner plates laid on top of each other, the cereal bowls stacked together, and the Tupperware mixing bowls grouped from the largest on the bottom to the smallest on top, with the lids organized by size next to them. Mama just slammed things in the cabinets, a bowl stacked on top of a plate and plastic containers shoved in edgeways. I'd have to fix it later. After sorting through to find two that weren't chipped, I took down two plates and a lemon-yellow mixing bowl.

I opened the fridge for eggs, bacon, and butter. Mama had been at work in there, too. I'd have to pay more attention around this house.

The eggs weren't on the right side of the middle shelf, where I liked them. The bacon was laying there half-open on the top shelf, not in the meat drawer. In the compartment on the door, the butter dish was empty except for smears. A stick of butter shoved beneath a head of lettuce—outside of the vegetable bin—was open, and I saw obvious indentations where fork tines had scraped off a pat. I shook my head at the ceiling and rummaged around to find a jar of pear preserves, which should have been on the far left of the top shelf, towards the front. More chores for later. When I had my own place, I'd be able to keep everything in proper order.

Arms full, and fixings clasped to my chest, I placed everything on the counter next to the stove and set to work, all the while singing the Beatles' *Till There Was You* under my breath. I stirred the skillet of scrambled eggs with the same wooden spoon Mama paddled me with when I was five years old. I'd been in trouble for pulling all the pots and pans into the yard and using the garden hose to create my own Marineland show from a plastic set of sea creatures—dolphins, a shark, tropical fish, a stingray, and two giant sea turtles.

The scent of buttered toast filled the air. I opened the oven to check on it. That smell was Aunt Jean, which reminded me that I wouldn't have to sneak around anymore when Jim made an honest woman out of me.

Breakfast in bed. I loaded our meal onto an aluminum pizza pan, and those words formed a tunnel down the hall. When I came out the other side, my new life began—the best part yet, the one I'd been waiting for ever since I was six years old, when Daddy lost his job and did the things he did and went to jail for attacking Mama and a policeman.

———

The next day was Saturday, and Jim showed up, right at my front door. The doorbell rang, and when I looked out the window, it shocked me so bad, I thought somebody must have died.

"What's wrong?" I practically shrieked at him.

"Don't tell me you've forgotten the two-month anniversary of our first date." He held his keys up and jingled them. "Got a surprise for you. Come on."

I threw my arms around him, without a thought about anyone seeing us. "I did too remember! Just thought you wouldn't."

He dropped his head and poked out his bottom lip. "Now, you've hurt my feelings."

I goosed him under the arm, and he pulled away from me, laughing. "Let me get my shoes."

We drove to a cow pasture on Morgan Dairy Road, near one of our old make-out spots. "Here we are!" He hopped out of the car. Wondering what he was up to, I opened my door and sunk my feet into soft grass. From the trunk, he pulled out a butterfly-shaped kite.

"Oh, my gosh! I've never flown one before." I squeezed my hands up under my chin.

He couldn't believe it. "You mean a kite like this one?"

"Not any kite."

"You're kidding me." I'd never seen him with his mouth dropped open.

"Cross my heart." I licked my pointer finger and made an x over my left breast. A gust of wind blew the kite from his hands, but it was already attached to a ball of twine, so it only skittered a few yards away.

"Then you're in for a treat." While he untangled the cord, I breathed in the spring air and raised my face to a powder blue sky. Lowering my eyes, I saw purple clover blanketing the ground as far as I could see.

"Ready." With the multi-colored kite gripped in one hand, he handed me the ball. Several feet of string lay unwound on the ground between us. "I'm going to start running. As the wind catches the kite, let more out. Got it?"

Wind ruffled his dark hair. Two spots of color on his cheeks accentuated his twinkling eyes. I nodded and felt my love for him surge through every square inch of my body.

He leaned in quick as Jack Be Nimble, kissed me on the tip of my nose, and sprinted off with the kite held aloft, over his head. At first, the wind just battered the kite straight out behind him. But as he ran, the breeze rose up under it.

I frantically pulled foot after foot of twine, trying to keep up. A blast of air swirled across the meadow. The kite flew out of Jim's hands and the cord tightened so fast it almost jerked the ball from my hands as Jim yelled, "Hold on!"

The kite tugged and billowed and was the most incredible thing I'd ever seen. Its swooping motion paralleled the way Jim made me feel.

He ran to me with an enormous smile covering his face. "First try! Whatcha think of that?" Then he took the ball and drew me in next to him, my back pressed up against his body as we swayed together in the wind, with the kite soaring into the sky.

———

On Sunday morning, I sat on my bed, up on my knees, mooning over the butterfly-shaped kite. I'd thumb-tacked it to the wall over my bed, with its psychedelic tail curled down, so I could wrap it around my finger and remember our special day. Everything went right yesterday. I hadn't messed up one time to cause him to act ugly. In fact, since he'd begun coming to my house, he hadn't gotten mad. Not once. That's what it would be like when we had our own place and got to be with each other all the time.

I twisted the kite's tail around my fist. Sometimes I wondered why we never went to his house. But I figured maybe he was embarrassed by where he lived. I could help him fix it, but I was too scared to broach the subject. He still didn't like me asking questions. I lay back on my bed listening to my Beatles' record and dreaming of a time when we'd spend all our anniversaries together, when Mama burst in.

"Cut that infernal racket off." She crossed to the record player and stopped John and Paul mid-lyric with a screech, as she jerked the needle across the 45.

"Mama!" I jumped from the bed.

"Don't Mama me. When were you gonna tell me you're fooling around with Jimmy Ledbetter?" Her blue eyes tinted to steel gray, and her forehead wrinkled up. I blinked and counted to three.

"Answer me, and I want the truth, missy. I've finally heard the news that everyone in town seems to know, except me. How long's this been going on?" Mama pointed to the bed for me to sit. I continued standing.

"Sit down. We're having a talk, and I'm not leaving until I learn what I want to know." She snapped her fingers and jabbed at me, then at the bed.

"I won't quit seeing him." I lifted my chin.

"What?" The tip of her nose and both cheeks glowed pink.

"I can tell where this is going, so I'm gonna let you know right off. I don't know what you have against him, but it won't change my mind." I stood, hands on my hips. With Mama, I knew I needed to take a firm stance, or she'd roll all over me.

"I see." Mama sat on my bed, crossed her legs, and her foot swung to the rhythm of a grandfather clock's pendulum.

"You do?" I eased down onto the edge of the bed next to her, with my right leg shaking the same as the jiggler on top of Mama's pressure cooker.

"So, you're going to see him no matter what?" She wasn't acting the way I would have imagined. I thought she'd be hysterical and set down ultimatums.

"Yep." Maybe she realized I'm grown up.

"Even though he's married?"

"He is not!" I sprang from the bed.

"It's true." Mama looked me straight in the eyes as she said it, then glanced away, rubbing the back of her neck and twisting her head from side to side.

I took a backward step, then collapsed to the floor, sobbing. Mama came and sat next to me and let me cry. She didn't try to touch me or talk while I bawled my eyes out.

The tears slowed, and I raised my swollen face to her. My voice started as a whisper and accelerated so fast it ended in a shriek, "You're lying. You don't have anybody, and you don't want me to have anyone, either." With the last words, spittle sprayed onto her.

She wiped her face with one hand and pushed herself off the floor into a standing position. "I wish it wasn't true as much as you do."

It couldn't be. My brain was doing the equations, even when I tried to stop it. Everything added up. That explained why I'd never been to his house, why he saw me at odd times, and why he acted so secretively.

I refused to look at Mama, crawled onto my bed, and curled up on my side, my back to her. "Leave me alone. I don't ever want to talk to you again."

"That's not gonna hurt my feelings, given the way you speak to me." She closed the door on her way out.

Twenty-Six

The next morning, weak daylight seeped into my bedroom. My fairy alarm clock read 7:06. I pulled the covers over my head and lay in the suffocating dark, the way I used to do at night when I was a scared kid. Back then, I never realized why I was so afraid. Daddy. I'd been a fool to believe I deserved a real life.

When Jim tapped at my bedroom window, the me who managed to drag herself from the mattress and open the window for him wasn't Jim's Mary Alice. I hadn't showered or brushed my teeth or combed my hair. And I wasn't the girl who answered quickly, the way Jim liked. I was just Alice, the girl who always knew about Daddy and who saw Jim for what he was, long before I was willing to.

Alice had spent the night spinning all the combination locks in my brain to unbolt the compartments and vaults where I'd stored all my reservations about Jim. There'd been no time to sleep, as I poured over all the signs I'd captured and then chosen to deny.

Unsealing the truth about Jim unblocked everything Daddy had done. I couldn't shove the memories of him into my rabbit hole. I had to face them. So, when I saw the Jim I loved, and now also hated, clamber through the window, I turned and trundled back to bed, without saying a word.

"What took you so long to let me in? It's frigging raining out there if you haven't noticed from your warm little bed."

I lay under the covers, facing away from him.

"What's crawled up your butt? On the rag or something?" His perturbed voice meant nothing to me.

I turned and saw him grab my heart-covered robe from the bedpost and use it to dry his sopping wet hair. What a douche bag.

I sat up in bed. "You smell like a dog."

"What the hell did you say?" He stood dripping on the carpet, the robe hanging limp in his hand.

"You're married." The words came out in a flat monotone.

"What?" He dropped my housecoat to the floor.

"I know you're married." My fists balled up. I pushed them together as hard as I could, to stop my first impulse—to punch him.

"I never told you I wasn't married." His tone and posture recovered their self-satisfied bearing, and he stripped off his wet shirt.

I wasn't swayed by his unflinching display. "Put your clothes back on and get out of here."

He snatched his shirt from the floor, took a step towards the window, and spoke facing it. "You aren't even giving me a chance to explain?"

"Explain what." My tone came out a comment instead of a question.

"If you're so cold you won't even hear my side ..." He moved another step towards the window.

Stop listening to him! Alice screamed at me. His shoulders were curled forward. I'd never seen him this way. "How you think you're getting out of this one?"

He whirled around. "Because we're separated, for Christ's sake. Getting divorced. I told her it was over when I met you. I was going to tell you when the papers were finalized. I was trying to protect you until it was all said and done." He looked at the floor and shook his head back and forth.

I picked at my sheets, wondering if I believed him. *Are you crazy? He's lying again.* No, it's me who's ruined it all. I should run to him and apologize for being distrustful.

Thoughts about Daddy came steaming in with a strength I couldn't bear. If I was left all alone, I'd never make it. And here was Jim, right in front of me—the only person who ever cared about me. So what if he was married? Plenty of people got divorced. I sat up in bed, with my mind working double-time to lock Daddy back up. I couldn't endure feeling crazy, like the girls in *I Never Promised You a Rose Garden* and *The Bell Jar*.

Jim bent down on his knees by the side of my bed and cradled my hands in his. "Baby, I don't want to lose you."

His words pushed my thoughts about Daddy back down. As long as I stared into Jim's eyes, Daddy was gone. Jim needed me. He wanted me. He didn't want to lose me. Somehow, through all the bedlam inside me, I realized I had to hold on to somebody, or I'd slip away and cease to exist.

My thoughts bubbled and rolled. What if I worked hard to be different? Then he'd change. I'd stand up to him, not saying yes when I didn't mean it. Hadn't that been lying to him? Hadn't I been just as dishonest? If I gave him another chance, he'd treat me better. I'd be stronger. We'd both be different. We'd get married, just the way I planned.

And that decision gave me the strength to round up all my thoughts of Daddy and plunge them deep into the rabbit hole. I pushed Alice in there, too, and locked them both away, so I didn't go crazy and end up in the loony bin the way Daddy had said.

Feeling weightless, I rose up and took Jim in my arms. I rocked us back and forth until he moved with me onto the bed, and we became one.

Twenty-Seven

When I came out of the bathroom later that day, Mama was home and on the phone. Eavesdropping wasn't normally my style, but I needed to know what she was saying about Jim and me. She hadn't mentioned anything about him since yesterday morning, but I knew my mama, and she wouldn't let this drop. Her way was to let things cool off, so that I let down my guard. Then, out of the blue, she'd spring on me.

I crept down the hall. From the sound of it, she was talking to Lucille, and I only made out bits and pieces.

"... can't allow it ... that hoodlum ... revved up Dodge barreling down Rockmart Highway ... deals dope from the trunk of his car ... I tell her she can't see him, she'll think it's my apron string talking ... Jean gets wind of this, it'll kill her."

I couldn't listen anymore. I stole back to my room and flopped onto the bed. No matter what else happened, Aunt Jean couldn't know about Jim and me. Mama was right about that. But she was so wrong about Jim.

When she burst into my room, I knew what it meant. But I still didn't know what to do.

"Come in here with me. I need to talk to you." She motioned for me to follow her into the den.

"We got nothing to talk about." I said it strong. Inside, I was quaking.

"We'll talk about whatever I want, whenever I say so, young lady. Get your ass up off that bed right now." I hadn't seen her face blazing like this since the last night Daddy was home.

Nobody disputed Mama's ultimatums. I had to do whatever it took to convince her Jim and me weren't negotiable before she issued a proclamation.

I screamed at her before I realized what I was doing. "I got the right to see whoever I want!"

She came at me so fast that I threw my arms up for protection. It was a good thing because she grabbed both of my arms and shook me. "Don't tell me about your rights. Sandy Middleton called me at work today. Told me she saw that hoodlum leaving my house at ten o'clock in the morning. When you were supposed to be in school."

She shoved me. My head recoiled on the headboard. Mama had never laid a hand on me before.

Her face was six inches from mine. "I'm your mother, and it's my duty to protect you. I won't stand by and watch you ruin your life." She slapped the wall above my head with both hands. The smack was earsplitting. I ducked and scrambled to the far side of the mattress.

She lunged at me and ended up halfway across my bed, bracing herself on stiff arms. "You ain't got sense one. It's up to me to take this situation under control." Rising from the bed, she towered over me. "I forbid you to see him."

"No!" I came up on my knees, beating my fists into my thighs. "You can't do that!"

"Oh yes I can, and I am. You brought this on yourself." She pivoted and covered the distance to the hall in two strides. With her hand on my doorknob, she turned back to me. "No phone calls. As for school, you've got a few weeks left this year. I'll drive you and pick you up myself. You'll come back to the store with me every afternoon and go in with me on Saturday." It was like she was ticking off a list. "This summer, you can get yourself a job, with the same driving arrangements, or you can sit in the back office of the store all damn day long, for all I care." My slamming door reverberated with such force that the full-length mirror mounted on the back of it cracked.

I charged from my bed and kicked the door so hard that I stove my big toe in.

She couldn't do this. I wouldn't let her. Limping around my room, toe throbbing, I gathered clothes and shoes and jammed them into my Scooby Doo tote bag. Where was Jim's St. Christopher necklace and phone number? I found the chain and medallion on the floor between my bed and nightstand. The paper he'd scrawled on yesterday was tucked under my phone. He'd torn a strip from my composition book and curled the slip into my hand. "Here's all the proof I can give you that I'm separated."

Crossing the room, I slipped the necklace on and crammed his number into my pocket. I didn't hesitate as I opened the window, crawled out, and hobbled across the backyard and through the woods.

I limped all the way to Carolyn's. When I got there, her parents' car was gone but her VW was in the drive.

I rang the bell, sending up silent pleas that Carolyn would be home. She answered the door but didn't look that happy to see me. We'd barely spoken to each other for three weeks.

"Can I use your phone?" I was still panting from the walk over. My toe throbbed.

"That's all you're here for?" The disgust was evident in her voice.

"Carolyn, you don't know what's happened. Can you just help me?" She glanced at my carryall. Sweat ran in rivulets from my temples, down my cheeks, to the creases of my neck.

"All right. Come on in. Jeez, Mary Alice, what's going on?" Concern flickered across her face.

"Mama and I had a bad fight. I don't want to talk about it." I must have walked down this hall with Carolyn in front of me a thousand times, but today it was a place I'd never been.

Her back drew up rigid, and she spoke without turning to me, "Of course not. Why would I think you'd talk to me about anything anymore?"

She handed me her pink phone.

"Carolyn …" I wanted to explain, but she cut me off.

"Forget it. Use the phone and go back to ignoring me." She held her eyes wide open. "You've made it exceedingly clear that I'm nothing to you. Lately, I don't even know who you are."

Why did she have to pick today to make a statement? I felt utterly forsaken by everyone. Hunching my shoulders, I turned my back to her, so she didn't see that I was about to cry. As his phone rang, I mouthed "please" silently. What if he wasn't there? He answered on the third ring. "Jim, I need you to come get me. Please."

He must have heard the panic in my voice. "Where are you?"

"Carolyn's. Her house is …."

"I know where she lives. Give me twenty minutes." He hung up.

"He's picking me up here. Won't be long. I'll wait out front, so he knows which house is yours."

The corner of Carolyn's mouth trembled, but her face remained harsh. "Want me to wait with you?"

Nothing would be better, but I knew how he felt about her. I didn't want him saying anything mean to her, and I couldn't deal with another crisis today. "He might not like that."

The quiver at her lips set into a straight line. "Wouldn't want that, now, would we?" Her contempt was obvious. "What's happened to you? I never thought you'd be a doormat for some guy!"

"I am not!" We'd always despised that kind of girl. "And he's not 'some guy.' I'm going to marry him."

She didn't act surprised or happy for me. Just stood there shaking her head and biting her bottom lip. "What have you got yourself into?"

When I left her room, she didn't even say goodbye.

For the first fifteen minutes, I sat against Carolyn's car, on the far side, where Mama couldn't see me if she drove by. Carolyn calling me a doormat really stung. Maybe I was careful to do what Jim wanted, but everything was fine between us that way. Was that being smart, or letting him walk all over me, like Carolyn said?

The last five minutes, I sat at the end of her drive, looking up the road, hoping Mama hadn't discovered I was gone. I expected to see her any second.

When I saw Jim's car, I looked towards Carolyn's bedroom window, half expecting her to be staring out, but there wasn't even a flutter of her curtains. He pulled into the drive. I tossed my tote into the back and slumped down into the front seat. "Mama banned me from seeing you." I burst into tears.

"Tell her you'll see whoever you want." Backing out and holding his hand over his right ear, he continued, "And stop your caterwauling. I got a headache."

"You don't know my mama." Nobody understood.

"What is it you want me to do?" He sounded aggravated.

"She was going to drive me to and from school and make me stay at the store with her. I'd be a prisoner and never get to see you." I pushed the pads of my thumbs underneath my brow bones and concentrated on the patterns of flashing light in the dark of my head. He didn't say anything.

Without opening my eyes, I asked, "Can't I stay with you?" What in the world was I going to do if he said no? He'd probably been lying to me and was living with his wife.

I felt the weight of his hand on my thigh. "Look at me." He didn't sound annoyed anymore. "You sure?"

I couldn't believe what I was hearing. "Oh, Jim, I'm positive."

He squeezed my leg. "You move in with me—you can't go running back to Mama."

I slid across the seat and threw my arms around him. "Course not. Why would I?"

He draped his arm over my shoulders. "All right, then. Let's get you home."

Home. I lay my head in the curve of his neck. Everything was going to be perfect.

He chuckled. "I'll warn you. The place is a mess. Needs a woman's touch, for sure."

"It can't be that bad. I'll help you." It was everything I'd dreamed of, without the wedding. I wouldn't be able to face Aunt Jean. Then there was Mama. I'd have to call her.

"You can fix it up while I'm at work. Couldn't have better timing. I got on at Georgia Kraft. Whatcha think of that?" He swiveled his head and beamed at me. "Best paying job I ever had."

"That's great!" I smacked a big kiss on his cheek.

"Fair warning. It's swing shift and I'm starting tomorrow on first, for training." He glanced at me with eyebrows raised. "Sure you won't mind all the crazy hours?"

"Nothing matters as long as we're together." I slid my hand under his ponytail and rubbed the back of his neck.

We headed up Shorter Avenue towards West Rome. turned left onto Burnett Ferry Road, went about a mile, then bore right into a trailer park. I never pictured him in a trailer, always saw him in a run-down, white frame house in the country, with a front porch and a big oak tree shading the yard.

He pulled up to the sixth one on the right. A dozen little barefoot kids were in the road, playing kickball with a dime store ball, not paying any attention to his car. "Filthy brats don't have a lick of sense." He didn't say it mean, just tired, and it jarred me how much it sounded like a combination of Daddy and what Mama said to me earlier.

I climbed the metal platform, up into his trailer, the excitement building with each step. He unlocked the door, then swooped down, lifted me, and carried me across the threshold.

The first thing that registered was the stench, like rotten garbage. I held my breath while he twirled me around, kissing me. "It's not much, but it's ours!" He sat me down and grabbed my hand. I only had time to glance around and see a tiny living room with worn brown plaid furniture, a miniscule kitchen with dishes overflowing in the sink. Beer cans sat everywhere. They covered the short kitchen counter, the glass-top end table, and the skinny coffee table. He pulled me through a hallway so narrow that I almost had to turn sideways, into the bedroom.

"Not much" was an understatement. This place needed me as much as Jim did. I'd get both of them spic and span in a couple of weeks. As we fell to his bed, the musty odor told me it was best that I blur my eyes, so I didn't have to look at the sheets.

Twenty-Eight

Later that night, when Jim went out for cigarettes and a gallon of milk, I covered his nasty couch with a clean sheet, sat down, and called Mama.

"You've had me worried sick to death." She sounded like all her breath was captured in her throat.

"I'm fine." I twisted the edge of the cotton sheet tight around my finger and watched the tip turn purple.

"Fine! I get hold of you and you'll be anything but fine! Where the hell are you?" Her words flew fast.

"At Jim's."

"I'm coming after you." Her voice was two notches higher than usual. "Where does he live?"

"No, Mama. I'm staying." I couldn't believe how firm I sounded.

"Over my dead body." Now she spoke in slow, even measures. "You get your ass home or I'm calling the police."

I was afraid of that, so I'd prepared myself. "You do it, and I'll just run off again. You can't keep me there against my will, and you know it, Mama."

"You are my daughter, my under-aged daughter. I'll do whatever I damn well please, whether you like it or not." She was screaming so loud, I had to hold the phone away from my ear.

"Mama."

"Tell that bastard he'll be sorry when I slap him with kidnapping and contributing to the delinquency of a minor!"

I banged the receiver against the arm of the sofa, then clamped it back to my ear. "Mama! Listen to me."

"No, you'll listen to me, young lady. You are out of your ever-loving mind."

I yelled into the phone. "Let me talk or I'm hanging up!"

"Then, talk." Her ragged breathing echoed down the line.

"I'm not coming home. I love him. Why can't you be happy for me?"

"Happy! I'll rot in hell before I stand by and let you ruin your life! Either he brings you home tonight or I'll see he's thrown under the damn jail. Get here by tomorrow, and I won't even have to tell your Aunt Jean." She kept talking, but the sound of Jim's car engine outside took all of my attention.

"I'm hanging up now. I love you, Mama."

"Don't you …." When I pushed the button down on the phone's base, she was still hollering on the other end. I replaced the receiver, laid my head on my knees, and cried.

His car door slammed, so I jumped up and ran to the bathroom to wash my face. Jim came in while I was drying my eyes on a mildewed towel.

He pressed his hand into the small of my back and pulled me close to him. "My little girl's not getting homesick?"

"No!" I hiccupped. "And I don't like being called little girl."

I thought it might make him mad, but he just laughed and cupped my butt cheeks. "Rrrrrrrrr, I got me a tiger."

I pulled away. "I called Mama to let her know I'm all right."

He patted my head. "Good for you."

"Don't make fun of me. She said she'd have you arrested unless you brought me home tonight." I burst out crying and buried my face in his shirt.

He cradled my chin in his palm and lifted my head. "Honey, she has to find us first. This is a buddy's place. No one knows where I am." He tilted his head at me and crossed his eyes with such a goofy look I had to laugh. "Better, much better. Have you forgotten we're celebrating?"

I pulled at the roll of toilet paper and honked my nose. "I'm sorry."

"Honeymoon's over before it started. You're already snot-faced in front of me." He grinned and pinched my tush.

I batted my hand at his chest. "Oh, you. It's the happiest day of my life. I'm just …."

"A bundle of nerves? A train wreck?" He held up his hand and ticked off smart ass replies. "A worrywart? A fraidy cat?" He threw his forearm over his eyes. "Oh, my God, you're not ... having a nervous breakdown!" He peeked over his arm. "Are you?"

"You turkey." I felt my face getting hot. "Okay, you're right. Make you happy?"

He wrapped his arms around me and kissed me—the sweetest kiss he'd ever given. "I am one happy man. Don't you know that?"

From the light in his eyes and the relaxed curve of his shoulders, I saw he meant it.

"You know, you gotta lighten up. Come on out of the bathroom." He pulled me in front of him and guided me down the hall. "There are far more lovely rooms in my humble abode. Join me in the sure-to-be-cleaner-soon living room. Have a beer with me." I jerked my head over my shoulder at him.

When he saw the shock on my face, he threw his hands up and waved them. "Oh-my-God, it's the end of times." He shook his head and looked at me like I was a child who needed to be brought in out of the rain. "Sweetheart, I don't know what century you've been living in, but a little tonic is sure to cure what ails you. Especially if you're in the midst of a complete nervous collapse. We can't act too soon!" He grabbed my hand and propelled me down the hall.

Around ten o'clock, after sipping down two sour beers and feeling light-headed, Jim led me to the bed, saying, "Oh, no, you don't. I'm loving up on that luscious bod of yours before you get too tipsy. My shift starts at seven-thirty, and I want to get there early. Make a good impression on my first day."

That's when I realized he couldn't drive me to school. But I'd meant what I said. Nothing mattered, as long as we were together.

—

The first day, while Jim was gone to work, I opened all the windows to air out the place and wiped down all the counters with some Lysol I'd found under the kitchen sink. I cleaned the bathroom until it shone and did the same to the fridge, tossing out unrecognizable food concealed by green-brown mold. In the closet were several sets of sheets. I changed the bed and covered the living room bucket chair with the bottom sheet matching the mint green top sheet I'd thrown over the couch.

By the time Jim got home at four-fifteen, I'd taken all the garbage to the dumpster and was smelling sweet from my shower. When he came through the door, stinking with the strong, noxious odor of the paper mill, my damp hair hung down my back smelling of Johnson's baby shampoo. I hugged him up tight.

With his arm locked around my waist, he stared first at my face and then at the trailer. "Look at my beautiful baby and my clean house."

"I've never been so happy." It was as if a shower of sunlight poured from my crown to the soles of my feet.

He cleaned up and took me out for pizza. It was a real treat, to rejoice in us being together and for his new job. Afterwards, we drove to the A&P for some food and cleaning supplies before going home to crawl under the sheets. As we drifted off to sleep, all I could think of was how everything was like a dream come true.

The second day, I cooked breakfast for him and burned the sausage. Mama and I never ate it, but Tennessee Pride patties were Jim's favorites. He popped the charred pieces in his mouth and moaned with pleasure.

After he left, I spent all morning wiping all the fake wood paneling down in every room using a bucket of bleach I'd diluted with water. After one room, my eyes stung, and I had to go sit on the metal steps, coughing and gasping for air, before plunging back in.

Life fell into a rhythm. With no washer and no way to get to the Laundromat, each day I'd take down two of the grimy curtains, wash them in the bathtub, and hang them to dry on the metal steps, while I washed those two windows and did all the other chores. I'd rest in the afternoon. To take my mind off things, I liked to watch the kids Jim had called brats outside playing and fighting amongst themselves. For supper, I made the dinners I'd learned from Mama, Hamburger Helper and spaghetti, followed by hot dogs, corn dogs, and hamburgers.

Slowly, Jim began to talk about his soon-to-be-ex-wife. "You're a catch. Let me tell you. My ex, Denise, wouldn't lift a hand to cook or clean. You can't imagine the hell she put me through." I smiled and snuggled closer to him.

That first week, I also picked up the phone to call Mama every afternoon. But each time, I sat it back in the cradle, afraid of what she'd say.

———

On Wednesday of the second week, I sat on our sheet-draped couch, in our shabby-but-clean house, with nothing to do but think about school. Now was the time I'd be in Mrs. Owen's class. They'd be having reading circle. Instead of sitting here, I could be perched on a tiny chair with my knees up to my chin working with Bobby Dempsey on his phonics. How could I not have thought about him until today? He must think I'd forgotten all about him.

Now, I would fail eleventh grade. My GPA would be ruined. There would be no college scholarship. I had nobody to blame but myself. As much as I loved Jim, I'd underestimated how much I wanted to teach.

I sat there, staring at the vinyl door, thinking I should never have let Jim carry me over its threshold. In the distance, I heard the school bus braking. The sound of kids whooping it up grew louder with every second. Standing, I fixed myself a Coke and moved outside to sit on the metal steps. The kids were out in the street again. I'd noticed they all seemed to stay in the same clothes they'd worn to school. Those clothes looked the same as my play clothes Mama made me change into after school. She had always worked hard to make sure I had decent things to wear.

A group of eight boys played kickball, some convoluted version of the game ending in roughhousing more often than not. Four girls with a long, braided utility rope played jump rope. They'd started with Cinderella Dressed in Yeller and had progressed to School. But it was hard for them to play with two always having to turn the rope. When one of them failed a grade, making it someone else's turn, they were constantly changing out players.

I stood, dusted off the seat of my pants, and pulled down the hem of Jim's Georgia Bulldogs T-shirt—I was running out of clean clothes, even though I'd worn everything I brought twice—and walked over to them. One of the girls, who looked about twelve years old and was poured into a pair of bleach-stained, jean cut-offs, cut her eyes at me, wiped sweat from her thick neck, and stopped spinning the rope. It died down into a wiggly snake on the unpaved, dusty road. "Are you a new kid?" They all gawked at me.

I looked at the uneven bangs someone had cut way too high on her forehead. "Nope. I'm out of school."

Their little leader put one hand on her hip. "Are you one of Jim's 'nieces'?" Her friends snickered and looked at the ground. But not her. She stared me down. "Maybe another 'kissin' cousin'?"

I think the only thing that might have given away my shock was the way my head rocked back, before I replied, "Nope. But I know how to twirl a rope. You want my help or not?"

I could see her sizing up the situation. She nodded once. "I'm Jeannie. This here's Myra, Brenda, and Tammy." She held out the rope's end while the other girls peeked up and waggled their fingers in shy waves.

Taking the rope, I laid down my rules. "I don't want to jump, so that will help all of you get less turns at the rope. But I'm not keeping up with what grade you've reached, and I'm not here to settle any arguments. You start bickering, like I've heard for a week now, and I'm going back inside. Got it?" Jeannie bit her lip to keep from smiling. I had the best afternoon I'd had in ages.

———

On Friday of the second week, Jim was off. After I cooked breakfast and washed the dishes, he pulled me back into bed. Lying there in a glow, I broached the subject. "We have to wash clothes some time, and I need to go get more of my things. Can you take me today?"

He yawned. "My keys are on the kitchen table. Knock yourself out, Baby. I deserve a rest. That new foreman's been busting my balls for ten days." He petted my shoulder and rolled to his side, with his back turned to me. "Gonna take a little nap. You go on ahead." Turning his head towards me one more time, he said, "You'll be home to fix dinner, right?"

I plucked at the covers. "Yes. What you want? We're about out of everything. I need money for groceries and the laundry." I was hoping he'd go with me.

"Take it from my wallet. Make whatever your little heart desires." His eyes narrowed. "As long it don't break the bank. That damn Denise had shit-for-brains and would come back with steak and shrimp. You got sense enough to manage." His face met mine. "Oh, watch how you brake, the pedal's about on the fucking floorboard." He flipped over and pulled his knees up, in the position he always slept in.

"Well then, I think I'll stop by the library for some books. I need something to read."

He grunted. "See you when you get back."

"Next week, I really have to get to the health department to get the pill." I pulled at my earlobe.

"Whatever you need, Honey. You run on now." Punching his pillow, he settled his head on it and pulled my pillow on top of his head.

———

When I'd been gone for three weeks, I called Mama. Jim had phoned, saying he was "stopping for a few beers with the boys." The last couple of times he'd called with that message, he hadn't come home until after eleven o'clock.

I waited until eight-thirty, when she was sure to be home and have already eaten.

"Mama?" The receiver shook in my hand.

"You finally decide to let me know you aren't dead and lying in a ditch?" Her voice was laced tight.

"I was scared to call. You …"

She interrupted me, "Not too scared to come clean out your room though. Did you think I wouldn't notice? Think you could slink in and out, like a rat?" From the sound of it, she'd had a few beers.

"I didn't want a fuss." I concentrated on rubbing my finger over the side seam of my blue jeans.

"She didn't want to make a fuss." Mama barked a high, loud laugh.

"I'm sorry, Mama." My right leg started shaking.

"I'm sorry, Mama. You don't have a clue what you've put me through." I heard her take a gulp of something. "Do you?" She roared the last question.

"But Mama ...."

"I've been through hell. You hear me? Twenty-one days of sheer, unadulterated hell!" I heard glass breaking.

"Are you okay?" God, she was right. I was so scared of facing her, I didn't think about her there, waiting for me to call.

"Well, aren't you the sweetest? Asking about me." I'd never heard her this mean, except with Daddy. "I've got one question for you." There was a pause on the line.

"Yes?" Tears welled in my eyes, and a tremendous wave built over my head.

"Are you coming home?" Her voice broke on the last word. That harsh tone disappeared. In all my life, I never heard my mama sound crestfallen.

My answer sat way back on my tongue, trying not to be discovered. "Mama ...."

"I see." The strength came back into her inflection. "You always have been a hard-headed mule." As she continued, she gained steam. "Don't reckon that'll change now. You'll be eighteen soon enough. If you want to run out on me, after all I've done for you ... I'm washing my hands of you." The phone went dead. Sitting there, my ear buzzing from the dial tone, the wave broke, and sorrow pounded me.

———

Two months later, standing in the kitchen of Jim's dilapidated trailer—that I once wished to see so badly and now wished never to see again—my arms were crossed over Jim's oversized, red Georgia Bulldog T-shirt I'd come to live in. I clenched my jaw and squinted my eyes.

Jim gave me his Old West smile and said, "Ah, come on. I told you we'd talk about it. I been busy all week."

He reached to run his fingernails down my upper arm. I took a step back. His expression changed. "All right. You want the truth. I ran into my old buddy, Bill, last week. The guy works down at McMillin's." I didn't acknowledge him, so he continued.

"Saw him at Wal-Mart. He had all five of his brats with him. All alone with this army of kids. I never saw that many rug rats in my life. He's got one squalling in the buggy, reaching out to me with booger-drenched, sausage-link fingers, and two boys rolling in the aisles, duking it out. A real slug fest." Jim chuckled to himself. I tapped my fingers on the kitchen counter.

"Then one of 'em—couldn't have been more than four years old—tears off running down the aisle with her hand stuck out, high-fiving the Kotex packages. They're falling like dominoes, all over the floor. Before I can get to her, she's ripped open a pack like it's her birthday and is tossing them in the air." He doubled over, howling with laughter.

"I reached down to take the brat, and she bit me! Started yelling, 'Help! Help me!' Two women, must've been six foot five, the both of them, grabbed my arms and wrestled me to the ground before Bill could stop 'em." Jim took a breath and started to carry on, but I hadn't changed my deep-freeze stare. Did he really think I believed two women in Wal-Mart knocked him to the floor? He kicked at the sofa.

"Shit, Mary Alice. I didn't want to talk about this because I don't want no damn baby. I thought and I thought about it. Can't do it. Never was in the picture, Sugar. Whatever you're thinking, count me out." He paced across our cramped living room.

"Don't matter what you do or say, you have to get rid of it. I don't want it. You hear me?" He dropped onto the bucket chair and lit a cigarette. "You hear what I'm saying?"

"Get rid of it. Our baby." My top lip trembled. "You can't mean that."

He tapped his temple with the hand clenching his Winston. "Get it in your head. I'm dead serious." A plume of smoke rose above him.

"We can't do that." Alice spoke as my pupils filled up black.

"People do it every day. It's why they invented it. We just have to figure out how to pay for it." A moan started in the base of my throat and emerged a full-blown wail.

Jim jumped up, clamped his hand over my mouth, and held me around the waist with his other arm, my back pressed against his chest. "Shut the fuck up! You want the neighbors to call the police?"

My stomach heaved with sobs that made no sound. Jim rocked me, and when I wound down a little, he murmured, "We'll have a baby in a couple of years. You're the one's always talking about going to college. You'll see. You wouldn't want our kid growing up in this trailer park. Huh?" He released his grip around my waist and moved his hands up to my shoulders, so he could direct me to one of the mismatched chairs at our scratched-up wooden table. "There, you sit here. I'll get you a nice cold Coke."

Small dots of light flickered in front of me, and Alice blared inside my head. *Don't you hear him? Sounds so logical with his bullshit. How the hell did you get us into this?*

When he placed the fizzing drink in front of me, I still sat in the same position, staring straight ahead, with my eyes unfocused. He plopped down across from me with a cup of steaming coffee.

His tone was reassuring. "This won't change anything between us. In a few years, you won't even remember we almost got tied down with something we weren't ready for."

Won't change anything? Tied down with some "thing." Are you listening to this?

"I'll take care of you. You gotta trust me. It's not even real yet." He was talking about our child.

Jim tilted his chair back and wobbled on the two back legs, a small movement towards me, then away, before he said it, "I love you."

When I heard him finally say it, I thought, oh my God, he doesn't love me. Alice screamed in my ear, *Finally!*

"Did you listen to what I just said?" He brought his chair forward solid. His eyes focused on a spot to the left of my right ear.

"Yes." I spoke in a low voice, and swallowed two, three, four times to hold back the tears. The words I'd wanted to hear, dreamed of hearing, and now they didn't mean anything.

He turned his eyes straight on my face and slapped his hand down on the kitchen table. "Don't that mean nothing to you?"

I looked past him at the picture of grapes and an apple next to the fridge. In my head, I counted each grape, one, two, three, four, five, six … all the way to fifteen. No good. Fifteen wasn't a good number. I'd have to re-count. I'd allow myself to count the apple, too. Sixteen was okay. It was eight doubled. I could live with sixteen.

"Mary Alice!" Jim leaned over the table and grabbed me by the shoulders. "What the hell are you doing? Off in your own private la-la land again?"

I drew small circles on my jean leg, kept my finger moving in small patterns so Jim wouldn't notice, but just enough to hold myself in the zone. "Jim, I love you. I love you so much." Alice sent chills through my body.

"Well, damned if anybody'd know it from the crazy way you act. I thought you'd be happy. Hell, I thought you'd do anything but spaz out on me." He let go of my shoulders and gave me a little push.

I reached out with my right hand and tried to grip his hand, keeping my left hand at the side of my leg. The circles became figure eights—down and back, down and back, down and back. I felt the pattern twist up and over my feet and head.

"Don't be mad. I just wasn't sure you loved me." I reached for him, but he wouldn't let me touch him. "If you do, you'll want our baby." I pushed my fingernails into the table's soft wood, bearing down to make small marks, releasing, and moving down in a line of half-moons. The tip of my middle fingernail tore loose, and I brought it to my mouth to chew, then slid it between my lower middle teeth, and flicked my tongue against its sharp point.

"You got yourself confused between two separate balls of wax. I want you. Not some noose around my neck. And you gotta stop calling the nugget in your belly a baby. Ain't no baby yet. Just a mistake we can make right before it's too late." His horrible words matched his face: snarled lips and wide nostrils. I could see the black hairs he needed to clip.

Alice was right. "You don't love me. No matter how hard I try." I slouched lower in my seat, with my right leg jiggling so fast my glass rattled on the table. I imagined our roly-poly baby curled up in my stomach. "You want me to kill our baby."

Jim huffed and put his cigarette out in the coffee mug. "You're a nut case. I don't know why I bother with you. Seriously, Mary Alice. You're fucked up." He shook his head.

"I'll take care of the baby. It won't change anything between us." Running my fingers through my hair, I envisioned a cradle by the side of our bed.

Before I knew what was happening, he pushed the table with both hands and rocketed to his feet, towering over me. His mug and my glass fell, rolled to the floor, and shattered. The spilled Coke dripped onto my lap. "I've had my say. It's me or your accident. You decide to go through with this, you stupid, fucking cunt, and you're out on your ass, on your own."

I collapsed. A crack sounded as my skull hit the table. "Lord, at the drama." He lifted my head by the hair and leaned in face-to-face, smelling of coffee and cigarettes. "You either need to go act on-stage or get some professional help."

Alice jumped in front of me and snarled back at him, "I'm keeping our baby." He let go. My head fell and did not bounce as he stormed from the trailer. I couldn't move, couldn't think. Couldn't even hear Alice anymore. I was down the rabbit hole.

I don't know how much time passed before I became aware of the world around me. When I touched my forehead, there was a smear of blood on my fingertips.

The only sounds in the quiet house were the shrill neighborhood kids and the faucet dripping, where Jim hadn't fixed it. I was all by myself, with a speck in my belly, wishing I hadn't cut myself off from Mama and Aunt Jean and Carolyn. The light in the room faded as night came on. I sat staring at the blurred outline of the picture of grapes, counting the fruit, in the dark, alone.

Twenty-Nine

A week later, Jim still hadn't come back. I couldn't sleep, couldn't eat. Rent was due. Most of the food in the house had been eaten. The electric, water, and phone bills arrived, threatening to cut off service. Jim hadn't paid them for over thirty days. I didn't know where he was, had no way to get in contact with him, and didn't have a dime to my name.

Finally, the phone rang. "You still hell bent on catastrophe?"

"Jim, where are you?" I stood there feeling as if a giant pair of scissors had cut me in two. "I've been worried sick."

"Oh, now you care about me." There was so much background noise, it was hard to make out what he was saying.

"Please. Come home." I couldn't help crying. He didn't answer.

All I heard was music playing, people talking, and a woman's voice, "Come on, Sugar!"

I held the receiver with both hands, as close to my mouth and ear as I could. "Jim, listen. Let's talk. We can work this out." I sunk to the couch. "I miss you. Can you hear me?"

His voice came on the line. "This was a mistake."

"No! Don't hang up."

When he spoke, I could tell it was to someone else. "Give me five fucking minutes!" Then he was back. "Mary Alice?"

"I'm here. I'm listening."

"Sweetheart, you're a good kid, but I'm no good for you ...."

"No, don't do this. I love you. You love me. I know you do." Wherever he was, Lynyrd Skynyrd sang *Gimme Three Steps*.

His voice rose above the din. "Go home to your mama."

"No, I want you." Sobs shook through my chest. "I want us. You said I made you happy."

"I can't. Baby, I tried. Ain't got it in me. I gotta go."

"But what about me? I'm here with nothing!" I screamed into the phone.

"I'm back with Denise. You knew I was married." In the seconds that followed, I heard his intake of breath and him hissing the word "shit." Then he came back on the line. "Call your mama. She'll help you. Dammit! I really am sorry." He hung up.

I sat the receiver down in slow motion and curled up on the couch. Outside, a car backfired, the couple next door shouted at each other, and Jeannie and the girls sang in unison, "Last night or the night before, my boyfriend took me to the candy store. He bought me ice cream, he bought me cake. He brought me home with a belly ache. Mama, Mama, I feel sick. Call for the doctor quick, quick, quick."

———

The next morning, there was a manila envelope on the table. Inside the envelope were five one-hundred-dollar bills and a note reading: None of this was to hurt you. The whole world don't turn around your pretty head. Had a good run in a poker game. This money's to take care of your problem.

What was I going to do? I was sitting with my head on my knees when the front door opened and a huge, burly man-of-a-man in a black Harley jacket, with full blonde beard and wild hair, filled my front door. "Who the hell are you? Where's Jim?"

"I'm his girlfriend." I managed to squeak it out.

"I was just with Jim and Denise last night and he didn't mention you at all, Sugar Lips." The guy slumped down into a chair. "You gotta go. I need my place."

"Can't you give me more time?" Inside, Alice started to shiver. As the guy shook his head, I thought of the cash Jim just gave me. "Look. I have rent money, and don't you see everything I've done to clean the place? I'll leave it this way if you just give me time. Please." The man shook his shaggy head. "Please. I'm pregnant. Give me time to find a place to live."

"Okay. Okay. I'll give you two weeks. But you owe me last month's rent and this month's rent." He stood up as if it were settled.

I didn't want to anger him, but I didn't have that much money. "But you're only giving me two weeks, so I only need to pay you for two weeks of this last month."

"Fine! But you better not be here when I come back in two weeks." He stomped down the steps and roared away on his bike.

What was I going to do?

—

Finally, I decided I needed to get help. I rooted around the kitchen until I found a dime. Then I trudged to the corner phone booth. Who to call? Mama? Aunt Jean? Aunt Jean? Mama? I chose Aunt Jean.

"Mary Alice!" Loud and urgent. "Mary Alice! Where have you been? I been sick to death over you."

"I'm okay, Aunt Jean. I'm fine. But I need your help."

"Have you called your mama?" Her tone was brisk.

"Not yet. That's what I need your help with." I took a sip of Sprite. "I need a place to live."

"I'm sure your mama will be happy to take you back. She'll be thrilled."

"But she said she was washing her hands of me. She's not going to let me come back." Aunt Jean just didn't understand. "It's important. Very important."

"Yes, it's important that a teenage girl live with her mother."

"Aunt Jean?" I stalled.

"Yes?"

"I'm pregnant."

"I was afraid of that." Then, dead silence.

The moments spread out in the quiet. I pulled at my hair. "Well, say something!"

"I'll set up dinner with the three of us." I sighed with huge relief, and she continued, "But you have to get us there."

"I don't have a car."

"Let me see what I can do."

—

The next morning, a knock came on my door. I opened it to find a little old lady with Church of God hair. "Mary Alice?"

"That's me."

"I'm Mrs. Stover, from your Aunt Jean's church."

"Oh, yes, I remember you, Mrs. Stover. I sang in Mr. Stover's children's choir when I was little." They were both such nice people. "Come in. Come in." I ushered her to my sheet-covered couch.

"Your Aunt Jean tells me you need a vehicle to get back and forth from work. Reverend Stover and I have a used car we want to give you. We've provided it for missionaries in the past. No reason you can't have it now."

I stared at her with my mouth dropped. "Wh-what?"

She reached across and dropped keys into my hands. "There you go, Sweetheart. You take good care of that baby."

"Aunt Jean told you!" The words exploded before I could think.

"I won't say a word to anyone about your pregnancy. I promise you. I realize your mother doesn't know yet." With that, she rose, left, and climbed into another car driven by Reverend Stover. I waved bye to them and came out to look at my new car.

———

One week later, I pulled up in front of Aunt Jean's, as nervous as a locust beating its wings into a dust storm. Two days ago, I'd called her and spent an hour apologizing again for not contacting her all summer, breaking the news about the baby, and begging her to set up a meeting for us to go tell Mama. I gave her the good news about the job I got at Penney's but didn't tell her Jim had left me.

When I pulled into her drive, she was ready and waiting on the glider on the front porch. Before I stopped the car, she got up, so I stayed behind the wheel.

We were running late. I could barely breathe, just thinking of facing Mama. And it was no help this car didn't have air conditioning. In the late August heat, I was burning up, even with all the windows rolled down. The back of my shirt stuck to the vinyl seats.

Aunt Jean opened the door to the ten-year-old red Datsun Mrs. Stover had given me. "Lord have mercy. You don't think I'm crawling into that death trap." Her long neck bent down like a giraffe's as she peered in with a look of disgust at the interior: peeling headliner, missing floorboard mats, and the rusty hand-crank for a sunroof someone had cut out and installed on their own.

"Aunt Jean, as long as I'm working at Penney's, this wreck is all I can afford. I'm lucky to have it. I'm so grateful to have it. Come on, now. We've got to be at Mama's by seven o'clock." I shouldn't have been short with her, but I was tired and crabby from standing all day, so sick to my stomach I had been afraid I'd toss up in the garbage can under the layaway counter.

Aunt Jean drew herself up to a full six feet two inches, counting her usual tower of hair. She looked towards her dingy white frame house, towards the Bledsoe's next door, and I saw her chest rise and fall with a sigh she made sure I could map out to a count of eight. Her face appeared again. In the evening light, the sparse fuzz of whiskers over her top lip was illuminated.

"Don't just sit there. If I'm getting in, you gotta help me." Jarring from my reverie, I saw she'd jammed her skinny butt into the car, but her tall beehive had caught in the seat belt, and her long bird legs were still outside.

I jumped out, sprinted around the car, and reached to take her big-ass purse and a Tupperware cake saver from her arms. "Oh, Aunt Jean, I should've been over here helping you, but I was off on a fancy." Lately, I was more prone to daydreaming than ever.

"Humph." Aunt Jean shoved the cake towards me and lobbed the purse around sideways. It accidentally smacked me in the face.

I grabbed her stuff, while she lifted first one leg and then the other into the car's front seat. She had tried to fasten the seat belt three times before I could set all the stuff down on the gravel drive and come over to buckle her in.

Her eyes met mine. I could see the little whiskers at the corners of her mouth trembling just a tad, and I knew we were gonna have a good evening.

"Well, Miss Priss, if you're taking my life in your hands, then let's get on with it. Hand me my cake before the army ants march off with it. And be careful with my purse. I got your Mama's tonic in there."

"Is that what nearly cracked my head wide open?" I rubbed my cheek.

"Now don't go smarting off to your old Aunt Jean. We have a heap of talking to do before we reach your mama's. We gotta figure out our strategy."

As I put the cake in her lap, Aunt Jean tucked a stray strand of my brown hair behind my ear and whispered, "We can do this. You just never mind that belly that's shouting 'Baby' for all the world to see. I'll be there with you, and if your mama opens her mouth too wide, I'll fill it up with the old stories nobody cares to have aired out in the living room." Aunt Jean grabbed my hand and squeezed when I set her purse on the console between the two seats. "You hear me?"

I nodded, pushed my knuckles at the corners of my eyes, and wiped smudges of Maybelline off onto the faded work pants Jim had left at the trailer. Other than the five maternity dresses I'd bought at the thrift store to wear to work, I had nothing else that fit. I was afraid Mama would recognize those dresses for what they were, so I'd fastened his pants across my stomach with a looped rubber band and worn his huge Georgia Bulldogs' T-shirt.

Aunt Jean took several bobby pins out of her dome of hair and held them between her teeth while she worked to twist her hairdo back into place.

Those hair pins brought a memory to me, as fresh as it was at age seven, standing in Aunt Jean's kitchen. In the midst of sewing me a blue and green plaid dress, she had a row of straight pins clenched in her teeth looking like vibrating antenna, as if she'd popped insects into her mouth.

Thinking about it now, I remembered everything she'd done for me and all the times I'd told her what I was going to do for her "when I grew up." It looked as if I'd never be able to do anything to make up for all she'd done for me.

Driving down Maple Street, immersed in memory, I hadn't been listening to her. As I tuned back into the present, I realized she was drilling me with questions. "What are you planning to do? When your stomach gets so big you can't see your own shoes? How do you think you can hold a job standing on your feet all day? How did you get yourself into this mess to start with? When are you getting married so that baby has a last name?"

I pulled my shoulders in toward the steering wheel. "Aunt Jean, I got something I have to tell you." I took a deep breath. "Jim isn't going to marry me." I glanced at her.

"Why don't you pull over here in the Piggly Wiggly parking lot so we can talk?" Aunt Jean's voice came out smooth and steady.

My right cheek jerked twice. "Okay." I pulled in, parked, and faced her.

"Well?" She raised her eyebrows.

"I haven't known how to tell you." My voice trailed off. I dropped my head and told her in a low voice. "Jim's married and he's gone back to live with his wife. He gave me some money I used to pay the bills, but they were backed up to start with, and I've only got to the end of next week before the rent's due again. I can't afford the place by myself. I have to move out now." The truth flowed out in a soft rush.

Aunt Jean waited for me to wipe my eyes on my shirtsleeve before she spoke. "I wondered when you were gonna tell me."

"You knew?" My leg jerked and thwacked against the steering wheel.

"You know your mother tells me everything, and she wouldn't wait for the Lord's second coming to spread bad news. And you knew how I'd feel about this. That's why you've been avoiding me for months. I been teaching you the Bible since before you could walk into the church on your own two feet." Her lips were pressed so tight they'd disappeared.

"Yes, you have." My entire face flamed red.

"When we choose to disobey God's word, there's payment due, Mary Alice. What were you thinking, running around with a married man? You've been brought up better."

I squirmed in my seat, and a tear oozed from the corner of my eye. Aunt Jean reached over and brushed it away. "No, I'm not petting on you and condoning how you've been living. Sit yourself up straight and stop feeling sorry for yourself." Her face was no-nonsense. "What's done is done. It's between God and you and this baby. I reckon you have enough to worry about without hearing me tell you what you already know."

She gave my hand a brisk double pat that stung. "We're going to talk more about you running around with that hoodlum later. I've been a-praying over it, but that's an egg's not ready to crack yet. For now, we have to talk about tonight." She rummaged in her pocketbook, pulled out a pack of Wrigley's gum and popped a piece in her mouth. She chewed and talked. "Here's what we're gonna do. I'll handle your mother. You stick by my side. Don't leave yourself alone with her for more than a few minutes. She's mad as a hen. Bonnie King over at First National Bank was the one to tell her you were seeing that boy and now Bonnie was the one to tell her Jimmy moved back in with Denise." Clucking her tongue at me, she tucked her pack of gum back into her purse. "You should've told her yourself, before half the town knew. Makes her feel stupid. One thing your mama don't like is looking foolish. No, sirree."

Aunt Jean leaned in closer, and her spearmint scent surrounded me. "But she's had time now to cool her cornbread, and you have to ask your mama for help."

I pulled my bottom lip in and bit so hard it brought the tang of blood. "If I can't take care of this myself, Mama will never let me live it down, and you know it."

"Mary Alice, you're like a cat up in a tree, thinking it won't let the fireman touch it. Nobody climbed up there but you, and that's where you're gonna stay, unless you get some help." She took an embroidered cloth handkerchief from her bag and wiped at her top lip, beaded in sweat. "You know I'd do anything for you. But I'm not in any shape to help you with a little baby."

I shook my head and opened my mouth to talk, but she rushed in. "That's my baby sister, and I know her better'n you. She's your mother, and she loves you. Pretty soon you'll understand a mother's love. She's mad now. We'll explain to her that hounding you with what you've done wrong won't help this state of affairs." Aunt Jean wagged her finger at me. "Though I expect you'll mull this over long and hard.

It's up to you to live a righteous life from now on. This baby is all that matters. Be a good mother. That's how you're going to make up for your sins. All three of us will be a lot better off if we realize you've got yourself a baby, and there's no going back."

Her words daunted me. Until I heard them, I hadn't felt the full weight of my circumstances.

"You need your mama's help. Not for you, mind you, but for that baby you're bringing into the world." She swiped at her sweat-soaked neck again. It was sweltering in here. Liquid pooled between my breasts and down my back.

"My mama's never going to forgive me. She's washed her hands of me. She said so. And she'll never help me. Not in a million years." I beat my fist on the steering wheel so hard it beeped, and we both jumped, then burst out laughing.

"A million years pass mighty quick when a baby comes out crying and needing a warm bottle and dry diapers." Aunt Jean chuckled and wiped her eyes with her nasty handkerchief. "A million years pass in a blink of the good Lord's eyes. You do what I tell you and watch your mama real close. See if she don't start blinking, long before you would have thought possible."

The purple and blue scarf she wore had slipped up from her dress's neckline. I tucked it back in place and leaned over to kiss the side of her damp cheek. While I couldn't imagine my mama backing down for anything, I could envision loving my baby and my baby loving me the way I'd always loved my Aunt Jean.

Thirty

I never felt as strange as I did driving up to my own house that day. I'd been gone almost four months. Did I knock at the door? Or use my key?

Mama made my decision for me by opening the front door and standing there, waiting for us to come in. My breath started coming short and fast.

"You're going to be fine. Come help me out of this sardine can." Aunt Jean's voice was a lifeline. I opened the door for her and carried the cake and her purse, while she led the way.

"Something smells awful good in here." Aunt Jean wrapped her arms around Mama. "This is quite a treat—the three of us together. I made a carrot cake."

Mama refused to catch my eye as she answered Aunt Jean. "Well, you shouldn't have. I know how much work those are, all that grating and mixing." Mama was hugging Aunt Jean longer than usual. "But I'm not too sorry. You know it's my favorite." She leaned back, holding Aunt Jean away from her to ask, "Cream cheese frosting?"

"I don't rightly believe it's a true carrot cake without it. Now, I realize most people don't put pineapple in their batter, but that's why mine's so moist." They chatted away as if everything were normal. "Of course, that little secret is between the three of us." Aunt Jean reached for me and pulled me into the circle.

"Hey, Mama." My mind was a total blank on what to say. I held the cake container close to cover up my "bump."

She looked me up and down. "I see you're still dressing in men's rags." She gave a deep sigh. "I was hoping this run at being an adult would include some women's clothing."

"I'm gone for months and that's all you care about?" I narrowed my eyes at her.

Aunt Jean jumped in quickly, "I can see the two of you are overjoyed, after missing each other for so long. Let's carry on this reunion inside, where I can sit down."

The house was exactly as it was the day I left. I don't know what I expected, but it seemed like years had passed since then. After living in Jim's one-bedroom mobile home for over four months, our little house seemed huge. More than that, I was home. Jim's trailer always seemed like a landing place, on my way to somewhere else.

I put the cake on our kitchen counter and looked down. Mama rustled around in the kitchen. Would she notice my bump? Maybe this big shirt was doing its job.

Seated at the table, Aunt Jean held up her hand. "I'm going to ask the two of you for a favor."

Both of us turned to her. "I would like us to have a nice dinner, without any gnawing at each other." She looked from me to Mama. "Then, after we eat, we'll go into the den and have a nice, long talk. How's that sound?"

We both nodded. "Is there anything I can do to help?" I asked Mama.

"Nope. It's all ready. Come fix your plate." She waved her apron at Aunt Jean. "Jean, you stay put. I've got yours."

Compared to this spread of food, my meals for the last couple of months had been a sorry excuse. I always fixed whatever was cheap and quick: hot dogs with macaroni and cheese from a box, hamburgers with canned pork and beans, and grilled cheese with Campbell's tomato soup.

Tonight, Mama had cooked chicken and dumplings, fresh green beans, her homemade mac 'n cheese, sliced carrots in a buttery sauce, and fresh-baked buttermilk biscuits. She didn't cook often, but when she did, it was a family feast.

Based on how nervous I was at facing Mama, I thought I wouldn't eat a bite, but I wolfed her food down. "I see you've missed your Mama's cooking." Aunt Jean grinned at me.

I answered with a mouth full. "You can say that again. My dinners taste like sawdust compared to this." All three of us laughed. "Mama, I need to pay attention to how you fix everything."

She drew her shoulders back and smiled. "It's nothing difficult. Just takes some practice." Taking a swig of sweet tea, she continued, "It's a shame you missed the sweet corn season this summer. My creamed corn's always been your favorite."

I opened my mouth to ask why she was hell bent on rubbing my nose in it, but Aunt Jean must have caught my expression and spoke up first. "You know, I remember Mama teaching us how to make dumplings, but I never got the knack of it. You have the touch."

As I listened to them, I closed my eyes to keep tears from spilling over. Every inch of me had missed them like blue blazes.

—

After dinner, Aunt Jean stretched out on the couch while Mama and I cleaned the kitchen. We didn't say much, but our hands worked in unison from so many years of this routine. I'd volunteered to load the dishwasher, which would keep my bump out of sight. She emptied the pots and split up the leftovers into containers. "You want to take some of this food back to …" She paused. "… your house?"

"I'd love some. Thank you." I avoided her eye and started wiping down the counters and table, which kept my back to her. An awkward silence fell. "So, how's work?"

She continued dividing the meal into foil packets. "Since when did you ever care about my work?"

I sighed. "Well, then how's the weather?"

Cutting her eyes towards me, she took a dish towel and flicked it at me. "Partly cloudy with a chance of thunderstorms."

I washed the dish cloth out and hung it on the sink. "Sounds like we should plan for stormy weather." We both laughed.

"Maybe. Or maybe it will blow over." She wiped off the wet table, re-folded the towel, and slid it back onto its rod.

I crossed behind her on the way to the bathroom. We were so close we almost touched.

When I came back into the den, Mama and Aunt Jean sat on the couch, waiting for me. My stomach churned. Maybe I shouldn't have eaten so much after all. I perched on the edge of the recliner, waiting.

Aunt Jean spoke up first. "Marva, Mary Alice would like to talk to you."

Mama stared at me. "I'm right here, where I've been the whole time."

There was a knot in my throat as big as a plum. Aunt Jean nodded at me.

"Mama, I'm sorry for the way I left." I wished she didn't look so formidable, with her set jaw and her piercing blue eyes. "I know you've heard. Jim's gone back to his wife."

"You want to come back here?" She shook her head. "You spent your entire life running away from me. I never thought you'd come running to me." She sounded cold-hearted.

Aunt Jean waved her hand, that meant, "Go on."

"Yes. I want to come home." I jumped in surprise at how loudly I said it.

"Of course you can come home. What kind of mother do you think I am?" She held up one finger. "But ... only under the condition you don't see that boy. And you realize this is my house and my rules." Her shoulders were set straight back.

It took me a few seconds to realize she'd agreed so quickly. But when I did, I answered fast. "I understand. I won't see him." That was the easy part. "But I need to tell you something." Blood drummed in my ears. My mouth stuck closed.

"Well?"

I swallowed hard and ran my tongue around my teeth. I felt faint. "I'm going to have a baby."

I watched Mama's face pale by two shades. She whipped her head at Aunt Jean. "You knew this!"

Aunt Jean sat with her hands resting calmly in her lap. "It was for Mary Alice to tell you herself."

She turned her attention to me. I wanted to sink into the floor. "How could you do this to me?"

"I didn't mean to." I felt tears crawling in dry sockets.

"You hoed the row straight to his bed. Don't tell me you didn't mean to. You're not eight-years-old and just broke my Thanksgiving turkey platter. This won't mend with Super Glue." She pinched the bridge of her nose and squeezed her eyes shut.

"I wish I could change it, but I can't, Mama. I know I've done wrong, but what's done is done." Aunt Jean had advised me right. This was the way of thinking my mama understood.

Mama glared at the bump in my mid-section. "How did I miss it when you walked in the door? But you look like you've lost so much weight everywhere else, I thought it was messy clothes and junk food. I'm gonna take a wild guess the bastard's not willing to take responsibility for supporting it. Am I right?"

I chewed on my thumbnail, the last one not gnawed to the quick.

"I thought as much. I've had to be your mama and your daddy. Trust me, it's no cake walk." She paused. "Well then, I'll be the one to tell you this doesn't have to be a done deal. You've got options." Tightening her eyes into slits, she addressed Aunt Jean. "Jean, I'd appreciate it if you'd keep your mouth shut during this part of the conversation. If you don't like what you're hearing, feel free to leave the room any time."

Aunt Jean lifted her chin. "You don't worry about me. I'll be sitting here praying for God's will." She hesitated. "And I'd appreciate it if you keep your mouth shut."

In all my days, I'd never heard those two talk ugly to each other.

Mama drew her hands into fists. "I will hope it doesn't come to that. But, by God, I will do what I see fit for my daughter." Aunt Jean slipped her shoes on but remained sitting. Both of them turned their spotlight eyes on me. Aunt Jean closed her eyes and moved her lips in silent prayer.

"Like I was saying, you have ways out of this. Two obvious solutions. The first is the simplest. You have a planned miscarriage."

For a split second, I didn't know what she was talking about. When I finally understood, I clenched my fists and said, "An abortion! You're just like Jim!"

"Then the bastard and me have one thing in common."

Aunt Jean's lips moved faster, and the faintest noise reached me—those nonsense sounds she made, like the people at her church speaking in tongues.

Keeping a bead on me, Mama snapped at Aunt Jean. "Jean, cut the crap." The noises slowed, then stopped, but Aunt Jean's mouth still moved and an occasional, barely audible "sss" sound emerged. Mama turned to me. "It's a choice you have to consider. It would solve everything."

"I told him, and now I'm telling you. No."

She took a deep breath. "Why in the world wouldn't you at least think about it?"

"You can mark that one off your list because I'm over the three-month mark anyway ... probably four."

"Good God!" Dismay replaced the anger in Mama's voice. "Are you sure? For the love of Pete, why didn't you come to me sooner?"

"Anyway, I did consider it. No. I'm keeping my baby."

She tried a different tactic. "All right, one down." She glanced at Aunt Jean. "There's lots of good people can't have children of their own. They'd adopt your baby." Aunt Jean's eyes flew open, and her lips tightened into a straight line.

Mama came over to me, kneeled, and took my hands in hers. "You don't have to ruin your life. You could go live with your cousin Sally in Thomasville until the baby's born. Nobody'd ever have to know. We'd find a real good home with a couple who'd give it everything you're too young to provide."

She was so close I smelled her White Shoulders. I'd never seriously thought of adoption. Up until last week, I expected Jim to come back. Without him, I had no idea how I'd manage.

When I didn't respond, she stood and went back to the couch. "Who do you think's gonna raise that child?" she said, coming from another direction now. "You? Without even a high school diploma? If you're counting on me to wipe any more dirty butts, you have another think coming. I've done my share. Me all alone, barely having two cents to rub together and hoping they learned how to multiply." She took a mouthful of air and lit in again.

"You were born stubborn. Put the brakes on and refused to come out. Had to yank you out with forceps." I'd heard this all before, but now it took on new meaning. I imagined my baby with its feet and hands pressed up against the womb, refusing to move. At first, the initial idea of delivery scared me, but the image quickly seemed so funny I gave a nervous snicker.

Mama pressed her lips together and shook her head. "Must be something funny about this situation I'm not seeing."

My smile faltered. "You could be more sympathetic. It's a poor innocent baby."

Mama glowered at me. "I do believe that's exactly the point."

"Can't you give me two minutes to weigh out what you're saying?" I held my head in my hands.

The room grew blissfully quiet while I studied the tiny hole in the knee of Jim's work pants. What kind of mother would I be, anyway? I raised my eyes. "I'll think about it."

Aunt Jean broke in. "You don't want to do that."

"Jean ..." Mama sounded threatening.

"You had your say." Aunt Jean said to Mama. "Now I'll have mine, before she makes the worst decision of her life."

"I'm warning you, Jean. Stay out of this. You're biased. It makes you the last person should be talking to her."

"I'm just the person she needs to hear from." Aunt Jean said, lowering her voice. "God blessed you with this child. You give it away and won't a day go by you don't regret it. For the rest of your life, you'll wonder where she is, what she's doing, if she's really been taken care of."

"Stop it, Jean!" Mama shouted.

Aunt Jean barreled on, "Think long and hard before you act out of fear, instead of love. God will find a way to provide for you and this child."

Mama sprang to her feet. The overhead light cast her shadow over Aunt Jean. "Mary Alice is not you! You're talking about your life, not hers. It doesn't have to be like it was for you. Some people place their child in capable hands and live the rest of their lives realizing they made the right choice for the baby. I've always admired what you did."

Like it was for you. What you did. Every confusing thing they'd said during the last half hour began to fall in place. But it couldn't be. That was impossible.

Mama shifted her sights to me. "Putting your baby up for adoption would be the ultimate act of unselfishness on your part. Don't you see that?"

Aunt Jean turned to me. "If that's how your Mama wants it, then that's how it will be. Even if it means airing dirty laundry, I will not stand idly by and watch you make the same mistake I did." Every fourth word or so, she paused briefly to draw in uneven breaths.

"What are you saying?" Chills ran between my shoulder blades.

A tear trickled down Aunt Jean's cheek, her face tormented.

If I'd been given twenty years to prepare, I wouldn't have been ready for Aunt Jean's next words. "When I was sixteen years old, I found myself in the family way."

Keeping her eyes averted, she went on. "The boy had gone off to war. Three weeks after I began to suspect I had a problem; his family got the telegram. He'd been killed."

I swallowed hard and blinked fast, to keep from crying. Mama and I moved at the same time to go sit on either side of her.

She gripped our hands with her bony fingers and drew both onto her lap. "I didn't have a choice. Mama sent me to the Church of God Home for Unwed Mothers in Cleveland, Tennessee, to have the baby." She looked directly into my eyes and squeezed my hand. "It was a girl. After the doctor left, the delivery nurse took pity on me and let me hold her before they took her away. From the way her tiny fist clamped onto my finger and how she curled into my arms, I could tell she knew me, recognized I was her mama." She paused and drew in a ragged breath. "Right after, I went to work near there, at the Church of God Orphanage. They let me live there and help all those poor, abandoned children. I didn't come back home for years, until I got TB and had to enter Battey State, here in Rome. I've spent the rest of my life in the church, trying to make up for what I did. But I never will."

I laid my chin on her shoulder. "I'm so sorry."

"None as sorry as me, dear girl." Releasing my hand, she rested her head on top of mine. "None as sorry as me."

Part IV

So the Eyes of God
Know Where to Turn

Thirty-One

Moving back to Mama's was easier than I thought it would be. In my old bedroom, I packed up all my stuffed animals and took the posters down off my walls. Mama treated me even better than usual. The hard part was doing without Jim. I couldn't help thinking if only I could talk to him in person, he'd change his mind and come back. We'd be the family I always dreamed of. My child would have a daddy.

Sitting together after dinner, watching *Happy Days* on TV, I knew Mama wouldn't want to hear it, but I had to talk to her about it.

"Mama, I know you want me to have the baby adopted, but what if Jim comes around?" As soon as I saw the scorn on her face, I wished I hadn't said anything, but I forged on. "I know you don't want me seeing him, but he is the father. Wouldn't it be better for the baby if we were all together? If he got divorced and married me, you'd accept him then, wouldn't you?"

"Your head's in the clouds, along with your ass," Mama answered in disgust. "No man in that family ever did right by their women."

I took my feet off the coffee table. "But that's not true. His granddaddy, Raymond, was madly in love with the woman from Italy he married."

"What in God's name are you talking about? Raymond Ledbetter never married anyone from Italy." Mama's tone was incredulous. "Where'd you hear that nonsense?"

"Jim told me."

"Jim's lying or his brain's addled. Raymond Ledbetter married Nell Goodwin from Cartersville. Ran off with a waitress and left her with two babies. Nell worked with my mother at the textile mill and cleaned other people's houses on the weekend, just to make ends meet."

A weird feeling in my ears and head started pounding away. "Why are you saying that? It's not true. He married Maria. She died. He was wild with grief and drove his car into the gorge. Left Jim's daddy to be raised by his mother."

"Look, I don't know what line of bullshit that boy's been filling your head with, but his granddaddy, Raymond Ledbetter, lives up in Summerville. He never married any Italian, and he sure ain't dead … though there's quite a few folks who'd like your story better, including Jim's daddy. Raymond is one ornery bastard who never gave a shit for his own son."

I sank back in the recliner and stared at the overhead light. Suddenly, a ringing in my ears joined forces with my rolling stomach. Leaping up, I barely made it to the bathroom before tossing up my dinner.

Mama came into the bathroom, wet a washcloth, and held it to my forehead, then the back of my neck. "That boy's played you for a fool. He comes near this house, and I'll fill him with buckshot."

"Stoppit." I turned on the faucet and splashed my face with water. "There must be some kind of mix-up."

"Oh, there's been a mix-up, all right. And if I could get my hands around his lying throat, I'd choke the ever-loving life out of him." Mama pinched the bridge of her nose. The look she gave me was worn to the bone. "I know you're confused. I know it's not really your fault. You're too young for your own good. But you need to realize you've been taken advantage of. Then maybe you'll stop this foolish nonsense, thinking that scoundrel will come through for you and that speck in your belly." She wrapped her arms around me. "I'll help you find a good family."

I pushed her away and charged out of the bathroom. In my bedroom, I crawled under the covers and spent the rest of the night wrapped around myself, figuring out just what I could tell Jim to make him change his mind.

———

It had been a month since Jim left me. From watching Mama and Daddy, I'd learned that over time, the fire went out of an argument. I was betting Jim was thinking about me. By now, he had to be sick of

Denise, given the way he'd talked about her. We would work things out for the baby.

I was not going to end up living a life of regret, wishing I'd kept my baby, like Aunt Jean. If Jim and I could only talk, he'd see we all belong together. I had to do it for our baby, not for me. I had to try one more time.

When the plant whistle blew, I got out of my car and waited for Jim.

He saw me, turned to the two men walking out the gate beside him and said something. The laugh they gave made me sick at heart.

"What do you want?" He said it loud enough for the other guys to hear. They snickered again. I couldn't help the tears streaming down my face.

He grabbed my arm. "Get in the damn car and stop making a scene." Steering me by the elbow, he opened my driver's door and guided me into the seat. Then he came around to the passenger's side and got in. "Let's get this over with fast. Then I better not ever see your ass here again. I have to work with these men."

I stared at his filthy shirt and unshaven face. "What kind of person leaves the person they love, and their baby?"

He rolled down his window and lit a match on the sole of his steel-toed boot. After holding it to his cigarette, he flicked it out the open window. "You're a big girl." He glanced at my stomach. "Getting bigger every day, I see."

My throat felt full, but I didn't cry. I needed to stay focused on why I was there. "We have to talk about the baby." Just saying it, I felt stronger. "I know you. You don't want to be like our daddies. You have to live up to your responsibility."

Jim moved so fast towards me I raised my arms to protect myself, jerking backwards with such force I hit my head on the car door window.

"Jesus Christ! I ain't gonna smack you, though I ought to beat the living shit out of you."

Now I was scared. I was afraid to drop my guard.

Snatching my arms, he pinned them by my sides. "You listen to me and listen good. I said I'd stay if you got rid of it. I told you I didn't want it. I gave you the money to take care of things. But no, you had to wait around too late for that." The look on his face wasn't as much anger as it was hurt. "You ever think how I'd feel when you chose it over me? And now you've ruined our chances, you think I'm going to feel sorry for you?" I followed his gaze out the window, at the paper mill chimneys belching white smoke. I laid my hand against his cheek. He closed his eyes, and we sat that way for a few seconds.

But when he opened his eyes, his mean glint was back. "Yep. That's what you took away from me." He took my wrist and shoved my hand away. "I don't aim to be there when you pop out a screaming brat. Hell, I don't even know it's mine. You could have spread your legs for anyone. Sure did for me."

"How can you say that? I've never been with anyone else, and you know it."

"I don't know any such thing. You didn't even bleed the first time I had you." He drummed his fingers on the dashboard. Mill workers continued to surge out of the plant and through the parking lot. As they came by, each lit a cigarette or pulled a wad of tobacco from a pouch and pinched it in their cheeks, even the women.

"Please, Jim, for God's sake. I love you." I took his hand. He let me hold it. "I never wanted anybody but you." He shifted his gaze to me and brought his fingertips to my face. "I don't care what you've done before. I know you felt something for me. Together, we were both better off. We can make each other happy again." I thought I saw a flicker in his eyes before he turned his head away from me and let go of my hand.

When he turned back, he'd set his eyes hard again and sneered but didn't say a word. "Why don't you want me anymore?" It came out sounding so pathetic I despised myself.

"You're a noose around my neck, that's why." He held his hand to his Adam's apple. He didn't mean it. I know he didn't. But he sounded so much like Daddy I dropped my head to the steering wheel.

"Honey, I'm sick to death of your theatrics. You can win an Oscar without me, you hear?" He opened the door, got out, and slammed it. "Stay away from me. It's over."

I lifted my head. The face in the window didn't match his words. He was wiping at his eyes with the sleeve of his shirt. His top lip quivered. He made a movement, as if he were going to open the door again. Instead, he punched it. There was no impact to the car, just pain on his face.

Still, he left me there, without another word, sitting in the parking lot, crying. He was never going to change his mind.

—

When Mama pulled into the carport that night, I lay in my bed, feeling like I'd had all the stuffing knocked out of me. The customary sounds of her coming home drifted to my room, including the fridge opening. Most nights, the first thing she did was either pour a huge glass of iced tea or pop open a beer. I heard the crack of the ice tray handle and the clatter of cubes hitting the metal bowl we kept in the freezer.

In a few minutes, I heard her coming down the hall. She gave me her "what's up."

"I know I told you I wouldn't, but I went to see Jim. I thought maybe he'd change his mind." The ice in her glass clinked.

"I knew you would." The expression on her face didn't alter one bit.

"You did?" My mama constantly amazed me.

"Do any good?" She sipped her tea.

I shook my head.

"Didn't figure it would." Taking a huge gulp, she set her glass down on my nightstand and plopped onto the foot of my bed. "Let's talk."

"Okay." I knew what was coming.

"I've asked around a little. Real privately. An agency in Atlanta is set up for girls in situations just like yours. They handle everything. Even have a place for you to live, though I think you might like your cousin's better." As she talked, I thought about how she had never gotten involved in my schooling. Mama took care of me, but she didn't do things like Carolyn's mother did … PTA, school conferences, helping find the right college … and her lack of interest always hurt my feelings, but I also believed she meant it as a compliment. It was her way of saying she trusted me to handle my business. So, it meant a lot to me that she was trying to help now when I needed her help the most.

Yet, it made breaking the news to her that much harder. I held up my hand. Her voice dropped away. "Mama, I've decided to keep the baby." She cupped her hand over her top lip. "Here's why. I'm not going to end up like Aunt Jean."

The words poured out of her. "Jean thinks you keeping your baby will somehow make up for her decision. Over thirty years, I've watched that damn church cover her from head to foot in guilt. I swore I'd never end up that way. But, Mary Alice, you've got a good head on your shoulders … at least you did until you hooked up with that slimeball. And you don't have a cross nailed around your neck. God gave you brains so you could weigh things out." She reached over and took my hand. "You're feeling sorry for yourself. Think about the baby."

"I know what you're saying." What I wanted had nothing to do with the church. That was Aunt Jean's comfort, not mine. But I wasn't going to live my life regretting what I'd done and wondering where my baby was every day. The way I saw it, it was Aunt Jean's regrets that tied her to the church, not the other way around. "I know myself, Mama. If I gave this baby away, I'd never get over it."

"You can't look at it that way! You'd be giving the baby a good home, not 'giving it away.'"

I raised my eyes to the ceiling and covered my face. My cool hands felt good on my hot skin. Mama intended well, but she didn't know how I felt inside, how the feel of Daddy's hands on me would come out of nowhere sometimes, how it always seemed like everybody could "see" that stain on me, regardless of how hard I tried to hide. Every good grade I ever got meant nothing. I knew it was simply a matter of time before people figured out how worthless I really was. This baby was my chance to prove to myself I was good for something. I would give my baby all the love I never had, and all that love would fill up the rabbit hole inside me. I'd make up for being "me" by being the best mother my baby could ever have.

But I couldn't tell Mama that, so I explained it the best I could.

"I know I'm too young. I know you're trying to help me. But my child belongs with me. I will provide the best home. I'm keeping the baby, not to be selfish or stubborn or to go against you, Mama. I'm doing it because I am the best mother for my baby."

Mama sighed. "Well, I reckon I've seen that headstrong expression on your face enough times to recognize your mind's made up."

I bit my bottom lip and nodded.

"I can't say I'm happy with your decision. And I have to hope you might come to your senses. But you're my daughter, and I love you. We'll make it work, somehow." She leaned down and kissed me on the forehead.

—

Later that night, I awoke curled face down on my bed, with my knees up under me … the way I imagined my baby. Mama was calling for me and knocking on my door, "Mary Alice. You okay?"

"I'm fine, Mama. Just a bad dream." No different than most nights. When I finally got to sleep, I'd wake with a start and an overwhelming sense of panic.

"Are you sure?" Mama entered, clutching her faded green housecoat around her middle with one hand, and picking sleep out of her eyes with the other.

She crossed the room, turned on the lamp, and tapped my legs, signaling me to move over. "That must have been some nightmare," she said, dropping to the edge of the bed. "You were shouting. Tell me about it."

"You always said never tell a dream before breakfast or it'd come true."

"Come on, you can tell me." Mama always took great stock in dreams. She sounded like she really wanted to help.

"I only remember the end. I was crawling on all fours over a swinging bridge, across a deep gorge with a baby on my back. But then, the dream changed, and it was you with the baby. I was a little girl, running off ahead of you. You kept shouting for me to come back."

I didn't tell her, in the dream, I was also the baby on her back, clutching the neck of her shirt, the same as the time I rode a Shetland pony at the county fair and held onto its mane. "I dashed back to you, and we backed up, until we reached the safety of the cliff's edge."

Again, I held part of the dream back. As much as Mama had hated being stuck in the middle of that bridge, I liked it, because she was close to me, touching me.

"Mothers-to-be dream all kinds of crazy things. That dream's telling you how scared you are. In it, you're the mother, and the baby, and the little girl. It's telling you that you're going to be fine. You reached safety. It's also saying you're afraid to go forward." She kneaded her hand over the small of my spine. "Back aches?"

"A little."

"Thought mine would break in two, it hurt so bad when I was pregnant with you." Rubbing that spot, she asked, "Thirsty?"

I wanted her to stay here with me but realized my throat was parched. "I'll take some water."

She returned with a mug, and I thought she'd sit down and talk to me about the baby.

"Here you go. I know you asked for water, but it's chamomile tea instead, weakened down. Should help you sleep and settle your stomach." Mama yawned wide, without covering her mouth. "If you don't need anything else, I'm going back to bed. Gotta open up shop at seven tomorrow."

"No, nothing else." I hoped my disappointment didn't show through. I wanted to grab her hand and ask her to stay, but I didn't. "Thanks, Mama."

She stood in my door for a few seconds, then kissed the air at me and went back to bed.

Sipping the tea, I wondered what Mama would do if I went in there and crawled into bed beside her. Despite the fact I hadn't done that since I was six years old, I still felt tempted. But the possibility she'd push me away squelched that desire. Instead, I snapped my light off. Then I lay in bed, watching the shadows on the ceiling evolve into the shape of a baby buggy.

Thirty-Two

Grease popped on the back of my hand, and steam from the boiling corn on the cob rose into my sweat-drenched face. Mama's favorite dinner would be ready when she got home from work. She was so good to me yesterday when I told her about keeping the baby and again when I had the nightmare. I wanted to do something for her. And I hoped we could sit and talk about babies—having them and how to take care of them.

I'd checked out books from the downtown library, including Dr. Spock's Baby and Child Care. Some of the diagrams and general information helped, but Dr. Spock said I knew more than I thought I did. He must be mentally deranged.

For the first time in my life, I regretted tossing my naked Tiny Tears doll in the bottom of my closet. All the girls I'd made fun of for their baby dolls, play irons, and miniature stoves probably knew how to hold a baby, change its diaper, and feed it a bottle. I should go play with a five-year-old to learn how to take care of my baby.

At seven o'clock, with dinner on the table, I paced, waiting for Mama. The fried chicken hadn't crisped up and some of the pieces were more black than brown. The corn and a bowl of pinto beans heated from a can looked okay. But when I'd sliced the cornbread, it seemed gooey inside and the outside crust matched the fried chicken, a little burnt. What kind of mother was I going to make if I couldn't even cook a decent supper?

Hearing Mama's sputtering Ford Maverick pull into the driveway, I yanked off my red Kiss the Cook apron, and ran to sit at the table. I wanted to act nonchalant when she came in. The point was for her to think nothing special about her grown daughter cooking for her mother.

I wanted tonight to be the start of something new for Mama and me. No arguments. Just us, getting along.

She came through the door with frizzy hair and smeared lipstick. Walking in without a word, she headed straight to the fridge. She took a cold Budweiser, popped the top, and gulped half of it. Then, with eyes closed, she held the can upright against her forehead. When she opened them and saw me and the table, she grinned.

"Am I dreaming? Did I have a stroke before this beer could work its medicine, and this is all a mirage?"

"Well, it's not much, I'm afraid."

"Anything better than a pack of Tom's peanut butter crackers and a Tab would suit me fine right about now. Anything." She reached for her shoes. "Just let me get these damn torture devices off. Then I'll rinse the store's grease and rubber stink off my hands and neck and be right back."

She hobbled off towards the hall with the beer can in one hand, one shoe off and the other shoe on. I thought, there goes my mama. Without knowing why, I felt proud of her.

At her bedroom door, she turned and pointed a shoe at me. "You are growing up. Swear to God. Growing up right before my eyes. I'd never have believed it." Then she popped back out of the room, the tap, slap of her footsteps going down the hall.

I felt proud but confused. Hadn't she seen how responsible I'd been for years with my schoolwork?

My cold dinner shone with grease by the time Mama came back into the kitchen. I wrung my hands. "The chicken didn't turn out right. Neither did the cornbread. I made tea. Sweet. Two cups of sugar, the way you like it."

"Goodness. You always worry yourself to death over nothing." Mama threw her head back and cawed. Took me by the wrist and plopped me at the table. "Sit here and eat up, cause I'm famished. This looks delicious." She patted my hand. "You did good."

"Let me fix our drinks." I half-rose.

"No, ma'am. I got it. Appreciate your offer of tea, and I'll drink some later, but I'm gonna have my second beer right now. And if it goes down as smooth as the first, then it and my dinner's gonna make for one fine evening." She came back to the table with her can and a glass of milk for me. "You are drinking lots of milk, aren't you?"

It must have occurred to her she hadn't inquired much about my pregnancy, because she added, "Have you been to the doctor?"

"Just the county clinic when I took the test."

"Too bad you didn't sneak off to that clinic for some birth control pills." She sat down and forked a chicken thigh. "Well, you don't have to look like I just stabbed you. You know it's true." She broke off a piece of bread and scooped up some beans.

"Are you ever gonna stop bringing it up? Aunt Jean says you should never tell a person something they already know."

She stopped her fork mid-way to her mouth. "Is that so?"

I looked straight at her. "Yes. It is."

She nodded, as if considering it. "She just might have something there." Her forkful of beans went into her mouth. "But since that don't apply to something a body don't know, then do you reckon you'd be offended if we talk about cooking? Cooking, and how you time it to hit the table with it all hot at the same time."

At first, I thought she was being mean again. But when she sipped from her beer and brought it down, one side of her mouth crinkled up, and she blinked both eyes at me.

I giggled. "I told you I messed it up. Didn't I tell you?"

"You told me, but don't you always say I never listen?" Now, she laughed, cupped one hand over her ear, and leaned towards me. "Eh?"

It was good to see her like this, yawing back and forth with me. I filled my plate, selecting the most burned chicken thigh.

She picked it up and held it with thumb and index finger, up in front of my face. "Nope. You get yourself a decent piece. There's plenty. We can trim off the black part on a couple of these pieces. They'll make a fine cold lunch tomorrow." She dropped the burned piece back onto the platter.

I pierced another one and took a bite of corn. Except for being cold, it tasted pretty good. Not half bad. "About the doctor."

"Uh huh." She kept chewing and circled her fork in a "go ahead" motion.

I was about to split wide open with all my unanswered questions about this baby. "What do I do? See Dr. Baker? The clinic? I read about vitamins and checkups." The questions spilled out of me. "What else am I supposed to do? How do I know if something's wrong? That book I'm reading says I'll know how to take care of the baby. But I don't. I don't know how. What if I hold it wrong or drop it? I know I'll be a good mother, but how do I learn?"

Mama chewed and listened.

"I don't know how to sterilize baby bottles, but they have these Playtex ones you pop plastic sleeves onto. Are those safe? Do they work the same? The book says some babies have trouble sucking. How will I know? Or should I breastfeed?" My cheeks heated up. "The book says it's not needed, but I heard it's better for the baby. And what about diapers? Cloth or disposable? Are disposable too expensive? I'm sorry, Mama. I'll buy everything I can, and I'll pay you back for anything I can't. And I'll work. I'll get a better-paying job after the baby's born." I stopped to take a breath.

Mama set her fork down. "You're gonna make yourself sick. That baby will be fine. I'll show you what to do. Most of mothering just comes naturally. There're things you can't learn from a damn book. You change a diaper or give a baby its bath a couple of times and you'll feel like you've been doing it your whole life." She tapped her index finger against the wood grain laminate tabletop. "We don't always see eye-to-eye, the two of us."

She paused and looked at me like she hadn't since I was little. "But haven't I always made sure you had what you needed? Maybe not things you wanted. But have you ever gone without a meal or a place to live or clothes on your back or school supplies?"

"No, Mama. I never have." I thought about all the times I was so mad at her I could spit ten-penny nails. When I was little, I thought she should be home with me. But now I understood that the times I'd been so angry, she was at work, doing her best to keep us in this house and buy our food. For most of my life, she'd worked twelve hours a day, six days a week. I was exhausted after working four hours. How in the world was I going to take care of my baby?

I looked at Mama and saw a different person sitting there, across from the daughter she had to raise all alone, with no help from Daddy, just plenty of guff.

Scraping up the last of the pintos on my plate, I noticed the alternating line of dark and gray running down the side part in her hair where she needed another "Clairol fix," as she called it. Fine lines radiated from the corners of her blue eyes. "I never thought how hard it's been for you."

"No. You haven't."

"I must have been blind."

She drained the last gulp of beer. "That'll change soon enough."

Rising, she carried her empty plate with her. "I'm gonna have some of your tea. It'll be my dessert after the best meal I've had all week."

Mama was all angles, from her skinny frame outlined by sharp elbows, pointy knees, and elf-like ears to her way of turning on a conversation. It was her way, and for the first time in my life, I considered that just because I was all rounded, circling myself, questioning myself over and over, it didn't mean either of us was wrong.

Still, I wished I could follow one of her right angles. I'd like to think my situation through, come to a conclusion, and walk tall towards my decision, confident I'd made the correct turn.

With her glass of tea in hand, Mama headed towards the back of the house. "A nice long soak's exactly what the doctor ordered." She winked at me. "I appreciate you cooking dinner. Leave those dishes be until I get out of the tub. I'll get them later."

"I love you, Mama." The words shot out of my mouth.

She closed her eyes and stood so still I wondered what was wrong. But just as I was about to ask, she opened them, crossed the room in three steps, sat her tea down, and bent to wrap her arms around me. Recovering from my surprise, I got up from my chair. "I can hug you better standing up," I explained.

"Whatever you need to do. Mama's here for you." She drew me to her with both hands. For the first time ever, Mama wasn't the first one to let go.

Thirty-Three

Dr. Baker was Mama's doctor, had been since before I was born. He must have been over sixty years old. Wrinkles overlapped wrinkles around his eyes, and his puffy face was always red-tinged.

The first time I saw him, he breezed in and out of the exam room. For this second visit, I had my list of questions handy for when he came in, because he'd only given me about five minutes the time before.

I was sitting on the side of the examination table, swinging my bare feet, when he stepped inside the room in a big hurry.

"Miss Lydell." He tipped his head towards me. "How have you been?"

My long list of complaints was embarrassing, but he didn't give me much time, so I sputtered it all out. "I have a lot of gas and nausea, a pain running all the way from my hip to my knee, and I have to pee all the time."

He studied my chart without looking at me. "You're not going to stink up the room right now, are you?" He looked at me over his glasses, and I couldn't help giggling. "If you need to go, there's a toilet just around the corner."

The man was funny, but he hadn't answered my questions. "But Dr. Baker! You're not listening to me. That's not all."

He sat down with my chart on his knee. "Miss Lydell, I am all ears."

"My nose stays stopped up. I get such bad leg cramps I have to get out of bed and put weight on my heels, or the pain is so bad it keeps me awake. But that's nothing unusual. I can't sleep worth a flip." I glanced at the scrap of paper in my hands. "Oh, I'm constipated." I bet he thought I was a hypochondriac.

"That's the iron in your maternity vitamins. Eat more fresh vegetables and rice." He stood and pushed a little button to call the nurse. "Let's take a look." He never answered my concerns.

"But what about everything else?" It was hard to keep my voice from squeaking.

"You're five months pregnant. This is how your body reacts." He patted my shoulder. "Lay back and put your feet in the stirrups. Let me handle this. I'd let you know if anything was out of whack or if there was anything you could do to make it better." His nurse bustled into the room as he said, "The good news is this will be history in just a few short months."

———

A month later, I was ready with a new list. "I'm really worried this time. I'm getting super dizzy. So bad I worry about driving." I blushed when telling Dr. Baker, "There's dark spots on my nipples." Raising his gaze from my chart, he shifted from foot to foot, obviously waiting for me to hurry up and finish. "My biggest concern is my stomach cramps. My hands tingle, and my feet are numb, and I get so swollen."

"Lord, you young women scare yourselves to death. Those cramps are Braxton Hicks contractions. Your hormones are racing through your body like a filly at the Kentucky Derby." He squeezed my calf and checked how the skin reacted. "Yes, there's some edema presenting, but nothing to be overly concerned about. I knew one mother, the right side of her face swelled up three times the size of the left side. She looked a sight." He shook his head. "But it's all normal. Perfectly normal."

He tapped my record. "You've gained ten pounds in the last month."

That's good news. I lost twenty the first four months.

"Your blood pressure's up, and there's a trace of protein in your urine."

"I've never had high blood pressure. Should I be concerned? What does a trace of urine in my protein mean? I mean protein in my urine." My pen was ready to write his answers in the little composition book I brought to every exam.

"It's nothing to be concerned about as long as we keep an eye on it. Take the blood pressure medicine and diuretic I'm giving you. Avoid the salt." He scribbled on his prescription pad, scratched at his thin gray hair, and yawned. "Women have been having babies since the dawn of time. You need to calm down and put your feet up every chance you get. Are you still working?"

"I work at Penney's, in the layaway department."

He glanced up and actually looked me in the face. "On your feet all day?"

"Yes. But Mr. Bonner lets me bring in a high-backed stool to sit on when I'm not waiting on customers."

He looked back down. "Make sure you get plenty of rest. Drink lots of water. Come back in a month and we'll see how you're doing. You might need bed rest the last four to six weeks." Ripping the scripts off his pad, he added, "I'll start seeing you every two weeks after the next visit."

"But I planned on working until I had the baby." I pecked the pen against my notebook.

He sighed. "Young lady, I've been delivering babies for over thirty years, and I can assure you of one thing—plans change. The best thing you can do for yourself and your baby is to reduce your anxiety level. You're wound up as tight as a virgin on her wedding night."

My mouth was still open when the door closed behind him, leaving me sitting alone on the examination table with my pen still poised over my notepad, and a draft at my back where the paper gown didn't close.

Thirty-Four

For three months, I lived the same day over and over again. I woke up, nibbled on soda crackers, and sipped water. Then I raced to the bathroom to vomit.

Mama left for Firestone before I got out of bed. I was glad she didn't have to hear me barf. I'd read that morning sickness only lasted three months. At seven months pregnant, my stomach wasn't taking any part of that rule seriously. Sometimes I vomited on and off all day.

My feet and ankles were swollen up like puffer fish. The only shoes I could wear were loose-laced Keds two sizes too big.

And the rest of my body … sore boobs, flabby butt, and bloated stomach. I told Mama, "If I were a whale, you'd beach me."

"If you were a whale, you'd move a hell of a lot faster than you do now." Her reply made me laugh so hard I peed and had to change pants.

———

On the morning of December first, I dragged myself out of bed and flipped my calendar. Per the doctor's estimate, I was twenty-eight weeks pregnant. After I'd had my shower, the phone rang. I shambled down the hall, yawning. "Hello."

It was Aunt Jean. "Honey, can you pick up a few things for an old, ailing woman?"

I felt poorly myself this morning. The daily vomit session was over, but my stomach ached, and so did the small of my back. My feet and fingers felt like sausages. My face had been swollen for weeks, but today it was a pumpkin. If I looked closely, the right and the left sides were the same size, thank God, but they made me look like a walrus. Based on our bathroom scales, I'd gained another twenty pounds in the last four weeks, although I didn't see how, when I was still puking every day. I planned on asking Dr. Baker about it at my appointment the next day.

"I'll be right there, Aunt Jean. I don't have to be at work until noon."

"No reason for you to stay with me." She wheezed. "A few groceries and a quick visit are all I need. You have other things to do."

I stopped by the Piggly Wiggly to pick up some Tums, Sprite, Ritz crackers, and Campbell's chicken noodle soup. Inside the store, a man and woman had a baby girl dressed in a pink onesie and strapped into a baby carrier. They both bent over her cooing. Her rosebud mouth puckered in an O, while her little legs kicked up a storm.

I burst into tears and cried all the way to the check-out line. The clerk laid her hand on mine before counting out my change. "Honey, I don't know what's wrong, but it'll be all right. You need to settle down. It's not good for the baby." My sniffling burst into wails.

Tears streamed down my cheeks as I drove to Aunt Jean's. I wiped and wiped. I couldn't stop. My baby would never have a father.

———

"Lord have mercy, what's wrong?" Aunt Jean pushed herself up in her bed, coughed into a pale pink tissue, and sank back onto her pillow.

"I'm sorry. It's nothing. I got started and just can't quit." Dropping the grocery bag on her bedroom's faded linoleum, I flopped onto the blue and white flowery armchair by her bed. "Mama says it's hormones. Doctor says it's normal. I say I'm a total mess." I laughed, then buried my face in my hands, and started crying again.

Aunt Jean's bed springs creaked. She scuffed in her house shoes from her bedroom into the kitchen, ran the tap, and shuffled back. She sat on the mismatched rust-colored ottoman at the foot of my chair, tapped my arm, and handed me a wet, clean dishcloth. "Come on now." I wiped at my swollen face and hiccupped uncontrollably.

She motioned for me to move closer, put her knobby hand on the back of my head, and bowed hers. "Lord, anoint this child." She drew in harsh breaths between each sentence. "Show her and her unborn child Your merciful love. In Jesus' name. Amen." With every third word, I hiccupped, my shoulders jerked, and her hand bounced against my head.

Her prayer was shorter than I'd ever heard. She took both of my soggy hands in hers. "Child, I can't bear seeing you this way." Her voice was husky and choppy. "What can I do?"

"No, you're sick. We'll talk about it later. Stop trying to talk." I pulled my hands from hers.

"I'll be the judge of that. Tell me." Her bushy eyebrows were pulled down low.

"There's nothing you or anybody can do." I wiped the dish rag across my eyes, pulled a Kleenex from the side table next to us and blew two honks into it. "I've ruined my baby's life. Mama was right. I should give this baby two parents to love it."

"Get hold of yourself. Ask for strength." A whistling sound accompanied her words. "'All things are possible to him who believes.' Didn't I teach you that?" She was wheezing for breath even harder than usual, and the lenses of her black-rimmed frames had speckles of what looked like orange pulp.

"I'm sorry. I should be ashamed of myself. Let's get you back in bed." I rose from the chair and put my arm around her shoulders to help her.

She shrugged me off. "No, ma'am. Won't have you straining in your condition." Leaning forward, she pushed the chair with both hands to heft herself up, took the two steps to the bed, and slumped onto the mattress. Then, wheezing something awful, she motioned for me to get the dull green oxygen canister sitting in the corner.

I wheeled it over. She reached with trembling fingers for the nose tubing and inserted one knob into each nostril. Then she dropped her head back onto her pillow and closed her eyes. She took racking breaths, her face gray and washed-out.

Oh God, please don't let anything happen to my Aunt Jean. I'll straighten up. Won't bother her again with my petty problems. Just let her be okay. I sat on the edge of the bed and held her right hand. Her left was on her chest, rising and falling.

Slowly, her face lost its pallid tone, a bit of color brightened her cheeks, and her breaths came slower and easier. Her eyelids fluttered, and she squeezed my hand. I slipped my jacket off and hung it on her footboard. Next door, I heard Mr. Bledsoe calling his white Cairn terrier. "Boston! Here, boy!" He whistled and Boston's high-pitched yip carried across the yards.

I carefully removed her glasses and grabbed the Piggly Wiggly bag I'd dropped as I came in. Washing her glasses under the kitchen faucet, I remembered all the times I stood on a chair at that sink with my drying cloth, "chewing the fat," as Aunt Jean called it.

She still had the same striped dish towels. Where did she buy those? I dried her glasses on the towel and laid them on her kitchen table. The wooden table I loved had been shoved under the back window with its sides down. Yellowing Sunday School books and religious tracts covered it now, as well as home-canned peaches and boxes of greeting cards. In the middle of her kitchen, in its place, was our nasty old Formica table, which Mama replaced with another one almost like it. Mama was proud our new one had a "wood grain look." I couldn't stand it. It was all phony and nothing real.

I ran my finger along our old Formica table's smooth surface. It held no magic.

I pulled open the china cabinet door and noticed her supply of jelly glasses was getting low. She broke dishes with increasing frequency, like her hands couldn't hold them as tightly anymore. I made a note to buy her some lightweight, pretty tumblers next pay day, regardless of what else I needed to get the baby. Aunt Jean barely scraped by on her disability check.

When I returned with her eyeglasses and a Sprite, she took a few sips and handed the drink back to me. Settling back onto her pillow, she closed her eyes. I set the glass on her bed table, next a her box of Christmas cards she was in the midst of addressing. She looked so frail. "I'm calling Mama."

She opened one eye. "No, you're not. Give me my specs."

Mama answered on the second ring.

"Mama, Aunt Jean's having a breathing spell." Aunt Jean batted at my arm, so I stretched the phone's cord and moved farther away. Mama was asking me questions about Aunt Jean's color and her pulse, and I couldn't handle both of them at once.

"Her color's getting better, and I forgot to check her pulse. I'll do it when we hang up." Aunt Jean grabbed her Sunday devotional, rolled it up, and banged it on the little round table by her bed. "She's pitching a fit, but I can call my boss and tell him I need to stay here until one o'clock. Can you take a late lunch and stay with her for an hour or two after that?"

"I don't need …" Aunt Jean was interrupted by a coughing fit, and finished in a weak voice, "… no babysitter."

"Just a minute, Mama." I held the receiver to my leg and shook a finger at Aunt Jean. "You're making it worse. I'm just doing what you'd do for me. And this will get Mama out of the store for a few hours, okay?"

She let her breath out in a "harrumph," but her shoulders relaxed.

"Okay, Mama. She's willing to have us here for a while. Will that work?" Mama said she'd come by at one o'clock.

Aunt Jean's covers were all wrinkled and twisted. I straightened and tucked them under her arms. Those little whiskers at the corners of her mouth twitched. "Don't go thinking I'm Grandma or her wolf."

"Oh, Grandmama, what big teeth you have!"

"The better to eat you with." She lunged her head forward, just a little bit, and raised one curled claw in a tiny swipe through the air.

"You always know just what to say to make me laugh." I took a Kleenex and wiped away tiny dots of perspiration from her forehead. "Let's get you some soup."

"I'm not hungry."

"Is it chicken noodle or chicken and stars to please you today?"

"You think you're so smart." Her voice was getting raspy again.

"That's what you used to say." I wished I knew more about nursing, what to look for, when to really be alarmed.

"Well, I've changed my mind." She said it in a sassy way, but her eyelids were half-closed.

"Well, then you'd be right. I don't think I'm as smart as I used to be. But I am hungry enough for the three of us. I'm putting on some soup!" I patted my belly and went into the kitchen. She didn't utter a peep as I rattled around, getting out an old Club aluminum pot and her skinny, metal can opener.

Mama and had I bought her an electric can opener a few years back, but she held up one hand. "I don't favor new-fangled gadgets. My can opener's been turning round and round for me since before you ..." She pointed at me. "... were born. I like it. It likes me. Enough said."

Taking one of her spindly kitchen matches, I lit the stove's eye. I was still intimidated by her gas stove. It heated things faster than an electric range, and food seemed to stay hotter. What I couldn't shake were memories of the preacher at Aunt Jean's church talking about hellfire and damnation. As a kid, I'd veered clear of that stove and its flickering blue evil glow. The funny things we thought as kids somehow stick with us. I cupped my hand on my stomach. What would my baby remember?

I used Aunt Jean's crimped-up pizza pan as a bed tray and spooned soup into a bowl with a rooster painted on the bottom. These dishes were ours years ago. Now, Aunt Jean had all the pieces that survived. I laid a napkin on the pan and wondered what else Aunt Jean might like. Maybe some Jell-O would be good. I stooped down to look in the cabinet for a box of gelatin.

At that moment, the baby kicked, kicked so hard I saw my stomach move. I'd felt movement before. First, it had felt like bubbles inside me. Then, it felt like popcorn popping, then a big heart swaying to its own beat.

In the last couple of months, I'd felt movement and a few little kicks. But this was different. In fact, I'd been wondering why I hadn't felt more kicks and turns, like I'd read about other women having in their fifth and sixth months. When I questioned Dr. Baker about it, he'd reassured me every pregnancy was unique. "You're looking A-Okay."

I laid both hands on my belly, fingertips touching. Another kick. Rippling.

Soup forgotten, I dashed into Aunt Jean's bedroom, but she was asleep and snoring, her top lip quivering. I stood quietly by her bed, waiting for more movement, but there was none. Feeling my baby move filled me with such wonder and reverence I wished Mama were here. Or Jim. No, not Jim. But someone besides Jim, who would place his big, sun-tanned hands against my round stomach and look into my eyes, waiting with me for the miracle.

I turned to go back into the kitchen and saw the old Jesus picture on the wall, the one with the sheep. It'd been years since I noticed it hanging there. When I was in grade school, I thought Jesus and the sheep were alive. God, I was a weird little kid. I didn't even want to think about all the trouble I got into for taking the crucifix from the living room. What had I called it? Bird Jesus? No, that wasn't right.

Backing into the kitchen, I sagged into a kitchen chair. Sunlight came through the window over the sink and dust motes danced. A waltz. And every girl dust mote had a boy dust mote partner. It was too much to bear, and I dropped my head onto the table and sobbed in silence.

When my sides stopped hitching, I took a napkin from its holder and blew my nose. My baby would be just like me, no daddy. And I'd be the same as Mama, no one to love. It wasn't fair. Mama's voice in my head came in loud and clear, "The sooner you learn that life's not fair, the better off you're going to be." I smiled. It was awful when she was right.

The soup had grown stone cold. I dumped it back into the pan and turned the heat up to re-warm it. My stomach burned. I rubbed the small of my aching back with one hand, as I stirred soup with the other.

Bed springs creaked in the other room. I peeked my head around the doorframe. Aunt Jean's eyes were open. "Have a nice nap?"

She nodded.

"I'll have you some soup ready in two shakes of a lamb's tail."

She smiled. "Sounds good." Her voice was a little stronger.

I set my face into seriousness. "I made it myself. Plucked a chicken this morning while I was out plowing in the north forty."

That twitch at the corner of her mouth showed up. "I bet you did."

"I thought you didn't bet." I pulled my eyebrows down and cocked my head at her.

She laughed a half-bark. "Well. When you've seen as much water under the bridge as I have, it starts to cloud up, be not as crystal clear as it once was." A cough stopped her.

"Don't talk. I'll be right back." I took the entire pot of soup to my make-shift tray and poured broth into the bowl. Then I used my spoon to scoop out the cubes of chicken, bits of carrots, and soggy stars. I hurried the tray in to her.

"You need to eat this. It'll open up your chest." I motioned for her to sit up taller in bed, so I could hand her the food. "Let me freshen your drink."

As I set the tray on her lap, she motioned for me to bend down and planted a kiss on my forehead. Her lips felt chill to the touch. "You're my girl."

"You bet I am." The tears welled up in my eyes had nothing to do with sadness. Those tears rose from the love in my heart. All those times Aunt Jean said God sent me to her, so she'd have someone to love, I'd thought I was some sort of gift to her. Now I understood. What she'd given me, I'd never be able to repay.

Thirty-Five

"Are you two arguing over the Wish Book again?" Mama stood in the bedroom doorway.

Aunt Jean and I were piled up in her bed with the Sears catalog playing an old game of ours, where we each picked one item from each page. We hadn't even heard Mama come in.

"We aren't arguing. We're negotiating." Aunt Jean grinned at Mama. "Better than the days we used it for something else."

"Why do you have to remind me of that old outhouse!" Mama's voice boomed in Aunt Jean's small bedroom. Then she looked over at me. "Sorry I'm late. Had a customer who wouldn't stop yakking."

My watch read 12:55. "Yikes! I have to go." I gave Aunt Jean a big kiss on the cheek. "Love you. Be good." It took me two tries to roll myself up and off the bed. When I finally got up, my dress was bunched underneath my butt. I pulled the hem down and rubbed my belly.

"You feel okay?" Aunt Jean pushed her glasses up with her index finger and peered at me. Mama pivoted with her detective eyes.

I dismissed her question with a wave of my hand. "Sure."

Turning from them, I pretended to be looking for my purse and took the opportunity to take slow, steady breaths to stop my dizziness.

When I felt my head clear and my stomach unclench, I grabbed my pocketbook and pointed at Aunt Jean. "Remember, Mama's a menace at this game. Don't let her take that red scarf out from under you."

"You hear how she talks about me?" Mama petitioned Aunt Jean, before draping her jacket over the chair and blowing air kisses to me as I left. "I'll shop for baby clothes, even if you do mistreat me."

———

I didn't mind working at J.C. Penney's. I took layaway payments and wrapped presents. We weren't very busy. Usually, I ran the whole department by myself.

When I got to work that day, Mrs. Leonard, who worked in the accounting office, brought a wedding present for me to wrap. I carried the stack of sheets and towels to the back room, which was full of giant rolls of twenty-four-inch-wide wrapping paper. I selected one of our largest boxes from under the table and assembled it. Then I lined it with white tissue paper and filled it with her items.

I grasped both sides of the gift wrap's edge and pulled, using just the right pressure to roll off enough paper without wasting or tearing it. I'd done this so many times I could eyeball the box and guesstimate the paper I'd need. The spindle had a long, serrated edge, and I cut the paper in one fell swoop. I loved the ripping noise.

It took no time to fold the gift wrap over the box and tape it in place, complete with mitered ends. The last step was making ribbon bow ties into fluffed-out chrysanthemum shapes and sticking them on the box.

I delivered the finished product to Mrs. Leonard's ooh's and ah's and returned to my station.

Where were the customers tonight? My job wasn't bad, except for the slow times, and it was our busiest season, with Christmas twenty-four days away. Since I'd caught up the layaway records, I had nothing to do. I stood looking out at the racks of women's clothing, holding my aching back, and wondering what I was going to do about my situation. No matter how I analyzed the options, there just wasn't a solution. I couldn't afford an apartment on my salary as a gift wrap girl. I didn't want to be a drain on Mama. Aunt Jean had no room, and she wasn't up to a baby anyway. Carolyn was a senior and not even talking to me. And I'd promised myself I'd never see Jim again.

I looked up and saw Mrs. Stover at the window. I hadn't seen her since she and Mr. Stover gave me my car. Immediately, I came out of the office and gave her a gigantic hug. "Mrs. Stover, thank you so much for my car. I'm overwhelmed. You saved my life."

"What a nice surprise, Mary Alice. I didn't know you were working here." Mrs. Stover placed her hands on my shoulders. "Let me look at you." She glanced at my mid-section.

"Yes, ma'am. I've been here a few months." Since I got pregnant, I hadn't seen any of Aunt Jean's church members. Now Mrs. Stover was sure to think me scandalous. Hopefully, she wouldn't start preaching at me.

She rooted around in her purse and pulled out a yellow layaway slip and a five-dollar bill. "This is on Mr. Stover's new coat I'm giving him for Christmas."

"What a nice gift." I took the payment and skimmed through the index box to find her layaway slip. "You've been paying on it regular for two months now. Only one more payment after this one."

"Your aunt tells me you're a hard worker and turning out to be a good cook."

I twisted around to face her. "She did?" Maybe Mrs. Stover wouldn't think me a disgrace, after all.

"She certainly did, and I think it's admirable. You cannot feed a growing child from a box." She made a tsking noise. "All these young women, fixing Hamburger Helper for their families. What's the world coming to? You're bringing a child of God into this world. The body is a temple." Her double chin trembled as she spoke. "If you want to feed your little one hamburger with noodles, just cook them up fresh. It's really easy …."

She was going into great detail about how to dice an onion and sauté it, when I realized I'd peed myself. Just a little. The trickle inched down my leg. I wished I had on pants, instead of a maternity dress. Good thing I was behind the counter. It was quite a relief when Mrs. Stover finished her recipe advice and tootled away.

I called out to the accounting department on my way to the ladies' room. "Mrs. Leonard, I'm sorry. I have to run to the bathroom. Can you listen out for customers?"

"Sure thing."

In the bathroom, a cramp doubled me over. I opened the stall, pulled down my panties and felt immediate relief when my urine flowed.

I wiped. Pink goo on the white toilet paper. I wiped again. More pink goo. I was only seven months pregnant. Too early for my "show." This was a bad sign.

After wiping away the gunk, I wrapped toilet paper around my hand to form a pad and used it as a make-shift Kotex. While washing my hands, a trickle went down my right leg. When I backed away from the sink to look, another pale pink rivulet dribbled to my left knee.

Another cramp hit so hard I grabbed the sink to steady myself.

With blurred vision, I looked again. And there were more trickles. Two became four, then six. Was my water breaking? It couldn't be— but it was.

Thirty-Six

At first, I couldn't move. All I could do was stand there looking at my feet. I stood rooted there for a few minutes, until Mrs. Leonard came into the bathroom.

One look at my face and her gaze moved down to my feet. "Oh, my Lord." The rivulets had gained speed and formed a pink-tinged puddle on the bathroom tiles.

I forced myself to form words, "What do I do?" Nothing had prepared me for this.

When she realized what was happening, she took charge. "We get you to the hospital. That's what. Can you walk?"

I nodded.

"Good, you start heading downstairs. I'll get Delores to come help you. I'll bring my car around front." Before dashing out, she pulled me into a warm hug. "It will be okay. Nothing to worry about. Nothing at all." Her words beat in time to the pounding in my head.

Before I'd made my way ten feet from the bathroom, Delores and the other three women from the office surrounded me, petting my hands and whisking me away. They cloistered around me as I struggled across the second floor and down the elevator. By the time we reached the first floor, every step sent pain up my spine and across my belly. My lower back and tailbone hurt as bad as they did when I fell on my butt roller skating years ago.

The racks and shelves of merchandise and holiday decorations were blurred as I passed, a daze that matched my brain. I felt as if I couldn't breathe. I snorted like a pony.

The women helping me huddled so close we moved across the sales floor as a herd.

We burst through the plate-glass double doors onto Broad Street. I gulped in the chill December air. My entourage opened Mrs. Leonard's passenger door and fussed me into the Ford Pinto. Mrs. Leonard chanted, "Hurry-it-up. Hurry-it-up." I thought of pregnant horses galloping across a wide open plain, the sound of their hooves echoing in my head.

Mrs. Edwards tried to stretch a seat belt around me, and I knocked her hands away. "No, no, no."

My bodyguards slammed the car door shut. One final "God bless you, child," from Delores, and we were off.

Mrs. Leonard had the heat on high. The hot air blowing in my face smothered me. Ever since the time Daddy touched me in his truck, I hadn't been able to stand car heat. It made me want to jump out the window. Even though it wasn't my car, I searched the dash instruments and flipped the heat off.

The smothering heat took a few minutes to evaporate. I pulled my head closer to my knees, trying to stave off the state of. The floorboard was littered with gum wrappers, dried leaves, and—oh, God, no—a receipt from Jim's Transmission. Call me superstitious, but Jim was the last word I wanted to see. It was another bad omen. I dragged my foot over the receipt and crushed it under my heel.

Through sheer will, I pulled myself up and looked out the window. At what felt like sixty miles per hour, we were flying across the Second Avenue Bridge over the Oostanaula River. Dizziness washed over me. The sight of that dirty, muddy, tobacco-brown water was too much. A third bad sign.

Acid rose in my throat. I heaved and vomited, all over my legs and the hem of my dress. Flecks of noodle stars and carrots dotted my bare calves, socks, and tennis shoes. As I continued to gag and dry heave, the floorboard flotsam sloshed in my puked-up chicken soup.

The stench was overpowering. Mrs. Leonard gagged, rolled her window all the way down, and the car filled with freezing cold fresh air.

I used my hands to swab chunks from my tongue and add them to the mess smeared onto my dress. Tendrils of hair had snaked their way into my mouth. I plucked them out and turned to Mrs. Leonard, "I'm sorry."

"I don't care. Not one iota." She gripped the steering wheel and barely flicked her eyes towards me. "Almost there."

Another blast of pain coursed around my abdomen as if someone had harnessed me and was pulling the leather tighter and tighter.

Though it was less than a mile from Penney's to Floyd Medical Center, every bump made it feel like fifty. I'd wanted natural childbirth, but my doctor was against it. Mama wasn't too keen on the idea either. I'd planned to do it anyway, but ended up not having a coach to attend lessons with me.

Without those classes, I didn't know what to do now, except try to breathe. Every book I'd read talked about breathing. None of the books had warned me the pain would be so bad it would take my breath away.

Nothing had ever seemed as beautiful as the hospital's sign that blurred in and out of focus. Mrs. Leonard screeched to a stop. The car door opened and a burly guy at least six feet two in olive green scrubs took one look at me and practically lifted me from the seat into a wheelchair. His shirt smelled like cigarettes, Daddy's and Jim's stink. No more bad omens!

I didn't know it would hurt this much. People claim pain is white hot or flaming red. For me, this agony was a noxious, flashing green strobe.

The motion of the stretcher sent my world spinning. An attendant wheeled me into an examination room, and a blood pressure cuff squeezed my upper arm.

"220 over 120." Unbelievably high. Hearing it, I knew from all my reading that my baby and I were in grave danger.

The doctor came in, but in all his medical jargon, I only understood two words: Preeclampsia and Induce.

Both the baby and I could die. That's when Alice and I prayed. Take me, God. Just let my baby live.

Thirty-Seven

When I woke up, it took a while to figure out where I was. Crisscross tape held an IV in place on my left hand. It hurt, but no pain could have matched the smoldering fire filling my head.

My eyes felt tied shut. I could only open them a crack before a taut line pulled them closed again.

My mouth was so dry. My lips felt swollen and chapped. When I parted them, they made a popping noise. I couldn't feel my feet, but I could wiggle my toes.

"Mary Alice!" Mama's voice, urgent, like I'd done something wrong.

I forced my eyes open and squinted across my immobilized left arm and the gleaming metal bed rail. All I could see was an open door and white blurs passing in the hall. I tried to turn my head to the right, but a jolt of pain fixed it in place. I groaned and closed my eyes.

The click, click, click that was my mother's heels moved from my right to my left. When I opened my eyes again and saw her, I remembered seeing her in the delivery room.

"Push. Mary Alice, push!" It was the tone she used when telling Daddy to leave. Her get-off-my-Goddamn-porch voice.

I pushed. That's all I remembered. Mama gripping my hand and commanding me. Pain bashing my body.

"Honey."

She never called me honey. Not honey. Not baby. Not sweetie. None of the endearments Aunt Jean used. It must mean the baby died. I moaned and whipped my head back and forth, regardless of the pain. "No, no, no."

"Wake up, baby." She shook my shoulder. "Wake up."

It was Aunt Jean's voice coming from my mama. My baby was dead. "Please, no." The sound scratched. "My baby."

"She's in the nursery. Intensive care."

"What?" I wrenched my eyes open. Mama stood beside the bed with her dark hair frizzed out and her lips pale pink without their usual tangerine lipstick. "What?" I said it again, louder.

"Listen to me." Back to the command tone. Back to my mama.

I did as she said.

She reached out to me but couldn't hold the hand with the IV. So I moved my right arm across my chest. She clutched that hand, holding it firmly without hurting. When she spoke, the words went through her skin into my hand, up my arm, and inside my heart. "Your baby is very sick. They're doing everything they can for her."

"She's alive?"

"Yes." The word was strong and irrefutable and mine.

Yes was the world. "Yes." I hissed it. I tasted it.

"She is." Mama squeezed my hand. "But …."

"Let me see her." I tried to move. Made an effort to sit up. "I have to see her."

Mama pushed me back. "Lie down."

"No. Let me go." I didn't have the strength and flopped back onto the pillow. I was a drum with one thousand fists pounding me.

"Listen." Her voice drilled a hole through my head and pinned me to the pillow. "You're sick. You have to be still. I'll talk to them, find out when you can see her."

I lay without moving. I had to be still and build my strength.

"Good." She snaked her hand around the bedrail, pulled up the white remote with its thick cord. Then she pushed the button marked with a symbol of a nurse's head. A tiny red light went on. I reached for the remote, and Mama handed it to me. Holding it with one hand, I jabbed the button with my thumb and stared at the remote, moving my eyes around and around the rectangular outline of a nurse's cap. As I traced, I counted. Every time I made it to eight, I punched the button again, until there was an answer.

"Yes." A hollow sound that meant no.

"We need to see the nurse." Mama answered for me.

"She'll be there shortly." The red light on my remote went out.

"Mary Alice, I'll tell you what I know if you promise to stay calm. Okay?" I looked closely at Mama. Her face was shiny, devoid of make-up, not even a swipe of blush across her high-boned cheeks. Puffy folds almost enveloped her blood-shot eyes. From the waist down, her red-and-white-striped dress drooped in wrinkles.

I nodded.

She pulled up a chair and sat down. "Do you remember coming to the hospital yesterday?"

Thinking was like scrambled eggs. "No." An image of Mrs. Leonard's car flitted across my mind. "Yes. Oh, I do."

"Your blood pressure shot up. You went into labor early. They had to induce, or you both would have died." She stopped for a minute. "You understand?"

My ears were like a radio with someone turning the volume up and down.

"If it hadn't worked, they would have done a C-section." Mama screwed her face up, and for a minute, I was afraid she would cry. "You were mostly out of it, but you pushed your little heart out. I was so proud of you." Mama never tossed around praise. Even in the midst of straining to find out about my daughter, I felt a rush of satisfaction.

"They wanted to take you to surgery, but I told them, 'You don't know my daughter. She can do this.'" She grinned Aunt Jean's twitchy grin. "There's times when it pays to be hard-headed."

I smiled despite myself, and it gave me the courage to ask, "The baby?" I forced my tongue around my lips.

Mama stood up, crossed to the other side of my bed, and pulled the hospital tray over my stomach. She tried to put the straw between my lips, but I still couldn't turn my head to the right without it exploding. So she wheeled the tray around to the other side of the bed and brought the tall thermal mug to me, its straw sticking out from the lid.

I sucked and swallowed and felt the cold-water race down my parched throat. Sucked and swallowed again. Shook my head when she offered a third sip.

She held onto the mug and continued, "You had her yesterday at 6:57 p.m. I don't know what kind of medicine they've got you on, but you slept for over twenty-four hours." She paused and twiddled with the straw. "She weighed two pounds, nine ounces."

I thought I must have heard her wrong. But the part of me that knew it was true ratcheted in my head.

Her sad eyes told me more than her words. "She's so tiny, sugar. Maybe too small to make it. They won't know for a while."

The gravity holding my body ceased to exist. The ground beneath me turned into a spinning vortex. It threatened to pull me down into my rabbit hole. I struggled to stay present, but couldn't feel the bed beneath me. With my right fist, I knocked against my thigh. I had to keep myself together for my daughter.

The door opened, and a razor thin woman entered the room. She didn't say a word, just came over and snatched the chart hanging at the foot of my bed. Her eyes ticked back and forth over the page. She tsk, tsk'd as she reviewed my medical information. Ignoring me, she glared at Mama when she stepped over to fiddle with the IV controls. Then she stood with her shoulders held back and hands behind her. "You called?"

Rather than being intimidated, I was furious. Behind her, I saw Mama looking her up and down from head to foot, and I knew if I wanted to be the first to speak, I better hurry.

"I want to see my baby." I was surprised at how firmly those words came out.

"Impossible. She is in the NICU in an incubator and must not be disturbed. You may see her tomorrow for three visits of five minutes each. Once in the morning. Once after lunch. And again after dinner." She broadcast like a robot from hell.

My body trembled with anger. "I'm not waiting until tomorrow to see my baby."

"You must do what's best for the infant. She is sleeping. Surely, you would not want to jeopardize her health and well-being." Her nostrils expanded and contracted with each word. I wanted to jam my IV needle through them.

"Where is she?" My voice got louder and higher. "I'm her mother, and I'm going to see her."

The nurse relaxed her shoulders a bit. "You are also ill. You have to settle down, get a good night's sleep. Then you'll be well enough to see her tomorrow. I will get a sedative for you." She made a sharp left turn and started from the room.

"Stop." Mama stood and pointed at the nurse. "What the hell is wrong with you? My daughter almost died. She just had a baby and hasn't even got to see her yet. Looking at you, I don't believe you're anybody's mother. But for Christ's sake, you will not talk to my daughter that way, especially after what she's been through. Where the fuck is your supervisor?"

"I will not tolerate vulgarity." She whipped around to face Mama. "You are a visitor in this hospital. If you cannot follow rules, you will be asked to leave."

Mama stepped towards her. "I'll be leaving my child here alone with you over your dead body. Either you get somebody else in here to talk to us, or I'll go find the head of this racket and talk to him about my friend, the lawyer."

"Fine." Each word was clipped. "I will be happy to have the head nurse explain what must be done to insure your daughter's and granddaughter's health. She has much more important duties, but with some families, she's used to getting involved." Her dyed jet-black hair was pulled back so tightly in a bun it lifted the corners of her narrow eyes.

She left before Mama could throw a chair at her.

The minute the door closed, I felt frantic. "Mama, I have to see her now. What if I never get to see her?" I started crawling toward the foot of the bed. Each movement sent shooting pains.

Mama was up and onto the bed before I got halfway there. She wrapped her arms around me. I pushed at her. She held on.

"Let me go." I rose up on my knees, though my bottom hurt badly. I thought it would split open. She continued restraining me, and I pummeled her shoulder blades. The IV tore away from my hand.

Mama pulled me in tighter. "Let me go!" Drops of blood fell from my nose to my hand.

Mama drew in a sharp breath and pushed me onto my back. I hit the pillow with a whomp. She straddled me, with her face directly over mine. "Settle down! Right now."

My thick tongue made the words come out slurred. "I'm fine."

"You are not fine." With each word, she slapped the pillow by my ear. "Women have tough deliveries all the time. When your doctor told me you had preeclampsia, I didn't know what it meant. But he explained that, even now, your blood pressure could shoot sky high again. You could die from a stroke." Perched above me, with a knee on either side of my chest and her shirt-waist dress gathered up onto her thighs, she pressed her right palm across her forehead and clenched her eyes shut. Her left fist gripped her bodice. It was one of the scariest sights I'd ever seen.

"Mama?" A memory flashed of Mama slumped on the kitchen floor, Daddy screaming, and blue lights shining off the walls. I took her right hand away from her brow. It trembled. "I'm sorry." Every time my heartbeat, a thumping inflated my balloon head.

She shifted her weight off me and sat on her haunches, next to me on the mattress. "You have to calm down. Promise me you'll keep yourself under control."

Her eyes were wild, and she clutched my hand so hard it hurt. "I—will—not—lose—you—again! Do you hear me?"

I was too shocked to speak right away. My mama did not care this much. Her outpouring of emotion dumbfounded me. I nodded. "I promise."

"I know we have our differences …" Tears sprung to her eyes. "… but you and Jean are all I got."

Mama took my face in her hands, the same as Aunt Jean would have. "You've always been high-strung. But now, you're grown, a mother. Mothers pull themselves up and put one foot in front of the other. There's always gonna be something'll try to scare you senseless or beat you down, but you just keep moving forward." She released my hand and cupped my chin. "So, tell me right now that you'll be a mother."

No way did I want to vow to be stoic like Mama. But I didn't have a choice. She was right. "I will." I slumped into her arms. "Oh, God, Mama."

"My little hushpuppy." Mama stroked my hair the way she did when I was five. "I'll take you to her. You'll see her tonight. I swear to God."

Yes, I wanted to see her right that second. But I'd drained every reserve. My body was so heavy I sank back onto the pillow, closed my eyes, and counted: touching the fingers on my right hand, from one to five, then five to one, over and over. It must have lulled me to sleep, because I awoke to Mama's voice.

She was talking to someone else in the room. "I don't know who that bitch nurse was—been up here with my sister many a time and I've never seen the likes of her—but you make sure she doesn't step foot in this room again. She should be ashamed. So should you for keeping somebody like that on staff. I'm telling you one thing ... as soon as we get my daughter calmed down enough, she's going to see her baby, and I mean tonight."

Mama's voice was the voice of God, coming out of her with an unimaginable force. For once, I was glad my mama was someone with the power to smite.

Thirty-Eight

A half-hour later, an attendant came in with a wheelchair and rolled me to the Neonatal Intensive Care Unit. A two-foot-wide white sign with black lettering was posted on the honeydew-green colored walls above the family's sink and again at the door:

INFECTION CONTROL:
NEONATAL INTENSIVE CARE UNIT VISITING GUIDELINES
Babies in the neonatal unit are particularly vulnerable to falling ill because they are sick or premature.
Gowning and handwashing by all attendants and visitors are required to prevent neonatal morbidity and mortality.

HANDWASHING PROCEDURE:
1. Remove all jewelry (watches, rings, bracelets).
2. Roll sleeves up to elbows.
3. Use antiseptic soap provided.
4. Scrub from fingertips to elbows for a full 2 minutes.

GOWNS:
Located in the lockers. Opens to the back.
Handling of neonates should be minimized.
ANYONE WHO HAS BEEN EXPOSED TO A CONTAGIOUS DISEASE MAY NOT ENTER
Note: If you are visiting more than one baby, please wash your hands before handling each infant.
These precautions protect and provide safety to all of our babies.
Their ability to fight infections is much less than yours!

I still had on my hospital gown. Before we left my room, a new nurse came in and removed what was left of the taped-on mess where I'd yanked out my IV. I threw on the red robe covered with tiny white hearts that Mama brought me from home.

When I tried to roll up my sleeves, I was all thumbs. Mama lent a hand. It was the first time she'd helped me with my clothing since I started school, when she insisted on pulling galoshes over my winter shoes. Our eyes met, and she squeezed my upper arm.

"Chin up." She turned on the water before pushing up her dress sleeves.

The soap smelled strong and reminded me of the kind Jim had washed his hands with after working on his car. I closed my eyes and breathed in and out as I scrubbed my hands and arms and counted off the seconds. One one-thousand, two one-thousand, three one-thousand … all the way to 120 one-thousands. The sign in front of me seemed to expand and recede. Mama had said I was on strong medicine. I didn't know if it was the drugs or fear or a combination of both that made solid things move and all the spit in my mouth dry up.

Mama cleared her throat and jarred me from staring at the sign. She had finished washing up and had a frayed green gown held out to me. When I raised my arms, she slid the wide sleeves up over my robe. I turned, and she looped it in the back, the way Aunt Jean used to tie the wide bows of my church dresses. It gave me fuzzy memories. I remembered my shiny black patent leather Mary Janes and thin, white dress socks, which reminded me of Dorothy's dazzling ruby red slippers. I looked down at my hospital socks and Mama's black pumps and touched my heels together three times, thinking, there's no place like home, there's no place like home.

Mama brought me back to the present. "Are you ready?" Mama's expression was the same as the last time Aunt Jean was here in the cardiac unit. She tried to look composed, but a spasm at the corner of her right eye flickered.

I wanted to run away. At the same time, I didn't want another second to pass without seeing my baby. Swallowing hard, I nodded. Blood roared in my ears.

Mama opened the door. The room was filled with a row of incubators, all resembling giant acrylic shoe boxes mounted on stands. Each had two round cut-outs on each side and seemed illuminated by a spotlight. I grimaced. Neon lights flooded the room way too bright. It was much noisier than I expected. Nurses talking to each other, and the sound of whooshing air, clicks, and beeps.

Between each incubator were machines, monitor screens, and buttons of every size and color waiting to be pushed. I felt like I was in a space lab. But as my eyes adjusted, I saw a sky-blue baby quilt printed with pink bunnies draped over the top of one incubator. A teddy bear hung from an IV pole near another.

A nurse met us at the door. Her mouth was moving, but the loud buzzing in my head made it impossible to understand a word she said. Mama picked up my wrist and held it out to her. The nurse checked my identification bracelet. She was a plump, older woman who smiled and directed us to an incubator in the corner.

We edged up to the clear machine. My baby lay face up on a solid white blanket with a pair of thick pink and blue stripes. One set ran just under her shoulders and the other at her feet. Her diaper, as little as a doll's, swallowed her whole. I looked away.

In my fifth-grade class, I once operated a filmstrip about Australia by turning the knob to advance each slide in time with a 45-rpm record. Flick, flick, flick, we went down under and saw photos of Aborigines, The Great Barrier Reef, Ayers Rock, koala bears, platypuses, and kangaroos. Then there was a close-up of a baby kangaroo, a joey, on the outside of its mother's lower belly. It reminded me of a skinned, pink worm with nubby forelegs, no back legs, and eyes just specks of black on each side of its unformed head. The record announced it weighed less than a lump of sugar. After birth, it had to crawl up its mother's belly and into her pouch, where it would stay and develop for nine months before going out into the world.

My baby looked so much like that joey that the room wavered. My crepe paper legs stumbled. Mama placed a firm grip under my elbow.

I looked at her again. I could have held my daughter in one hand. She was that tiny.

And she was covered in contraptions. A white tube down her throat. Black wires crisscrossing her tummy and disappearing down into her diaper.

The clear oxygen tube above her mouth and inside each nostril was a miniature of Aunt Jean's. Strips of white, gauzy tape held it in place.

Both of her little arms were taped onto foam board splints, as if she'd been pinned to a child's flip flops.

I couldn't even see her hands. They were both encased in bandages with a yellow vial of some sort poking out the ends. Another rolled-up blanket supported her little knees.

Her toes were the first things I saw clearly after the tubes and wires. Though unbelievably small—her entire foot wasn't much wider than my thumb—she had perfectly formed toes. I counted the miniscule, gleaming toenails. One, two, three, four, five, six, seven, eight, nine, ten.

The nurse came to my side and lay her hand on the top of the incubator. Her tone was firm, yet kind. "Your little girl is holding her own. She's been stable since I came on duty."

I saw my baby as if looking through a camera's viewfinder, in snapshots. Her slightly caved-in chest, indented in the shape of a capital I. Her blue veins beneath translucent pink skin. The misshapen top of her head, almost in a point. The down cap of fine brown hair with her scalp shining through. Her closed eyes, little mounds with an equator line etched across the center of each. The furrowed forehead, same as a little old man's.

Then I saw her as a whole, and the sight was overwhelming. I was right to begin with. She was my little kangaroo joey worm.

I put my hand up to my mouth. My knuckles knocked into my top teeth. I gasped for air. Mama reached for me. I flailed at her. The nurse grabbed my wrists and pulled them down.

"Look at me." Her grip was powerful. She jerked me towards her. "Your baby will react to your emotions. Do you understand me? You have to be strong for her."

I saw this woman: her tightly permed silver hair, her strong chin, and her metallic gray eyes. She could rule the world.

I turned to Mama. She stared from me to the baby and back again The expression on her face was one reserved for car crashes.

My legs folded under me. Mama bolted to help the nurse lower me into a rocking chair nearby.

My baby. After all my bold talk about being the best for her, I was terrified. I wasn't enough. I'd let her down. She'd picked the wrong mother.

Thirty-Nine

The television in my hospital room was up high, on a mount attached to the wall by an upside-down V-shaped bracket. I focused on the three shiny flat-head screws at the tips and apex of the inverted V. Instead of sleeping, I counted the three screws over and over … one, two, three, one, two, three. As long as I counted, I didn't imagine my baby covered in wires, tubes, and tape.

When I allowed myself to take my attention off the TV support, I saw Mama curled up on the empty hospital bed next to me. One of the sisters from Aunt Jean's church worked in administration here, and she got us a semi-private room with two beds and arranged it so I'd be the only patient. The sound of Mama's pff, pfff, pffff snoring matched the rhythm of my counting. My eyelids drooped from the whooze they must have put into the IV that was back in my arm. The three screws became six. I counted from one to six until I dropped off to sleep.

I woke up when a nurse came in and turned on the fluorescent light above the headboard. This nurse was a well-oiled machine with all her movements programmed: take the pulse, the blood pressure, and the temperature, check the IV bag, and rattle the thermal mug of ice water. Not mean, but efficient. Speaking in a low voice, she nodded toward the IV pole. "You need to drink plenty of fluids. Then we can take Stanley the Snake away."

I was in slow motion and hadn't gotten past the feel of the blood pressure cuff on my upper arm when I realized she'd already finished.

"Do you need anything?" She stood by my bed with her body poised to turn and leave.

"No, ma'am." I coughed, and the movement sent sharp pains down through my abdomen.

"Hold your stomach when you cough. It won't hurt as bad." Her eyes looked more friendly than I'd first thought.

Another cough shook me, and I interlaced my hands across my lower belly and applied pressure. It did help. I nodded to thank her. She tipped her head my way, and she was gone, on to her rounds and the next patient.

As soon as she left the room, I realized I needed to go to the bathroom. I thought Mama was asleep, but she must not have been. When I lowered the side rail, she was up in a flash and at my side.

"What are you doing? You don't need to walk by yourself until the IV's out and you're off the sedatives." She scooted behind me, wrapped her right arm around my waist, and gripped the IV pole with her left. "Let's take it slow."

Mama tried to move her feet in time with mine, but I started and stumbled so much she tripped over her own big toes.

"Shall we dance? Cha, cha cha." I said it without looking at her and wiggled my behind.

"Can you dance is more like it. I'm not gonna have anything to walk on, much less tango, when your two left feet get through with me." Mama grabbed the back of my gown and guided me firmly. "On the count of two, we move. Ready?"

She gave me an all-serious look, and I started giggling, but the movement made my stomach hurt, and I wrapped my arms around my middle.

"Any day now." Her words sounded tough, but her voice was gentle.

"Don't make me laugh." I held my lower belly with both hands and leaned forward.

"Don't ...," she broke out in laughter, "... bust a gut."

As we laughed, she got all the way behind me so she could reach around with both hands and help me hold my abdomen. I alternated between peals and groans.

"Okay. On two." I moved her hands away and laced my fingers around the pole. I counted off, "One, two, three, one, two, three ..."

We shuffled to the bathroom, and no vaudeville act could have done it better. From the toilet, I looked up at Mama. She had her back turned to me for my privacy, and I felt a swell of love for her.

Mama cleared her throat. "Do you need another Kotex?"
"I do."
She left but came right back with a pad the size of a small paperback book.
"It's Kotex for King Kong. Well, Mrs. Kong."
I laughed, and then I thought about my baby. My body turned cold all over. How could we be laughing with her laying in there fighting for her life? Weariness washed through me. I grabbed hold of the sink to pull myself up. I told Mama, "I can make it on my own."
She ducked behind me and grappled with my gown and the pole, just like she did on the way in. "I know you can. But it takes a fool to refuse help when the devil's at the front door and somebody knows the back way." She squeezed my waist. "You let me help you the next few days and then you can take over. She should be home in a couple of months."
I knew this should sound really good coming from my mama, but I was filled with a ghastly chill that seemed even to cover my vision. Everything looked as if I saw it from behind a giant sheet of ice. "Months?"
"Mary Alice, she was born two months early. I'm sure she won't be home for over a month, at the least." Mama was right again. I would have to toughen up if I was going to be the mother my baby needed.
A half-hour later, I sat in a tub of hot water on an inflated, plastic donut, having a Sitz bath. Mama and the nurse insisted it would help heal my episiotomy. I'd been promised breakfast after this and then a visit to see my baby.
After I got in there, I didn't want to leave. Warm and alone, a wet washcloth covered my face. I could count my breaths and not have to think.
Then I heard Aunt Jean's voice, and the icy cold engulfing me took on tiny cracks. Grabbing a towel, I made a hasty effort to dry off and throw my gown on. Then I was out the door and into her arms. I clenched my eyes tight so I didn't start crying and break down this wall I'd built. I gave her a final squeeze, but she still held me tight. Always, I could depend on Aunt Jean to be the last one to let go. As she

continued to clasp me to her, I smiled at Mama. Though I'd have never thought it before, I now knew Mama would never let go, either.

Mama ushered Aunt Jean into the cushioned chair by my bedside and tucked me between my sheets. Aunt Jean had on her Sunday best, a dove gray dress with a full skirt and narrow belt sewn from the same fabric. She probably made it from a Butterick pattern. It buttoned up the front to just below her chin. Devoid of make-up or jewelry, she seemed regal sitting there with her bee-hive gray hair looking like a crown.

"Brother Stover drove me over here. He's visiting with the sick. I want you to know I've had the prayer chain going from Biloxi, Mississippi, to Jacksonville, Florida. Even called Miss Ida May Foster in Alexandria, Virginia. She's as close to being a Yankee as they come, but she's praying for your little girl all the same." The number of friends Aunt Jean had constantly amazed me, and with her seldom leaving the house except for church and the grocery. She considered the long-distance charges as part of her church tithe.

"I've come to see my great-niece." She said it like there was nothing wrong. "And to bring you presents." She handed me a small package wrapped in the Sunday funny papers. Opening the card first, I saw it was pure Aunt Jean, trying to help me the only way she knew how.

> For My Dear Girl,
> When you feel yourself in need, remember God is with you, always. "I can do all things through Christ which strengtheneth me." Philippians 4:13
> With much love on the birth of your own baby girl,
> Aunt Jean

"Ah, Aunt Jean."

"Well, go on, open it." She waved the backs of her fingers at me.

Lifting a tiny lid, I revealed a little girl's delicate necklace with a tiny gold cross lying on white cotton batting. "Oh, Aunt Jean. It's so dainty and beautiful."

She crooked her finger at me and beamed. "I know you'll have to keep it back until she's older. But I saw it at Kessler's and wanted her to have it. It looks so much like the one I bought for you when you were born."

My eyes misted up. "I still have it. Keep it in my jewelry box with the thumb-sized booklet of the Lord's Prayer you gave me."

She grabbed my hand and gave it a squeeze. "Now let's see what play-pretty the Stovers have sent you."

Mama handed me the present and I took a minute to just hold it. It had pink paper dotted with white storks and a huge pink ribbon Sister Stover tied herself. It was real satin, and I stroked it with my thumb and forefinger. The wrap job exceeded my best work. Each fold was crisp, every piece of tape uniform and evenly spaced. "It's too pretty to open."

I pulled the pink satin bow, and it glided from the package. When I unwrapped it and eased the top off of the white box, a rainbow of pink, blue, yellow, and green was nestled inside. I lifted the crocheted afghan and let its folds fall over my chest. "It's beautiful. I've never seen a pattern like this. So intricate. And it's so much softer than most blankets."

The yarn had the silky feel of angora when I rubbed my hand over it. "How can I ever thank them? They've given me so much."

"They're happy to do it. You've been a Dearheart of the church since you were yea high." She held her hand up at the side of her chair, and I imagined my little girl standing that tall at age two. A hopeful thought.

"And that's not their only gift." She leaned towards me in a conspirator's gesture. "I let them know the pickle you're in. That you'll have to go home while your baby is still here at the hospital. All that driving back and forth three times a day just to see her. Brother Stover's niece went through something similar just last year."

She took a deep breath before belting out, "The Stovers have a furnished garage apartment off East Main Street and it's not rented right now. It's only one bedroom and a walk-up, not in a very good neighborhood. But it's yours to use, as long as your baby's in the hospital, and it's a skip and a jump over the Etowah River Bridge from there to here." She sat back in triumph. "How's that for a prayer chain?"

I couldn't believe it. "You're serious?"

"Yes, ma'am." She opened the drawer to my nightstand, took out the Bible, and laid her hand on it.

It was the truth. "I'll never be able to pay them back. First, the car and now an apartment."

"They don't want you to." She shook her finger at me the same as she did when I was little and she caught me climbing the tree in her backyard. "And don't you even think about it. They'd be offended if you offered. This is part of their mission work, and they're honored to help you. Sometimes they let traveling revivalists and missionaries stay there, so it's all equipped with dishes, pots and pans, and linens. You can move in as soon as the hospital releases you." Digging in her purse, she pulled out a silver key ring in the shape of a cross and handed it to me. One bronze key dangled on the fob, and a laminated card read, "7B E. Glover St."

"I don't know what to say. I'm flabbergasted." The key shone in my palm.

"Say thank you, and when you have the chance to help somebody, don't forget all the blessings God sent your way when you were in need." She ran her tongue across her top lip, and Mama poured her a cup of water.

"I was told you haven't named her yet. Is that true?" She looked at me like she couldn't believe it, took a sip of water, and sat straight up, waiting for my answer.

"But ...." My heart beat faster.

"Well, name her now. She has to have a name. So the eyes of God know where to turn when we pray for her."

I surprised myself by answering right away. "Rebecca."

Before I came to the hospital, I hadn't decided on a name. A short list of possibilities sat on my bedside table, but Rebecca hadn't been one of my choices. I had no idea why it popped out.

"A fine biblical name. Rebecca what?"

"I don't know." My mind was a complete blank. I couldn't think of any of the names I'd poured over in the preceding weeks.

"Well, Rebecca will do for now. Shall we pray?" I saw Mama standing behind Aunt Jean with her jaw clenched in a "here she goes again" look. I dropped my head and laced my hands under my chin. We needed all the prayers we could get.

———

Aunt Jean and I stood at the neonatal ICU sink, just finishing up washing and gowning. Last night, it seemed like the process took forever. This morning, it took no time at all. Maybe it was because my head was clearer, and I knew what I was walking into.

I plucked the sleeve of Aunt Jean's dress between my thumb and forefinger and used it to pull her ear down towards me. "Now, Aunt Jean, how she looks ... it might be a shock to you."

She cupped my chin in one hand and looked straight at me with her wide-lensed glasses magnifying her eyes three times their normal size. "Sweetheart, she won't look like anything but love to me because she's my dear heart's own flesh and blood."

I nodded, but I didn't think she was really prepared for this.

When we entered the room, it didn't seem as bright as it did last night. I looked for the nice, gray-haired nurse, but there were two new nurses on shift. One was a guy and that surprised me. I'd never seen a male nurse, but his green scrubs were the same as all the other nurses. He had a shock of red hair against pale, freckled skin. "Mary Alice Lydell, here to see my baby. This is my Aunt Jean." He checked my ID bracelet and directed me to my baby. I waved him away. "I know where she is." That came out sharper than intended. My insides were tumbling stones. "Sorry. I'm nervous."

"Well, hello Nervous, I'm Gilbert, but everyone calls me Gil. Let me know if you need anything." He winked and headed over to another baby. I liked him immediately.

As we walked towards her incubator, a chill buzzed up and down my spine, the backs of my legs, and clear down my arms. But I didn't want Aunt Jean to think me a coward, and the nurse from last night said Rebecca would know what I felt. She was way too little to feel this kind of cold. I thought about sunshine coming through a window and imagined I stood in a beam with her in my arms. I'd warmed up by the time we reached her.

She was the same as last night. Aunt Jean and I stood, looking at her. I got the notion we were standing by a coffin at a funeral, and panic started to set in until Aunt Jean spoke.

"My, my, isn't she the most beautiful thing you ever saw?" I looked at Aunt Jean and saw she was gazing at Rebecca with her mouth and eyes set all soft like when I was little and she tucked me in bed. It sent a spark through me that ignited every cell in my body.

I focused all of my heightened intensity on Rebecca. I took her in, from the tips of her toes to the slight curl of hair at the crown of her head, and I didn't see wires and tubes and tape. All I saw was love.

Reaching in one of those open portholes, I touched the soft skin at the crook of her elbow with the tip of my index finger. When I did, she opened her eyes, and I yanked my hand back. Steel-gray eyes looked straight at me, and I sensed an immediate connection that went from her to me, like the beam of sunshine I'd been thinking about, only coming out of her and into me. I felt her clear though my body and tears of joy began to fall from my eyes.

Without thinking once about what I was doing, I started singing. "Hush little baby, don't say a word, Mama's gonna buy you a mockingbird." While I crooned, she closed her eyes and her body relaxed, without me even touching her.

She knew me. She knew I was her mother.

I was intent on Rebecca and jumped when I realized Gil had joined us. "I touched her. Is that okay?" My voice came out in a whisper.

"She's tougher than she looks. Just be careful. Avoid the breathing tube, that white one down her throat, and her IV, the one at her hand, and, of course, the feeding tube needs to stay taped in place. Those other wires are monitoring her vitals." He motioned for me to go ahead, as if it were easy.

I turned to Aunt Jean. She smiled, urging me on. I extended my right pointer finger and reached in through the opening nearest her feet.

Using the tip of my finger, I touched her leg as gently as possible. I barely rubbed her. Still, she jerked, and I pulled away so fast I jostled the incubator, which totally flustered me.

I was stepping back, away from her, when Aunt Jean took both of her hands and cupped them around my face, the same as she did when I was little. She held so firmly it hurt a bit, but not enough to cause real pain. She kissed my right cheek and talked to me under her breath. "Mary Alice, your child needs comforting."

I felt her strength coursing through me and drew two deep breaths. Then I squeezed both of Aunt Jean's hands in mine. "Thank you. I can do this."

"Yes, ma'am. I know you can. She don't want anybody else but you." Aunt Jean took a step backwards and Gil went to the nurse's station, leaving Rebecca to me.

Rebecca's face was screwed up tight. This time, I moved my finger in fast and started to sing, "Hush-a-bye don't you cry. Go to sleep my little baby." I ran my finger down her leg as tenderly as possible. All I wanted to do was calm her down. I kept the tune going and reached in with both hands.

At first, it seemed I couldn't get to her due to all the contraptions inside her and around her. But my fingers found the way. I stroked her legs and massaged the soles of her feet with my right thumb. "Sssshhh. Now, now." Over and over. And, slowly she settled down, the same as a wind-up doll.

She fell asleep, and I experienced a fullness in my chest I'd never felt in my life. I loved her.

I loved her so much it felt as if my heart would split open and winged songs fly out. The closest I'd ever come to this feeling was with Aunt Jean, but this … this was another world's love that made my scalp tingle, and my feet hold firm to the ground.

I turned to look for Aunt Jean and Gil, to ask how long it'd be before I could hold her. Aunt Jean had pulled up a chair and sat there rocking. "It come right to you what to do, now, didn't it?" She raised those bushy eyebrows, but not in a mean way, not in a told-you-so kind of way.

I held my palms out to her. "It's like my hands knew better than I did."

She grasped them to help her get up out of the chair. "You need to be remembering the good Lord is moving through you, guiding you, there for you every moment." Her head turned toward Rebecca and her lips set in a straight line. "That's one itsy bitsy baby, sweetie. She's going to need every ounce of her mother, with a huge heaping of grace from above."

Turning back to see her lying there, all the medical gizmos didn't look nearly as foreign as they did before. "I know." With those words, I was flooded with the certainty I would be the mother Rebecca needed.

Forty

The hospital released me a week after I arrived. Mama would be coming to get me during her lunch break. We'd pick up my car from behind Penney's and go to my new apartment. I had a half-hour to visit my little pumpkin before then.

Gil leaned over her crib, wiping the creases under her arm. "Watch. There's really not much to it."

"I bet it's harder than you make it look."

"Your first, right?" He flipped her to one side and washed her back.

I blurted it out. "Yes, and I don't know the first thing about babies."

"Okay, then you can jump right in. You do the legs and feet." He passed me a wipe.

I dabbed between each of her infinitesimally small toes. She pulled them away from me.

"They all hate it when you wash their piggies," Gil said as he pulled out a fresh blanket. "Let me tell you, the veteran moms—the ones whose first babies did not have a NICU stay—say they didn't know what to do either. Not until someone showed them or they did it enough times. Besides, a lot of your worries are normal for any new mother, not just a new preemie mother." Everything he said reassured me in every way possible. "Hey, I have some cafeteria coupons for you."

"Gee, Gil, thanks. I appreciate you and everything you've been doing for Rebecca and me. Oh, I almost forgot to tell you! Guess what?" He raised his eyebrows. "I'm going home." I laid my hand on her sweet head. "But I can't stand leaving without her."

"We're taking good care of her, Mary." An alarm sounded across the room, and he turned and strode away towards it.

Nobody'd ever called me Mary before. Always Mary Alice, and I'd always hated the name. But Mary had a soft sound to it. I wondered if I could change my name.

Putting my lips to the porthole nearest her head, I whispered, "I love you the mostest, forever and ever and a day."

That's when I knew what her full name would be. Rebecca Jean Lydell, after Aunt Jean. And I'd call her Becky! Because she was much too little for a three-syllable name.

"Time for all good mommies to go eat their lunches and take their afternoon naps." Gil's voice echoed in the NICU as he stood by the double doors, pointing at his wristwatch.

I held my eyes open as wide as possible so I could take in every inch, every Becky curve, and store it in my mind to last me until after dinner.

Mama wasn't due for another ten minutes. I used the family waiting room phone to call Aunt Jean. "Guess what? I've named her."

"You picked out a middle name?" When I told her, there was a pause on the other end, then her voice came on all husky. "I'm speechless."

"Well, that's a first!" I giggled into the receiver.

"You're a rascal, but I am deeply honored. I can't begin to tell you what it means to me, seeing you with your daughter. Helps to make things right for me and mine. I guess that might sound nutty."

"No, Aunt Jean. It doesn't. But there's one thing I don't understand." I waited for her to ask.

"What's that?"

"You taught me that everything happens for a reason. Isn't that right?" Her pause again.

"Yes." Only the one word and the sound of her stop-and-start breathing.

"Then, can't you see you did the right thing? It wasn't like it is for me. People won't look at me like I'm a 'fallen woman.' If I'd been in the same boat back then, wouldn't your advice have been entirely different?" I spoke from a place of conviction and hoped she could hear that.

"I've wrestled with this for longer than you've been on this Earth. But seeing you go through similar circumstances has brought it all back, like it was just yesterday. I'd forgotten how young I was when it happened. I hadn't remembered a lot of things that have come back to me now." Her voice broke and I could tell she was crying. "I vowed to hang onto every moment I had with you. I told you before, and it was the truth, God sent you to me when I needed you the most."

Wiping tears from the corners of my eyes, I had to clear my throat before telling her, "He sent us to each other, Aunt Jean. He sent us to each other."

———

While I waited out front for Mama, a group of teenage Candy Stripe volunteers went by in their showy pink and white uniforms. All of them giggling about boys and talking about movies and football games. What would Becky think of me if she knew I was jealous? But those days were over for me, and I did envy them.

When I got in the car with Mama and told her Becky's name, she goosed my knee and said, "You can call her what you want. I'm calling her Speck. Cause that's what she is, same as I told you when you were pregnant. Just a little scrap of a girl." She looked pleased with herself. "She's a fighter. Our little Speck."

"I don't want you calling her an odd name like that." I spoke up quickly, trying to nip that idea right away.

"Why not? It's cute." Mama merged onto Turner McCall Boulevard.

"It's not a name, that's why. It's a size. Maybe 'extra-small' would be just as good."

"She's my granddaughter, and I'll call her what I like." She shot a look at me.

"She's my daughter, and I get to name her. You had your chance with me, and you blew it!" I was serious, but I still laughed as I said it.

"What's wrong with your name? It's a perfectly good name." She pulled up next to my old Datsun.

"I'll see you at the apartment." After the last week, it felt so good to be doing something normal, even if it was quibbling with my mama.

I cranked my car and let excitement fill me as I drove down South Broad Street with Mama's car behind me, over the river, past Myrtle Hill Cemetery, and past the old McCall Hospital where I was born.

When the road split, I bore left onto East Main, left onto Glover Street, past a convenience store on the corner, and there the garage was on the left. It sat back to the side of a house. I parked my car, flew up the steps, and fit the key in the lock. The key chain clinked against the doorframe.

When I threw the door open and flipped on the light, I saw the cutest little apartment ever. The living room was filled with windows, a poofy green couch, an end table, a rocker, and a floor lamp. I walked inside and my shoes tapped on hardwood floors. It smelled like lemons.

Through the living room was the kitchen, the size of a cracker box, but with a handful of cabinets and a little table with two chairs. The walls glowed a pale golden shade. Lots of people must like yellow kitchens, and this was definitely a sign, a good one.

I heard Mama yelling, "Yoo hoo," at the front door.

"I'm in the kitchen!" No dishwasher. I'd gotten spoiled again at Mama's. But I'd lived for months without one at Jim's. It was no big deal.

Back in the living room, Mama was still standing in the doorway, nodding her approval. "Come on!" I grabbed her hand and pulled her into the bedroom, which was as big as mine at home, but not the blue walls I'd dreamed of. These were a nice, conservative beige matched with a chocolate brown bedspread.

I spun around in the middle of the bedroom floor. "Can you believe it?"

Mama perched on the end of the bed and bounced. "Seems like a firm mattress, too." Looking up at me, she spoke in a soft tone. "You deserve some good luck."

I looked around at my new home. This was more than good luck. It was a miracle. My focus stopped above the dresser, and I burst out laughing and dropped to the bed, rolling at the hilarity of it all. It was a crucifix. It looked like the one I took from Aunt Jean's house all those years ago.

Mama frowned, not understanding, until I pointed, and she turned her head. She tumbled onto the bed next to me. "I hope to God you keep your hands off that one!" We both rolled laughing. "Come on, let's get your stuff out of my car and fix ourselves a sandwich, so I can get back to work."

We ate peanut butter and jelly sandwiches, washed down with two Cokes she'd brought from the store.

At Mama's car, I wrapped my arms around her. "Thank you so much for lunch and for helping me and everything."

"I'm relieved you have a decent place to stay near the hospital." She put her hands on my shoulders, as if she were giving me marching orders. "Now. Penney's is holding your job. But there's no telling when you'll be able to go back to work, with her so sick." A car went by on Glover with the engine making a knocking noise. "I know you've saved some money from your paychecks you can use towards your food and gas, but you let me know if you need anything. I'm right around the corner at Firestone. You just holler." Next door, a metallic purple Mustang skid into the convenience store lot, and four guys opened their doors and fell out, whooping and acting like fools.

Mama tucked a loose strand behind my ear. "Now, I want you to watch yourself here. I think it's safe enough. But it is a rough neighborhood. My only concern is you driving down South Broad, coming home late from the hospital. Keep your eyes open and your car doors locked. And when you get here, you watch yourself, and go straight from the car into the house and bolt the door."

"I will." Other than the store next door and the East Main traffic, the street seemed quiet, and the houses were kept up. There were even Christmas decorations on most of the porches.

I hadn't thought much about Christmas. It would be here in a couple of weeks. I wished Becky could be home by then, but I knew it wasn't possible. I would make the best of it anyway.

"Ho, ho, ho, Mama!" I took her hands and pulled her around in a circle on the drive.

"Ho, ho yourself. I'm off to work. You skedaddle upstairs and take a nap before you have to drive back to the hospital. It wouldn't hurt you to call me every night when you get back here, either. Let me know you're home safe."

Next door, the hooligans left the store with brown paper bags clutched in their hands, singing a raunchy version of Jingle Bells. She turned to get in her car. I stopped her and tucked the tag back under her blouse collar. "I'll call you." Using my pinkie, I wiped at a smear of mascara underneath her left eye. "Think you can handle things without me?"

She bit her lip and put on her tough look. "You and Speck will be home before you know it. Until then, I'll lounge around enjoying my freedom." Ducking her head to get into the car, I heard her sniff. Before she drove away, she rummaged in her purse, pulled out a Kleenex, and blew her nose. She cranked the car, rolled down her window, and shouted at me before pulling out of the drive, "Damn allergies!"

Forty-One

For three days, I followed almost the same routine as Becky—sleeping and eating, plus seeing my little girl. I talked on the phone to Mama and Aunt Jean every day, and Mama came by to visit Becky once.

But after a few days, I was much stronger and that left a lot of hours with nothing to do. Gil warned me I had at least two months of these days before she'd be able to come home.

So, after visiting Becky the morning of her ten-day birthday, I was seriously stir-crazy and ready to try something different. I got into my car and drove to my old Saturday stomping grounds—the library.

Next door to the library was a bronze statue of Romulus and Remus in front of the city auditorium. It was a huge rendition of two naked little boys suckling a she wolf's extremely prominent teats. Rome was named after Rome, Italy, because of the town's seven hills and three rivers. Our city forefathers must have been drinking Coca Cola before they took the cocaine out, because all similarity ended there.

Nonetheless, back in the 1920's, Mussolini sent this replica of artwork from his city of Rome. The church folk found it indecent and had raised a stink about it for fifty years. I thought it was gorgeous in front of the stately brick building with huge white columns—one of the only touches of class in this crappy town. Aunt Jean said they used to put diapers on the twins, and she thought they still should.

The wolf disappeared from sight as I climbed the library steps. I pulled open the heavy doors and walked into the cool and quiet. I loved the smell but could never exactly identify the odor.

First, I decided to go to the children's section. It was such a cheerful place. Cut-outs of submarines, rocket ships, and old-fashioned biplanes hung from the ceiling. A group of seven children and four mothers sat in a semi-circle on a brightly colored carpet printed with the alphabet, numbers, and a hopscotch board. An older woman read *The Little Engine That Could*, which both Mama and Aunt Jean had read to me a hundred times. Someday, Becky and I would be sitting in that group. I'd share all my favorites with her and teach her how to read before she even started school, so she didn't have to waste one day without books.

I'd always favored children's books and knew I'd find something light to read here. In ten minutes, I headed back upstairs with *The Secret Garden*.

Next, I looked up publications about premature babies and spent a good hour perusing and reading sections on infant and child development. Two books looked especially promising, and I added them to my stack.

I thought about Mama telling me to think positive. The woman at the reference desk had helped me before, so I went to her.

I was almost embarrassed to ask. "Are there any books written about thinking positive?"

She peered over her oval-shaped wire-rim glasses. "Oh, many. But the most famous is *The Power of Positive Thinking* by Norman Vincent Peale. I'd recommend you start there." She jotted the Dewey Decimal code, 248.4 Pea, on a slip of paper for me.

I was getting hungry. I hurried to the 200's and found it in no time. There were several copies on the shelf. I grabbed one and was trucking down the aisles, heading for the check-out, when a book in the 300's section literally shone at me as I zoomed by. Putting my brakes on, I came to a standstill and re-traced my steps. I couldn't help being curious. The only thing I'd ever had shine at me was Aunt Jean's Jesus, but I was just a little girl then.

When I reached the book, I saw it wasn't really gleaming or anything fantastical, but the spine did have a luster to it. I jerked my hand back when I touched it and drew my breath in fast. The title was *Father-Daughter Sex Abuse*. Every ounce of my body told me to run as fast as I could. But I was drawn to the book, as surely as Aladdin was compelled to rub the lamp. Someone had written a book about this. That meant I wasn't the only one.

I looked up and down the aisle. No one in sight. I set my other three books down on a half-filled shelf. Shaking, I lifted the volume. The cover design was strange—old-fashioned, pink wallpaper torn so the title showed through. I opened it by chance to the table of contents. Four words took my breath away: Incest: A Common Occurrence. I trembled so badly I almost dropped it. I glanced around again, to make sure no one was watching, and slid the book into my purse. I had to read it but was too ashamed for the check-out person to see the title. I wasn't stealing it. I'd bring it back.

Snatching up all the books, I trotted to the front, checked out, and practically ran to my car. Back at the apartment, I slid the book under my mattress, until I could get up the nerve to read it. Then I flung out my arms and started spinning in circles, the way I used to do in my bedroom. As I spun, it was like that book began to transmit the old Alice voice. *Read it right now. Take it out and open it. Any section will do. You've come too far to chicken out now.*

But, if I read that book, if I faced the truth, I might crawl into my rabbit hole and never come out. If I truly came to terms with what Daddy did, it might destroy me.

Only thing crazy about you is thinking that way! Didn't believe you had it in you to be Becky's mother, but now you know you do. You can do this.

The room righted. My heart slowed its frantic beating. The Alice voice made sense. Why had I shoved her down the rabbit hole?

Fear. Pure and simple. There is no Alice Girl. Just me, and this is the part of me that knows. The time has come. I have to let this side of me have its say and stop dismissing it as a lunatic named Alice. As soon as those thoughts formed in my mind, I had an image of tight-faced Alice—with her hair in her eyes, in her sloppy, men's clothing—lining herself up in front of me, like a life-size paper doll. I inhaled her into my pores, starting at my toes and speeding up through my body, until she fused into my brain. I imagined a sound like a bubble popping at the crown of my head. And then, I was one. I wasn't Mary Alice anymore and there was no Alice. We were just one girl named Mary.

I lifted the mattress and pulled the book out. On the first page, I read: "Do you think you're crazy? Do you think you're bad, that something's wrong with you deep down inside and if people knew they'd abandon you? ... Children who've been abused often don't connect what happened to them as a child with their current problems. Understanding the connection will frequently enable you to get unstuck and move on with your life. This is an optimistic book. It will help you sort out what was, what is, and what can be."

I flipped through and passages jumped from the page: Most abused children grow up thinking the abuse occurred because of themselves ... but it was a problem with your abuser, not with you. No child is ever to blame for the abuse.

Alice, my voice of reason, had been telling me all along there was nothing wrong with me, that it was all him. And I'd shoved her aside. It might take a while, but I'd do whatever it took to get past this, for Becky and for me.

For now, I had to get back to the hospital. My daughter came first.

I slipped the hardback into my nightstand drawer. As I went into the kitchen, I thought about it waiting there for me. I was ready to listen to whatever it had to tell me about Daddy.

—

That afternoon, as I approached her incubator, it was like Becky knew I was there. She waved her little flip-flop hand. Someone had drawn a purple smiley face on the side of her bilirubin light. I reached in and smoothed my fingertip over the curve of her elbow. "Hey, little Tater Tot."

Upon hearing my voice, she opened her marble gray eyes. Her furrowed brow reminded me of a little old woman.

"What's the matter? Don't like being called Tater Tot? Well, I don't blame you. Okay, you're my little scrapper. You like that?" Out of the blue, I started warbling a song Mama used to sing to me about three little fishes and a mommy fish. Becky blinked and kicked when I got to the funny part, "Boop, boop, dittum, datum, wattum, choo!"

"Where'd you learn that old Andrews Sisters' tune?" Gil came up behind me with an armload of infant blankets.

"Didn't know anyone sang it except my mama." We both laughed.

"Let me put these up, and I have great news." He started away from me, but I butted in.

"Oh, no. Great news first, then you can do your laundry."

He laid the blankets on a shelf. "What was I thinking? Guess I forgot how demanding you are! Okay, Troublemaker, how would you like to hold your daughter?" Every freckle on his face stood out as he pulled over the rocking chair.

"You don't mean it?" I be-bopped in place.

He grinned and lifted the top of her incubator.

"You do mean it!" I could have done the conga around the NICU and circled each baby. My arms began to tingle.

"Okay, wildcat, sit yourself down, and I'll hand her over." He swiftly bundled her up papoose-style, including her arms. Only her head was visible. "She's not used to space travel. It may cause her discomfort, but she'll be fine. No worries."

He gathered the wires so they emerged in one grouping at the side of her head, minimizing what I'd have to deal with when holding her.

My bundle of Becky came closer, and I started feeling twitchy. "What do I do?" I clasped my hands to my chest and looked to Gil in dismay. "She's so little. How do I hold her? What if I hurt her?"

Standing right in front of me with Becky in his arms, he was the picture of an unruffled owl. His big, aqua green eyes soothed me. "Slow down. You won't hurt her, and you'll be an old pro in no time. Now, take a second and get yourself ready."

Bringing my arms down, I laid my hands on top of each other and held my elbows out. I pushed my feet down steady, so the rocker stayed put, took an opera singer's breath, all the way down to my navel, and looked at Gil. "Ready."

"Here she comes." His tone was hushed and reassuring. Slowly, he lowered her into my arms. "There you go. That's right. Keep her neck supported."

Her weight transferred to my forearms. Such a wee little girl.

"You got her. Lift her head a tad more." He adjusted her tubing, so it was free and clear of my chair.

I'd held dolls, even a baby or two. They always felt stiff, and I'd endured the ordeal for a few minutes. But from the moment Gil laid Becky's head into the curve of my arm, I had the sense I'd been holding her all my life.

She was part of me. Like our bodies were still united. Her eyes flickered open and met mine. The connection from hers to mine felt as solid as a telephone wire. I felt the line flowing down into my solar plexus like an open link of communication. Everything else in the room faded away as we rocked.

—

"Mama, you can't believe how it felt to hold her. I was scared, but then I wasn't. It was incredible. I can't even describe it." I pumped my potato masher up and down and around the pot, dolloped in more butter and pummeled some more.

"Don't let me forget, I took Jean to lunch today and she sent her camera to you. It's in my purse. She said pictures are long over-due." Mama turned down the eye under the boiling black-eyed peas. "I know you find this hard to believe, but I do know how it feels to hold your daughter for the first time."

I flashed a look of apology at her. "I know, but I can't believe it. I had no idea it would change everything. I mean … everything!" I flung open my arms and whipped potatoes spattered from the masher in my hand to the top two cabinet doors. "Whoops!"

Mama wet a dish cloth and wiped down the wood surface. "It's so good to see you feeling happy. But if you get any more excited, we won't get a bite to eat."

"I am, Mama. I'm dancing inside, and it's spilling out." I salted and peppered the potatoes, swirled my finger around the inside of the pot and held it out for Mama, who licked it off.

"Just right. I see I taught you something." She opened the oven door and pulled out the cornbread. "We'll butter this and be ready to eat."

"I know it's not much but I'm so glad you're here to celebrate me coming home." Crossing to the fridge, I pulled out my salads: two canned pear halves on saucers, each filled with a glob of mayonnaise and sprinkled with grated cheddar cheese. "Sorry there's no meat."

We fixed our plates and ate quickly. I think both of us were starved. Mama jabbed peas with her fork tines, which reminded me of how I used to eat them.

"Do you remember me eating with a toothpick?" I shook my head.

She chuckled. "Who could forget? You've always had your ways." Then she used her fork to separate the food on her plate into quadrants and mimicked a little girl's voice. "Ewww, it's touching."

Feeling sheepish, I rubbed my left eye with my knuckle and feigned a shudder at Mama. The problem was I still did those sorts of nutty things and I had to stop. "I'm definitely going to pay for my raising." Mama didn't look like she was gloating, but she did appear self-satisfied.

I slapped my hand against the table. "Back to Becky and away from all my dippy quirks. We can expect her home sometime between the end of January and mid-February."

Mama brought her attention down to her plate and chewed. When she looked back up, she appeared to be watching me with care. "When are you going to tell Jim?"

"Jim?" My good mood faltered. "Why would I tell Jim?"

She set her fork down and pressed her index finger against her lips. Silence lasted for three beats. "He's her father."

Anger prickled up my neck to the top of my head. "No. He lost his right to her. He doesn't want her, anyway. I'm never talking to him again, and Becky's no concern of his."

"Can't we talk about this?" Her tone was curt, but not snippy. I couldn't avoid the topic forever. We both sighed. "Let's go into the living room and get comfortable."

I rose and dusted cornbread crumbs from my fingertips. "Just leave your plate here. I'll get the dishes later."

"You don't have to look so dire." Mama slid her free hand around my waist as we stepped into the other room, each of us bringing our tumblers of tea.

We plunked down on the sofa. "Broaching that subject is like pouring lye soap in my eyes."

"No, it's opening them big browns of yours and seeing the world for what it is." She set her glass onto a Piggly Wiggly circular lying on the end table. I gripped mine, rubbed my thumb up and down its condensation, and felt the urge to count.

"Mary Alice, when people discuss a problem, it don't mean they're going to actually do everything they consider. Let's just talk about your predicament. Okay?" She had dark circles under her eyes and little red spider veins at the sides of her nostrils I hadn't noticed before. "How do you think you're going to dodge telling Jim about Becky?" I opened my mouth, and she intervened. "Hear me out, first. Then I'll listen."

My mama through and through … I was to listen, and then, and only then, I got a chance to talk.

"You're going to need help tending to Becky. Now, more than ever. We don't know what kind of care she's going to need. How do you plan to live? This is half Jim's responsibility. He has to come through with child support, if nothing else."

I shook my head. "I tried to talk to him about his 'responsibility,' and I thought he was going to hit me, for real. It was an ugly scene."

"He ever lays a hand on you or Becky, and his days are over." Mama gritted her teeth. "But you've got to be practical. With her sick, you can't work for a while. This is going to come up when you file for welfare and food stamps. Then they'll prove paternity and take him to court." She narrowed her eyes. "Or we could kill the bastard for his Social Security. Those checks come as regular as rain."

I drew my chin up. "Somehow, I don't think a dead Daddy and her mother and grandmother in prison will be in Becky's best interest."

Mama threw one arm above her head. "Good God, I was joking. Why do you have to be so damned serious all the time? Like you've got a gold-plated spike eternally stuck up your ass."

I turned my head away from her and stared off into the kitchen. I imagined Becky in a highchair at that table, rubbing pureed carrots into her hair.

"I know what it's like to struggle with money. When it feels like the monthly bills are a leather belt that won't fasten in the middle, no matter how hard you stretch both sides of it." She rocked her head from side-to-side. "Your daddy never hit a lick at a snake to help me. It's hard. You don't have a clue how tough it is." With her hands propped on her stomach, she tapped the tips of her fingers together. "We'll make the son of a bitch do his duty."

"Mama, I know. I realize I don't have an inkling how I'll get by. But, if Daddy hadn't been in prison and had paid child support, would the money have been worth you having to put up with his shit all the time?" I saw a flash of something in her eyes, and she shifted her frown to her knees.

Now I was the one biding my time for her response. She bit on her lips and scratched behind her ear, then met my gaze straight on.

"I gotta admit—hell, no! I think I'd rather have pounded my skull with a ball-peen hammer every morning." Her laugh was a barking sound, and I joined in with a twitter. Mama gave me a quick, one-armed hug around my shoulders. "Ya got a point there, gal."

Then she drummed her fingers on the end table. "That's enough serious talk for one night. I'm exhausted. Let me help you clean up, then I'm heading home."

"I got it, Mama." She followed me into the kitchen.

"Nope. Four hands can do triple the work of two. It's a mathematical mystery, but true. We'll get this done in no time." I filled the sink with suds, while she cleared the table.

After Mama traipsed down the stairs, I locked up and got ready for bed, and my book.

The morning seemed like two days ago. Settling back against the headboard, I rotated my pillow lengthwise, stuffed it behind me for support, and pulled out *Father-Daughter Sexual Abuse*. Holding it, I knew I needed help to tackle it. I set it down and first opened *The Power of Positive Thinking*.

Reading along in the first chapter, the book spooked me out by quoting the same Bible verse Aunt Jean wrote in my gift card, "I can do all things through Christ, which strengtheneth me." Philippians 4:13.

I didn't know if this was the book I was looking for after all. I didn't know it'd be religious. But what were the odds Aunt Jean and the book would quote the same Bible verse? I decided to give it a try and ignore the religious parts as best I could.

It was a fast read, and I flew through it to the mid-way point. I liked what it said about changing what I was thinking and making a list of what I did have. I ran through the list in my head: Becky, Mama, Aunt Jean, Mrs. Stover's apartment, Gil, the doctors and hospital, books, the library, and a car that started. Plenty of people had a lot less. I had to stop focusing on what I didn't have, when all this was right in front of me. And, I could add one more thing to the list—one day, I would find a way to go back to school. Getting my degree would make it possible to take care of Becky by myself.

The book gave me specific things to do. It said to stamp my mind with a picture of myself succeeding, and when a negative thought came to mind, to deliberately voice a positive one to cancel it out. I'd been imagining voices in my head since before I could remember. The difference was switching out what I said to myself. I'd done it just yesterday when I pictured Becky in my arms in a sunbeam.

It was funny, this book wasn't that different from *The Little Engine That Could*. Mama's voice came to me clearly, "I think I can. I think I can. I know I can. I know I can."

Lifting the book, I told myself these two books would change my life. I was strong enough to handle whatever came. If I had my doubts, I just had to keep talking to myself until it became the truth.

I flipped it open and read: "Sexual abuse is when any adult forces, tricks, threatens, or coerces a child to have any kind of sexual contact with him/her ... the most harmful sexual abuse is perpetuated by a parent."

But I don't think Daddy ever did it. Was just touching me the same? Only three pages later I found: "You may have a tendency to minimize what happened, such as 'But it couldn't have been incest, he didn't rape me, he only fondled my breasts, or only touched my genitals.'"

I stared at the page. The book couldn't be clearer. It was exactly what had happened to me. I never thought of what Daddy did as "incest." The idea sent me reeling.

Turning the pages with increasing speed, I flew through sections, key phrases catching my eye: children push the memories away; you may have "gone into a trance" when being sexually abused, by mentally dissociating yourself from your body, thus learning coping skills that served a valuable purpose then, but now interfere with your ability to function as a healthy adult.

I shook so badly I bit my tongue. Couldn't quit shaking. The people who wrote this book knew all about "forgetting," the fog, the time machine, the floating, the counting.

The icy cold I felt mirrored the deep freeze I underwent at thirteen, on the day Daddy came back. The difference was a growing anger in the pit of my stomach. He'd caused all the crazy things I did.

One thing the book said was the most important: "You reacted normally to an abnormal situation, but those behaviors aren't serving you now. The key is to realize this and stop looking for someone to come rescue you. The abuse wasn't your fault, but it is your responsibility to work through recovery." I'd done all kind of nutty things for a good reason, but I had to stop all of them now, for Becky and for me.

I went into the bathroom, took a scalding hot shower, looked at myself in the mirror, and said out loud, "It wasn't my fault." The noise echoed off the tan bathroom tiles. My head knew it was the truth, but after all these years, it would take my heart a while to grapple with it.

For my whole life, inside my head, the memories of him touching me had been lined-up dominos, just waiting to be knocked over. It had taken every ounce of my energy to wall off what he did. I protected myself from knowing, because I thought if I tipped one truth of it, all the pieces would fall down. I'd go down the rabbit hole forever.

That book explained me to myself.

All along, I'd believed it happened because I was so bad. I thought there was no way a father could treat his daughter that way unless something was horribly wrong with her. I had it backwards, and he planned it that way. Every bit of it was Daddy's doing and he was the shameful one. He was the man, out of everybody in the world, who was supposed to take care of me.

The book said to get counseling and to replace negative thought patterns with positive ones. As soon as I could, I'd check to see if anyone offered free counseling or if Mama's insurance covered it. Until then, it was up to me to figure out how to get better. The Positive Thinking book would help me change my thinking. Every time I thought badly of myself, I would turn it around on its head. I put both books into my nightstand drawer and switched off my bedside lamp.

With the lights out, a moonbeam came through my window and across the bed. I focused on that blue-white gleam and imagined Becky's sweet little face, then transformed that visage the way I fancied she would look at age six, with her top two teeth missing and pigtails. I drifted off thinking I needed to learn how to braid her hair.

Forty-Two

As I was leaving the NICU on Christmas Eve morning, I heard my name. "Mary Alice!"

"Carolyn?" She was sitting in the NICU waiting area with a huge present in her lap. With everything that had happened in my life since last April, it seemed like years since I'd seen her.

She sat twirling her hair. She always did that when she was nervous. As I came closer, I saw she looked the same, and the familiarity was wonderfully, blessedly comforting. I ran the last few steps to her. She'd only half-risen from her seat, but I reached to grab her anyway.

"Wait." She sat the box down and circled her arms around me.

Tears coursed down my face. Somehow, seeing Carolyn made everything that had transpired more real.

"I'm sorry. I didn't know you were here until a couple of days ago. I don't know what to do or what to say. I've been such a jerk." She wiped at her smeared mascara with the side of her thumb.

"No, please don't. I'm the one who's sorry." We stood stiffly, facing each other, so I pulled up a chair. We sat knee-to-knee, gripping each other's hands. "I was out of my head. And then I lost my mind." We laughed.

"Tell me about your baby." Her wide, unblinking blue eyes showed fear, and, for once, she was the one tapping her leather boot, instead of me jiggling mine. She had "the look" I'd seen on other people's faces in this waiting room, a cross between concern and discomfort. No one ever seemed to know what to say to the parents.

I smiled wide. "You may wish you hadn't asked that one. She's got me dancing steps I never knew before. My gosh, I wish you could see her. I bet there's never been such a little baby with such a big personality. Mama says as soon as she's walking, we're putting boxing gloves on her and putting her in the ring. She's a tiny, adorable dynamo. They even took her IV out this morning. I got to hold her hand for the first time!"

"Ahhh, that's so sweet." In her white holiday sweater with sequins, Carolyn could have been the winter wonderland queen. Looking down at my wrinkled shirt, I saw myself the way Carolyn must see me, a Dickins' charwoman. More importantly, I saw myself the way Becky would see her mother. I would have to take better care of myself.

"Here." Carolyn handed me the present. "I hope you don't already have it."

I chuckled and thought, fat chance of that, but said, "Oh, I bet I don't." Inside the box was an infant bathtub with a non-skid bottom filled with baby towels, washcloths, baby soap and shampoo, and a bright yellow rubber duck. I held each item up and again fought back the tears. "Oh, Carolyn. Thank you. She needs all of this, and it looks so pretty with the pink and yellow things spilling out of the blue tub, like a flower arrangement. The happiest day of my life will be when I take her home and give her a bath in this tub."

She blushed. "I'm really sorry you've had such a hard time."

I heaved a deep sigh. "It's Becky who's had it bad. I just need to grow up."

Her foot wasn't tapping anymore. Instead, she leaned forward, and her eyes drooped with sadness. "It's funny. You were never one of the girls who talked about having babies. Now look at you. You're a great mom."

"Hmm." I tipped my head towards her and gave a half-grin. "I don't know about that, but I'm learning every day."

She took a small Christmas present from her purse. "This one's for you."

"But I don't have anything for you."

She waved me away and shrugged. "Get real."

I unwrapped it and lifted a silver chain from the small jewelry box.

316 • Birdhouse Jesus

"It's a mother's necklace with her birthstone, a blue topaz." A pendant the color of the Gulf of Mexico sparkled at me. "I remembered you like silver, not gold."

I really was going to cry. "You can't imagine what this means." I turned the back of my neck to her. "Help me put it on."

She fastened the clasp, and I heard her question from behind my ear. "When will she get to go home?"

"Maybe in about a month."

She gave a quick intake of breath. "Sorry. I just didn't know it would be that long. Oh, my goodness."

I grasped her hand. "It will go by quickly." As much as I loved seeing Carolyn, I felt exhausted. Her visit had brought up so many emotions. "I'm super glad you came. What are you doing tonight and tomorrow for Christmas?"

"Tonight's dinner at Grandma Townsend's with all of Dad's clan, and tomorrow is Christmas lunch with Mom's family at Nana Turner's. It's a very special celebration of kinship." She used a sarcastic tone. "I'm really looking forward to Aunt Mildred, who always runs her fingers around the bottom of the iced cakes and licks off the frosting. Lovely." She leaned her head to one side so far, her right ear touched her shoulder. I'd forgotten that habit of hers, and it made me laugh.

"I've missed you." I stood up, so she'd take my cue and know it was okay to leave.

She followed suit. "When are you home? I don't know whether to come here or there to see you, and when is best?"

I shook my head. "That's a long story. It might be a while, but I'll call you when I can. I promise." We embraced, then I pulled her away from me at arm's length. "You're going to be Auntie Carolyn. Becky's going to love you! But I'm warning you … no baby talk. None. Nada. Capiche?"

"No babbling? But they love baby talk." She swung her long gleam of hair forward, over both shoulders, and pouted her lips.

I lifted the giant box with the bathing supplies. "Come on. We'll walk to the parking lot together. And I'm serious. None of your prattle to my little Einstein." I grinned at her. "Now tell me all about your senior year but give me the Reader's Digest condensed version. Because I seriously need to get home and lie down before I cook for tomorrow, and you have a wild party to attend."

A cute guy dressed in green scrubs passed us in the hall. Carolyn and I turned to each other at the same time with did-you-catch-that looks. We burst out giggling. I hadn't clowned around with a friend in so long it made me remember I was still just seventeen. For once, I agreed with Mama, some fun would do me good. But from now on, I was watching the kind of fun I had.

—

On Christmas Day I woke up at six and bounced out of bed. Becky's first Christmas! I couldn't wait for next year, when she'd be toddling around and excited by all the bright lights.

In the shower, I looked down and saw my belly had shrunk. There was an outward curve to my lower stomach that I didn't have before pregnancy, but it wasn't that bad.

I hadn't worn jeans since August. Dashing into the bedroom, I pulled a pair from my closet and slid them over my rump. I had to lie down on the bed to zip them, but they were on, and they'd stretch out more in an hour or so. I slipped on a red sweater Mama had given me, and I was in regular clothes again. If I could have managed more than baby steps in those tight jeans, I would have danced a jig.

First, I drove to the hospital. The streets were deserted, and the halls empty. Gil said they sent any patient who could be released home for the holidays. But in the NICU, three of us parents rushed up at the same time, and when I went through the double doors, there were two couples already at the incubators. Full house.

A Christmas angel dangled from Becky's IV pole and protected her. Her brown curls shone under the NICU lights. She wasn't simply beautiful, she was radiant.

"Merry, merry Christmas. Wake up, sleepy head." I tickled her earlobe, and she flicked her hand at mine. "Oh, no. You're not brushing your mom off on Christmas morning." I stroked my fingertip down her cheek. She wiggled and peeked one eye open at me. "There's my girl."

I pulled a gift I'd wrapped in silver paper from my pocketbook and flashed it in front of Becky's eyes. She blinked and twitched her eyes. "Ooooh … shiny! What could it be? Want me to open it for you? All right, but next year, you're opening it yourself." I ripped open the package and showed her the book cover, *Babies*. "Tater tots, just like you. See the brother holding his baby sister. Wait 'til you come home. We're going to read so many stories." I opened the book and began to read, showing Becky each page.

"Are you already reading to that baby?" Gil had on a Santa hat with bright green stars pinned to it with diaper pins.

"Can't start too young. Merry Christmas!" I pulled a gift wrapped in the same silver paper I used for Becky's from my tote bag and held it out to him.

The look on his face was pleasure mixed with bashfulness. "No, you didn't need to do this. Really."

"Are you trying to spoil my fun?" I lifted my eyebrows at him.

"You're incorrigible." He opened the present, a piece of artwork I had made and mounted in a dime store frame.

"I saw your peace sign bracelet and thought you might like it." I tapped my fingers on the side seam of my jean leg while he examined the collage I'd made from a photo of him holding Becky. In it, he sported a goofy grin. Encircling the picture were symbols I'd cut from discarded magazines in the waiting room: peace signs, rainbow flowers and mushrooms, neon pink hearts, bright yellow smiley faces, and a VW camper decorated in psychedelic colors, driven by a green alien. At the top, I'd used a thick black magic marker to pen in "Peace, Love, & Nursing." At the bottom, I printed, "Living it every day."

He looked up at me with a bewildered expression, his mouth open and eyes squinting. "I'm stunned." His gaze went back to the artwork, and he shook his head. "You hand-made this … mind-blowing."

"I wanted you to remember Becky. So, you like it?" I shifted from foot to foot.

"Do I like it?" Holding the frame by his side, he enveloped me in a bear hug. "It's the coolest gift anyone ever gave me."

My whole face lifted. "Who would have thought a guy would show me how to be a mother?" His arms around me felt a little too good. I was relieved when he pulled back. Not that we'd ever be anything but friends. I was just hug-starved.

"Whoa. I hate to burst your bubble, but there's going to be a whole lot more to mothering when you leave here. I don't know diddly squat about anything but nursing." One of the other kid's monitor went off, and he trotted away, dropping the picture off at the nurse's station.

I turned back to Becky. "Okay, Scrapper, I'll be back this afternoon with your grandma and Aunt Jean. We decided it'd be best if we ate our Christmas feast first, then came back to see you. Sleep tight; don't let the bedbugs bite." I waved at Gil on the way out, and he jingled the ball of his Santa hat at me.

—

"Aunt Jean, I'm here." I went into her bedroom without waiting for an answer. She was all dressed and sitting on her chair with her Bible. Her slippered feet were propped on the ottoman. I plopped a kiss on her cheek, turned my face for the peck from her, and threw my winter coat over her bed post.

"Merry Christmas, dear heart." She took her house shoes off and handed them to me. "Put these in my bag. My arches are already hurting, and I may want to wear them at your mama's."

"You look so pretty, but that red satin blouse is a little daring, don't you think?" I talked as I gathered her parcels.

She finished putting on her black patent pumps and swatted her hand at me. "You had on a big coat when you came in. I didn't notice how slim and trim you're looking in your sweater."

She rose and pressed her palms to the small of her back. "I've got everything that goes to your Mama's laid out on the kitchen table."

"I'll start loading the car." Four runs later, I had everything in my Datsun. In addition to a tote full of stuff, she had a humongous stack of presents, a red velvet cake, and my favorite, fresh creamed corn. "Aunt Jean, who are all these presents for?"

"Just load the car, and you'll find out soon enough." She gave me a secret holiday grin.

On the last trip to load the car, we went together and climbed into my tiny vehicle. She had a short coughing fit before we reached downtown.

"You okay?" She held her hand up to indicate she was fine and hacked into her handkerchief. "Are you warm enough? I could turn the heater up." I had the heater on as low as it would go and really didn't want hot air blowing in this car.

"No, the cold helps my chest." Her cough settled. "So, we have a new cook for this year's Christmas dinner. Tell me what treat you made us."

Relieved that she didn't want the heat, even though it really was cold, I shivered and smiled as I listed my goodies. "It's not much. I took the easy stuff this year. Deviled eggs. A pecan pie. Congealed salad."

"You know I love pecan pie." Her eyes lit up.

"Yes, ma'am. That's why I made it." I turned into my drive.

She roused and peered out the windshield. "Is this your place?"

"Sure is, and it's so cute, Aunt Jean. Maybe you can see it one day, but I sure don't want you climbing steps right now." She leaned her head sideways and took a gander at the flight of stairs.

"I'll have to agree with you. They look mighty steep."

A couple of trips up and down the stairs for the food and my two piddly gifts, and we were back on the road. "Please tell Mrs. Stover how grateful I am for this apartment." I frowned. "I hope she knows how long Becky will be at the hospital."

Aunt Jean laid her hand on my right knee. "Listen to me. You're don't worry a hair on your head about the Stovers and that apartment. They want you to use it as long as need be. They're more comfortable than most and are happy they can afford to help …. I know you know how to keep confidences." Her voice dropped down low.

I snapped my head toward her with a quizzical look. "Of course."

"I met Sister Stover at the home in Tennessee. If not for each other, I don't know how we'd have made it all these years. Her baby went to an aunt of hers, who was barren, and started wearing maternity clothes the day Sister Stover went into the home."

"Oh, Aunt Jean. I had no idea."

"And that's the way it's to stay. No one, and I mean no one but me, not even Reverend Stover, knows the truth." She lifted her nose and took a deep breath. "Her baby grew up thinking of her as a cousin. I'd talked her into breaking the truth to her when she was old enough to understand, but her sweet girl died of pneumonia when she was ten years old." She closed her eyes and prayed, "Bless her dear soul and that of her grieving mother's."

Driving down Cave Spring Street, it was all I could do not to stop the car. "I'm so sorry. No wonder she's helped me so much."

"That's absolutely true. And you remember that. Every day she can help you is a blessing to her. I have faith you'll keep her trust. I wouldn't have told you without it. She told me if the time was ever right, I could tell you."

"I would never tell another soul. No matter what. I think she's a saint."

Aunt Jean grunted. "Let's not go overboard. I also know she likes her muscadine wine from time to time, and you know how I feel about evil spirits."

I turned my head and looked at Floyd Junior College as we whizzed by so she wouldn't see the amusement on my face. "You are a mess! I thought she was your dearest friend."

"The truth's the truth. Not many saints in this world. We're all human." Her voice rebounded in the small hull of the car. "Keeps it interesting, wouldn't you say?"

With those words, we turned into Mama's driveway. Mama came out to help me unload the car. Leave it to Mama to be different. No red for her today. She had on a black, long-sleeved dress with blue and green paisley stitching across the bodice and a full skirt with tiny pleats cinched at her narrow waist.

With my arms heaped full, I nodded. "It's all Aunt Jean's. I don't know what she's gone and done." I walked through the door, and the aroma of turkey and dressing was so powerful I started salivating. "Oh, Mama. That smells scrumptious."

The three of us worked as one body with six hands to warm up the corn and Mama's green beans, cut the pie and cake, set the table, slice the turkey, cut the giblets up into the gravy, put the rolls in the oven with the sweet potato casserole, and get spoons in all the food.

Finally, our feast was ready and our plates piled high. After the blessing, all we heard for a few minutes were the sounds of three sets of chewing teeth. Aunt Jean broke the spell, "We all sound like cows in the field! Where's our manners?"

Between bites, I let them know about Carolyn coming to the hospital. Aunt Jean caught us up on church gossip.

"I can't eat another bite." I unsnapped my jeans, right there at the table.

Aunt Jean fanned herself with her napkin and gulped down more iced tea. "My skirt has an elastic waist, otherwise there would have been an explosion on my side of the table."

Mama burped, and we all broke out laughing. "Excuse me. Highest compliments to the chefs." Mama and I started clearing the table. "Jean, go rest on the couch for a spell. Mary Alice and I will clean up, then we'll open presents."

I thought it was as good a time as any to break my news. "Mama, I'd like to drop the 'Alice' part of my name."

She dropped her plate into the sink. "What?"

I blushed. "Can you just call me Mary? I never have liked the name Alice. This is the perfect time because Becky will only ever hear me called Mary." We stood there, surrounded by dirty dishes, staring at each other. I'd always felt like two girls, and Becky needed one mother. Alice had already become part of me. But I couldn't explain that to Mama.

"Well, for heaven's sake." Mama called out to Aunt Jean, who had toddled out of the kitchen and was admiring the Christmas tree. "Did you hear what your niece just said?"

"I did." She bent to lift a gift from under the branches and appeared to be studying the name tag.

"It's really no big whup, Mama. It's still my name, only it's halved. I'm not a little kid anymore." I turned and set my armload on the counter and started loading the dishwasher.

"I don't know how I'll ever remember to call you something different from your name, but I'll give it a go." Mama pulled out old Cool Whip and butter bowls to divvy up the food. "Who did we think we were cooking for?"

I couldn't believe she was letting it go that easily. "We could have fed an entire clan with all this food."

"Think we might get away with this again next year, Mary?" She sounded out "Mary" in two long syllables.

It took a while to clear, clean, and package all the food into thirds. When we finished, Mama took off her apron and washed her hands. "That's some good eating for all of us the next few days. Might give me time enough to see a man!"

I didn't believe Aunt Jean heard her because Aunt Jean rattled off, "Sure does help me. Thank you for the turkey. I know it costs the most."

Mama announced, "I'll pass out presents since Mary Alice … oops, I mean Mary, is now an official grown-up." She moved across the room on the sure feet of a dancer and put Elvis Presley's Christmas album on our old stereo. "This will put us in the mood."

She was having so much fun, I cast my eyes on her and was sure she'd been nipping at the bourbon I knew was hidden in the cabinet above the fridge.

My pile multiplied into a small mountain. I was curious and started sorting through them, and it quickly became clear most of them were for Becky, which eased my mind to no end.

While Mama played Santa, Aunt Jean slipped her shoes off. "Honey, go get those house slippers for me. My feet are done for the day."

I retrieved her house shoes, and we all settled into our seats, with Becky's hoard surrounding my chair.

"Mary Al …." Mama rolled her eyes to the ceiling. "Mary, you open yours and Becky's first."

I was dying to tear into them. "I can't believe this! There's a whole heap to Becky from the North Rome Church of God and the women at J.C. Penney's. What does that mean?"

Aunt Jean grinned. "It means Sister Stover took up a collection from the women at the church and bought you the things you need." She winked at me. "The things she always wanted to buy, but never had children."

"I don't know what to say."

"Don't say anything. We're all on pins and needles here. Open away, girl." Mama waved with both hands for me to get on with it.

"I really want to open Becky's last. Is that okay? This is the only baby shower I'm going to get."

Mama looked at the ceiling. "Always want your own way, don't you?"

"Ah, Mama, I'm not trying to be difficult, but I want to watch you open yours first."

Aunt Jean looked from Mama to me and lifted a green package with red poinsettias from the floor next to her feet. "This is to me from Marva." The sound of paper ripping joined Elvis singing *Blue Christmas*. She spread the multi-colored scarf out across her lap. "It's as pretty as a stained-glass window." She turned to Mama. "Now, you open one."

"Don't either of you think I can't see what's going on here." Mama cut her eyes from Aunt Jean to me but took the small box from me. Her expression changed when she saw what was inside. "What an angel." She showed Aunt Jean the framed photo of Becky. "I'm taking this to work and sitting it by the register. Then, I can see her all day."

It was the same design I did for Gil, but with Becky alone in the photo. Her little hand was up by the side of her face with my huge finger curled in it.

"Aunt Jean, open mine next. It's the silver one." After seeing it was the same photo, Aunt Jean showed Mama, and they compared.

For Mama's present, the magazine cut-outs framing the photo were of yellow and white daisies and red roses, her favorite flowers. Aunt Jean's had pictures of lions and lambs.

"These are very special. Looks like you worked hard to put them together." Aunt Jean tapped the picture frame glass. I let my breath out. I could tell they really liked them. "Now, Miss Priss, we aren't waiting any longer for you to open one."

From Aunt Jean, I ended up with a new tote bag she made from nursery rhyme fabric, and a box of chocolate-covered cherries. For as long as I could remember, she'd bought me the same candy for Christmas. It was the kind with all liquid centers, just the way I liked.

Mama had gotten me two more sweaters, one navy blue and one Kelly green. They both had V-necks, and at first, I felt piqued, because she was trying to change the way I dressed. She knew I didn't like low-cut things, though I had to admit these weren't really immodest at all. It was just I usually wore crew necks. But then I thought about my visit with Carolyn at the hospital and told myself Becky's mom shouldn't dress like a boy. "Thanks, Mama. What pretty colors."

Aunt Jean got a new black purse, and Mama had a set of dishcloths and towels, the same blue-and-white-stripe as Aunt Jean's, and a potholder mitten that covered her entire hand.

Mama was especially proud of that mitten, and she snapped it claw-like at Aunt Jean. "I've always wanted one of these. My old crocheted squares are worn thin, and even when I double them up, it scorches my fingers." She focused her blue stare at me. "Now, can you finally open those baby presents before they turn to stone?" Mama actually looked excited. She almost bounced in her seat.

From the church, there were boxes of baby clothes, diapers, and crib sheets. Some were new and some were used, and I was grateful for each.

From Penney's, a huge box contained a car seat. All those women had gone in together to get it for me. The card read, "For all your danger-filled drives."

Mama and Aunt Jean ooohed and aaahed with each package opened, and I passed the boxes around so they could inspect my loot.

Aunt Jean's packages were filled with a children's Bible stories book and hand sewn items: a baby quilt and three burp cloths from the same nursery rhyme pattern she used for my tote bag, and four dresses, in varying sizes.

"Look familiar?" Aunt Jean's lip twitched.

I gazed in astonishment. "They're miniatures of the ones you made me for school. Aunt Jean, it's the same blue-and-green-plaid and red-and-blue-striped fabric." I held them up for Mama to see.

"Jean, how adorable." Mama rubbed at her eyes. "Brings back the days."

"You know I'm a pack rat. Had some swatches and ends of bolts left over for a decade, literally. Thought it would be special to make Becky dresses like yours." She brought her hands down on her thighs and dipped her chin in a self-satisfied motion.

"But this had to have taken you forever. You didn't even know she'd be a girl." I held the tiny dresses up to my chest.

"You didn't realize, but I knew all along she was a girl." She tilted her head in a canny manner.

Becky's last presents were from Mama. First, a diaper bag made from blue jean material. "Oh, Mama. It's so me, just my style." Two huge boxes contained an umbrella stroller and a baby swing. "Wow! You knew I needed these. I didn't think I'd ever be able to afford the swing."

"Best babysitter you can get." Mama had her hands clenched between her knees and had leaned forward expectantly the whole time I'd been opening her packages.

The last two gifts were ABC blocks and a mobile. I opened the mobile, wound the music box, and held it up. *Mary Had a Little Lamb* tinkled through the room, and a cow, pig, sheep, horse, and duck circled around and around. I swallowed and swallowed but the tears streamed down my cheeks, anyway. Holding the mobile, with it still playing, I dashed to Mama, sat right in her lap the way I hadn't done since I was six years old, and lay my head on her shoulder. "It's everything I needed. I didn't even have to ask you. You heard me talking about wanting these things. You remembered." *Mary Had a Little Lamb* played slower and slower, until the last note sounded with a ping.

Mama ran her fingers through my hair. "Of course, I listened to you." She murmured in my ear. "Don't you know I realize how smart you are? You've never asked for anything you didn't need." I snuggled into her and thought about all the good in my life. Thinking this way was bound to bring even more.

———

By the time we all visited with Becky, and I drove Aunt Jean home, night was falling and most of the houses were lit up with holiday lights. I'd turned the car heat to low fan and the lowest-level warmth, as a concession to help me get over my panic, step by step.

I slowed to a crawl at the statue of Romulus and Remus in front of the city auditorium. Someone had tied a Santa hat on the head of the wolf and green garland around her throat. The twins had red bows stuck on their privates.

When I passed by Penney's, I pulled into a parking space and remembered all I could about the day Becky was born, which wasn't much. Something about horses and the inside of Mrs. Leonard's car. I was delirious. Twenty-five days had never seemed like such a long time before. I was a different person from the girl who climbed into that Pinto.

In my apartment, it felt strange to be alone on Christmas night. I went into my bedroom with a cup of hot tea and looked at the photos of Becky I'd stuck all around the edges of the mirror. In my favorite, she had a dopey expression, but I loved it. Taking down the latest one and holding it to the light, I almost dropped my mug. Something about her face resembled Jim's. I guess I hadn't noticed before, because of all the tape holding the feeding tube in place.

Looking at it brought up an image of Jim, and my feelings surprised me. In spite of all he'd put me through, I got that pitty-pat in my chest. How could I still have feelings for that bastard? My voice of reason answered for me: because you're a loving person.

Facing my own reflection in my bedroom mirror, I said it out loud, "I am lovable." Despite my best effort, my voice cracked in the middle of "lovable." It was one thing if your mama loved you, or your aunt or best friend, but I'd never had a man who cared about me. Hell, if they'd just treated me with indifference, it would have been an improvement.

In the back of my mind, I heard, but Gil treats me good and what about Jeff in eighth grade?

I argued with myself that both of them were nice to everyone.

But that voice disputed me. Isn't it enough? Start with a nice guy who's your friend. Then, maybe, one day, you'll meet someone who loves you. My voice of reason sounded irrational.

Forty-Three

New Year's Day, my little girl was turning one —one-month-old. I was the first to arrive in the NICU and waved at Gil on my way in. Becky bicycled her feet when I reached her side, and I sang, "They say it's your birthday. We're gonna have a good time." Gil was passing by and stuck his head over to sing along, but neither of us knew all the words, and we tapered off into a really lame ending.

"No typical 'happy birthday to you,' huh?" He'd had a haircut. His head was now covered in short red spikes.

"I always think the Happy Birthday song sounds like drowning dogs." I scrunched my nose.

He laughed. "You are so weird. But I prefer the Beatles' version, too. So, you're a fan of the boys from Liverpool?"

"John's my guy." I motioned for him to come closer and spoke in a lower tone. "He's Becky's father. That's why I can't let anyone know."

Gil burst out laughing. "Mystery solved."

"It was a mad fling." I said it in the worst British accent a good Southern girl could muster.

"Hey, hey. Earlier, the monitor showed a dip, like she was starting apnea, but she caught herself. Recovered on her own." His voice raised in excitement.

"That's really good, right?" I wrapped my arms around her incubator and hugged it.

He mimicked my rotten Brit accent. "A bloody fantastic sign."

———

I left the hospital and drove to Mama's alone. Aunt Jean wasn't feeling well enough to come, and I planned to take her some food later.

Passing by Carolyn's house jogged my memory. I hadn't called her since our Christmas Eve visit. But seeing her house made me realize Carolyn represented graduation and college, while I faced diapers and bottles. How would Carolyn ever understand my life now?

When I came through the front door, I saw Mama's tree was still up, and she'd arranged Becky's presents in stacks underneath.

Mama had fixed our traditional New Year's meal: greens and black-eyed peas to represent the dollars and change we'd have in the coming year. After we finished eating, she went into her bedroom and came back with a shoe box.

"I have a surprise." Mama motioned for me to join her on the couch. "After seeing Becky on Christmas Day, I haven't been able to get over how much she resembles the way you looked as a baby. So, I pulled down all the old photos from the top of my closet and found your baby pictures."

"Oh, wow!" I leaned close to Mama as she lifted the lid from the Florsheim shoe box. I guess she'd shown me all these photos when I was a kid, but I didn't really care until now.

"That's the one I wanted you to see the most." She pointed to my eyes and forehead in the picture. "Becky's the spitting image of you as a baby. Down to the dark curls. You remember how I used to roll your top curl on a foam roller every night when you were little?"

Immersed in the uncanny likeness, I didn't answer, just held it closer. "You'd think this was Becky in the picture."

"Look at this one with your Aunt Jean holding you and grinning! Doesn't she look proud as punch?" Mama passed one that looked as if it were taken in a hospital room.

"I look pitiful in this one, but you have to remember it was a rough delivery," Mama said. I rubbed the nobs on my forehead and wondered what kind of brain damage forceps caused. "But I didn't have the time you did of it."

The shot showed Mama sitting up tall in a hospital bed and looking down at me in her arms. I didn't think she looked pitiful at all. The look on her face was pure joy and made my throat close up. Why didn't I remember ever seeing these photos?

"Here's you and your daddy." I hesitated before taking it from her. She heaved a deep sigh. "I know you don't remember him the way he was then. So puffed up. Even sang *Rock-a-bye Baby* to you in his gruff voice."

I looked at him holding me, with a smile on his face, and I wanted to stomp on the damn picture, grind it into the dirt. Mama leaned closer and stroked her finger over his face and mine in the glossy.

"He wasn't always so bad, you know." She looked at me. "The Carl I knew then would have loved to see Becky now. That man played Ride A Little Horsy with you more than any daddy I ever saw. You both loved it so much. We used to dream of getting old together and spoiling our grandbabies." I gaped at her. Blood roared in my ears, and an Arctic finger raced down my spine. "I know that's probably hard for you to imagine. Wait until you get older. You'll see."

I flung the photo away from me. It caught a current of air and circled to the floor like a maple seed pod.

I screamed at her. "Thank God he will never touch my daughter!"

Mama leaned back. "What in the world?"

Shaking all over, I stood towering over her. "Don't you ever mention him again, after what he did to me. Do you understand me?"

"What in the world!" She drew her neck up, and her eye twitched. "What's gotten into you?"

I stood with my nails cutting into my palms, and Daddy's hands around my throat. His voice echoed in my head, "Don't tell."

Raising my hands to my neck, I felt my heartbeat hammering. Black dots dipped and dove in front of me. I spit the words out of my mouth. "He touched me!" The force of it sent an explosion through my head. I almost buckled from the pulsing at my temples.

Mama's expression didn't change. "What do you mean?" Then she wrinkled her forehead and pulled her eyelids down. "What are you trying to tell me?" The tic at the corner of her eye went into spasms.

Light in the room seemed to grow brighter and I heaved with each breath. "You know what I'm saying. He put his hands on me."

Mama shook her head back and forth emphatically. Her face and the tips of her ears bloomed blood red. "Mary Alice, your daddy was a low-lying snake and guilty of many things. But you can't expect me to believe such as this." She'd started out talking fast, but by the time she finished, she paced each word, and her skin tone had lost some of its initial redness. "You've always been high-strung, with an over-active imagination, taken to flights of fancy. I believe the stress of all you're going through has warped your brain."

There she was, in control, like she knew it all. "I am not crazy." I pummeled my fists on my thighs. "That's exactly what he said—that you'd send me away if I told. Then, when I was thirteen, he threatened to kill you if I told."

She slapped the side of the couch. "You need to get charge of yourself. What you're saying is nonsense. You're out of touch with reality. You haven't even seen him since you were six years old. Then he died in prison." As though dismissing me, she put the lid back on the photos and banged the box down on the coffee table.

"Oh, yes, I have. After Mamaw's funeral, he came to the house." The thought of it made my jaws send shooting pain down my neck and up through my eyes, as if even my bones were threatening me to shut my mouth.

Mama drew her head back and looked at me as if she really did fear for my sanity. "Your daddy couldn't even come home for his own mother's funeral. His brother Bobby told me. You have lost your senses. That man hasn't set foot in this town since he went to prison eleven years ago."

"What is wrong with you? Why would I lie?" I shouldn't have told. Should've known she wouldn't believe me. My shoulders slumped and the old fog sensation rolled over my vision. I started to un-focus my eyes, to zone out. But a white-hot fury shot out through me instead, and I faced her. "Any decent mother wouldn't call me crazy. She'd believe me."

"Don't tell me I'm not a good mother. I'll help you any way I can, but this is simply not true. You're talking craziness." She crossed her arms over her chest.

"With all we've been through, how can you sit there and refuse to give me any more credit than that? Why can't you accept what I'm telling you?"

She jumped up, and now she was the one yelling with her arms thrown akimbo. "It is not the truth because I would have known. That's why. It could not have gone on without me knowing. I would have done something."

"Who do you think you are? All-knowing-God?" My entire body howled inside. "I was just a little girl. He hunched on me like a dog, in my own bed. Put his hands in my panties." Saying these words out loud, I felt as exposed as if I were standing naked on the city auditorium steps in front of the whole town. My entire being said to cover my head in shame. I didn't want to cry, but tears gushed down my cheeks. I knocked them away with the side of my hand and told myself I would not be ashamed for things that weren't my fault.

She didn't say a word. Just averted her eyes and passed by me on her way into the kitchen.

My head throbbed. Without looking back at her, I grabbed my purse and coat and rushed out, slamming the door behind me, and scrambled into my car. Trembling with outrage, I couldn't get the damn key into the ignition. It took three attempts, and I punched the dash so hard the face of my radio cracked. Slamming the car into reverse, I stepped on the gas and screeched over the hump at the end of the driveway. I was water loosed from a dam. The trip home went by in a blur.

In my bedroom, I paced. The impact of each step caused the hardwood floor to reverberate. What was wrong with her? Why didn't she believe me? My rage escalated.

I seized a pillow from my bed and brought it over my head. Wham! It resounded against the mattress. Over and over, I swung it up and down with as much force as I possessed. Each wallop connected with my anguished wailing. "I'm not crazy!" When the pillow burst open and feathers stormed the air, I continued flailing. In time, the effort exhausted me, and I dropped to the bed, spent.

The grief of Mama not believing me was as unbearable as Daddy's hands. I curled in on myself, allowed my eyes to loosen, and sank into nothingness.

———

Coming to, the room receded into darkness. My old floaty feeling wasn't the comfort it once was. Instead, it disconcerted me. My eyes focused, and the clock numerals came into view. Nine-thirty. Becky! I'd missed afternoon and evening visiting hours.

Not once in thirty days had I wasted a chance to see her. Whether I wanted to or not, I heard Mama's voice in my head, "Mothers pull themselves up. They put one foot in front of the other and keep moving forward."

I sprinted to the bathroom, washed my face, ran a brush through my hair, and dabbed toothpaste into my mouth and squished it with my finger. Down the stairs, two steps at a time, I got into my car and onto the road to Becky.

In the NICU, Gil met me at the door with a look of concern. "Everything all right?"

"A family problem." Becky's bed and the curve of her back were illuminated in the corner.

"Visiting hours are over." He tugged on his earlobe. "Why don't you go get a good night's sleep and come back in the morning? She's fine. You look all done in, anyway."

"Please, let me see her. Just a few minutes." I looked at him with pleading eyes.

He glanced at the other nurse. "Five minutes. It's all I can do."

I dashed to Becky. Since they'd removed the breathing tube, she slept with her thumb curled in her mouth. Every few seconds, she did her dear little suckling movement. Gil had told me enough for me to know this was what we'd been looking for. She'd be able to start the nippling process soon, the first step to her coming home.

Reaching in, I enclosed her foot in my hand. She wrinkled her nose but didn't wake. "I love you so much. You're my dear girl." She had to be my only concern now. I had to get past Mama's and Daddy's betrayals. Leaning my forehead against the incubator's acrylic side and closing my eyes, I told her, "I will always believe you. And I will love you forever and ever and a day."

I heard someone approaching and straightened up. Gil ran his hand across his red spikes. "Sure you're okay?"

"I will be." I pushed my hair back behind my ears with both hands.

"She recovered another bout of apnea this afternoon." His tone was steady and soothing as he studied my face.

"That's such good news." Some of the tension in my body fell away.

He reached his hand out to me, and at first I didn't see the meal coupons. "Here's some more cafeteria passes." I took them from him, and his hand lingered on mine. "You're going to be okay, Mary."

I squeezed his hand. His kindness brought all my emotions barreling in on me, and what I wanted to do was lay my head against his chest and cry. But that was the last thing he deserved. I pulled away. "Thank you, Gil. You'll never know how much I appreciate this."

The swinging doors sounded out their usual swish as I exited. The corridor in front of me yawned into the distance. Before tonight, I'd always wished Mama were by my side to walk down it, the way she had on that first NICU visit. Now, I stepped into the blazing white light, alone.

336 • Birdhouse Jesus

Two days later, I was dressed for my morning visit and eating the last bite of toast when a rap came at my door. My hand froze mid-bite, but I quickly drew in a breath and went to the door.

It was Aunt Jean, bent at the waist and wheezing, with a drizzle of rain glistening on her black raincoat. "Oh, my goodness, come in. Come in here." I tucked my arm into the crook of her elbow and guided her to my couch. Ran to the kitchen and came back with a glass of water. "Take this. Sip."

I knelt on my knees and took one of her trembling hands while she tipped the glass to her lips. When she sat the tumbler down, she said, "Be fine. In a minute," and patted the seat next to hers.

While I worried about what she was going to say, I studied her hairdo and reached up to tuck a bobby pin back in place.

"You know why I'm here." A line of perspiration shone across the baby-fine hairs over her upper lip.

"I think so." I moved to the cushion beside her.

Her breathing had slowed. "Your poor mama can't eat or sleep. Hasn't been to work in two days. How could you do this to her?"

My first reaction was a flash of sore resentment. To her! What about me? But I thought Mama probably hadn't told her the truth. No telling what story she'd spun. Then Aunt Jean's message registered. My mama had missed work. That was unheard of. A wave of apprehension washed over me. "Is she sick?"

"You know full well what's troubling her." She scowled at me, and for a second, I shrunk to three feet tall and guilty of climbing on her rock wall.

But I wasn't the guilty one. "What's troubling her? Did she tell you what Daddy did?"

Aunt Jean sat her purse on the end table. "She told me what you said."

I narrowed my eyes. "And?"

"And we find that hard to believe." She said it looking me straight in the face. I could have crumpled then and there—my despair greater at her betrayal than Mama and Daddy's combined. I'd never have thought, in a million years, that she would have turned her back on me.

But I was not to be treated any old way they wanted. "You 'find that hard to believe.' I find that inexcusable." I stated it with no meanness on my face, but with much sorrow. I saw it shook her.

Still, she snapped open her purse and brought out a Church of God pamphlet titled, "Forgiveness: Jesus' Gift of Salvation." She laid it on the end table and tapped it with her index finger. "I hope this brings you back to the Lord." How could she renounce my claim in one breath and tell me to forgive in the next?

If I were the girl I used to be, if I weren't Becky's mother, I would have laid my head on her shoulder and cried my eyes out. I would have told her whatever she wanted to hear, for the sake of her love. It was only grace that allowed me to choose my love for Becky over my Aunt Jean's love for me.

"Don't you see you're asking me to forgive him for something you say he didn't do?" My voice bounced off the walls. I plucked the pamphlet up between my thumb and index finger and dropped it back into her pocketbook. "You'll be needing this more than me."

Now, she acted flustered, drumming her fingers on her purse, blinking her eyes repeatedly. "I don't know what's become of you. I even took up for you when you ran off with that married man."

"I feel the same as I always have for you. I love you dearly." As I said the words, a feeling of calm ebbed through me. No one, not even my Aunt Jean, was going to silence me any longer. I was free to speak my truth.

"Deep in your heart, I know you realize what I'm saying is true. When I was six years old and took your crucifix, I tried to tell you." The pain in her eyes made me want to stop, but I would not and could not. "You didn't want to hear it then, and you don't want to hear it now. Even so, it's the gospel truth, and I believe if you open your eyes, you'll see what's before you."

I wish I could say my heart matched those brave words. But, after losing Mama, and now Aunt Jean, it was ripped into fragments I only kept beating for my little girl. In the seconds before Aunt Jean spoke, some hope in me imagined she'd take it all back, throw her arms around my neck, and whisper in my ear, "My dear girl, I believe you. I am so sorry he did it. This is not your fault. We'll get through this together."

But it wasn't to be. "I love you. I'll pray for you." That's all she said, before rising and making her way down those steep stairs and into Mrs. Stover's waiting car.

I sat perfectly still and told myself I would survive, that the pain would subside one day, that a chest pierced with splinters could still draw air. I could not allow myself the luxury of feeling what I'd lost. Nothing could divert my waking moments from Becky. I would face all of this one day, when my daughter's life didn't depend on my sound mind. My rabbit hole had protected me from hopelessness before. It would serve a higher purpose now. I stuffed thoughts of Daddy, Mama, and Aunt Jean into the rabbit hole and barricaded the entrance.

In half an hour, I would leave for the hospital at my usual time, and when I did, I would have put this behind me, for now. Thirty minutes wasn't long for the job I had to do. I folded my hands in my lap and spent every sweep of the minute hand imagining cotton being stuffed inside my wounded chest—a temporary measure to get me by, until time had its chance to sear the raw edges and mend what would never be whole again.

Forty-Five

I wish I could report that in the following weeks I didn't drag myself around, putting on one of Mama's smiles for the customer, as I trudged my way to the hospital, as I held my daughter's first bottle, as I delighted in the news she would be home in about a week. That would be a lie. But I can say "acting as if" all was well went a long way.

By the time talk started about us going home at the end of January, I sincerely enjoyed my days. When I wasn't visiting Becky, I got the apartment ready for her, making sure Mama was at Firestone each time I went to gather our things.

After Aunt Jean's visit, I'd been worried the Stovers would kick me out, but a short note had come in the mail:

Dear Mary Alice,

Please stay in the apartment as long as you need it. I hope you don't mind. One of the hospital's nurses, Sister Roper, who attends church with us, lets us know how your little angel is doing. Praise God for how far He's brought her.

We are praying Jesus will re-unite your family. Your Aunt Jean worries about you. You should call her.

With the Lord's love,

The Stovers

I knew I should call Mama and Aunt Jean. But that would bring everything to a head. There was no way to focus on Becky if I stayed torn up about them. So I stored everything away until my life allowed time to figure out what to do about them. I didn't hear a peep from Mama. Aunt Jean sent a card every day. It always said the same thing: I'm praying for Becky and you. Love, Aunt Jean. But she didn't call.

Aunt Jean always said, "Busy hands are the devil's enemy." I kept myself occupied.

At the library, I delighted in sitting on the outskirts of the children's reading circle, dreaming of the day Becky and I could join the other mother-child pairs.

I devoured books about childcare and development.

A couple of trips to Family Services and I had myself set up for food stamps, a monthly welfare check, and her Medicaid. I told them I didn't know who the father was … the same as I'd done on her birth certificate. Becky and I would be able to scrape by until she was stable enough to leave her with a sitter.

I visited everyone at Penney's, thanking them for helping save our lives. Mrs. Leonard, the woman who'd driven me to the hospital, offered her daughter's used crib to me. She'd just had her third child and didn't intend to have any more. Mr. Bonner, the manager, said he was holding my job and had it filled temporarily with a college student who was taking a year between her studies.

I took long walks up and down Broad Street, remembering all the times Aunt Jean and I shopped at Kessler's and lunched at the Krystal.

I used that time the best I could, to prepare myself for Becky's homecoming.

———

On January 25, two days before the date set for us to go home, Becky's pediatrician came in while I was there for my morning visit.

"Miss Lydell, I'm delighted by Rebecca's progress. We'll want to monitor her closely after you go home, but my only serious concern is her vision. I've referred her to a pediatric ophthalmologist for some testing. Let me give you his name." He rummaged in his white coat for a pen.

"Why are you worried about her vision? I know you've mentioned problems with preemies, but she can see. I know she can." I'd been so relieved all the times Becky looked right at me or at one of her shiny toys.

He didn't respond at first, just scribbled a name on a prescription pad, tore it off, and handed it to me. Clearing his throat, he looked me in the eye. "Many times, mothers interpret an infant's ability to turn towards sound as an indication of their visual acuity. However, while I believe your daughter has rounded a corner on the respiratory and feeding ailments common for premature infants, I am not as confident that her vision is unimpaired." He patted my arm. "Let's not jump to any conclusions either way. That's what the experts are for. Dr. Looper is a fine physician. He'll take good care of you."

By then, I was accustomed to the abrupt flip of the doctors' white coat tails as an end to their conversations. They were constantly moving, and what I'd first thought of as callousness, even rudeness, I'd come to see as efficiency of time and emotion. I didn't know how they dealt with constant illness day in and day out.

I immediately went to the family room phone and made an appointment with the doctor. He could see us the week after next.

Two days later, Gil placed Becky into my arms and pointed me towards the exit. He smiled and shook his finger at me. "Remember, any mother worries over her baby. You have to relax. Trust yourself. She's been through more than most, but you're not going to break her. Babies are resilient."

I leaned in and kissed him square on the cheek. "I'll call you. We're two of your troubles you're not getting rid of." I said it as I approached those double doors for the last time.

He held his palm out to me. "Give me back that phone number. What was I thinking?"

"Too late, muchacho." I waved as I went through the doors. "And I'm only the beginning. Just wait until Becky learns to dial it herself!"

—

I looped the handle of Becky's carrier around my elbow and balanced her on my hip, with my pocketbook dangling from the crook of the other arm. Carefully, I mounted the apartment steps, one hand clenched for dear life on the railing. This would take some getting used to.

She kept squinting, and I told myself it was a normal reaction to sunlight, after being under artificial bulbs for so long. I still had much to learn about typical baby stuff.

At the landing, I pulled the key out of my pocket, glad I'd thought to stash it there. Once inside, I maneuvered to the bedroom, lifted her out of the contraption, and hugged her to my breast. "We're home, Tater Tot!"

Taking her to the mirror on the dresser, I showed her the two of us. "See the baby. That's Becky." My glowing face reflected next to her tiny, cherub features: delicate pink skin, dark head of hair, and heart-shaped lips. The baby in the mirror yawned wide. "You're not tuckering out on me already! You haven't even had the tour."

Next to my bed, Mrs. Leonard's used crib was made up with the yellow sheets and a bumper pad she'd sent with it. I'd mounted Becky's mobile onto the rail. I wound it up now and sang *Mary Had a Little Lamb* along with it, as the nursery rhyme characters circled. One drawer in the dresser held her clothes. Her diaper hanger hung from the bedroom closet door. Her swing filled the empty corner of the living room. Her toys stood ready in a small laundry basket, and a stack of children's library books sat on the end table. People had been so good to us. Despite everything that had happened, I still saw all the positives.

It was an indescribable freedom to hold her as long as I wanted, to walk with her from room to room, to talk to her in complete privacy. Within ten minutes, she was sound asleep.

I eased onto the rocker and held her. Stroked her little head and the silken skin of her cheeks and hands. As she slumbered, I rocked and made up a little verse I crooned over and over. "We can rock, and we can sing. We can do most anything." Becky and I were home.

Forty-Six

We fell into a routine those first few days at home. I followed her lead, and we spent long hours sleeping. Now I wasn't traveling back and forth to the hospital, time stretched and extended on each end and spread out around its middle.

Mama had been right. After two days of bathing and dressing Becky, changing her diapers, fixing bottles, and feeding her, those duties became habitual.

But interacting with her was never commonplace. Her personality was contagious. I sang. She snuggled closer. I dangled a toy in front of her face. Her eyes flickered. I tickled her toes. She wiggled all over.

I thought Mama or Aunt Jean might call me, but they didn't, so I poured all my energy into being present for Becky. Gil had been right. She was my primo girl. When she slept, her body relaxed into the mattress. When we played, she bobbed her head and kicked her feet. When she cried, she belted it out.

On our fifth day home, she slept less during the day and even took her pacifier more. It pleased me her sucking was getting stronger. Putting her to bed after dinner and a bath, she was usually totally relaxed, but that night she acted antsy and kept pulling her heels up to her bottom and mewling. Her whimpers turned to crying. Her sobs gave way to wailing.

I offered her the bottle. She wouldn't eat. I checked her diaper. All dry. I rocked her. I walked her. I held her to my breast, my shoulder, across my lap on her back, on her stomach. I checked her temperature. It was normal. I couldn't get her to burp. I gave her the pacifier. She spit it out. I tried everything.

Her cries became interspersed with hiccups. Taking her into my arms, I did my best to soothe her while I flipped through my childcare books. But those stupid things didn't help one bit. I'd tried everything they suggested. Why wouldn't she stop?

After 30 minutes, I wanted to pull my hair out. She yowled for so long I was both terrified something was wrong and frantic for her to stop. She'd pause for only a few minutes, draw her arms and legs up, and start in again.

I realized I was doing my old trick of un-focusing my eyes and going away. One minute I was rocking my screaming baby and the next I was pacing the floor, with no recollection of anything in-between. That scared me senseless. I couldn't space out for even one second. Becky was depending on me.

I had to calm myself down, so I laid her in the crib. She drew her knees up and bawled. I went into the living room, sat on the couch, took long, deep breaths, and thought, I can do this. Think. What could be the matter?

I'd never wanted to call my mama more than I did now. I picked up the phone and dialed. Aunt Jean answered on the first ring.

"Something's wrong with Becky." I slapped the phone cord against my leg as her high-pitched squeals sounded in the next room.

"What's wrong? Is that her crying?"

Hearing Aunt Jean's calm voice, the one that had gotten me through every day of my life, I broke down sobbing. "I've tried everything. She won't stop."

She asked me a dozen questions, from how long she'd been crying to how she'd been eating and sleeping and what I'd already tried.

"I think she has gas. That stuff hurts. Is her stomach distended?"

"Yes, I think so. But I tried burping her."

"Did you put her across your knees or your shoulder?"

"I tried both."

"Okay, try this. Hold her like a football. Drape her over your forearm, on her belly, with her head facing away from you and her bottom at your elbow. Then pat or rub her back."

"I'll have to put the phone down. I'll be back."

I rested her chin on my hand and straddled her legs over my forearm. She was too small to reach my elbow. I rubbed from the base of her spine up to her neck.

Within seconds, Becky simultaneously burped and expelled gas into her diaper. "That's the ticket." I rubbed circles with the flat of my hand on the small of her back. The gas rolled out of her. She hiccupped and whimpered while I placed her against my shoulder, all the while massaging her back, until she fell into an exhausted sleep.

I swaddled her in a blanket and laid her on her side. She twitched one shoulder and slept.

I hurried back to the phone. "Aunt Jean?"

She was still there. "Did it work?"

"Yes, I should have known. She's been fine for two weeks. I thought she was over her digestion problems. Because of me, she went through hours of pain. Anyone else would have helped her in two minutes." Tears leak down my face.

"I wouldn't say that. She could get gas again and nothing ease it." I barely heard her.

"I was crazy to think I could take care of her. I can't believe how stupid I am!" I knocked the heel of my hand against my forehead and gripped a handful of my hair.

"Stop it!" Her voice came out loud, sharp, and gruff. It was so unexpected coming from her that I stopped instantly. "Only thing stupid about you is belittling yourself. I know you're young, but you can handle this. You have to." She spoke in an exasperated tone. "Stop being so self-indulgent. Becky can't afford for you to coddle yourself. I know you. You're strong. You're smart. You love that little girl. And you're better than this kind of melodrama."

Her words stung and I was worn-out emotionally. "Thank you for helping me." I burst into tears and hung up the phone.

Forty-Seven

Becky's next few days weren't as smooth as the first few, but I was getting the hang of it. "Come on, Tater Tot. Let's go for a walk." It was a gorgeous day for February in North Georgia. The temperature had to be in the high fifties, and the sky was a shade of periwinkle we only saw on cool, clear days like this.

I had her umbrella stroller ready at the foot of the stairs. She wore a thick sleeper the church women gave me. Carrying her down in my arms, she felt strangely plump. I rested her on the sling seat, supported her tiny frame with towel rolls, and tucked Aunt Jean's nursery rhyme quilt up under her chin. A pink sun bonnet, pulled down low, shaded her face. "Just look at you. Your Grandma and Aunt Jean would love this." The thought was as tender as it was sad.

Halfway around the block, a white-haired lady walking with a cane stopped to admire Becky. "Well, who do we have here?"

"This is Becky. I'm Mary." It was her first introduction and the first time I gave my new name to someone. Blue eyes, marred by cataracts, peered at me.

"Pleased to meet you. I live down the street." She pointed in the opposite direction from the apartment. "Lived here over forty years. I'm Mrs. Westmoreland but I grew up down in Albany as a Dawson. Mama's people were up here, the Allens, of the bedding company, and she begged Daddy 'til he finally packed us up when I was fourteen and brought us here to South Rome. Times changed since then, I can tell you."

"I imagine you can." We both leaned over the stroller. Becky lay there, perfectly content, with her eyes wide under the brim of her hat.

"What a beautiful little girl." Mrs. Westmoreland held her lower back and straightened back up. "Some things never change, do they?"

"No, ma'am."

"Sugar and spice, and everything nice. I never had any girls. Had me snips and snails and puppy dog tails. My two ran me ragged." She looked off over my shoulder. "Them were the days. Let me tell you." Her voice sharpened as did the look of concentration on her face, and she leaned closer to me. "Goes by in the blink of an eye, young lady. You enjoy these times."

"I will." She'd brought a tear to both our eyes.

"Well, you better." She let loose a laugh. "Cause iffen you don't, regrets will paint your golden years black." With that, she tootled away.

As we finished our walk, I wondered again about calling Mama and going to see Aunt Jean. Mrs. Westmoreland made me miss them something horrible. Except, I felt hogtied. It wasn't the time to dredge all that up. My book said to do it when I was in a strong place. I wish it hadn't come out the way it did, at least for now. Maybe the three of us could agree not to talk about it for a while longer, until Becky got a little older. But I didn't want them to think I was backing down. It was important they took this seriously. I owed that to myself.

—

The day before Becky's eye doctor appointment, we were asleep for our afternoon nap. I was dreaming. Daddy was chopping down Mr. Hickory, with me up in my seat formed from three branches. I only had on my pink rosebud panties and couldn't decide if I should hold on tighter or jump. As I awoke, I became aware someone was banging on my back door.

Stumbling to my feet, I glanced over at Becky. She stirred but continued to doze.

At the door, I pulled back the curtain. Mama stood on the landing, her face the chalky gray color of rocks. My fingers flipped the lock, while I tried to gather my wits and prepare for a lambasting.

The second I swung it open, Mama barged in and grabbed hold of me with both arms, her head hung over my shoulder. I stiffened up and tried to pull away.

She wrapped herself around me in a stronghold. "No. Listen to me." She spoke facing away from me, her chin digging into my neck. "Your Aunt Jean died."

The world stopped.

Part V
What It Will Take

Forty-Eight

The drive home from Aunt Jean's funeral, under a cold, gray Georgia sky, was long and silent. Mama and I rode together. We'd maintained a balance of solace and civility during the days leading up to that graveside service at Sunset Hills Memorial Gardens. It was as if we'd made an unspoken truce to suspend our differences. We sat side by side at the mortician's desk at Jennings Funeral Home to make arrangements, stood united to greet family and friends at the viewing, and clutched each other's hands during the formal ceremony in the Church of God sanctuary. Mrs. Stover passed us tissue after tissue to replace the ones we soaked clear through.

I sensed a pining within us, but a wall trapped us on separate sides. I recognized the barrier for what it was—Daddy had engineered the entire structure, had laid each stone with his own hands, and carved his initials in the mortar. We just didn't know how to get around it.

With the funeral behind us, I felt the armistice being pulled from my fingers. The quiet in the car was anything but amicable.

When we made the funeral arrangements, I had called Gil to see if he knew of anyone who had experience with preemies and could keep Becky the day of the funeral. He offered to keep Becky himself.

We stopped by his place on the way back to my apartment. He lived in one of the walk-up flats carved out of a grand old house off Broad Street, on a steep hill, near the hospital, and in sight of the clock tower. He and I did little more than a hand-off of Becky and her diaper bag as he rushed to work, already half an hour late in relieving the nurse who agreed to take part of his shift.

With Becky in the back seat, Mama turned the heat up on high. The air blew in my face, and I experienced the old sensation of shrinking in the seat, my bleeding six-year-old legs stuck out in front of me, the smell of Daddy's bottles, Daddy growling, "Hold still," and my balloon head threatening to burst. I tried to shake it off, to tell myself it wasn't really happening, to repeat to myself, I'm safe. But I couldn't get oxygen to my lungs. In a flash, I cranked my window all the way down and poked my nose into the instant relief of fresh air. I took it in, but my stomach continued to roll.

I heard Mama behind me. "What's wrong with you? Becky …"

"I'm gonna be sick." Years of motherhood must have directed Mama to pull into a parking space on the cotton block. I just had time to throw open my door before I heaved onto the white line.

When I pulled my head back in, Mama handed me one of Becky's diapers she'd pulled from the diaper bag. She shifted to reverse. I wiped my mouth and rolled up my window, leaving it cracked open two inches.

As we passed McCall's Hospital, she asked, without taking her eyes from the road, "You better?"

"Yes."

At the apartment, Mama helped us upstairs. She got Becky down, while I washed my face and changed clothes. When I came out of the bathroom, Becky was asleep in her crib. Mama sat at the kitchen table, staring out the window. I fixed us both a Sprite and joined her. She didn't touch her glass.

Finally, she turned to me. "Are you ready to apologize?"

I sighed. "About what?"

"You know what." Her lips were turned under so tight none of the pink showed. She stared at me with flat and unblinking eyes.

"I can't change fact to fiction merely to suit you. I have nothing to be sorry about, except all of us losing each other." I pinched the bridge of my nose.

"You were born stubborn." She stood and headed to the door.

Watching her recede from me, my voice came out clear. "You've said that before, but I don't think you're seeing me the way I really am now."

On her way out, she fumbled with the deadbolt. I was amazed to find peace within myself. "I know you need to blame someone, but I'm not at fault."

Her response was the sound of her quick steps on the stairs and, down below, her car cranking. I rose and went to the window in time to see her taillights turning left onto the main road. Hopefully, she would go home and get some sleep. She looked bone tired.

—

My phone rang early the next morning. I was sitting on the couch with Becky propped up in my lap, reading her the book version of Old MacDonald Had a Farm. Whenever I made an animal sound, she'd jerk and blink and wiggle her mouth.

I shifted her to the crook of my left arm and answered the call.

"Mary Alice." Mama's voice, a bit tentative.

"Yes, Mama."

"I wonder if you can help me clean out Jean's place. I hate to do it now, but I only get two more bereavement days, and it's got to be done." By the time she finished, she sounded more sure of herself. Mama always felt at ease when doing her duty. I was glad. This would comfort her.

"Of course, I can. I'll get Becky's things together and meet you there. In half an hour?"

"You don't want me to pick you up?" Her voice came out tighter.

"Oh, no, that's not it. I need to run by the grocery on the way home. Thought I'd save you the trip." It would also ensure my own ride home, if things got too tense.

"See you there." She hung up without saying good-bye, but I didn't think it was out of spite. I interpreted it as her being distraught. I was sure she dreaded this as much as I did.

The drive to Aunt Jean's was the most peculiar event of my life. From my apartment to her little house on North Broad, I had to pass all our favorite haunts: Kessler's, the Krystal, the wide steps to the library, Piggly Wiggly, the Church of God, and the bus stop two blocks south of her front porch, where the glider sat empty.

Mama's car was already there. I parked behind hers and walked with Becky across the gravel drive and through the screen door, into the dark of the hall that split the house in two. In Aunt Jean's bedroom, that place where she'd spent most of her waking hours, Mama stood, her focus on the bed, her fist pressed to her mouth. A sound erupted from her throat, harsh and unintelligible.

I went to her, with Becky at my shoulder, and wrapped my free arm around her. She laid her head on my shoulder and wept. Low, guttural noises wracked her body.

Placing Becky on the bed surrounded by pillows, I put both hands flat on Mama's back and rocked her until she grew limp. I led her to the armchair and sat on the ottoman in front of her. She laid her head back and rested with her eyes closed.

Becky fussed behind me. I checked her diaper, changed her into a dry one, cradled her to my chest, and went to the kitchen to heat a bottle. The same Westinghouse refrigerator hummed. I knew if I opened the door, there'd be a glass barrel of pickles sitting high on the top shelf. I lit the gas stove and was not afraid.

While the bottle heated, I crossed to the ancient china cabinet and jerked on the door that always stuck. It opened, but not without its usual wobble and the dishes tinkling inside. Taking one of Aunt Jean's jelly glasses, I filled it at the tap and gazed out the window at Mr. Bledsoe's backyard and all his birdhouses.

I shook Becky's bottle onto the top of my hand. It was warm. I turned off the gas eye. The magical blue flame snuffed out. Propping the bottle against Becky's blanket, I lifted Mama's water in the other hand.

Mama was sitting up, her eyes brighter. When she saw me, she jumped up, took the glass, and motioned for me to use the chair to feed Becky.

"If only she were here." Mama's words sent a quick torrent springing from my eyes to splash onto Becky's upturned face.

I adjusted the bottle, wiped them away, and swallowed against the thickness in my throat. "If only."

Mama slipped off her flats, sat on the bed with her back against the old metal headboard, and brought her feet up under her. She took a deep breath. "I called your daddy's brother."

The indentation at the base of my neck fluttered. "You did?"

"Yes." She licked her lips. "He admitted Carl was released from prison a couple of months before Mamaw died. He did come home for the funeral. They kept all of it from me to avoid child support."

"I know." I felt our good scissors in my hand, the way the ring handles bit into my thumb as the blade shredded my orange shorts that day.

Her eyes darted in their sockets. I saw she was afraid, but she went on. "Why didn't you tell me?" Her voice broke on the first and last words.

I lifted Becky to my shoulder to burp her and gave my head a violent shake, to fight back tears. "Because I couldn't bear anyone knowing. Because he threatened me. Because I thought it was my fault. Because I thought you wouldn't love me anymore. He said you wouldn't." With my hands held firmly but gently against Becky's shoulder blades, I swayed back and forth.

"But I would have done something!" She held her arms out, beseeching.

I didn't speak. I did not say, *You wouldn't have believed me. You didn't believe me when I did tell you.* And in that moment, I forgave myself for not asking for help. Not opening her mouth had been the smartest thing that little girl could have done. Somehow, I'd known enough to protect myself at a time when I was too young to bear Mama and Aunt Jean not believing me. It almost destroyed me now.

Rather than confronting her complicity, I told my mama, "I don't have time anymore for what might or might not have been. I've got Becky to think of. I've got my whole life ahead of me. And one of the thousands of lessons Aunt Jean taught me was we can't live a life of regret." I brought Becky around to the crook of my arm and reached my hand out to Mama. She came to sit on the ottoman, our fingers laced together. "All we can do now is put one foot in front of the other and keep moving forward. That's what my mama taught me about mothers."

Mama clicked her teeth together, raised her chin as air hissed with her inhalation, squeezed her eyes shut, and twisted her head to one side. When she brought her head back down, her pupils were wide. I'd never seen her look young or vulnerable. "Mary Alice, I'm so sorry. I should have known something. And I should have believed you."

"You are? You believe me?" She nodded as tears streamed down her cheeks.

Through the core of my body, the rabbit hole filled with white light. Its walls disintegrated, and I gasped at the pressure burst loose in my chest. I breathed, and it seemed the air went clear down to my toes. I felt such sheer relief, such alleviation of all I'd carried for so long. I felt weightless.

I laughed and cried at the same time. Mama looked at me aghast, until I handed her Becky, raised my arms over my head, rolled my neck in loose circles, and repeated, "Oh, Mama, you can't imagine how it feels. I can't describe it. I'm a beam of light set free."

I remembered the song Aunt Jean and I used to sing, *This Little Light of Mine*, and I heard Aunt Jean's voice in my head, "Let it shine. Let it shine. Let it shine."

Becky woke up. Supporting her neck, Mama sat Becky up against her chest facing me. "I want Becky and you to come home."

"You do?" I grabbed a spit cloth, wiped drool from Becky's mouth, and patty-caked her hands.

"Yes, I do. There's no sense in the two of you living off by yourselves, when the three of us could be together." Her voice had the old no-nonsense tone.

"All right."

She drew her shoulders back. "You don't want your independence, your own place."

I drew my face up, all serious. "It takes a fool to refuse help when the devil's at the front door and somebody knows the back way."

We both burst out laughing and it startled Becky so much she screwed up her face and let out a cry of alarm. Mama turned Becky to face her and looked back and forth between the two of us. "This baby has some lungs on her."

"I'd say you're discovering that a little late in the game. You've got us moving back in, and I'm not letting you out of it." I arranged Becky's little fortress on Aunt Jean's bed so we could get to work.

Mama drew Becky to her, stroked her velvet cheek, and wasn't the least bit believable as she said, "We'll just send her to live with the elves if she can't be quiet. They'll know what to do with her." She rubbed Becky's tiny palm. Becky closed her hand around Mama's giant finger. "Ahhhh, just look at that."

I grinned from ear to ear. "I never would've believed it. You're smitten."

She jerked her head up at me. "I'm no such thing."

"Whatever you say, Mama." I took Becky and laid her in the makeshift crib. "Whatever you say."

"Where to start? She surely was a pack rat." As we turned to view the room, I saw the two of us reflected in the chifforobe's mirror. We looked like we belonged together.

Forty-Nine

For weeks after we lost Aunt Jean, I was numb, and the world seemed to have lost its shine. I did my best to keep my spirits up for all of us. Becky helped. She was a pure joy. Moving back to Mama's and Becky's daily schedule also helped me keep going. I knew what to do and when to do it. My duties demanded full attention, with no time for indulgences, as Aunt Jean would have reminded me. Except, I missed her so much. I was heartsick we'd been at odds when she died. During Becky's nap times, I wrote letters to Aunt Jean.

The first few were filled with remorse. I didn't need to wait for my golden years for my life to be painted black with regrets. Why hadn't I called her? It would have been so easy to pick up the phone, to drive Becky over to see her, to tell her I loved her, no matter how wrong she was about Daddy and how badly she'd handled it.

Then my writing turned angry. How could she leave me? And without giving us a chance to make amends. I hated that damn Church of God, with its unholy babble. I hated God for letting people die. I never hated Aunt Jean. I loved her.

After all those bitter letters, I poured my love for her out in long, looping missives. Despite her shortcomings, I adored my Aunt Jean. Everything good in me—that I'd now pass on to Becky—she'd sown. As I scrawled page after page, I felt no older than five, with my arms clutched around her long skirts, looking up at her, my heart bursting with love. If I could only pat her cheek again and tell her, "I love you the mostest."

I know exactly what she'd do. She'd lean in towards me, her eyes shining right back at me, and say, "Oh, no, you do not. I love you the mostest, forever and ever and a day."

Aunt Jean and I came into each other's lives just when we needed each other the most ... to have someone to love. She'd live on through the love I'd give Becky. She might not approve of every choice I'd make in life, but all my choices would be influenced by her.

I sat down one morning, while Mama was at work and Becky's mobile played its cheery tune and penned my last letter.

Dear Aunt Jean,

The last time I saw you, you wanted me to forgive. You'd be happy to see Mama and me now. I can't believe you missed us getting back together, that you'll miss seeing Becky grow up.

As for Daddy, I don't care if you understand or not, but I don't have to forgive him. Nobody has to forgive a father who molested them.

It's easy to forgive you. You may have missed all the clues when I was little, but who could have anticipated the unimaginable? When I finally did tell, I forgive you for siding with your baby sister. I would forgive you for not believing me, but it was clear you realized the truth, just couldn't admit it. I understand not being able to admit something. I even absolve you for thinking I have to forgive Daddy.

But me—it will take a miracle to forgive myself. It will take huge cathedrals rising up into the mist. I can't forgive not being there in the last days of your life, can't forgive wondering if you died thinking I didn't love you.

It will take you sitting down here next to me, clasping my hand, and saying, "There, there, now, you know your old Aunt Jean wouldn't hold anything against you. You're my girl, my dear girl." That's what it will take.

I'll need those words whispered in my ear before daybreak, those words entering through sleep's membrane and opening me up at the same time the chimes of my clock open my eyes.

One morning, when I least expect it, I pray I'll wake and breathe in your Listerine and White Shoulders. Then the shards lining my throat will be gone. The stays crushing my rib cage will be loosened. I'll know you were here. I'll know you forgive me. That's when I'll be able to forgive myself for not spending the time we'd been given, when I still had the chance.

My love forever and ever, and a day,

Mary

That letter saved me. In my act of writing it, she came to me. Of course that was what she would say, if only she could. She'd forgive me, allowing me to forgive myself. I knew, without a doubt, that she loved me, and I loved her. If only we'd been given more time, we would have risen above the human need to change truth into something easier to live with. I was sure of it.

Epilogue

At the end of February, the weather turned cold again. I had bundled Becky in her warmest clothes for the visit to Dr. Looper and had driven with care across town.

"Mary Lydell." A female nurse stood at the doorway. I had the urge to run, but rose and carried Becky back to the examination room.

"Oh, my, isn't she precious? And tiny. Had her home long?" She indicated I should place Becky on the scales.

"About a month." I watched the register with bated breath to see how much she weighed now.

"Five pounds, six ounces."

I beamed with pleasure. "That's great! She didn't gain much until we worked out her feeding, but I think she's averaging about five ounces a week now. That's normal, isn't it?"

The nurse smiled at me as she took Becky's temperature and checked her pulse. "If I could define 'normal,' I'd be a rich woman. But yes, I believe that's a good weight gain. She looks healthy, Mom." Annotating the chart, she told me the doctor would be in shortly and left the room.

To take my mind off the exam, I bounced Becky on my knee and sang a couple of her favorite songs. My eyes flicked back and forth between my sweet girl's happy face and the poster of a giant eye staring at me.

Dr. Looper gave a quick knock, then came in with Becky's chart in hand. He looked about fifty, with short brown hair threaded with gray. His thick glasses matched some of the kids in the waiting room. I thought he seemed a bit more at ease than the doctors I'd seen in the NICU and imagined that this environment must be less stressful. "I'll be examining your little one's eyes. Checking for Retinopathy of Prematurity, which is a vision impairment that can affect preemies. You'll hear it called ROP, for short." I nodded. "I'm going to put some drops in to dilate her eyes, then I'll be back. She will have some discomfort at first. Don't be surprised if she lets us know about it."

I held her while he administered the drops. Sure enough, she screamed bloody murder as he left the room, and for several minutes after. I thought back to my last eye exam and remembered those drops stinging like wildfire. She settled down as I held her close, jiggling her and humming.

In a few minutes, the doctor gave his quick knock entrance, lowered the lights in the room, snapped a spotlight on us, and looked into her eyes with a round lens held between his thumb and index finger. Becky and I both blinked against the glare.

"Um hum. Um hum," he murmured as he angled the lens, shifting its flashing surface to and fro, checking each eye. Then he flicked off the spot, brought up the overhead lights, and made some notes before addressing me. "Your daughter definitely has ROP. There are several stages to this, with some resulting in moderate vision impairments and some in more serious impairments, including blindness." He paused. I gaped at him and nodded my head up and down. "I see she weighed two pounds, nine ounces at delivery. That's just on the borderline for how we might expect her eyes will develop. Less than two pounds, seven, and my prognosis wouldn't be as good. Given her birth weight and the progress she's made to date, we're going to have to follow her closely to see how serious this is. I'm hoping she'll have some functional vision and can assure you I'll do everything possible to help her retain whatever vision we can."

I couldn't speak. All I could do was hold Becky close to me and blink.

His tone softened. "I realize it's hard to be prepared for this kind of news. Do you have any questions?"

I shook my head.

"You will most likely have questions later. I want you to feel free to call me. I'll see her back in six to eight weeks." He laid his hand on my shoulder. "I'll have the nurse give you some materials to read." His hand squeezed my upper arm. I barely felt it. "These children adapt to their vision. She won't even know what she's lost until she gets older."

"Thank you." The words skimmed ever so softly over Becky's head and out into the room.

"You're welcome. If you have questions before your next appointment, please don't hesitate to call, or even come in." The door shut behind him.

I turned Becky in my lap, to face me, and peered into her eyes. She looked fine. She was looking right at me. Wasn't she? I turned her sideways in my lap, pulled my head back, then popped it back in front of her. She bobbled her head. I pulled a toy from my blue jean diaper bag and dangled it in front of her. When I moved it to the side, her head turned toward it. Didn't it?

The door opened and the nurse came in with some brochures. "Here you go, sweetheart." She made sure my fingers closed around them. "Doctor Looper's also referred you to the Division of Blind Services. They have an early intervention program with vision teachers who'll work with you. It's important her lessons start right away. Understand?"

"Yes." I nodded and looked at the phone number she'd placed on top of the stack.

She smiled at me. "That's one beautiful little girl you've got there."

—

A year later, on Sunday, February 12, I sat in the living room, re-reading one of my books on low vision and young children. We still weren't sure how much Becky saw, but we knew she reacted to light and colors, and she appeared to see some forms or shapes. We really couldn't tell. All we knew was she had some vision, but it was impaired.

We visited her vision teacher, Barbara Costanzo, every week, and she showed me how important basic concepts were … up, down, in, out, under, and over. It made sense. How would you ever understand those directions when you couldn't see them? She also taught me how to use toys that lit up or had sound to improve Becky's vision tracking and to get her to lift her head. The toys provided stimulation for her instead of the self-stimulation most kids with vision impairment did, such as flapping their hands and pressing their eyes. I liked Barbara.

She knew her stuff, cracked jokes, and, like Gil, wouldn't let me indulge myself for a minute.

I'd spent the last year reading every book I could get my hands on about blindness, low vision, and training children with vision impairments. I had a real déjà vu moment the day I'd read a chapter about simple strategies adults used, like always keeping everything in the refrigerator and cabinets in the same place. Just the way I'd always done obsessively. It felt as if everything I'd gone though that resulted in my strange compulsions had prepared me for being Becky's mother. That made me happy to be me, quirks and all, as if everything that had happened served some purpose, instead of it being like a dog run down in the road. It was kind of spooky. Like fate.

I had my book open to a section on mobility, where it talked about being very specific about counting steps—counting, yes, I knew all about counting, another moment for the Twilight Zone music—when I heard the sounds I loved. Becky's singsong babbling, followed by Mama, "Boop, boop, dittum, datum, wattum, choo!" Becky's irresistible giggle spilled into the room.

"Mama." She called to me from my mama's embrace, with her arms held out toward the kitchen.

Those tousled curls and crooked little brown eyes, rising from the bib of her red OshKosh overalls, were the sweetest vision in the universe. "There's my sugar bear."

When she heard my voice, her outstretched hands turned towards me, and her fingers opened and closed. "Mama."

Mama sat her in my lap, along with a bottle. "Here's our girl."

Becky wrapped her arms around my neck and lay her cheek against mine. I sat the bottle next to me, breathed in Becky's baby powder, and tickled my fingers up her back. "Creepie mousie's coming to get you." She squealed.

Mama reached out and goosed her. Becky let Mama know what she thought by loosening one hand and batting it towards her, while making a high-pitched "eeee" sound.

"No, yourself." Mama wrapped her hand around Becky's, brought it to her mouth, and kissed it.

"Na-na." Mama's whole face lit up. It was Becky's latest word, and Mama was beside herself every time she heard her say it.

"That's right. Nana loves her Speck." Mama gently scratched her nails on Becky's palm. Becky tittered, drew her arms away from both of us, and sat on my lap.

"Baba." She patted her hands.

"Yes, ma'am. Here you go." I cradled her and handed her the bottle. She slurped it down.

"That girl's an eater." Mama looked satisfied. We'd been through a lot to get Becky to eat and stabilize her weight. Those pudgy fingers wrapped around her bottle were quite a sight to see.

"Wonder where she gets it?" I eyed Mama.

"We do come from a long line of women-who-can-eat. How do you reckon we stay so skinny?" She dropped to the couch, held her leg up, and twisted her foot from right to left.

"Speak for yourself. You and Aunt Jean fall in that bracket. I reside in the land of women-who-can-eat-and-everybody-can-tell." I sighed and looked at the photo on the coffee table, the one Gil took of the four of us Christmas before last. "I miss her."

Mama leaned towards me. "We'll always miss her."

I squeezed Becky closer to me. She wiggle-waggled her feet, the way she did when she was purely happy. The sound of her suckling mixed with the smell of Mama's White Shoulders was too good for words. "I think Aunt Jean would be real proud of us."

"She would be pleased as punch." Mama reached over and lifted my chin up using her index finger. We were eye-to-eye. "And so am I."

Mama skittered off into her bedroom and came back with a hand full of envelopes. She had to see I was puzzled, but she just winked at me, held the packets aloft, shook the entire bundle, and sunk to the couch.

"What do you have there?" Becky tossed her bottle to the floor and squirmed. I set her down and she crawled to her play corner Barbara helped me design. It was filled with toys that had different textures and sounds. But Becky's favorite was the little table she could pull up on.

Mama crooked her finger for me to come to her. Now I was curious. I joined Mama on the couch while Becky rolled a toy ice cream truck back and forth to make the bell ring.

"Now." Mama tapped the letters against the coffee table. "I've been at work."

I narrowed my eyes at her, confounded. "What's this about?"

Mama leaned her head against the back of the couch and gave me a loving smile, one usually reserved for her Speck. "You are such a good mother. I've watched you with Becky and felt so proud. It was that Miss Barbara who got me to thinking about it."

"Becky's vision teacher?"

"When I met her at the picnic last fall, the one with all the kids getting vision service." I nodded. "She told me what a good mother you are, but also what a good teacher. And I said, 'You know, she always wanted to be a teacher. Had the grades for it, too. Smart as a whip.' Barbara said it was a shame, and I agreed. But the more I thought about it, the more I thought, 'Why's it have to be that way?'"

Becky rolled onto her back and stuck one foot into her mouth. Mama and I both laughed.

"So, I did some investigating of my own." That wink again.

"Mama, I know you're going somewhere with this, but I'm totally confused."

She slapped one envelope on the table. "That's a letter of recommendation from your school principal." Slapped a second envelope down. "That one's from your guidance counselor, Mrs. Snow." A third. "Mr. Bonner, your manager at Penney's." A fourth. "Mrs. Owen, the teacher where you served as an aid. She wrote a humdinger of one and made the initial call to Floyd Junior College for me." She carefully laid the fifth one down. "That's your acceptance letter from Floyd Junior, dependent on you passing your GED." She balanced the sixth one on top. "That is the name and address of a perfectly lovely, retired nurse Gil introduced me to who babysits children with special needs." And another, number seven. "I tucked some paperwork in there where you can apply for some sort of childcare assistance from one of the state's rinky-dinky programs to get mothers off welfare." And the last one, the eighth, she placed in my hands. "And this is a letter from Berry College saying they'll offer a full scholarship into their teaching program, after you complete one year at Floyd Junior with satisfactory grades."

My stomach shook. Mama shimmered through my tear-filled vision. I clutched the envelopes in astonishment. "Mama!" It was too much to take in at once.

She smiled, her teeth gleaming. "Too good to be true?"

"Mama, how did you … what did you … I can't believe this!" I shrieked and toppled onto her, folded her into my arms. I leapt from her and spun in a circle, clasping the letter to my chest. "Whoo Hoo!"

Becky giggled and hooted from her spot on the floor.

I dashed back to Mama and pulled her to her feet, hugged her to me, and rocked our bodies from side-to-side. "I'm gonna be a teacher."

She raised her hands to my hair and tucked a stray lock behind my ear, in a movement so reminiscent of Aunt Jean my heart did a double beat. "You already are a teacher. You're just getting the training to go with it." She took my face in her hands. "You deserve this."

"Oh, Mama. It's a dream come true. When I was little, I wanted to be a teacher because I liked to read, because I loved books. And then, when I tutored Bobby, I thought I wanted to be a teacher because I was good at it. But now, I know the real reason." I gripped her hands in mine. "I want to teach because teachers changed my life and Becky's life. It's like Mrs. Owen taught me, it's not just about teaching, it's inspiring children's futures. It's hope for tomorrow. Think of it, Mama. I could even learn to be a vision teacher, like Miss Barbara, and help other kids like Becky."

"Honey, you're stubborn enough to be anything your little heart desires."

I rubbed at the nobs at my hairline, my bumps caused by the forceps. "You've always said I was born hard-headed."

Becky gurgled. We both turned in time to see her pull herself up at her little table and stand unassisted for a full five seconds, before falling onto her tush.

368 • Birdhouse Jesus

"Did you see that?" Mama scooped her up and bounced her. "Look at you, our little Speck! Before you know it, you'll be the next one carting yourself off to college, leaving your old Nana here all alone."

"You'll have to spend lots of nights at Lucille's, won't you?" I poked her in the arm.

"You've always been too smart for your own good, you know that?" She giddy-upped into the kitchen with Becky, neighing like a horse, the two of them giggling fools.

I looked at the tower of envelopes that represented all the legwork Mama had done for me. Those envelopes were my salvation and Mama made it all possible. There were eight of them. Eight! My lucky number. The symbol of infinity but upright. The limitless. The eternal. Forever and ever, and a day.

About the Author

Terri Chastain 1957 – 2022

Terri was born on February 27, 1957 in Rome, Georgia. She received her bachelor's degree from Berry College in Rome in 1979. She and her husband, Joseph Wayne Chastain, raised three children: Brian, Michelle, and Winter.

Terri was passionate about her work in the nonprofit community. She spent twenty-five years in the Orlando area fundraising and teaching fundraising. Terri also was active in the creative writing community for over thirty years with several poems published. Terri loved Central Florida and had a passion for the Canadian Rockies and her special place, St. Augustine, Florida

Birdhouse Jesus is her first novel.

Made in the USA
Columbia, SC
30 November 2023

26935895R00224